Book Three of the Petrovo Series

JANE MARLOW

I0689540

The
Yellow
Ticket

RIVER GROVE
BOOKS

Published by River Grove Books
Austin, TX
www.rivergrovebooks.com

Distributed by River Grove Books

Design and composition by Greenleaf Book Group
Cover design by Greenleaf Book Group
Cover image: Two women ©iStockphoto.com/clu. Old birdcage with open door and passport used under license from Shutterstock.com. Yellow ticket photo courtesy of Altenmann, Wikimedia.

Cataloging-in-Publication data is available.

Print ISBN: 978-1-63299-219-2

eBook ISBN: 978-1-63299-220-8

First Edition

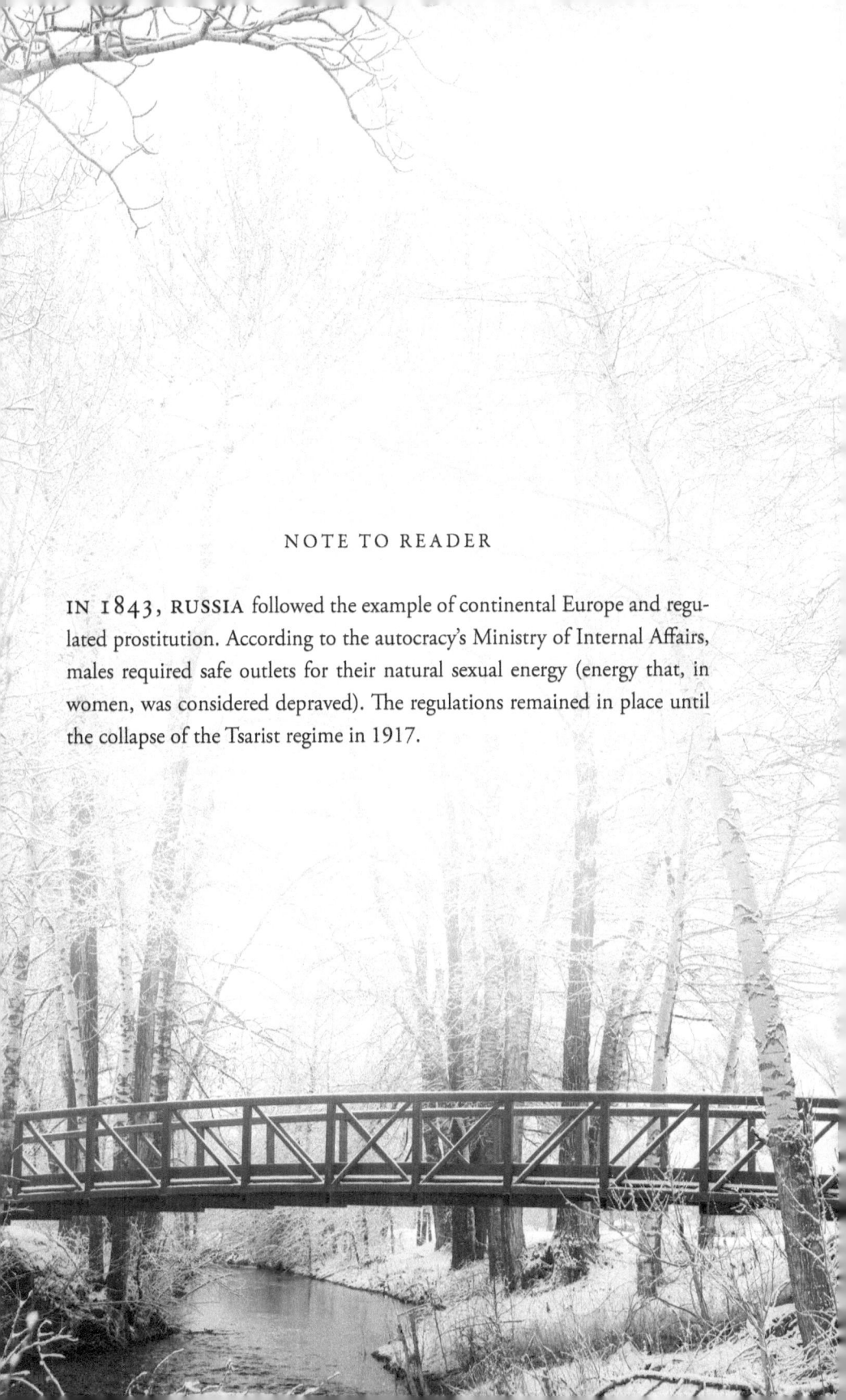

NOTE TO READER

IN 1843, RUSSIA followed the example of continental Europe and regulated prostitution. According to the autocracy's Ministry of Internal Affairs, males required safe outlets for their natural sexual energy (energy that, in women, was considered depraved). The regulations remained in place until the collapse of the Tsarist regime in 1917.

CHAPTER 1

September
1867

MONSIEUR SHELGUNOV'S CIGARETTE case is buffing to an elegant shine when I halt my rag in midstroke. I tilt my ear toward the whine of the hinges struggling under the heft of the mahogany front door. Boot heels snap across the marble floor of the foyer.

No footfalls trail after him. He has come home alone, once again depositing Madame and the children into someone else's care.

My throat clamps against the rising nausea. During my early employment at the Shelgunov household, the click of his boots was horrifying. The sound is no longer frightening; it's merely loathsome.

The first time he abused me, I had freshly turned sixteen and been living with the family only a few weeks. After the beast took what he wanted, I stripped the soiled sheets from the mattress and retched into them.

During the past year and a half, the soul-crushing task has become part of my list of unofficial duties in this house built of stone and vanity. But Shelgunov's lechery no longer paralyzes me with fear and shame. I, Anna Vorontsova, have built a protective wall of hatred around myself.

The footfalls draw closer until they're clicking the kitchen's pine boards behind me. I drop the polishing rag and cigarette case into the pocket of my apron. Nikolai Osipovich Shelgunov grabs my shoulder with one hand. The heel of his other hand slams against the back of my head. He thrusts me forward at the waist, jamming the side of my face into the raw chicken juice that coats the butcher block. My teeth cut into my cheek.

The hand on my shoulder moves down to the skirt of my servant's dress, which he tosses up and across my back. As he fiddles with his trousers, I brace for the tearing pain, the feeling of being ripped open.

He bores into me. My insides feel like they're being gashed. *Oh, Mother of God! The hurt is fearsome! Please make it quick! Quick!*

The cutting pain ebbs to raw chafing as he pounds me like the cur dog that he is. I sink into my trustworthy response of separating myself from the body he defiles. My thoughts focus on my afternoon chores.

His boots. He wants all nine pairs oiled before the cold sets in. Even as my hands grip the edges of the chopping block, my fingertips rehearse rubbing in the lanolin, then buffing the leather.

I glance through the French doors to the blue milk-glass vase on the glossy breakfast table. The maroon chrysanthemums are starting to droop. Madame will expect the sagging blooms to be replaced. I wonder which flowers remain in the garden after last night's hoarfrost.

As he grinds into me, I call upon every morsel of my imagination to climb the stairs to the twins' bedrooms and tidy the toy-strewn disarray.

Nikolai Osipovich Shelgunov humps in earnest, and my thoughts go to this evening's meal. Before Sveta left for her monthly Sunday afternoon off, she set aside most of tonight's supper in the larder—crayfish soup, apple bread, preserved dates—leaving me with only the chicken to prepare.

As my thoughts braise the imaginary chicken, my employer's breathing becomes ragged. He's close to finishing.

"You despicable bastard!" The female screech rattles the freshly polished silverware.

I bolt upright, pitching Shelgunov off-balance. He grabs the chopping block with one hand and his trousers with the other.

At the kitchen door, his wife twirls her drawstring reticule above her head. Once it gains full momentum, she cuts the purse loose. Its strands of shiny beads whiz past her husband's ear and smack into the white Dutch tiling of the new stove.

I slink toward the safety of the cranny between the cupboard and the pie chest.

"Rozaliya, I thought . . . " He grapples with the buttons on his pants. "I thought—"

"I know exactly what you thought!" Her heaving chest must be close to ripping the hooks and eyes off her beaded silk bodice. "You thought I was securely stashed away at my sister's while you enjoyed a little afternoon tryst! You thought I was too stupid to figure out what was happening in my own house! You thought—"

His hands reach out, slowly fanning up and down. "Calm down and allow me to explain."

"Shut your filthy, lying, stinking mouth! You promised on your very soul that this would never happen again!" Her eyes blaze as they seek me out in my narrow hideaway. Scanning me from head to toe, she snorts. "At least the last one was pretty!"

Madame snatches off her blue velvet hat and, with a strong backhand, launches it at her spouse's head. He ducks, allowing it to soar safely past, its satin ribbons casting fluttering trails. "Tell me," she snarls, "are you exercising your cock with Sveta also?"

Shelgunov squares his shoulders. "Certainly not. Sveta is old and fat."

Shifting her searing eyes toward me, Madame flings her head like an irate mare. Her hairpiece comes loose from its auburn up-sweep and catches on her silver earring, where it dangles like a one-sided pigtail. "And you, Anna! You're nothing but a tramp! That's why your village ousted you to Moscow. To think I allowed an unscrupulous trollop to live in my home and help raise my children!"

She rears back an open hand and steps in my direction.

Her husband catches her arm. "Roza, darling, let's discuss this in private."

Madame throws off his hand and brings forth words from deep within her throat. "Never. Touch. Me. Again."

Shelgunov grabs both her wrists and brings them to his chest. "I want to talk to you, husband to wife, in a mature fashion."

She yanks loose from his grasp and points a menacing finger at me. "And you, you little whore! Out of this house immediately!"

"Yes, yes, my love, of course." His voice drops to its most silky, cajoling timbre. "But what's most important right now is you and me. Come with me, and we'll sort this out." He places a hand on the small of her back and presses her toward the French doors and the breakfast room.

"What if I had brought the children home with me?" she shrieks while being strong-armed from the kitchen, her hairpiece swinging from her ear like a flamboyant jewel.

He closes the double doors behind them and leads her to one side of the room, away from my line of view. Fierce words filter through the doors.

In the safety of the cubbyhole, I slide my back down the wall until I'm sitting on the pine planks, knees at my chest. I use my apron to mop the chicken juice from my cheeks.

Out of this house immediately!

Cold, stark despair clutches me. "Oh holy Mary, Mother of God," I whisper. "I've nowhere to go!"

My pleas are interrupted by a piercing "You scoundrel!"

I look up to see slender fingers latch onto the blue milk-glass vase on the table. But Madame's aim is off. Rather than hitting her husband, the vase smashes into one of the French doors. A pane of glass shatters to the floor, mixing with shards from the vase. Water-laden chrysanthemum leaves cling forlornly to the remaining glass below the burst pane.

Now it's Monsieur's turn to fume. "Rozaliya! That vase came from France! Do you have any idea what I paid for it?"

My forehead drops onto my knees, and my stomach cinches into a nauseated ball. "Sacred Mother of God," I murmur, "have pity on me, your most humble servant."

Madame's footsteps stomp up the staircase to the second floor.

"I beg you, Holy Mother." Tears fall onto my servant's dress. "No rubles. Nowhere to live."

CHAPTER 2

September

1867

THE FADED GRAY eyes want to help, but they have little to offer. "I'm sorry, truly I am, but I don't know anyone in need of a house girl."

Sitting cross-legged in the scattered straw of the stable, I drop my head back against the plank wall. "Oh, Fenechka, what am I to do?"

Fenechka is the head housekeeper for the family next door to the Shelgunovs. She's my sole friend, if indeed a friend is someone you wave to across the fence—someone who occasionally offers seasoned advice, such as how to remove India ink from a linen tablecloth or retrieve a marble stuck up a child's nose. In addition to her domestic duties, Fenechka has a self-appointed responsibility: keeping watch over the comings and goings of the wealthy and almost-wealthy on the north side of Moscow.

Sitting shoulder to shoulder with me, Fenechka interlaces her fingers atop her broad belly. "When a position comes open, ol' Fenechka is always the first to know." The housekeeper's jolly face lapses into a sober expression. "But you'll need references."

"As Shelgunov was shoving me out the door, he whispered that any employers should contact him directly—that he'd give me a good referral."

"Well, I should hope so." Fenechka's fleshy finger pokes a springy silver curl back under her starched white cap.

"Fenechka, I need to ask you something." My eyes cast about the stable's dim corners. Assured that the only creature within earshot is the mare, I unbutton my gray coat and reach into my apron's pocket. "I . . . I . . . I didn't steal it. I really didn't. You must believe me. It simply slipped my mind."

"Untie your tongue and get to the point, child." Fenechka's good-natured Slavic face puckers into matronly smile lines.

"An accident. Truly." I ease my hand from inside my coat and hold it palm up to Fenechka.

The woman stretches her double chin to better scrutinize the crumpled object. "A rag? You're worried you'll get caught thieving a rag?"

"No. This." I peel back the cloth's edges as tenderly as though I'm removing swaddling from a newborn. "I was polishing it when he came home. You can understand, can't you, how scared I was when Rozaliya Yakovlevna began hurling things? And then how fast he tossed me out? I'm not a thief, I swear by all the saints." I fall into my habit of nibbling on my lower lip.

The big-hearted woman pats my knee. "You're no more a thief than is an ant that picks up scattered crumbs." She peers at the item, her forehead furrowed like a ploughed field. "But Anna, darling, I still can't make out what it is."

My thumb and index finger gingerly raise the shiny rectangle from the rag so the flickering light can find it. "A cigarette case. Silver."

"Ahhh."

"Will it fetch enough rubles to get me back to my village?" Tears sting my eyes. "I must go home. I must!"

"The case is worth a pocketful of rubles, easily. Let me have a look at it." As Fenechka takes the rag and its contents, her smile falls away. "Oh. This will bring you next to nothing."

"What?" My chest sags as if a hole were punched in it.

A stout finger directs my attention to the engraving across the lid. "Do you know what it says?"

I pull my lower lip even farther between my teeth and shake my head.

"I'm not sure either, but I suspect they're Shelgunov's initials. A pawnshop will assume the case is stolen. The initials make it too easy for the owner to identify it, and the shop owner won't risk his reputation. Plus, who would pay good money for a cigarette case with someone else's initials on it?"

A groan rumbles in my throat as my hands go to my temples. "Can the initials be rubbed away somehow?"

"Don't know. But I doubt it."

I close my eyes and watch my hope grow dark, like a flame smothered.

Fenechka rewraps the cigarette case. "Put your mind at ease. Just give Fenechka a little time to sniff out a good position for you." She puts her nose straight up into the air and draws in three rowdy snorts as though she might catch a whiff of something more promising than horse dung.

Fenechka heaves her girth and stands. I follow suit and fold myself into her staunch arms, aching to linger there, shielded from the world's harshness. Reluctantly, I pull away. "But you agree, don't you, that I should sell the case? Even if it's only worth a couple of rubles?"

"Personally, I'd sneak up on Shelgunov while he's sleeping and snap it shut on his balls."

My initial gasp is followed by a giggle.

Fenechka continues, "You might try the pawnshops near Sukharevskaya Square. You'll be safe enough during daylight. You've been there?"

"Yes, on errands." I hug Fenechka, then draw back and kiss her three times, alternating cheeks. "You're my guardian angel."

"Then heed this angel's advice and sleep in the loft. It's warmer up there. And Petya won't find you if he comes checking on the horse."

Up the steep ladder the housekeeper hauls items she borrowed from her employer: two blankets, a lantern with matches, and a loaf of bread stored in a tin, safe from greedy mice.

I join her, carrying a tattered pair of felt winter boots, a hand-knitted shawl, a comb, and a pair of gloves with worn-away fingertips—all of which I brought to Moscow from my home village, Petrovo. In addition to these items, I tote a muslin servant's dress and apron, a sleeping chemise that Madame insisted I wear at night, and galoshes that I bought secondhand after hoarding several months' wages. I'm wearing the remainder of my possessions: lace-up ankle boots plus a woolen servant's dress, coat, and stockings.

Fenechka assures me that life will look better in the morning and bids me good night. I extinguish the lantern and, still in my coat, curl up like a worm in the loft's straw, the blankets pulled high. Outside, a loose board on the carriage house thumps in the breeze. The leaves piled against the wall crackle with the rooting of some night animal. I know these sounds well. They're the sounds of my family's rough-hewn hut, sounds I took for granted all those years.

I brush back a tear of remorse.

Oh, Mamasha, I never meant to bring shame on our family. Moscow is so mean and horrible. Please take me back.

FENECHKA WAS CORRECT. The pawnbroker accuses me of stealing the cigarette case.

I draw back in mock horror. "That's altogether not true. It's from my father. It's all I received when he passed on. I so hate to part with it."

"And what was your father's name?"

Incapable of putting a name with each of the three initials, I unwittingly chew on my lower lip.

"I'll give you fifty kopeks."

My neck arches back. "Your offer is an insult."

"The only thing I can do with this cigarette holder is sell it to a silversmith, who'll melt down the metal." With a single finger, he pushes it back across the counter to me.

I stare at the case, loath to pick it back up. "Certainly you can do better than fifty kopeks."

The dealer's eyes shift from indifferent to unfriendly. "I don't have time to dicker. One ruble. My final offer."

The tears well in my eyes as I stuff the paper ruble into my skirt pocket.

"I MUST LEAVE soon, before Petya finds me. And they'll blame you, and I can't suffer that to happen. But Mother of God, what am I to do?" Sitting with Fenechka amid the straw in the loft, I hiccup back a sob.

"First thing to do is eat the stew while it'll still warm your insides."

I pull off my gloves, cup one hand around the comforting heat of the bowl, and use the other to dip a chunk of bread into the thick gravy. The warmth of the savory mutton and vegetables chases away the chill.

Fenechka leans forward, props an elbow on her ample thighs, and rests her chin on her knuckles. "What were your duties for Shelgunov? What are your qualifications?"

"Cleaning—house, clothes, dishes, windows, anything. Tending to children."

"Can you cook?"

"Only peasant food. Not the food rich people eat. Sveta did the cooking." Another possibility comes to me. "But I'm strong. I don't look it, but I am. I've hauled buckets and buckets of water. And I can mend."

Fenechka's eyes brighten. "You can sew?"

"Oh, yes. In Petrovo, I made all my clothes and my brothers' clothes. And I let out Rozaliya Yakovlevna's dresses when she gained weight. I can sew anything."

"There you go! Three jobs we can look for—maid, governess, seamstress."

"You mean, a seamstress in a shop?"

"Possibly."

"But how? Where?" I tear off another hunk of bread to sop up the final dab of gravy.

A long, pensive breath blows through Fenechka's pursed lips. "I'll put out the word that you're looking for employment. In the meantime, the quickest place to find day work is Khitrov Market." Fenechka describes how laborers—men and women desperate for rubles to hold body and soul together—gather in the open-air market each morning, hoping to meet up with employers in need of workers. "Mainly men looking for labor, but also women hoping for work as washerwomen, servants, cigarette makers, and the like."

My hopes all but vanish. "I've heard about Khitrov Market."

"What you heard is probably true." The wise woman's voice grows stern. "It's a cesspool of flophouses and gambling dens, full of drunkards and cutthroats. If you give it a try, you must be careful and look sharp. Constantly. And watch out for the children—pickpockets, every one of them."

I set aside my bowl, alarm coursing through me. "And you think I should go there?"

"It's your best chance for finding temporary work." Fenechka's nod is firm. "Leave here before sunup. It's a long walk, and the employers do their picking early. Follow the Boulevard Ring to the east side of the city, near the Yauza River. Don't take any money with you, not even a kopek. And don't go inside any building."

As Fenechka climbs down the ladder, I coil up in my bed of straw. In the impenetrable blackness of the stable, I cry tears that I fear will never stop.

CHAPTER 3

September
1867

THE SUN HAS yet to break above the stone buildings near the center of the city. I look down at the vast, low-lying square of Khitrov Market, its numerous bonfires sending up a haze of smoke while the nearby Yauza River hurls mist into the air. Although the combined vapors are as thick as milk, I can make out the square's ragged crush of people.

I silently plea-bargain with the Holy Mother. Please, Our Lady, if you find me work, I'll do anything. I swear by all that is holy, I'll give part of my wages to the Church every week, and I'll give alms to the poor, and I'll take bread to the needy and . . . and . . . I'll do anything!

With reluctant steps, I venture into the disorder, clamor, and stench of the slum market. While sidestepping a puddle of vomit, I'm almost knocked down by a man yelling, "Bastard!" as he chases another fellow through the crowd.

A hand latches onto the hem of my coat. I swirl to face the assailant. But the hand belongs to a filth-encrusted woman, not much older than me, who sits cross-legged on the cold cobblestones, encased in a blanket. Her anguished eyes are sunk deep in her skull. Under the tatters of her blanket, she clutches a tiny bundled baby.

"For the love of God, help me!" she wails.

When I respond, "I have nothing to give you, sister," her skeptical eyes travel the length of my tailored woolen coat.

I try to step away, but the woman's wart-laden fingers hold fast on the gray wool. "In the name of Christ! I beg you!"

The agony in the young mother's voice tears at my heart. "I swear to you, my pockets are empty."

The woman's ashen eyelids sag as her fist releases the wool and drops to her lap.

"I'd help you if I could," I insist to the despondent mother. "But maybe you can help me. Where do people gather when looking for work?"

Barely lifting her fleshless hand, the woman flicks her fingers toward the far end of the square. "But you won't find no work down there." Her bloodless lips curl into a sneer as she looks me over from top to bottom. "Too bad you got that thing on your face. Otherwise your pockets could be jangling with kopeks tonight."

Old instincts erupt, and my gloved hand flies to turn up my coat's collar to hide my cheek's teardrop-shaped birthmark, the size and color of a strawberry. Repulsed by the woman's vulgar insinuation about the kopeks, I back away and resume threading my way through the hordes of pleading beggars and urchins, their faces filthier than Moscow's streets. Men with purposeful steps push aside stumbling drunks. Women huddle near huge, simmering pots. Young ragamuffins chase one another and shout obscenities as they weave between wagons, stringy horses, and vagrants warming themselves beside meager fires. I sort through the ruckus of voices.

"Need good workers to haul rocks!"

"Day laborer wanted."

"Seeking men to work the barges."

"Looking for an honest man with horse and wagon."

I hear no mention of women's work.

I cautiously approach a pockmarked woman seated on a stool, hunched over a sizzling frying pan. "Excuse me. Is there any women's work to be had here?"

The woman looks up from her skillet, one bloodshot eye focused on me, the other covered with a black patch. "What kind of work?"

I mimic Fenechka's lofty words. "I've worked as a seamstress, a governess, and a maid."

The woman's eye skims across the horde of hungry, hopeful men. "Don't see none of that right now. Maybe later." She shrugs. "No way to know."

"Later? Do you think I should wait here and see what happens?"

The old crone scratches at a sore on her neck, her mocking expression implying, *Unless you have other pressing matters of importance to tend to . . .*

"You see, this is my first time here."

"Talk to the others." She nods toward the menagerie of lean-to booths and stalls made of weatherworn canvas. "Somebody might know of something." Her eye strays down my thick, tailored coat. "If you're not too fussy." Her attention returns to the rancid sausage hissing in the pan.

My teeth gnaw at my lower lip as I scan the teaming rabble. The tightening knot of dismay in my stomach threatens to spew out my breakfast of bread and a pear.

I approach a young man selling firewood. "Excuse me. Can women find work here? I've been employed as a seamstress, a governess, and a maid."

I ask the question of a toothless fishmonger. Then I travel down the line of sellers: dried fruits, sewing notions, baskets, hand-knitted scarves, cracked glasses and crockery, old clothes, felt boots, tallow candles.

When my last morsel of strength crumples, I drop onto a shamble of a bench that was just vacated by two seedy-looking women. A sudden gust creates a flurry of golden leaves, the only sign of color in the dismal squalor.

My attention is snared by two girls, no more than thirteen years of age and clothed only in dresses despite the stiff wind. They pass a bottle of vodka between themselves as they wave and giggle suggestively at several men throwing dice nearby.

Atop a battered wood fence, a scrawny cat crouches with its tail wrapped around its feet. Its unblinking, feral eyes stare long and hard at me until it's distracted by a man shoving aside a pack of children as he chases a young boy.

"Thief!" the man bellows. After he races past, the displaced children resume warming their bare feet in fresh horse dung. When I glance back at the fence, the cat is gone.

This is a Hell darker than any I've ever imagined.

Across Moscow, church bells chime one o'clock. Prospective employers are disappearing, as are most of the work seekers. I've been on my feet since before sunup, and the return walk to the stable will take an hour. There's no reason to remain here.

I rise from the bench, only to have my way obstructed by two young men, neither much older than me. They have the glassy-eyed look of vodka—and taunting grins that are bound and determined to find trouble.

"Looking for work?" one asks, his nose, large and hooked like a hawk's, leaking green snot.

On guard, I merely shrug a shoulder.

"What kind of work?" asks the second guy, his head cocked so a thick mop of greasy brown hair falls rakishly across his forehead.

"Excuse me. I best be on my way." I step to the side, but they move to block me. My mind blazes with fright.

"Hold on, little thing," Hawk-Nose says, his breath a fog of alcohol. He turns to the other guy. "Didn't old Unkovskii say he needs to replace one of his laundresses?"

"That's right." The second guy nods. "So, little thing, certainly you're able to wash laundry?" When I don't answer, he continues. "Tucked away in the basement, washing clothes, that blotch on your face won't matter."

"That blotch doesn't bother me," Hawk-Nose snickers. "Bother you, Pasha?"

"Not a bit. Come along with us, little thing. We'll take you to Unkovskii."

As Hawk-Nose turns sideways and spews a fountain of brackish spit, I shove myself, elbows flailing, through the gap between him and Pasha. I sprint through the disarray of unwashed bodies, sidestepping steamy cesspools, and giving wide berth to a fistfight between two teenage ruffians.

Only when I'm outside the slum market's gate do I slow my pace. As I trudge uphill, past tenements and skinny dogs, my chest heaves and my legs grow more leaden with every step. My insides curdle at the thought of ever dragging myself back to Moscow's underbelly again to rub elbows with the crawling dregs of humanity.

The sky grows moody and overcast, and my wind-stung eyes are half-blinded with tears. I'm so utterly alone and defenseless in Moscow.

If only I knew my letters. If only!

Oh, Mama, why didn't you allow me to go to school? I begged and begged, but you'd have none of it. *It's a woman's business to look after the pots, not read books.* When I sniveled that you weren't being fair, you responded with your customary *No one said life is fair.*

How close I came to unraveling the mystery of books! I ache as I think of the time in Petrovo, two years ago, when the estate owner's twenty-one-year-old daughter, Elena Stepanovna Maximova, broke both legs and needed a nursemaid. Who, out of the entire village, did she select? Me, Anna Vorontsova. And for six magical weeks, I—a timid, gangly fourteen-year-old—lived in the splendid estate house high on the hill, taking care of the young mademoiselle and watching how wealthy people conduct their lives. And almost learning to read.

For an hour or two every day, Mademoiselle Elena sat in her wheelchair while I scrunched up against the arm of the divan, and we'd go over the name of each letter and its pronunciation. With time, I could actually read a few words from the family's dusty childhood books. But once Mademoiselle could walk again, my assistance was no longer needed. The tutoring ceased and so did my recollection of the alphabet.

Other than fuzzy memories, all that remains of those remarkable weeks is the wool coat I'm wearing now, which Mademoiselle Elena gave to me because it no longer fit her.

BOTH MY SPIRITS and the sun are at their lowest when Fenechka's head pops through the passage in the floor of the loft. "Aha. The look on your face tells me Khitrov Market was not the answer to our prayers."

My face twists into a deeper grimace, pushing more tears from my eyes.

"No need to fret, Anna, darling. Ol' Fenechka has a plan." Her stocky arm hoists a large iron pot onto the wooden planks by its wire loop handle. "But first, take this while I go back to the house to get your supper. Special victuals tonight—tongue and potatoes." She disappears down the ladder.

Removing the pot's lid, I'm blasted by steam. As I wave away the vapor, my forehead wrinkles. The pot contains nothing but hot water.

I close my eyes and linger over the soothing mist as it works magic on my wind-burned face. My chest fills with the reviving steam.

Fenechka's words rush at me from all directions.

No need to fret . . .

A plan . . .

CHAPTER 4

September
1867

FENECHKA RETURNS TO the loft with the promised tongue and potatoes as well as an apple.

My stomach clamors as I pick up my spoon, but I'm too nervous to eat. "Tell me," I plead in a voice softer than a whisper.

"Stop chewing your lip, or you'll have a bloody scab when you meet your prospective employer."

"Who is it?"

"Viktorya Borisovna Vialtseva. An old hag who still puts on airs, even though she's a widow without two kopeks to rub together and relies on the generosity of her children to make ends meet. Rumor has it that her housekeeper quit her."

"I'll go first thing in the morning!" I pop an egg-sized bite of potato into my mouth.

Fenechka's pudgy finger sketches a map on the dusty floorboards. "You'll know the house when you see it—the most rundown one on the street."

"How many servants are there?"

The gritty map-finger rises up. "Maid, cook, butler, gardener, hairdresser, nursemaid. All rolled into one tiny package named Anna."

I lift a light-hearted shoulder. "Can't be much work to take care of one woman."

"And her grandson."

I say a silent prayer of gratitude, then ask what the pot of hot water is for.

"You. Scrub up for tomorrow. You smell like you live in a barn."

WITH FEIGNED CONFIDENCE, I tap the tarnished bronze knocker.

The wooden porch, although large enough to accommodate a single rocking chair, is empty. The railing's peeling white paint reveals its previous color was gray. Numerous dark, crusty splotches are dried on the painted floorboards of the porch, leading me to wonder if Viktorya Borisovna Vialtseva owns a goose.

I try to peer inconspicuously through the cracked glass of the door's oval window before rapping the knocker again.

"Show some patience," comes a brittle squawk. "I'm an old woman."

The door, however, isn't opened by an old woman. Before me is a boy at the threshold of manhood, a year or two younger than my age of seventeen. The red of his unruly hair matches the chafed rawness of his covey of pimples. His flabby body slouches against the door's frame. The odor of fried onions wafts through the doorway.

I smile. "Hello. I heard this household has need of a housekeeper."

His "Oh" is flat and disinterested. Then he blinks as if struck by an epiphany. "O-o-o-h-h." His grin, which is best described as a leer, displays yellowed front teeth so large and bucked, they could belong to a mule.

"Who is it?" The female voice inside is churlish.

The young man's head turns halfway around, as though it's seated upon the neck bones of a barn owl. "Girl wanting Olya's position."

He steps aside, motioning me to enter. After I edge past him, he leans out the doorway and sends an arc of tobacco-stained spit onto the porch.

Manners as good as the presumed goose, I silently scoff. If any good came from living with the Shelgunovs, it's my familiarity with the conduct of civil society.

The boy leads me partway down a hallway, then left through a double-door archway into a sitting room laden with the scent of mothballs. The sole light comes from its two windows, their heavy draperies partially open. In a cushioned armchair sits a thin, pinched-faced, gray-haired woman wearing a dressing gown with fur encircling the collar and cuffs—Viktorya Borisovna Vialtseva, I assume. Her dour eyes scrutinize my every step.

The woman's tremulous hand reaches for a cane leaning against the small side table, which is topped with a swan-shaped flower vase and an unlit colored-glass lamp. On the floor at the other side of her chair sits a dented brass spittoon.

With unexpected agility and speed, the woman jabs the cane's tip in the direction of a divan, its seat cushions shiny and smooth from longtime use. Assuming that's where I'm supposed to sit, I settle into a hollow in one of the cushions. My head drops forward as I unbutton my coat, allowing my shielded eyes to scan the dim room.

Other than Vialtseva's armchair and the stiff-backed divan, furnishings are limited to an austere wooden rocker, a square grand piano, and a spindle-legged corner table hosting an embroidered towel, several unlit votive candles, and the

Icon of the Mother of God. Crocheted doilies with yellowed edges are strewn across every horizontal surface.

When the mule-toothed boy drops into the rocking chair, his grandmother's dagger-shaped finger points at him, then flicks toward the hallway. "Close the doors behind you."

As her grandson sulks into the hallway, Vialtseva's rheumy eyes return to me and remain there, unwavering, while she fumbles in the pocket of her high-necked black dress. Eventually a tin snuffbox emerges, and she takes a pinch.

Since Vialtseva doesn't appear inclined to initiate conversation, I begin with "I heard you have an opening for a housekeeper."

"Where'd you hear that?" The woman has the warmth of a snake.

"From Fenechka, a friend of mine. She said—"

"Don't know any Fenechka."

"—that you are in need of someone to clean and cook and mend. I have years of experience doing all those things."

The old woman curls her upper lip to display teeth the same color and size as her grandson's. "*Years* of experience, eh? What did you do, start while you were still in your mother's belly?" Her bony hand gives a dismissive wave. "Your exaggerations don't impress me."

Feeling myself wilt, I lift my chin. "I can supply references."

"Listen, girlie, I'm a fragile old lady. I need more than a housekeeper. I need someone who can tend to my ailments."

"Oh, I've done that." My voice rings with truthfulness. "The owner of the village where I was raised, he had a daughter in a wheelchair. I took care of her. Tended to her every need and learned lots about medicines."

"What's that on your cheek? Looks like a squashed strawberry."

"It's just a mark I was born with, that's all."

"When I was a girl, those were called 'Satan's stains.'"

I recoil. The long-ago taunts of my childhood playmates ring with the intensity of Moscow's hundred church bells. The memories are as oppressive as the parlor's stale, overheated air.

"Do you mind if I remove my coat? The room is so . . . cozy."

In response to Vialtseva's one-shoulder shrug, I drape my wool coat over the arm of the divan and smooth the wrinkles from the skirt of my gray servant's dress. "Please tell me how I can best be of service to you."

"You're not hired yet, girlie. We need to discuss a few things."

I nod agreeably.

Her gnarled forefinger swipes the surface of the side table. "I expect cleanliness." She brandishes the underside of her finger to me. "No dust. No dust balls under the furniture." She grabs the cane's handle and thumps its tip on the floor. "Our clothes and bed linens will be clean and mended."

She thumps the cane again.

"The door will be politely answered and guests treated with courtesy."

Thump.

"The washbasins will always have water. Likewise, the chamber pots will be emptied."

Thump.

"You'll cook the foods that Vasily Terentievich and I enjoy. And that food will be wholesome and tasty. Vasily is a growing boy and will require extra attention from you."

Thump.

"In exchange for your duties, you'll receive a ruble a week plus your meals and a mattress on the hallway floor behind the kitchen."

One ruble a week. I can't do arithmetic, but I know months and months would be required to afford passage back to Petrovo, even in the bed of a hay wagon. "But Madame, those services are worth at least two rubles a week."

"Bah! One ruble and no more. Look around. This is a small house. No stairs to climb. Just Vasily and me to look after. No crying babies. No grubby children."

"The going rate is two r—"

"Enough! There are plenty of girls waiting in line for this position. Away with you." She thumps the cane twice.

My stomach tightens in panic. "In that case, I require off every Sunday afternoon." My teeth tug on my lower lip. I'm certain I'm demanding too much.

The old shrew's perceptive eyes inspect me while her gnarled fingers twiddle with a brooch pinning her collar together at the top of her neck. At long last, she gives a nod that could be interpreted as approval of my spunk. "Maybe you're older than you look." She rests her cane across her lap. "I'll meet that condition, but we need to discuss your duties regarding Vasily. It's important that you get acquainted with my grandson. As I said, he'll require extra attention from you."

"In what ways, Madame Vialtseva?"

"First, he likes his privacy and prefers to live by himself in the room above the carriage house. A typical young man, he disdains neatness, so simply allow him to live in his squalor. I warn you, though, you'll need to cook large portions. He eats like a horse." As if to reinforce her statement, she curls her lips to expose her mulish teeth.

"Is there anything else I need to know?"

"Oh, yes. You need to know all the conditions of your employment." Vialtseva wraps a claw around each end of the cane that lies across her thighs.

"Vasily is at that certain age when boys are naturally curious, especially about women. Do you understand what I'm saying?"

I nod.

"I doubt that you do. As his grandmother, I want to protect him from unhealthy practices. Self-stimulation. Prostitutes. Those types of things. However, boys will be boys, especially when they have urges that demand to be met. It's best to tend to those needs safely at home."

A poisonous taste fills my mouth. "You're saying . . . you're saying you want *me* to meet those needs?"

"At least you have the wherewithal to put two and two together."

My arm involuntarily flings itself across my stomach as nausea roils.

Mother of God! I've already whored myself to Nikolai Osipovich Shelgunov. Now I'm being asked to do more of the same. With Shelgunov, I had no alternative. But if I agree to it this time, the choice will be of my own free will. I'll be no better than a prostitute.

As if through a muffling fog, I hear a crusty "Lost your tongue? Hurry up. I've a long line of girls I can choose from."

A battle wages for my soul. Food. A place to live. Life's essentials. Plus, I would no longer be jeopardizing Fenechka by remaining in the stable. I could take the job and continue to look for a position elsewhere.

But Vialtseva's terms are depraved! They violate the very roots of my upbringing. It's a deadly sin—a sin so vile, I'll be damned to Hell.

To say yes to Vialtseva would mean spurning God-ordained principles. To say no would mean choosing righteousness and, along with it, starvation.

One choice saves my life. The other saves my soul.

All around me is silence, except for the ticking of a clock pendulum in the hallway. My eyes close. I have no choice but to accept the old biddy's conditions.

The stillness is broken by footsteps at the parlor's doorway, followed by a knock. When the door opens, there stands the very topic of conversation: pimple-faced, repugnant, mule-toothed, randy Vasily.

"I'm sorry to interrupt, Grandmother, but the men are here to pick up the piano."

"Tell them to come in. And show her"—Vialtseva renders a scornful tilt of her head—"to the door."

"Wait!" I frantically seek two things: words that won't come and time to think that isn't available. "Maybe . . . perhaps you'd be willing to take me through your house, so that I can better understand my new duties."

The woman's shrewd eyes turn toward me as her bony fingers flick Vasily away.

When the boy is out of earshot, I make certain my voice is low and coldly sober. "Under these conditions." I hold up a palm facing Vialtseva. "Hand only." Courtesy of Shelgunov, I'm familiar with the various ways men can be satisfied.

The gray head shakes resolutely. "He'll want more."

I lengthen my spine and hold my head erect. "Ain't risking a baby."

Vialtseva's jaw slides to one side in thought. "There are other ways."

I thrust my out-turned palm further forward. "Hand only."

Three pairs of heavy feet tromp into the room. "This it?" one of the men asks regarding the piano.

Vialtseva briefly nods to the man, then tells me, "Help me up. I'll show you the house. Do you have a name?"

I GATHER MY possessions into a burlap sack, then slump in the hay to wait for Fenechka. Dread of my new employment lies so heavy on my chest, my breath comes in fits and starts.

Eyelids closed, I try to fend off the foreboding by taking refuge in gilded memories. Wild strawberries in the woods, ripe for picking. A river made expressly for swimming and ice slides. My cousin Platon's little hand in mine.

All had been well until that one blunder that caused my entire future to collapse. I step outside myself and watch fifteen-year-old Anna at the evening circle dances on Petrovo's village square, during the first year that the boys from the neighboring village attended. Any of the girls would have leapt at the chance to be Tomas's girlfriend, but the boy's blinding smile settled on me. How could I help but be flattered? The only attention I received from the local boys was stinging ridicule of my birthmark as well as my blond hair, an oddity in a village where everyone's hair was a shade of brown.

But Tomas told me that he loved how my silky hair shimmered in the sunlight. And that he could spend an eternity gazing into my soulful blue eyes. He promised to give me his grandmother's cross that she had worn around her neck every day until she died.

My heart has always been too generous to say no to a request. Especially to a boy with a bewitching smile. When an evening of dancing drew to a close, he and I would hold hands and wander into a field of green barley or sneak into the barn. He'd stroke my hair and say soft, dreamy words. I allowed him to kiss me and, as the summer progressed, lift my skirt. His fingers did amazing things to me, and in due course, the inevitable happened.

Twice we lay together in the hay barn before summer yielded to the north wind. The dances stopped, and families huddled close to their massive stoves. By the time the Advent fast began in November, I knew a baby was growing inside me.

In a tiny village with two dirt roads and fifty-two thatched-roof huts, the memory of a peasant's sins lasts generations. I was fully aware that, according to Petrovo's collective consciousness, the shameless behavior of a promiscuous girl weakened the moral sinews that held together the family and, by extension, the village.

To this day, I can hear the outrage in Mama's voice and picture the tears in her eyes when she declared that if word of my pregnancy filtered through the village, my neighbors would shear off my long braid and tar my skirt. I'd be tied behind a cart and paraded past every hut in Petrovo while insults and garbage were hurled at me. I'd be shunned as a marriage partner and condemned to the life of a destitute spinster. Even beyond that, my family's reputation would be so tainted, we'd lose our standing in the village.

So Mama secretly sought the aid of a midwife in another village. The abortion, however, was a butchery. My insides were so torn that I bled for a week and was sick with fever. In a hut where a dozen people lived shoulder to shoulder, even the dullest member of my family was able to piece the puzzle together. It was only a matter of time before the gossip spilled into the village.

During my convalescence, God decided that death would take the owner of the estate that included my little village. The Count's extended family traveled from Moscow to attend his funeral. Mama spotted an opportunity to shield me and the rest of the family from Petrovo's merciless retribution. She pleaded with the dead Count's visiting cousin, Valeryan Kirillovich Shelgunov, to take me back to Moscow as a family servant. The carriage journey of several weeks would be sufficiently long that there could be no return.

Valeryan Kirillovich had no need of an additional servant, but another Moscow cousin, who did not attend the funeral, was looking for a reliable housekeeper and nanny. That cousin, to my eventual dismay, was Nikolai Osipovich Shelgunov.

THE AFTERNOON SHADOWS are lengthening as I fold myself into Fenech-ka's stalwart arms and sniffle my thank-yous and goodbyes. I make no mention of Vialtseva's vile demands.

When I finally tear myself away, I set off without a glance at the towering Shelgunov house next door. I put it behind me, just as someday I'll put mean old Vialtseva and her ill-mannered grandson behind me.

Not only is that currently an impossibility, but I fully believe the mule-toothed boy won't remain content with the terms his grandmother accepted. At some point, I'll have to fend him off. Is he the violent type? I'm suddenly burning hot, even as autumn's chilly twilight darkens. Fueled by self-loathing, sweat breaks out under my coat. I'm only seventeen years old, but I'm a harlot all the same—one who has slaughtered an unborn child and whose livelihood depends on fulfilling the wanton desires of men.

It's not too late, I remind myself. I could turn back right now. Vialtseva can't trace me, not that she would even try. I could return to Fenechka's warm meals and reassuring guidance. I could go back to where it's safe, and—

"Good evening, mademoiselle."

CHAPTER 5

September
1867

I REEL BACK, clutching my sack to my belly. A man stands to my right, less than three strides away.

"I apologize for startling you." He flicks the stub of a cigarette into the street, then touches the brim of his cap with his fingertips. "I thought you saw me here."

"My mind was elsewhere."

"I can't blame a lady for being jittery when she's alone after dark. After all, that's why, as a policeman, I'm here. Perhaps you'll feel safer if I escort you to your destination?"

I take note of the metal insignia on his cap, as well as the heavy police baton peeking out beneath his short leather jacket. The warm concern in his voice slows my racing heart.

"I know most of the residents and shopkeepers in this area. I don't recall seeing you." He runs a thumb and forefinger along his jaw.

"New to the neighborhood. Just headed down this block, so you needn't trouble yourself. Thank you, though." I resume walking, but at a quickened pace. How could I allow him to escort me when I'm not sure of my own destination? To Vialtseva's or back to the stable?

He falls into step beside me. "No trouble whatsoever. It's what I'm paid to do."

I'm distrustful of everyone I encounter in Moscow, and understandably so. My first fifteen years were confined to a village where everyone knew everyone else, from birth until death. Here in this big city, we are all strangers to each other.

Entering the reassuring glow of a streetlamp, I make a quick assessment. The man's clean-shaven face boasts a firm jaw. His boyishly blond hair pokes from beneath his cap, in stark contrast to the lines around his eyes, which suggest he's well into midlife.

"I think you'll find this section of town to be quite pleasant," he says. "Safe. Quiet. An unpretentious neighborhood to raise children. Do you have children?"

"No."

"I've found the residents to be quite friendly. You see, I step in if the on-duty policeman becomes ill or has other troubles. That way, I've become familiar with various parts of the city."

"Oh."

"I enjoy the diversity." His voice lowers. "And I think gaining experience in the assorted neighborhoods will help my chances of advancement." He chuckles at his disclosure.

We're only two houses shy of Vialtseva's time-worn cottage, and I'm still tempted to turn tail and run back to the stable. I need to be rid of the policeman so I can think clearly. I stop walking and pivot toward him. "Thank you for escorting me."

He turns to face me but says nothing.

I give a courteous nod of my head. "Good night."

He glances at the house behind me. "You live with the Trediakovsky family?"

"N-n-no. With Viktorya Borisovna Vialtseva."

"Ahhh. Then you're replacing Olya."

"Yes."

He resumes walking toward Vialtseva's while I trail behind him, my mind flying in all directions. I could turn and run away, but that's a ridiculously childish thing to do. Not to mention, the policeman could easily outrun me if he had a mind to.

Or I could tell him that I've forgotten something, then go back to the stable. But it's growing terribly dark, and my nerves are already in tatters.

Or I could continue onward to Vialtseva's.

I lower my eyes with modesty. "Being a servant, I use the back entrance."

"Oh, of course." He proceeds to walk around the side of the building, leaving me with no choice but to follow.

At the back stairs, I turn and thank him. "I feel safer knowing you're on duty. Good night."

He lifts his cap. "My pleasure, mademoiselle." He stands arrow-straight as he waits for me to climb the steps.

When I reach the door, I pause and glance over my shoulder in the ridiculous hope that he has disappeared. I run my upper teeth across my lower lip. If I enter this house, I'll be making a pact with the Devil.

Goosebumps race the length of my body as my knuckles rap on the door. Then I turn the handle.

CHAPTER 6

December
1867

I CARRY THE goblet of Bordeaux to the bedroom, just as I do every evening. Vialtseva, suffering from a stuffy head and a congested chest, is engulfed by the mounds of pillows propped against the carved headboard.

The old crone's claw reaches for the wineglass but halts halfway when a coughing fit takes hold. When the hacking subsides, she seizes the goblet. "Sun's barely set and I'm already worn out. I'd better get a good night's rest." Her implication is that if she doesn't, the blame falls on me and retribution will be exacted.

Hands clasped in front of my apron, I stand beside the bed while Vialtseva takes a sip. During the two and a half months I've been here, the routine has become familiar and loathsome.

"Fetch the doctor tomorrow. This cough is unbearable, and your liniment isn't helping." Her voice contains a perpetual scowl.

"Yes, Madame." I itch to remind the crotchety old hag that the smelly liniment I rubbed on her sunken chest is her own, not mine.

Vialtseva's next swallow of wine is followed by a long stretch of nose blowing. When the undertaking is complete, her head drops against the pillows, and her chest billows from the exertion.

When fully recuperated from her honking and trumpeting, Vialtseva shakes the wadded handkerchief at me. "What have you done to these hankies?"

"Pardon?"

"My nose is raw from them. They were never this rough when Olya was here. Heavens above, girl, these are made of silk. Instead, they feel like"—she rubs a corner of the fabric between her thumb and forefinger—"woven pig bristles."

"I washed them just as you instructed. First cold water, followed by the second washing in lukewarm water. Then rinsed in cold water."

"Are you making certain they dry gradually? I told you before—dry them gradually."

"I'll be sure to do that." *You old witch.*

After Vialtseva takes another sip, I ask, hoping to hasten the fourth and final swallow, "Is there anything else, Madame?"

"I want poached fish for dinner tomorrow. Make sure it's fresh. Not like that rank sturgeon you bought last time."

"Yes, Madame. Will that be all?" I hope it is, as I'm in no mood this evening to massage her swollen feet.

"Take Vasily some cheese and biscuits. He and some chums are studying for an examination tomorrow."

I curtsy, my heart sinking at the thought of trudging across the cold, dark yard to the carriage house. I had envisioned putting my achy feet beside the fire in the parlor and savoring a steaming glass of tea before retiring early to my bleak little mattress in the back hallway.

I scurry from the bedroom and the decaying old woman, closing the door precisely halfway, as per Vialtseva's preference. I gather the food and kitchenware in a basket, don my galoshes and gray wool coat, and trudge on the snow-packed track across the backyard to the dilapidated two-story structure. The bottom level is a long-empty carriage stall, and the top is Vasily's single-room bachelor flat. Raucous laughter from the diligent students spills down the wooden steps.

I send a quick prayer of gratitude to the Blessed Virgin that the dimwitted oaf has friends visiting tonight, so I won't have to . . . I grind my teeth, refusing to finish the thought, even in the privacy of my own mind.

In the dim light of the sickle moon, I clutch the railing and climb the stairs, which are thick with snow and ice. I knock on the door. "It's Anna. With your food."

"Yeah," Vasily's nasal voice replies.

The metal doorknob is ice-cold against my bare fingertips. I turn it one way, then the other, arguing with it until the cantankerous latch loosens its grip.

Vasily and his two friends are seated at the small, square table. Although open books occupy part of the table's scarred top, they're hard to locate among the wine bottles and dirty dishes. One of the boys, Maks, is a frequent visitor. He's reed-thin with pimples that match Vasily's. I don't recognize the other fellow, a greasy-haired boy with red suspenders and a finger digging about in his nose.

"Your grandmother sent this to help you study." I set the basket on the floorboards and begin stacking the food-crusted dishes to make room on the table. After backhanding the crumbs off the table, I reach down to empty the basket of its contents: tin of biscuits, block of cheese, knife, cutting board. Not one of the three boys lifts a finger to help.

"I'll need more coal tomorrow," Vasily informs me, exposing flecks of tobacco caught between his buckteeth.

"Will there be anything else?" I ask.

"Hey!" Maks's bellow fills the small room. "You're not leaving already? Have a drink with us and play some cards." The back of his hand shoves a half-empty wine bottle in my direction.

"I have work to do, just as you have studying to do." When I turn and bend over to lower the stacked dishes into the basket, Maks smacks my backside.

I'm both shocked and thrown off-balance. The pile of dishes sails from my hands and shatters on the floor.

My every muscle cringes. Vialtseva will skin me alive. And Vasily won't accept a thimbleful of responsibility.

A hand tugs the skirt of my coat. I twist around to see it belongs to the red-suspendered fellow. I grab the wool material and yank it from his grasp. "All of you, keep your hands to yourselves!"

Red Suspenders takes on a penitent look and pats his knee. "Come here, sweetheart, and let me make it up to you." The corners of his mouth, moist with saliva, curve into a smile.

Foolishly, I look to Vasily to end the harassment. But the gutless simpleton, true to his nature, grins and entwines his fingers behind his head.

Is this merely a cat-and-mouse game? Or are they drunk enough to take advantage of me?

"Oh, Anna, forgive us," Maks drones. "We don't mean any harm. Sometimes we get carried away." He contributes some brown spittle to the spittoon beside his chair. "Vasily was just telling us about the extra attention you bestow on him."

Red Suspenders chimes in. "Sounds like a most congenial arrangement."

"Oh, it is." Vasily's head bobs like it's atop a spring. "It is."

I spin to face the door, intent on a quick escape, but Maks bounds from his chair and blocks my way. He takes a step toward me, then a second. My heart hammers as my feet scuff backward until I encounter the edge of the table.

Red Suspenders clasps his hands flat across his chest and leans back to balance on his chair's two rear legs. "Why not just lift that skirt of yours and show us what Vasily's been getting?"

My head whirls toward Vasily. "What kind of lies have you been telling them?"

"Come on," Red Suspenders continues. "Olya at least gave us a peek."

Maks winks. "But we were hoping for more from you."

Vasily comes to life. "That's enough from the two of you!"

I look at him with gratitude. Maybe he's not a complete good-for-naught dullard. But my thankfulness is short-lived.

"She's for my use only. If you want any samples, you'll have to pay me."

Red Suspenders' eyes rove from the top of my head to my galoshes, then back up to linger on the heavy gray wool that covers my chest. "She ain't worth much."

I try to sidestep Maks and move to the door, but he brashly crosses his arms and moves step for step with me. "How about two for the price of one?" he calls to Vasily. Then he lowers his voice to me. "You ever taken on two at one time, sweetheart?" His chest is rising and flattening like a fireplace bellows.

My eyes dart to and fro. I can't watch all of them at the same time—the two at the table and Maks on my opposite side. "Vasily, this has gone too far. End it now." Try as I might to keep my voice low and commanding, it trills with fright.

Vasily straightens his slouch, proud that for once in his shiftless life, he possesses something someone else might want. "She's not interested in your two-for-one idea. She goes to the highest bidder." His open palm smacks the table, causing the empty wine bottles to shudder and the biscuits to jump inside their tin.

My attention is caught by the gleam of lamplight off a trembling sliver of metal. The cheese knife is only the length of my longest finger, but I recently sharpened it. It could do damage.

"My bid?" Maks unfolds one arm so his fingernails can contemplatively rake his greasy, pimply cheeks. "Not much."

Red Suspenders again takes measure of me. "She's prettier than Olya, I'll say that much. But she's too skinny for my taste."

I give the boys only half an ear. I'm calculating my distance from the cheese knife (an arm's length) versus my distance from Maks (two strides). Red Suspenders, tilted back in his chair, is too unstable to move quickly. Vasily's mind, whether sober or soused, is always slow to react.

Lines appear between Vasily's eyebrows as he considers his friends' appraisals and watches his prestige ebb away. After due consideration, he curls up one side of his mouth while his head makes tiny nods of agreement. "True, she's not worth much. But she's at least worth enough to slip me some answers during the exam tomorrow." His comment is addressed to Red Suspenders, who apparently has more to offer in the classroom than does Maks.

I wipe my moist palms on my coat.

"I want to see the entire parcel before I commit," Red Suspenders sneers.

I lunge and grab the knife, then spin toward Maks, my outstretched arm wielding the knife in a huge arc.

Maks hurtles away from the flashing blade. I have just enough room to dash past him.

There's a clamor at the table. I fling a glance in that direction. Only Vasily is visible. Red Suspenders has toppled his chair backward.

My eyes and the knife are pointed at Maks as my left hand tries to turn the doorknob. It slips in my sweaty palm. I grip harder and wrench it. The latch won't loosen.

I crank the knob in the opposite direction. The latch holds firm. *Open!* my insides scream as I jiggle the knob. *Open!*

Maks starts to close the short distance between him and me. My clammy hand wrenches the handle back and forth. Suddenly the latch releases its hold.

The freedom of bracing cold air washes over me.

I grip the railing and angle my feet sideways to keep from slipping down the narrow, ice-slicked steps. I dare to breathe only when I reach the bottom. No one follows me.

Fits of laughter spill from above, along with the words *yellow-haired bitch*. Raucous shrieks chase me as I run across the yard. Once in the house, I slam the bolt into its latch and fall back against the door, my chest heaving.

Were they laughing because they had gotten all they wanted—to frighten me nearly to death? Had it been their idea of youthful amusement, picking on someone merely because they could? Or would liquor and bravado have fueled them to commit despicable deeds?

My coat weighs as heavy on me as a bear's hide. The room is clogged with Vialtseva's pungent liniment. The house itself feels oppressive, as if laden with years of malevolence. I need air, wholesome air that hasn't been fouled by Vialtseva or those abominable dolts.

I drape my knitted shawl over my head and tie it beneath my chin. Silent footsteps carry me out the front door.

As I plunge into the hushed, deserted blackness, I wonder why the streetlamps aren't lit. Perhaps the lamplighter hasn't had enough time to make all his rounds, now that winter's darkness falls so early.

I glance behind to make sure the boys aren't following. Although I'm still shaken by their threats, the brisk night makes me feel cleaner and safer than I ever feel inside that dungeon of gloom and tyranny that Vialtseva calls home.

I vow to visit Fenechka this Sunday. Perhaps she knows of another opening for a domestic servant, a house inhabited by virtuous, kindhearted people.

I turn up the collar of my coat and, having forgotten my gloves, dig my hands deep into its pockets.

"Good evening."

My breath stalls. I stand as still as a statue, my eyes whisking about wildly. First, I see the burning tip of a cigarette, then the inky outline of a man.

CHAPTER 7

December

1867

IT'S THE POLICEMAN, leaning casually against the pole of a streetlamp.

My sigh of relief and *Good evening* emerge in a single white stream.

I've encountered him only once since my first day at Vialtseva's, but we didn't speak. He merely tipped his hat, and I returned the greeting with a nod.

"You're out late tonight." He pulls himself upright from the lamppost and moves toward me, his boots crunching on packed snow. "Headed somewhere?" He halts a couple of paces from me.

"No. Just taking in a bit of night air."

"A little nippy for that, I'd say." He pushes back his cap with a gloved finger. The dull moonlight falls on his face, and I'm taken aback. His gaze is fixed and piercing, like that of a cat stalking its prey. His eyes had seemed so kind and helpful that first day. Is the difference merely twilight versus pitch-darkness?

"A bit nippy, yes, but Madame Vialtseva keeps her house a little warm for my liking."

I resume walking, and he joins me, asking polite questions. Is working for Vialtseva what I expected? Have I become familiar with the neighborhood?

"You must enjoy walking at night. I see you quite often." He takes a deep pull on his cigarette before tossing it into the snow.

My brow wrinkles. *Quite often?* The first time our paths crossed was at dusk. The only other instance occurred when I was returning from the market, my handbasket loaded with purchases. It was at sunset, which, during the short days of winter, certainly couldn't be termed "night."

"I'd best be getting back. Madame is feeling a bit under the weather."

"Yes, on frosty nights like this, it seems you should be home, sitting by the fire, doing embroidery. Isn't that what respectable women do?"

Unease creeps through my bones. "As I said, I'm headed there now."

Before I can take a step in the return direction, his hand grabs my wrist and tightens like a noose. "Just a moment. I expect an answer."

Frightened prickles race down my spine. I make certain my voice is apologetic.

"I'm sorry, sir. I thought I answered your questions." Why does this policeman think ill of me?

"I'm curious about these walks, these strolls. Whom do you stroll with?" His lips, barely moving, are stamped with a cold dryness.

"No one."

He takes a step closer, then another, forcing me to move backward until I'm against an iron fence. In heart-thumping confusion, I blurt, "I'm just a servant who works in the house all day and needs a touch of fresh air. Please allow me to go home."

"Walking alone at night could be indicative of unseemly behavior." The man's jeer reveals teeth as sharp as a wolf's. He releases my wrist, only to seize the collar of my coat. "You know what I think? I think you work all day. And part of the night, too."

My spine goes rigid, and my head swings in fear. What is he insinuating?

His hand plunges from my collar to my upper arm and encircles it. He hustles me down the street, trapping me between him and the iron fence.

Terror courses through me like wildfire. I try to pull back, but he keeps dragging me along with him.

"That tight-fisted old crone doesn't pay you enough to keep a chicken alive. Which gives me grounds for suspicion that you're a nocturnal butterfly."

"A what?"

"You supplement your wages with your *strolls*, don't you?"

The fence ends at the mouth of an alley, into which he pushes me. He thrusts me face-first against a building and presses himself full-length along my backside, grinding my cheek into the cold bricks.

My garbled words tumble out chaotically. "Sir, if you'd just listen to me. Please, let me go. Please! I've done nothing. I swear."

"You aren't going anywhere." His breath is hot on my cheek. "Not until I see your yellow ticket."

"What?" I rasp, unable to take a full breath. My ribs, crushed between the policeman and the building, feel as if they could snap.

"Where's your yellow ticket?"

"I don't know what you're talking about. Truly!"

"Give me your goddamned yellow ticket!"

"Ticket?"

He takes a half step back from me, and life-giving air rushes down my throat.

His hand goes to the top of my head, and his fingers curl under the shawl. He yanks it backward to my neck, then twists. The double knot holds under my chin. He winds the material tighter.

My hands fly to the knot. *Breath! I need breath!* I strain to wedge my fingers under the knot, desperate to pull it away from my throat. But his hold is too strong.

Only after his long, low snigger slices the freezing air does the policeman release the shawl. He spins me around to face him, and lays a forearm across my neck, pinning me against the building. I wheeze, sucking in only partial breaths. With both hands, I try to pull his arm from my neck, but he's too powerful.

Using his teeth, he removes the glove from his free hand. He switches arms across my throat and repeats the process on this other hand. He shoves one glove deep into my mouth; the other he tucks into his coat pocket. His hips and thighs press hard against me.

With an unhurried gentleness, his free hand undoes the shawl's knot. Bit by slow bit, he pulls one end of the shawl downward until it falls from my neck to the ground. His forearm remains across my throat.

"You're a cute little blue-eyed liar. But not very smart. You still insist you don't have a yellow ticket, huh?"

Frantic with fear, I shake my head. What's he going to do? Take me to jail? Rape me? Kill me?

His mouth gloats while his hand moves to the lapel of my coat. With the same languid motion he used to remove my shawl, he undoes the top button.

My shoulders hunch, and my arms draw tight against my sides as I pull myself inward. My legs clasp together. My hands seek protection in my pockets. My fingers strike something hard, cold, and smooth.

The cheese knife.

"You have two choices." The policeman's head swings back and forth dolefully. "You can either show me a yellow ticket. Or you can oblige me like you oblige that witless grandson of Vialtseva."

His fingers calmly work at the second button.

My heart pulsates wildly. I can barely think over its pounding. The knife. I used it once tonight. If I use it again, I'll have to do more than threaten.

Can I do it? Me, who never in my life hurt a single creature?

His hand drops to the third button, just above my waist.

I'll have to be quick. And strong.

My fingers discern the knife's handle and the sharp side of the blade.

He undoes the fourth button and slips a hand inside my coat. His palm covers my breast. His sigh is only just audible.

But Nikolai Osipovich Shelgunov taught me what that sigh means. It means a man's attention is focused on one thing and dulled to everything else.

This allows me a brief moment to plan. Knife straight up. Plunge under the jaw. Right where it meets the underside of his chin. Jab like my brothers did when they bled out a sheep.

I tilt my head back as if I'm succumbing to his hands. From under hooded eyes, I watch him study my elongated neck.

I let my shoulders fall as though in surrender, disguising the motion of my hand gripping the handle.

Warm steam rolls from between his lips as an animal noise rises from deep in his throat.

Both my arms move simultaneously. One hand jerks the knife from my pocket while the other one wrenches his glove from my mouth.

The knife speeds upward, though I misjudge the distance. It nicks his jawbone, then veers up his cheek. I feel the drag of the skin as the blade slices.

Quicker than I can react, he seizes my wrist and squeezes until my fist opens. The knife falls into the snow.

Suddenly, it isn't pitch black. Someone is across the street. It's the lamplighter. He just flared up a lamp.

My attacker's hand leaps across my mouth. My teeth, partially apart, close down on a finger with all their force.

His hand jerks back just long enough for me to scream.

His fist smacks the side of my mouth, knocking me down. Points of light shoot through a haze. Amid that fog, I see a figure run up to us.

"What's going on here?" the lamplighter puffs.

I reach out a hand toward him. My tongue forms thick words. "Help me."

"That bitch stabbed me."

"Stabbed you?" The lamplighter is incredulous. "That little thing stabbed you?"

The policeman kicks away my outstretched arm. He kneels beside me and punches a knee into the center of my back, securing me to the ground. The breath flies out of me.

He picks up the cheese knife, and I hear my shawl being slashed. He yanks my hands behind my back and ties them together with a strip of my shawl. My braid is yanked, lifting my face from the snow, and he shoves a corner of the shawl's remains into my mouth.

Nooo! my throat tries to wail.

"I was in the process of arresting her."

Help! I struggle to scream, but only muffled sounds emerge.

"Arresting her?" The middle-aged man grows increasingly flabbergasted as each detail is unveiled.

"She sliced my face."

"She sliced your face?"

The policeman rises and wipes his bloody cheek with the back of his free hand. He stares at the glistening stain, then flings his hand as if to cast off the offending substance.

The lamplighter strokes his chin as his eyes trace the invisible droplets of blood through the air. "Why'd she slice you?"

The policeman's voice drops to a confidential, man-to-man tone. "No yellow ticket."

"You don't say." Hands braced on his thighs, the lamplighter bends forward at the waist for a closer look at me. I squirm and struggle, with screams trapped in my throat.

"I'm Officer Shestov, by the way. And I want to thank you for showing up just when you did."

The lamplighter straightens and nods his affirmation that he's pleased to have helped an officer of the law in imminent danger.

"If you'll excuse me now, I have to take her to the station house."

CHAPTER 8

December
1867

LIKE CAGED CHICKENS on market day, women fill the damp, squalid cell. Some stand. Some crouch. Some lay curled on the filthy floor. The lucky ones occupy the sparse benches. My bruised cheek throbs, my headache pounds all the way to my toes, and I shiver with cold even though I have my coat on.

I stand cowering against the wall, keeping as much distance as possible between me and the reeking stink of Moscow's lowest inhabitants. I was raised among people who smelled of hard work and village life. Sweat, manure, and stove smoke were part and parcel of my everyday world back home. But those smells are a far cry from the putrid stench of unwashed bodies, festering sores, fresh vomit, and pools of urine.

Home. The word echoes forlornly in my throbbing head.

Where is home now? Not Petrovo. Not Shelgunov's house. Not Vialtseva's.

No home. No employment. No rubles. No helping hand from a kindly neighbor. No one to rescue me from this dungeon.

My eyelids quiver as I realize those problems are behind me now. I'll be supplied with a gruesome place to live and barely enough food to keep my body alive. As surely as a cat pounces on a mouse, I'll be found guilty of assaulting a police officer.

Prison will be my new home.

Time crawls by—an hour, maybe two. Rats and cockroaches vie for space on the grimy floor. Four seasoned prisoners squat and roll dice in a corner. Women leave the cell and are replaced with new arrivals, most of whom seem quite familiar with the place. I become numb to everything except hopeless anguish.

Crouched on the floor beside me is a somnolent girl of about fifteen. When she collapses and her face splats into her own vomit, I move to another wall. I've been standing too long, and my legs are about to give way. I lower myself onto the disgusting floor and lean the back of my aching head against the wall. I close my eyes, unwilling to look at the morose wretchedness that surrounds me—women who are stuporous, boisterous, shaky, decayed.

Two new arrivals stumble into the cell and slump to the floor beside me. One asks, "Hey, you the blondie that knifed Shestov?"

I look at the woman but then quickly glance away from the weeping sore on her lip.

"From what I hear, you gashed that maggot real good," the second woman splutters while her dirty fingernails claw at whatever is crawling about in her thin hair.

"Next time, aim for his balls, not his face," the first one suggests.

The two of them giggle, drop their foreheads onto their upraised knees, and simultaneously sink into oblivion.

Time refuses to budge. The cold from the stone floor creeps into my bones, so I stand up again, kicking away a bold rat in the process.

More women arrive, including a stoop-shouldered old woman not much bigger around than one of the bars of the cell. As she enters, her quivering, liver-spotted hand pinches the guard's cheek.

"Aniska, you behave yourself." His dull tone implies he's uttered these words to her many a time.

The ancient woman hobbles on her cane toward me, and I long to disappear into myself. She tilts her fissured face up toward mine and pinches my bruised cheek with frosty, brittle fingers. I clench my teeth to keep from crying out in pain.

"Look at those rosy cheeks. You must be a blushing bride." Her grin is a black hole. "Is that why you're here—getting ready for your wedding?" Receiving no response, the old dame taps my shoulder with her cane. "Bashful on your wedding day, are you?"

The guard reissues his listless directive for the woman to behave herself. Then he admits a hefty-framed woman in her early twenties. As the door bangs shut behind the newcomer, she tells the guard, "You have my gratitude for showing me the way. Coulda never found it by myself."

The guard warns, "Watch your sharp tongue with me, Irina."

A handful of the women call their greetings.

"Hello, Irina!"

"You're looking good."

"How's life going?"

The husky woman responds. "Life's been good since I got off the streets." A head taller than anyone in the cell, she isn't so much fat as she is bulky. As she slides out of her coat, I see arms that rival my father's.

Irina singles out one of the women. "Why don't you join us at the house, Faina?"

"Naw. As an *odinochka*, whatever I make is mine to keep."

"That may be true," Irina replies, "but it's a dangerous life out there on the streets. We got an opening. Let me know, and I'll talk to Sophia Mikhailovna."

Irina glances about and spots the old woman rapping me with her cane. "Hey, Aniska, stop harassing that girl. Look, here's an empty spot on the bench where you can sit down." She points a commanding index finger at a young woman sitting on a bench, then jerks her thumb backward over her shoulder and quips, "Thanks for warming the seat for her."

The young woman vacates her spot while bestowing Irina with the nastiest of scowls.

Irina takes the shriveled Aniska by the elbow and helps ease her frail body onto the bench.

Following a weary sigh, the old woman lifts her right hand and studies her yellowed palm. The index finger of her left hand goes to the outside edge of her right thumb and slowly traces the outline of each leathered finger, like a cat cleaning each of its toes. When she reaches the outer edge of her little finger, she retraces her fingers backward until she reaches her thumb.

I watch as she continues the ritual, scrutinizing the palm of her left hand and running her right index finger up and down each finger, from thumb to pinkie, then back again. Satisfied that the palms have received adequate attention, she flips her right hand and stares at its wrinkled back, her left index finger slowly tracing each knobby finger—out, over, down.

The big woman approaches me with an open smile, rolling her eyes in Aniska's direction and twirling her finger at her temple. She folds her arms across her generous bosom and looks downward at me, even though we're both standing. "Name's Irina."

"Anna," I croak, my throat raging for something to drink.

"You new?"

"My first time here."

"They get you without a yellow ticket?"

I take measure of this Irina woman. Her clothes and hair are clean. No visible sores. She was kind to the old lady. She gives off a scent that reminds me of the rose garden behind the Shelgunov house. I so want to trust this woman. Yet it makes no sense to trust someone who is so at ease in a jail cell.

"I don't even know what a yellow ticket is. I was just walking. Just walking, that's all. The policeman, he asked to see my yellow ticket and when I didn't have one, he . . . he . . ."

"It's all right. You'll feel better if you talk about it. And trust me, Anna, nothing you say will offend my tender sensibilities."

I don't know what *tender sensibilities* are, but I find deep comfort in the sound of my own name in this alien place. "He tried to rape me. But I cut his face with my knife. He might have killed me except the lamplighter came upon us."

"Which one of our fine officers was it?"

"I think his name is Shestov."

A long, loud whistle comes from the woman. "You knifed Shestov?" She gives my shoulder a congratulatory slap that nearly buckles my knees. "He give you that bruise on your cheek?"

I nod.

"That hell-smoked devil!" Irina, with a colorful array of obscenities, describes how the crooked policeman routinely exploits his position for his own gain, through everything from bribery to extortion. "The filthy pig's specialty is using the yellow ticket as a threat to get what he wants from young girls. You just happened to walk by the wrong policeman. A bad piece of luck, for sure."

"But what exactly is a yellow ticket?"

"You're fresh from the country, aren't you?" Irina winks. "A yellow ticket is a license. All prostitutes are supposed to have one. Otherwise, you're illegal. Of course, a lot of women get away without having a yellow ticket 'cause they just do it every now and again to earn a few extra rubles. But if you're a full-fledged odinochka, or if you are in a house like me, eventually you wind up with one."

"Odinochka?"

"You're as green as grass!" Despite the jibe, her smile is friendly. "A streetwalker. An independent prostitute."

Our conversation is interrupted when Aniska rises to her unsteady feet and repeatedly thumps her cane against the wall. A couple of nearby women calm her down. Once again seated, she resumes counting her fingers.

"She's well known," I observe.

"Everyone knows Aniska, poor old gal. She's the ancient queen of this hellhole."

I grin ever so slightly. "She asked me if it was my wedding day."

Irina's belly heaves with laughter. "That's a good one!"

"What's wrong with her? Just crazy?"

"Long history. She worked in one of the houses for years. When she got too old to attract good customers, she was forced onto the street. Somewhere along the way, she went mad. Some say it's from syphilis. The police mostly ignore her, but every so often she winds up here when she creates too much of a ruckus. Which, conveniently for her, is usually in the freezing dead of winter." Irina chuckles, and I try my best to do the same. "She's nutty, but she's not as bad as some. Some women are just plain diabolically crazy."

I don't know what *diabolically* means, but I let it pass.

Irina leans back against the wall, folds her arms, and crosses her ankles, like she's settling in for a lengthy stay. "So what do you do, Anna, when you're not in jail? You a servant?" Following my nod, she asks, "Are you happy with your employer?"

Don't cry, I tell myself. *Not in front of this group of hardened women.* With brute determination, I suck back the tears and tell Irina about the miserable treatment I received from Vialtseva, including my extra responsibilities with Vasily. "I can't return to that old biddy's house."

Irina pats my hand. "You're an attractive girl. How old are you?"

"Seventeen."

"Those blue eyes are bewitching. Why not join our house? We got an opening."

I must have heard incorrectly. Was I just asked to become a prostitute? I let out a protracted breath. "Oh, I . . . I don't think so." My mouth goes dry as I shake my aching head. "I'd like to find a job as a seamstress."

"A seamstress." Irina looks at me with pity. "Newcomers start out in dank, dark cellars, pushing the needle twelve hours a day until their fingers are bloody. And you'll live a half step above starvation. You're far better off joining a reputable house like ours. We take care of each other."

"But the thought of men pawing me . . . ?"

"Oh." Irina's voice is flat. "You a virgin?" The final word seems to stick on her tongue, like it's from a foreign language.

"N-n-no." I describe Shelgunov's demands.

"Well, then, you're no stranger to men. And you don't have lice, do you? Our madam has no tolerance for lice."

While Irina gives my scalp a thorough inspection, she discusses her proposition as offhandedly as if she were reviewing tomorrow's dinner menu. "There's eight of us girls plus the owner, Sophia Mikhailovna, but she doesn't serve customers anymore. And Grisha lives in the house too. You'll like him. He tends bar, takes care of all the heavy work, and keeps the customers entertained while they're waiting for us."

Irina pauses, and I stare wide-eyed at her like I'm a complete dimwit.

"Sophia Mikhailovna expects a lot from us. But she wields her sword justly, which is more than I can say for most madams. Ours is a reputable house. Decent customers. Decent food. A hardworking girl can make fifty rubles a month plus free room and board. And one more thing. Sophia Mikhailovna has contacts. She can probably get you out of this hellhole."

My mind reels, first in one direction and then in the other.

> Fifty rubles a month!
> GODLESS ACTS!
> Good food.
> MEN PAWING AT ME.
> A warm bed.
> PREGNANCY.
> An honest employer.
> DISEASE.
> Safety.
> SIN.
> Hope.
> WHORE.

And of immediate concern, Irina's statement: *Sophia Mikhailovna has contacts . . . get you out of this hellhole.* Leaving with Sophia Mikhailovna is probably my only way out of this loathsome cell.

"I don't know . . . " I clutch my parched throat. "What about this?" I raise a finger to the red blotch on my cheek.

"Cover it with makeup." Irina shrugs a hefty shoulder. "Hell, Sophia Mikhailovna will probably like you better because of it."

I can't make sense of that last comment.

Irina continues, "Your other option is to get a job in a factory, where you'll work twelve hours a day, get raped by the boss, and you still can't feed yourself 'cause you're paid half what a man makes."

"Irina! This is the last time I'm bailing you out of this pigsty!"

A woman, whom I assume is Sophia Mikhailovna, and who looks to be in her midthirties, blows like a gale into the cellblock corridor. A fur-trimmed scarlet cloak drapes over her arm, partially covering layers of flouncing vermillion dress fabric. A sturdy corset cinches her waist and elevates her breasts. The woman's brown hair, held in place with gem-studded combs, is piled high like a crown. Waddling behind her is a roly-poly guard.

"I knew she'd rescue me," Irina whispers. "Do you want me to talk to her about taking you on?"

I go lightheaded, as if all my blood has drained to my feet. My teeth tug frantically at my lower lip.

Irina squeezes my hand. "No reason to be fearful. You'll see."

The jewel-headed madam swooshes up to the cell and taps her foot while the guard opens the door. Irina exits, and she and her madam talk outside the cell, their voices low. At one point, the older woman sweeps a keen gaze over me. I instantly lower my eyes. The two women walk down the corridor of cells, leaving me to my thoughts.

What should I do? Irina's offer is the most vile of propositions. But perhaps there's no other way out of the quagmire my life has become.

What would it be like to live in a house of . . . of . . . prostitution? I try to imagine it: Having a life of my own, not one dictated by people like despicable Shelgunov and peevish Vialtseva. Being surrounded by nice friends and lovely clothes. Looking forward to a secure future.

But how do prostitutes keep from getting pregnant? They must know secret ways to prevent babies. Besides, my mother, still angry over my immoral behavior, said that my botched abortion probably left me with a barren womb.

No! No! How could I even consider such an evil choice, damnable by an eternity in Hell?

But what of it? I've already prostituted myself. The worm is already in the apple, is it not?

I'm still debating with myself when the roly-poly guard returns and calls, "Anna Vorontsova." With relief beyond measure, I leave the cell and trail after him to where Sophia Mikhailovna stands, hands on her hips, icily looking down at an officer seated behind a desk.

I stand to one side, next to Irina, my nervous fingers tugging the tail of my braid.

"Shestov is lower than an earthworm, and you know it," Sophia Mikhailovna spouts.

The officer runs his fingers through his oiled hair. "Your opinion of him doesn't change the fact she attacked him with a knife."

"That girl was carrying a knife to protect herself on the very streets that snake is supposedly safeguarding. But instead, she had to protect herself against his act of raw aggression. You, Chizhov, know perfectly well that Shestov is worthless to the citizens of this city. He's too busy accosting young girls and taking bribes and getting kickbacks."

"That's nothing but hearsay, and it's irrelevant to the charges against that girl."

"Shestov is harmful to the interests of civil society and makes a mockery of the law!" Sophia Mikhailovna bends forward and plants her splayed fingertips on the desk. Her tone turns confidential. "Look. There's the girl now. You can see for yourself, she's a trembling child, an innocent victim of all that is wrong with this city. Look into those blue eyes. Do they belong to a brutish murderer?"

"Shestov's testimony was that she—"

"Shestov's testimony?" Sophia Mikhailovna snorts. "You'd be lucky to get even a thimbleful of truth from that wad of scum. You believe a known blasphemer over a young girl, fresh from her native village, naïve to the ways of life in this decadent city?"

"Your sweetness-and-innocence tale doesn't impress me."

"Then maybe this will. Remember that incident with Liudmila Dmitrievna last year? You were lucky not to have lost your own job because of Shestov's nasty little indiscretion." She straightens her back and gives an elegant wave of her gloved hand.

"Those charges were never proved!" The officer's neck veins bulge.

"That's true. But I doubt your supervisor will tolerate any more scandals involving Officer Shestov. Such as attempted rape."

Tight-jawed, Chizhov glares at the woman. His white knuckles clutch the edge of his desk. "Even if we drop the assault charges, the fact remains that she is operating without a yellow ticket."

Sophia Mikhailovna cocks a hip. "Since when do citizens need a yellow ticket to partake of a walk?"

"Taking a walk is a far cry from walking the streets, which is what she was doing."

"Prove it. Besides, she'll be down at the medical-police tomorrow to get her ticket. She just this very day joined my house. She'll be all legal and proper by this time tomorrow."

"That doesn't excuse the fact she was operating without a license, a transgression of the law." The deepening red of Chizhov's cheeks is visible even through his wide sideburns.

As Chizhov's furor rises, Sophia Mikhailovna's voice becomes increasingly unflappable. "For once in your vapid life behind that desk, act like you have at least some intelligence. Failure to carry a yellow ticket is not a criminal offense, even for a known prostitute. You can impose fines, but you can't lock her up for it. She's being improperly detained."

Chizhov slams both palms against his desktop. "Take her out of here! And I'll be checking with the medical-police to make sure she gets her sweet, naïve ass registered!"

"You do that," coos Sophia Mikhailovna. "And make sure you write 'Charges dropped' on her record." She slips her cloak over her shoulders. When Chizhov sits motionless, she prompts, "There's your pen. There's your ink pot. Let's not dawdle."

Chizhov scribbles on a piece of paper and flings it into an overflowing basket. "I'll see you burn in Hell for your lies!"

"In due time."

Sophia Mikhailovna lifts the fur-lined hood of her cloak over her piled hair. Then she and her layers of skirts glide out of the building. Irina takes me by the elbow, just as she did with old Aniska. "Come along. You're free."

I pause, but only for a moment. What choice have I but to follow?

CHAPTER 9

December
1867

THE FRIGID NIGHTTIME is like a blast of freedom, and I thank God for it.

Sophia Mikhailovna's strides are long and fast. Gently falling snow mutes the city's incessant clamor but not the madam's words as she promptly sets about upbraiding Irina. "I'm fed up with your reckless behavior. I'm—"

"It wasn't my fault. I was—"

"Hold your tongue until I finish speaking. This is my last warning: One more fight, one more arrest, and I'm through with you."

"Is that a threat?" Irina's bold belligerence cleaves the frozen air.

"It's an expression of my intent." Sophia Mikhailovna goes silent for a moment, allowing her restrained tone to make its impression on the towering woman. "I'm confiscating your wages until your jail fine is paid off. And you're under house confinement until such time. Is that understood?"

"House confinement? You can't do that."

"According to whom?" Sophia Mikhailovna turns her attention to me. "I was told that you've exchanged sex for pay. Is that correct?"

Exchanged sex for pay? The madam has converted the vile act into a business transaction! But after all, I suppose that's what it was. "Yes, that's correct. And I'm very grateful for what you did at the police station."

"You can show your appreciation by working hard and honestly. Don't make me regret having bet on this horse."

What does she mean? I'm a horse?

While we cross the bridge to the south side of the city, the madam explains the house rules. Sex is an instrument of barter. There can be no sex without payment. A customer is allowed thirty minutes maximum. It's the girl's responsibility to promptly, as she describes it, "get it out, get it up, get it off."

It takes me a few moments to grasp what she means by this.

"Commit that saying to memory," she orders as we cross a street, picking our way through the slushy tracks left by sledge runners. "Get it out, get it up, get it off. Engrave it in your brain."

She warns that drunkenness in her girls isn't tolerated. Also, at the first suggestion that a girl stole money from a customer, she is dismissed.

"By law, I am required to provide lodging, heat, light, plentiful and healthful food, and sufficient linen. I furnish basic sheets, blankets, and pillowcases plus a coverlet. If you prefer lavish bedding, you'll have to supply your own. I expect you to change your bed linens daily, or more often if needed. A housekeeper comes in a couple of hours every day to tidy up the common areas. Each girl is responsible for keeping her room clean, and her body and clothes odor free. There's a public bath a block away. Use it. Is that understood?"

"Yes."

"Cooking is shared equally by all the girls. Over the years, I have found that my girls keep a slimmer figure if they're required to prepare their own food rather than having a hired cook. I keep the larder stocked with the basics—flour, salt, cabbage, vinegar, potatoes, lard, kasha, honey, tea, fresh meat or fish. If you want fancy foods, you'll have to buy them yourself. Is that understood?"

"Yes."

"Select your dresses and undergarments with care. One needs to get in and out of clothes quickly. Same with your hairstyle—elegant but simple. Primping can't consume too much time. Buy dresses with form-fitting bodices. Focus on—"

"Excuse me," I squeak. "What's a bodice?"

"The part of the gown from the neck to the waist. You want it to accentuate your attributes." Her eyes skim the length of my body. "Well, do what you can." She picks up where she left off. "Focus on dresses with skirts that drape over the hips. Stay away from garments that require a cage crinoline—that's an enormous, rigid petticoat underneath your dress. I'll assign someone to take you shopping tomorrow. Purchase only one dress, until we see if you work out. Understood?"

"Yes."

"I cut fifty-fifty with my girls. Most madams keep sixty-five or even seventy-five percent, but I pay extra since I expect you to do your own cooking. Understood?"

Fifty-fifty? Seventy-five percent? I have no inkling what those words mean, but I'm too exhausted to grasp an explanation. "Yes."

"I expect you to follow the regulations of the medical-police—or at least the regulations that are reasonable."

"I understand," I say, preempting her question, unable to care at this moment who the *medical-police* are or about the meaning of *regulations*.

"I run a good house." Her strides slow. "Here we are. 903 Sviatoslavsky Prospekt."

The two-story structure melds in with the other shoulder-to-shoulder buildings of cut stone and brick. Facing the street are three tall windows at ground level and three directly above them on the second story. Not a glimmer of light escapes through any of them.

At the front corner of the building, the yardman doffs his hat to us. I trail after the women down a side passageway of cobblestones. As we pass by an entry with a gaslight beside it, Sophia Mikhailovna's gloved fingers flutter toward the ornate, varnished wood door.

"This is the Gentlemen's Entrance."

At the end of the walkway, we round the building's corner to the back. Sophia Mikhailovna points a gloved finger at a nondescript painted door. "This is your entrance."

I take a deep breath as I cross the threshold. My new home. A whorehouse.

Immediately inside the door, narrow stairs jut off to our right and disappear, curving behind the hallway's wall as they head toward the front of the house. We, too, head toward the front of the house, along the hallway's long runner. Sophia Mikhailovna's fingertips lightly brush a closed door on the left. "My apartment. No one enters it without knocking. And when I'm not in it, it's locked."

A few strides farther, the hallway ends at a closed door, so we veer left through a doorless archway into the kitchen. "Take a seat," Sophia Mikhailovna directs me. Then she and Irina leave the room via a second doorway, this one with a door.

I drape my coat over one of the spindle-back chairs that surround the trestle table and lower myself onto the seat. I glance about the supposed den of iniquity. There's a third doorway, covered with a curtain, and I assume it leads to the larder. Next to the blue-tiled stove are narrow shelves attached to the wall. Alongside the shelves is a painted corner cupboard with punched tin doors. Various pots hang from hooks. It's a kitchen that's as commonplace as potatoes.

My forearm rests atop the table, and I'm on the verge of dropping my aching forehead into the crook of my elbow when Sophia Mikhailovna reenters through the same door she exited. "And bring a bit of ice," she calls over her shoulder.

No sooner is she seated in the chair across the table from me than a massive frame fills the doorway. The man is built like a male Irina—a bit fleshy around his middle, but otherwise endowed with muscles that strain against his shirt. I peg his age to be mid- or late twenties. His hair is the same shade of red as his beard. A gold chain hangs around his neck, at the bottom of which is a flip-open watch that rests against his slight paunch.

"This is Grisha," Sophia Mikhailovna says as she wraps his ice in a towel. "He socializes with the gentlemen, offers them drinks, and protects you women.

Grisha, meet Anna." After Grisha and I exchange greetings, she thanks him for the ice and hands it to me.

"Yes, thank you, Grisha," I stammer, wondering what to do with the package of ice.

Sophia Mikhailovna points to her cheek.

"Oh!" I sputter as I apply the soothing cold to my bruise.

Sophia Mikhailovna instructs Grisha to allow us a few minutes to talk alone. "Then summon a sledge and driver to take Anna to her former residence to pick up a few belongings. Don't pay the cabbie until he returns with her."

I protest. "There's really no reason for all of that. I own almost nothing, so there's no need for me to go to the house." This is basically true—plus the fact that I never again want to step foot in that sinister place.

"Do you have your passport with you now?"

Oh my goodness!

I shake my head slowly. How in Heaven's name did I forget about my passport!

"Then you need to retrieve it. You'll turn in your passport to the medical-police. Do you—"

I lowered the ice from my cheek. "Turn in my . . . my passport?"

"Yes, in exchange for your yellow ticket."

"I have to turn in my passport?" I must have misheard. Passports are never voluntarily relinquished; they're too precious.

"Yes, if you want a license. And you need a license to work here." Sophia Mikhailovna motions for me to replace the ice against my face.

Suddenly the yellow ticket becomes a very perilous item. I must give up part of my identity in order to possess one. How will I ever get the passport back? Without one, I can't go anywhere outside of Moscow. I would be unable to travel back to Petrovo.

Sophia Mikhailovna nods at Grisha, and the stalwart man leaves the kitchen. "Grisha has the proportions of a bull and the disposition of a lamb," she muses. "Unless he gets angry. He's very protective of us. That's exactly what makes him so valuable."

Her long fingers smooth flyaway wisps of hair.

"Working hours begin in late afternoon, and they're over when the last customer leaves, anywhere from midnight on a slow evening like tonight to sunrise on weekends and holidays. You are expected to be here every day during working hours unless I approve otherwise. During off-hours, you are free to leave the house. You're also free to go anywhere in this house except my apartment. Is all that understood?"

"Yes."

"When we came in the door, you may have noticed some narrow stairs. That back stairway leads to the second floor, where the girls' rooms are located. Then it continues to the attic, where Grisha sleeps. The latrines and the clotheslines are in the back courtyard, which we share with three other buildings. Do you have any questions?"

My frazzled brain is too weary to ask any question except one. "Can I have a drink? I'm very thirsty."

"Of course. That is, assuming by 'drink' you mean kvass and not liquor."

I greedily slurp the humble, grain-based drink.

Furrows of disapproval flicker across the face of my new employer. "I will assign Maria, one of the women here, to set straight your grammar and table etiquette. You'll follow her guidance."

I nod, nibbling my lower lip. I sense I'm already being chastened.

"You are on probation for six weeks. Failure to abide by any of my rules will result in your dismissal. Is that fully understood?"

I give a single dip of my head at the ominous prospect.

Sophia Mikhailovna's features unexpectedly soften, becoming almost maternal. "All the girls are fretful when they first start. Tomorrow morning I plan to visit my sister, but during the afternoon I'll show you how to cover up that red mark on your face as well as your bruised cheek. And I'll give you a few tips to make your nights easier."

Sophia Mikhailovna absentmindedly fingers the string of pearls that lies above her generous display of cleavage.

"Tomorrow you'll purchase a nice gown using my credit. I'll keep your wages until you have paid me back the entire amount plus fifty percent. If you leave here without paying your debts, it's within my rights to have you arrested. And I'll see to it that you are."

I nod, even though she used the perplexing word again: *percent.*

"When you return this evening, your bed will be waiting for you in room number 2. The numbers are on the doors. Can you read numbers?"

"Little numbers," I reply, but my attention is centered on the term *bed.* A bed with a clean coverlet and a soft pillow. A bed that offers me safety and warmth. Quite unlike the filthy wool blanket on that smelly mattress on the floor of Vialtseva's back hallway.

"Make sure your drapes are closed at dusk, and keep them closed all night. Don't *ever* go into a room with its door closed unless it's your own. Is that understood?" Sophia Mikhailovna eyes me, her protégé, as if to ascertain whether she's dealing with a girl so simple-minded that she can't deduce why it's a breach of manners to open closed doors in a brothel.

"The Gentlemen's Entrance, which you saw on the side of the building, is kept locked and bolted from the time the last customer leaves until four o'clock the following afternoon. And there's never any reason to unbolt the door in the front of the building along the street. Do you remember this address? Listen closely: 903 Sviatoslavsky Prospekt, located in the Zamoskvorechye neighborhood. Repeat the address."

I do so, my voice childlike.

Sophia Mikhailovna shifts subjects. "Are you familiar with money—how many kopeks in a ruble, what a ten-kopek coin looks like, things of that nature?" At my nod, she continues. "Good. Some village girls have never seen money before. How you people function without money is beyond me."

I'm of the opinion we functioned quite well, and I ache to be back in my village where conversations didn't include words like *credit* and *license* and *instruments of barter*.

"Tomorrow while you're shopping, I want you to keep in mind this expression: 'It's all in the wrapping.'"

"All in the wrapping?" My spent mind can't decipher the meaning.

"The 'wrapping' is your looks. Your appeal. The fascination you hold for men. It's what gets them excited." Sophia Mikhailovna's lips twitch impatiently as she scrutinizes the vacant look on my face. "The wrapping is how you present yourself."

Grisha announces that he has secured a cab. I hand the ice and towel to Sophia Mikhailovna and promise to do a good job, although I have only the haziest notion of what the job entails.

Following Grisha out of the kitchen, I gasp as I enter a room that's awash in red.

Three overstuffed burgundy divans . . .
Several Voltaire chairs with brick-red fabric . . .
Maroon tiles surrounding the fireplace . . .
Scarlet velvet drapes with gold tassels . . .
A massive Oriental carpet with a flame-red background . . .
Crimson-and-gold wallpaper above a wood wainscot . . .

Everything boasts some shade of red—even the globes on the gas wall lamps and the fonts of the oil lamps. Oh, my soul, what might Mamasha say if she knew I was here!

"This is the Grand Salon." Grisha's voice is hushed, probably because a man is sitting on one of the divans. "We're required to wear proper attire in the Grand Salon during business hours."

I follow his lead and keep my voice low. "Four o'clock until the last customer leaves," I quote, but I have no idea what *proper attire* is.

"The drapes can be opened only during nonbusiness hours," he says. "On the outer side of the drapes are shutters that cover the bottom half of the windows. The shutters always remain closed."

Grisha points to the far side of the room where a shiny banister and red-carpeted stairs lead to the second floor. "The rooms are upstairs. Did Sophia Mikhailovna tell you your number?"

"Two."

Grisha leads me toward a door that's heavy with carvings plus an oval window that stretches almost the door's entire height. Next to the closed door is a wide window that extends from Grisha's thighs to the top of his head. I look through the window and see a teeny, gaslit square room, with the length of each wall approximately the height of a person. On the far side of the tiny room is the ornate exterior door on the side passageway that Sophia Mikhailovna described as the Gentlemen's Entrance.

Grisha opens the door with the oval glass and carved wood. We stand in our positions for a long, awkward moment before his free arm sweeps in a wide arc, prompting me to pass through the doorway. My cheeks heat with embarrassment as I recall male guests of the Shelgunovs performing this gesture for the wives. Opening the door is a politeness of some sort.

While we stand in the tiny room, he explains it's called an *antechamber*. "If you turn around, you'll see that across the room, tucked under the stairs, is the bar. That's where I spend my evenings. From there, I can see every person who enters the house, thanks to the door window and the wall window. I keep you girls under close watch—and very safe."

"But why is the main entrance on the side of the building rather than in front, along the street?"

"Against regulations to have a door directly facing the street."

There's that word again. "Regulations?"

"Against the law," he simplifies. We exit through the Gentlemen's Entrance and walk to the front of the building. Grisha offers his log-sized arm to help me into the hired sledge. His smile is kind when he says, "You'll be fine. Most of the women here are nice. You'll like them."

I'm tempted to ask which ones aren't nice, but the driver slaps the reins and sets the horse in motion.

CHAPTER 10

December
1867

THE POUNDING ON my door wakes me from a slumber so sound, it must be like the sleep of the dead. I grapple for my bearings, then stumble across the inky room toward the blade of light beneath my door.

I'm greeted by an exuberantly chipper Irina. "Time to be up, sleepyhead! A new day, a new life!" She gestures toward a woman who, standing beside sturdy Irina, looks the size of a wood sprite. "This is Athena. She'll take you shopping for clothes."

"You dress, then breakfast, then shopping." In addition to an unusual name, Athena has a thick foreign accent. "Porridge on stove."

I rub the deep slumber from my eyes. Athena has a thick mane of black hair and a neck as graceful as a swan's.

She points to herself. "Room 8. Door open, you ready shopping."

After assuring her that I'll hurry and closing the door, I slide the heavy drapes across their rod and squint at the street banked with sunlit snow. My breath paints a fog on the cool glass.

In contrast to the hush of last night, wagons and drays rumble along Sviatoslavsky Prospekt. Horses clip-clop and people scurry past buildings occupied by stores at the street level. The second-floor windows are shielded with various curtains, shades, and shutters.

I turn to face my room and cuddle myself in my own arms. I have a room all to myself!

My small bed plus the armoire, washbasin, and dressing table and chair take up almost the entire floor. I can see myself in two mirrors—one above the vanity and one full-length gilded glass affixed to the armoire's door. Three walls are painted, while one is papered with prints of rosy-cheeked cherubs whose long-lashed eyes pine after scantily clothed nymphs.

I pick up the pillow and hug it. A pillow! Pillows were unknown in Petrovo's huts, and I wasn't given one at either Shelgunov's or Vialtseva's house—although a couple of times I did lay my head on one, just to see what its feather-filled softness felt like.

As I smooth the calico bedspread, my thoughts take on sharp-edged images of faceless men rutting in my precious bed. I turn away before the picture can fully unfold.

After I pull on my wool servant's dress and plait my braid, I double-check the drawer where I placed my passport upon returning from Vialtseva's last night. While I was there, I picked up my few articles of clothing, including the second of my two servant's dresses. Thank heavens, the old biddy snored the whole time I tiptoed through her grim, sagging house.

I go downstairs to the kitchen, where two women are seated at the kitchen table. Irina bites into an apple while the other woman chatters. I go bug-eyed when I spot, sitting on Irina's shoulder, a large gray bird with a fearfully huge beak. His profile to me, he inspects me with a beady eye.

Irina kicks out the chair next to her. "Have a seat. This is Maria. And"—she raises her occupied shoulder—"this is Sasha."

If I remember correctly, Maria is supposed to teach me good grammar.

Maria jumps up from her seat and bustles to the stove. "I'll get you some porridge."

"No need to bother," I insist. "I'll get it." Maria reminds me of my mother— the same worried hazel eyes with two furrows between her eyebrows. She's not nearly as old as Mama, but older than I would expect to be working in a brothel.

"It's the least I can do for the woman who cut Shestov! Across the face, no less!" Maria's eyes are wide with awe as she ladles the porridge into a bowl. "You must be very brave."

Me, brave?

I gingerly slide onto the chair, careful not to rile the bird with the beak curved like a scythe, and probably as sharp as one. Looking about the table, I note the mismatched bowls and cups. None are the quality of Shelgunov's tableware.

"Tell me the whole story from start to finish." Maria places the steaming groats, a spoon, and a jar of honey in front of me, then retakes her seat. "Did Shestov put that bruise on your face?"

While my eyes swing like a clock pendulum between Maria and the intimidating bird, I give an abbreviated version of the incident. I pass over the reason a knife happened to be in my pocket.

Maria delights in the story. "But I wish you'd aimed for his nuts instead of his face!"

I laugh for the first time in my new home. "You're not the first person to say that."

"That vulture will stop at nothing. He'd kill a man at the drop of a hat."

"And he'd drop the hat." Irina offers Sasha a teeny bit of apple in her palm. He wraps his hawklike beak around the fruit.

"I pray I never meet that man again," I tell Maria. "And I pray I never go to jail again. And I thank God for Irina's help."

"God had little to do with it," Irina quips.

Maria gives Irina a sideways glance and makes the sign of the cross. "It was obviously God's will, or it wouldn't have occurred." She turns to address me. "You'll find that we take care of one another here. If you ever want to borrow something or need advice or maybe a shoulder to cry on, one of us is ready to help."

"Well, I do have a question. Why is that bird in the kitchen?"

"The first person up in the morning lets him out of his cage. He gets lonely."

Irina's answer does nothing to answer my query. "But why isn't he outside?"

"In this weather?" Irina's eyebrows rise almost to her hairline.

My confusion swells. "Yes. Like the other birds."

Irina roars with laughter that sends Sasha flapping wildly across the room. He procures a safe overview from atop the cupboard. "Now I understand your question. He's a parrot. A pet."

"Like a lapdog?"

"Exactly. Except he talks."

Sasha is giving me a suspicious, one-eyed stare, and I give a similar one to Irina. "You mean, he talks bird language?"

"No. He talks people language."

My teeth tug at my lower lip. Is Irina making fun of me? I look to maternal Maria for answers.

"It's true. Parrots imitate people. They say all sorts of things."

I break into a joyful smile. Friendly women. A talking bird. My own room. I feel better about life than I have at any time during the previous two years.

ATHENA DOESN'T MINCE her broken-Russian words when she tells me I need eye-popping undergarments that will push up my small breasts. She recommends a corset with front-opening stays. "Quicker off. Quicker back on." She pauses for a moment in thought. "Although some men just leave on."

In addition to the corset, I follow Athena's guidance in selecting some under-drawers and stockings. My eyes are drawn to white stockings, but Athena tells me that white silk stockings are considered appropriate only when wearing a white dress. Instead, I choose neutral colors—one pair each of gray and cream.

Neutral shades may be best for stockings, but the same doesn't hold true for petticoats. I gape at the bold colors trimmed with scarlet scalloping, braid, and even velvet. Those types of petticoats certainly weren't found in Rozaliya Yakov-levna Shelgunova's oversized closets. And I don't believe Viktorya Borisovna Vialt-seva even owned a petticoat. Athena gives a heartfelt sigh of disappointment when I prudishly chose a pallid beige with modest ruffles of the same color.

Regarding dresses, Athena advises against plunging necklines. "You no have melons." She points to a gown's bodice—a word, I'm proud to say, I remember from last evening—with vertical piping that tapers to a V below the waist. "This good for you. Make your small waist look even more smaller. Plus, it fasten in front. Quicker, yes, but also make men heat up fast when they unbutton."

Oh, my. I have so very much to learn.

I also select a couple of decorative hairpins and combs, a pair of satin shoes, felt carpet slippers, three handkerchiefs, a pair of earrings, a hairbrush, and a warm shawl to replace the one Shestov destroyed last evening.

My head swoons at the expense of these items. Yet no rubles exchange hands. Athena, however, pays for her sole purchase—a pair of stockings.

The two of us with our bundles and boxes are almost out the door when Athena stops short. "Dressing gown. You must have."

My fingers run over the luxurious fabrics in countless styles and colors. A bold, deep hue that falls in seductive folds? Or pastel with delicate embroidery? I finally settle on a teal-blue velvet with pleated satin flouncing at the bottom of the sleeves and a matching satin sash at the waist.

Athena nods. "Make your blue eyes even more beautiful."

I'm continually baffled that so many people in Moscow admire my blue eyes. When I was growing up in Petrovo, a village of brown-eyed brunettes, my blue eyes and blond hair were as desirable as a clubfoot. Given the choice, I'd choose the warm, gentle sable of Athena's dark-lashed eyes.

"Accept sisterly advice?" Athena asks as we tread through newly fallen snow that is already sooty and packed by feet, hooves, and sleigh runners.

"Of course."

"You did good shopping. No buy extra much. Next, do this: end debt soon. If don't end debt, you work every night for Sophia Mikhailovna and not for you.

End debt to Sophia Mikhailovna. I go to secondhand store and I pay cash for clothes. I take you there another time, if you want."

"Yes," I nod. "I would very much appreciate that."

"Other girls buy more, always more—clothes, jewelry, liqueurs, cigarettes. They never end debt. Madam get rich like Jew banker."

"Sophia Mikhailovna hired a cab for me last night. Do you think the cost will be taken from my earnings?"

"Only if she tell you first. You treat her fair, she treat you fair." Athena shakes her fist beside her glorious head of hair. "But she rule with rod of iron. No drunkenness. No opium-eaters. No lazy. No dirty body. No stealing. No fighting other girls. Very fair, but rod of iron."

I don't know what *opium-eaters* are, but rather than displaying more of my ignorance, I ask Athena how long she's been at the house.

"Two years. First thing I do—end debt." Athena describes how she had been raised in poverty in Greece and, at age thirteen, traded her virginity to a well-to-do uncle for food. She later got pregnant by a neighborhood boy, but, after they were married, she miscarried the baby. When she became pregnant a second time, her husband disappeared.

She arrived in Moscow at age twenty, having left her young son in the care of her parents. She'd been assured that she could make good money as a prostitute, a promise that held true. Some men slip her an extra ruble when she drapes a toga about her, places a bracelet around her upper arm, and garlands her head with a wreath of flowers.

"They say I look like Greek goddess." Athena laughs without arrogance. "No togas in Greece. Only in Rome. Men so stupid."

I don't have the faintest notion what a toga is or what a Greek goddess looks like. And the only thing I know about Greece and Rome is that they are both very far away. But I fully believe that Athena's liquid eyes, her sculpted face, and her willowy body earn purses full of rubles.

The Greek goddess goes on to say that within a couple of years, she'll have saved enough rubles to return to her home village, open a little shop, and provide a comfortable life for her son.

Athena links her arm with mine. "You be like me. End debt."

"I will," I promise both Athena and myself.

"Room 2 lucky room."

"Lucky room?"

"Was my room. Warm. Coal stove in hallway by door. Room lucky at bring in rubles, too." Athena explains that after she built up her list of customers, Sophia Mikhailovna moved her to one of the five large rooms that line the back of the building. Getting a larger room is the equivalent of a promotion.

Curious about my neighbors along the front hallway, I ask, "Who's in rooms 1 and 3?"

"Dunka, room 1. But she no sleep there. Only work there."

I wait for Athena to clarify the peculiar statement, but she reveals no more.

"And room 3?"

"Pelageya."

Nothing at all is revealed about her.

CHAPTER 11

December
1867

WHEN ATHENA AND I arrive back at 903 Sviatoslavsky Prospekt, Grisha is behind the counter. Sophia Mikhailovna, dressed in royal purple for the evening hours, is seated on one of the bar's three stools. Athena promptly goes upstairs, and our madam tells me, "Get yourself some potato soup from the stove, and bring it to Grisha's bar so we can begin your education."

As I fill a soup bowl, I ponder Sophia Mikhailovna's expression, *Grisha's bar*. It seems to be an odd choice of words, since he's merely an employee. Or so I assume.

As soon as I boost myself onto the stool's soft seat, Sophia Mikhailovna gets down to business. "Notice the bellpull."

I look about but can't locate a bellpull. Finally, Grisha pulls a tasseled cord that lies camouflaged against the wall of the same shade of crimson.

Sophia Mikhailovna instructs, "Listen closely."

Grisha gives another pull, and I hear a sedate tinkling in the upstairs hallway.

"It means a customer is waiting. It means *Get downstairs*. Is that understood?"

I nod while I spoon the thick soup between my lips.

"Liquor is illegal in brothels, so we have none here. Isn't that correct, Grisha?"

"No liquor at all." The exaggerated, solemn sway of Grisha's heavy head makes me grin. "Except for the open bottles in this hidden panel." His knuckles rap a waist-high wooden cabinet that's seated on the floor. Atop the cabinet's shellacked counter are a samovar, several rows of glasses, and a wooden box with drawers. "As far as the police are concerned"—he gives me a conspiring wink—"complimentary tea is the only drink in the house."

Sophia Mikhailovna continues, "Drinking during working hours is grounds for an employee's dismissal. Chronic inebriation will also result in termination. Is that understood?"

"Yes."

"And any liquor consumed from my inventory will be debited to your account."

The word *debited* is unknown to me, but I assume it means the girl pays for the liquor. I give yet another nod.

"That's a beautiful box." I point to the miniature chest of five drawers on the counter next to the glasses. Its gleaming wood reminds me of the jewelry box belonging to Shelgunov's wife.

Sophia Mikhailovna responds, "Grisha also sells quality cigars to patrons. He keeps them in that humidor."

"In what?"

Grisha places his open palm atop the box. "A humidor contains the correct amount of moisture to keep the cigars fresh."

"The liquor and the cigars bring in almost as many rubles as the upstairs services," explains Sophia Mikhailovna. "You are expected to encourage their consumption. Plus, a little alcohol loosens up the customers, especially the timid ones, so the time they require upstairs is shortened. Grisha keeps a flawless account of how long each girl is with a customer."

Grisha recites lines that seem well rehearsed. "Thirty minutes." He points at the watch resting against his stomach on a pendant. "Any longer and I go upstairs to check that the customer isn't giving you trouble. As our employer says, you need to *get it out, get it up, and get it off* within half an hour."

"Do be careful what you say," Sophia Mikhailovna warns Grisha, though her tone is mild. "You know that rascal"—she nods toward the birdcage that sits along the front wall—"repeats everything he hears. I doubt our customers would appreciate that little ditty."

"You're quite a rogue," Grisha teases the bird.

In his cage, Sasha, enjoying the agreeable companionship, bobs his head and repeats, "Little ditty."

My eyes grow round. The bird really can talk!

Sophia Mikhailovna asks if I'd like more potato soup. "Now would be a good time to get some."

When I return with a full bowl, Grisha's and Sophia Mikhailovna's low voices are deep in conversation. As I retake my seat, Grisha excuses himself and leaves to bring in more coal. His role in my orientation appears to be over.

With cool efficiency, Sophia Mikhailovna resumes my education. "The bar is only part of the design of the Grand Salon. The fine furniture, the heavy curtains, each and every item has the customer's desires in mind. And what are those desires?"

The madam doesn't wait for her pupil to respond.

"Men don't come here to ease their physical needs. That's not the primary purpose, although they expect to get their money's worth. First and foremost, they come here to find a momentary hideaway from their daily misfortunes. They hunger for an escape from the grayness of their daily lives. That's why everything is decorated in red and gold. It diverts them from the darkness of their habitual worries."

Sophia Mikhailovna's voice becomes lofty as she flings her arms out from her sides as though she's soaring. "Every man searches for revelry, for escape. This house becomes his kingdom. He is its sovereign."

Her arms drop as she abruptly terminates her flight through the kingdom. Her voice lowers, possibly in deference to the bird. "Men come here for a woman. Partially for sex, of course. But also for a clandestine evening. The purpose of this house is not to provide a venue for debauchery."

Clandestine, venue, and *debauchery* mean nothing to me, but I don't interrupt.

"Rather, we meet the physical and emotional needs of men. While a man is here, he's pampered. That's your job. Coddle them. Indulge them. Make them omnipotent for thirty minutes, maximum."

Omnipotent. Another one of those mysterious words, but I grasp the general concept.

Sophia Mikhailovna swings from the lofty to the down-to-earth. "That's what I expect from you—to give honest service in exchange for honest rubles. Is that understood?"

"Yes."

"Bestow special attention on sober, upstanding men. Particularly those who tip well." Sophia Mikhailovna leans close to me and locks her eyes with mine. "Plant your garden wisely, and you'll harvest it again and again." Abruptly, she stands. "Let's get to work on your clothing, makeup, and hair—the tools of your trade." Then she clicks her tongue and mutters, "That braid, it has to go."

I trail after the madam to the top staircase landing, where she grabs my shoulders and pivots me to the left. I'm facing a gigantic wall mirror the size of a barn door, its golden frame adorned with glitzy curlicues. In its gold-veined glass, my eyes first fall on Sophia Mikhailovna with her purple gown and regal bearing. Next to her is a beanpole girl who's as colorless as a fish's underbelly and as completely devoid of elegance as the pockmarked women at Khitrov Market. How will I ever attract customers in this house of beautiful women?

"Take note of two things," Sophia Mikhailovna instructs. "First, your disgusting habit of chewing on your lip."

I'm chagrined that the mirror has caught me in the act.

"Second, you walk as though boulders weigh on your shoulders." From behind me, she places a hand on each of my shoulders again and, with thumbs digging into them, wrenches backward.

"Standing erect not only propels the bust forward, but also portrays elegance and confidence. Comport yourself with dignity." The madam's fingertips skim over the crown of my head and tug back on my forehead, placing my neck in straight alignment with the rest of my body.

Long after Sophia Mikhailovna releases my forehead, I continue to stare at the image. I hadn't realized how slumped I was, as if trying to hide myself. Have I been doing that the whole of my life?

Once we're in my room, Sophia Mikhailovna tells me to put on my evening clothes while she looks over the day's purchases.

A subtle shake of her head is accompanied by a *tsk*. "Always remember what I told you last night—it's all in the wrapping. Downstairs, we must concentrate on elaborate concealment made as beguiling as possible. The curves Mother Nature gave you are to be enriched by the proper choice of corset. Once upstairs, a man's interest is piqued by what lies under the dress—your selection of which, I must say, is as boring as stewed turnips. You'll get the job done faster with lace-trimmed camisoles and French corsets and brightly colored petticoats. Here's an important lesson for you to commit to memory: Clothes lie. Use that lie to your advantage."

Sophia Mikhailovna strides to the bed and motions me to sit beside her. When I move as gracefully in my new gown and shoes as a drunk peasant, she demonstrates how to properly walk . . . lower myself to sitting . . . sit . . . and rise from sitting.

Once we're settled side by side, she details the fee charged for each type of service. Normally, she informs me, the men hand the rubles directly to her, but if she happens to be absent, the money is given to Grisha. This statement implies a great deal of trust, leaving me yet again to wonder about the relationship between the employer and her employee.

"Is the monetary part of your job understood?"

"Yes."

"Then let's move on to how the government meddles with us. Prostitution is illegal but regulated. Which allows the government to talk out of both sides of its mouth."

I understand no part of those statements.

Sophia Mikhailovna's tone is contemptuous as she explains the government has thirty rules that madams must obey, whereas prostitutes have only eleven. One of the regulations requires girls to examine their clients prior to any sexual acts.

"Needless to say, the rule is ridiculous. After all, most of the activity is performed in quite a hasty manner in a darkened room. Nevertheless," she acknowledges, "the rule isn't without its particular merit. For your own protection, if you encounter a poxed or unclean customer, pleasantly but firmly refuse service. Understood?"

I nod.

"Which brings us to the precautionary arts."

Precautionary arts? Neither word has meaning for me.

"Even if the man appears clean, try to sponge him with permanganate of potash. Some men will tolerate the washing. Most won't."

She pauses for my nod.

"At the end of his visit, your final task, which you must never omit, is to look the man over before he exits your room. I never want it said that this house sent someone home with rouge on his collar."

I nod again.

"Once the transaction is executed and he leaves, you must douche yourself immediately with the permanganate. It prevents disease as well as pregnancy. This routine must be performed after every encounter. Every. Encounter." Her fingers toy with the string of pearls about her neck. "Some girls prefer to use bichloride of mercury or dilute carbolic acid. But I personally prefer the permanganate of potash. When diluted with water, it's such an attractive purple."

I'm altogether baffled.

She then describes how to tuck absorbent material in my vagina (another new word) to hide the monthly scourge. "Most girls don't miss but one night of work a month."

Sophia's instructions seem unending.

"The tools of your trade are clothing and makeup. We've already discussed clothing." She sets to work on my face. "Usually I tell the girls to use only powder and rouge, as both can be quickly reapplied between customers. But you'll need something more to conceal that port-wine stain on your face. And for the next few nights, that bruise on your cheek."

She coats my face with something that's as thick as mud. Then she smears on a second layer. When I finally peer into the hand mirror, an unknown mask looks back at me.

"By the way," Sophia Mikhailovna says, "the handle on that mirror is mother-of-pearl. You break it, you pay for it."

Next, she unbraids my hair, which lies pale as flax like a blanket across my back. I yearn to have Athena's dark, lustrous tresses.

Sophia Mikhailovna whisks my hair in what she calls a "fashionable upsweep," which I'll never be able to replicate. "You have two tasks after the man leaves. We've already covered the first one. What is it?"

"The purple liquid."

"Correct. But by the way, to attract the right type of clientele, you must begin speaking in complete sentences, not fragments."

I nod.

"The second task is to make yourself presentable. Take a quick but thorough look in the mirror, and tidy your face and hair. Notice the towel and cake of soap on the washbasin. Sponge off the sweat that the customer leaves on your skin. Not only will your body have a more appealing scent, but your clothes will require fewer cleanings. Before your evening begins, be certain your washbasin has water."

Her instructions are endless. "Rinse your mouth several times an evening. It keeps your breath sweet. And of course, dipping snuff is strictly forbidden."

"I understand."

"Keep your room tidy. No hatboxes, tins of rouge, ribbons, bric-a-brac. Perfume bottles are acceptable, but not in excessive numbers. Empty your bedpan prior to your first customer and as needed throughout the evening. Keep your bedframe pulled away from the wall, so as to not disturb your neighbor."

"Yes, Madame."

"I supply lamp oil. Wax candles create exotic lighting that enhances a woman's features and makes her skin glow. If you want candlelight, I have thick candles that will last an entire evening. I'll deduct the cost from your earnings. But they will pay for themselves by speeding things up, allowing you time for an extra customer each night."

She opens the top drawer of the chest and pulls out, one by one, a shoehorn, a clothes brush, a file for my fingernails, and a sleep mask for my eyes.

"I expect all of these items to still be in this drawer after you leave this house."

After I leave? But I just got here!

The faint tinkling of Grisha's bell filters into my room. Customers have arrived.

Sophia Mikhailovna says, "Take a final look at yourself, cleanse your mouth, and find a smile to put on your face. Then walk with elegance and confidence down the stairs. Have you any questions?"

No questions, but my mind is a rat's nest of confused thoughts.

Before closing the door, she adds, "If any customer becomes belligerent, alert Grisha immediately." She tosses a silver whistle to me. "Keep it handy."

I stare into the armoire's mirror. The image staring back can't be me! Piled hair. Cinched waist. Glittery earrings. Preposterous rouge. The costume looks silly. I'm just an unsightly girl pretending to be a beguiling woman. I no longer look plain. Rather, I look just plain ridiculous.

I slump backward onto the bed and cover my face with my hands. Shopping, clothes, hairstyles, new friends, talking bird . . . all that is over and done. Now is the moment I've banned from my thoughts all day—the heart-stopping reality of what I'm undertaking.

I remind myself that I have no choice. I must try. Please, most forgiving God, help me get through tonight.

My hand claps over my mouth. What am I asking? For God's help in this wicked, shameful endeavor? Why not just plead, *God, please help me sin splendidly?*

The skin over my spine twitches. I leap from the bed and swirl to look over my shoulder. I'm certain I felt fingers on my back. The fingers of the village boy Tomas Katkov. Of Nikolai Osipovich Shelgunov. Of Vasily Vialtsev. Of the policeman Shestov. Of the men who will be here tonight.

The men tonight. Who will be the first? His hands on my body. His breath on my face. His foulness on my sheets.

My stomach curls around itself. A sour taste rises to my mouth.

I've sold myself, body and soul, and it was my own doing.

Mamasha, I'm so sorry, so very sorry for the wrong I did. Please let me come home!

I choke back the tears, knowing they'll accomplish nothing except to ruin Sophia Mikhailovna's makeup.

I know what I need to do tonight. The same thing I did with Shelgunov. I need to hollow out my mind, my feelings, my soul.

CHAPTER 12

December
1867

HALFWAY DOWN THE staircase, fear freezes my next step. Below me, the Grand Salon is empty except for a man talking with Grisha at the bar and Sasha preening himself in his cage.

The world feels like it's closing in, about to smother me. Anxiety cinches my belly. I try to take a deep breath, but my new stays won't budge. Instead, I swallow, although I'm not sure why. My mouth is as dry as chaff that's been winnowed from the grain.

My clammy hand grips the glossy banister as I will my foot onto the next step. Then the next. And the next. After reaching the bottom of the stairs without my legs buckling beneath me, I place one squeamish foot in front of the other.

The middle-aged man turns toward me and strokes his forked beard. His pear-shaped torso is turned out in a frock coat.

So, this will be my first customer.

But that assumption is immediately dispelled by Grisha, who introduces the man as Timofei Ivanov, "a favorite friend of Matryna's."

"Oh," I stammer. "Sh-should I go upstairs and tell Matryna?" Not that I know which room is Matryna's.

"Don't bother," the favorite friend replies. "She'll be down soon enough."

Grisha asks, "Meanwhile, Timofei Ivanov, how about another glass of wine while we wait?"

Timofei Ivanov gives me a long, disconcerting appraisal. "Only if you'll join us."

I accept a glass of tea and scan the man's face. Odd—he doesn't have any eyebrows.

Grisha and Timofei Ivanov have barely started a comradely critique of Moscow's mayor, Prince A. A. Shcherbatov, when a red-haired woman, presumably Matryna, retrieves her favorite friend. I note his swagger as he ascends the stairs. Then my eyes wander to the deserted entrance vestibule.

"Evenings start out slow," Grisha says, then asks if my shopping went well.

I nod. "Athena was most helpful. Quite sisterly in her advice."

"She's good-hearted, that's the truth. Too bad she's bound and determined to return to Greece. She's the only one around here who can cook worth a copper kopek. Wait till you taste her stew." His eyes close and his paw of a hand makes slow circles beneath his nose, wafting up an imaginary aroma. "Cinnamon. Cloves. A splash of wine." His eyes pop open. "And for dessert—layers of pastry as thin as leaves, all dripping with honey and walnuts." He wipes his bearded chin as though the gooey concoction is dribbling down it.

"Maybe she'll teach someone before she leaves," I say.

Grisha guffaws. "Saints help us, it's only on their good days that the other ladies can boil an egg."

Ladies? I've heard the females in the house referred to as women and girls. But not as ladies. I search for irony in Grisha's voice but find none—although his chubby cheeks seem perpetually puckered in anticipation of a good laugh.

Two young men enter the Grand Salon. They stomp the snow from their boots and hang their overcoats and caps on the wall hooks.

My throat constricts, choking back the nausea.

Grisha greets them with a robust "Good evening, messieurs. What can I get you to drink?"

The young men order shots of vodka and blow the cold from their cupped hands. Grisha gestures with his head, implying that I should escort them to two divans that face each other on the far side of the room. As I step forward, Grisha slyly tugs the bellpull.

I lower myself stiffly onto a burgundy divan, my erratic heart pummeling my breastbone. After the two men exchange apprehensive looks, one sits next to me while the other takes a seat on the opposite divan. To be truthful, the term *men* is a bit of an exaggeration. They're more like callow teenagers who recently shed their milk teeth.

I smile at them. Their return grins are uneasy. I frantically search for something to say to bridge the silence. How I wish I were still chatting with Grisha about Greek pastries!

With a rustling of silk, two women descend the staircase. One is the brightly rouged Irina. The other is a snippet of a girl, half the size of Irina. I guess her to be my age, maybe a year or two older. A skimming glance between the two women apparently achieves some sort of communication because they separate, with Irina heading to the bar and the girl coming toward us.

Her peacock-blue gown is adorned with a single white ribbon, which flutters from a waist no bigger around than a custard dish. She sedately positions herself next to the young man on the other divan, her eyes as bright as fireflies and her cheeks as smooth as rose petals. She's like a featherweight doll that could be tossed single-handedly onto a bed, then twirled around into any position desired.

Despite her fledgling appearance, the pixie takes control like a seasoned expert. "Good evening, fellows. I'm Dunyasha. I see you've met Anna."

I'm startled that the elfin woman knows my name. But then again, in a house with eight women, gossip is sure to fly like a bird on the wing.

Dunyasha asks if this is their first visit and emphatically declares her hope to see them often in the future.

Sophia Mikhailovna makes her entrance and sweeps toward us with fluid grace. She stands between the two divans and extends her arms outward from her sides, inviting each of the seated young men to grasp a hand. Once she has hold of them, her grip is steadfast.

"Welcome to my house, gentlemen. I believe you're new here." The madam's voice oozes with a sultry creaminess like none I've ever heard. "I run a clean establishment, one that caters to genteel and discreet men such as yourselves. Upstairs services start at three rubles. You are our guests, and we want to please you in every way possible. It's our firm desire." Her buttery voice provocatively adds weight to the last two words.

Her warm smile is almost maternal as she continues to clutch their hands. "Grisha, in honor of their first visit, please refill these gentlemen's glasses. On the house."

Dunyasha inhales what I assume is feigned surprise at the madam's generosity and squeezes the forearm of her soon-to-be customer. "Of course, the police frown on partaking of liquor here, so let's keep it our little secret." Her delicate mouth gasps as three fingertips quickly veil the *O* of her lips. She leans closer to her young man, lightly places her hand on his thigh, and breathes, "You're not a policeman, are you?"

Even with my knotted stomach, racing heart, and hair-curling fear, I come close to snickering at the absurdly coquettish behavior. The boys, however, lap it up like cream.

Sophia Mikhailovna releases their hands at last and beams at me just a tiny moment longer than necessary. I take her cue to follow Dunyasha's lead. My smile is stiff but broad as I open a clenched hand and awkwardly lay it on my customer's arm.

As Sophia Mikhailovna retreats, she passes behind my divan. I feel a hand on one shoulder, followed by a gentle tug. I promptly throw my shoulders back and straighten my spine.

With fetching dimples, fluttering eyelashes, and dancing eyes, Dunyasha pulls conversation from the lads. "Oh, do go on," she breathily encourages as the two fellows talk about their work as apprentice painters. She squeals with laughter whenever they make the slightest semblance of a joke. In no time at all, her young man has his arm on the back of the divan behind her.

The moment the boys tip the last of their vodka, Grisha ambles over to the divans. "Would you fellows like another drink? Or would you prefer to go upstairs?"

The boys blush—first pink, then red, and finally as crimson as the walls. Dunyasha's fellow murmurs, "Upstairs."

After they hand their rubles to Grisha, Dunyasha rises and extends her hand to her customer. Again I follow her lead, my clammy hand gripping the second boy's hand, which is equally moist. As we head upstairs, I clutch the banister while the steps waver beneath me, as if I'm underwater.

I remind myself that this is what I must do in order to survive. *Many nice women do it,* I reassure myself. *Just look at Athena and Irina.*

Once we're alone in my room, the boy straight off begins nuzzling my neck and grabbing my breasts. In no time, I'm lying on my back, still clothed, the bottom of my skirt bunched under my chin. The boy's trousers are down at his ankles.

Nice women do it. To survive.

He's trying to enter me when suddenly there's a warm mess between my thighs.

He lies full-weight on top of me, regaining his breath, then stands to pull up his trousers. As I pull down my skirt, I wonder what would be appropriate to say at this moment. *Hope you enjoyed it,* maybe? Or perhaps *My goodness, that was fast?*

I open the door for him and muster the courage to brush my lips against his flushed cheek. "I hope to see you again."

His head pulses up and down.

"You're welcome to wait for your friend downstairs in the Grand Salon."

I gently close the door, turn, and look at my bed. All I have to do is sponge the stickiness from between my legs, straighten the rumpled bedcovers, and tidy my hair and makeup. There seems no reason to use the purple permanganate of potash. The difficult part will be finding the willpower to go back downstairs.

After I gather myself, I bring to bear every morsel of my resolve and descend the staircase. The Grand Salon is empty except for Grisha at his bar. I head for one of his stools.

"Things all right?" He tone is off-handed, yet his eyes are intense.

My shrug is nonchalant. "Sure." Grisha's furrowed forehead infers that my charade isn't fooling him. I add, "I'll be fine. It's kind of you to ask."

With nothing else to do, I glance about the room. My attention is caught by a potted plant next to the closed drapes of a front window. More accurately, it's a pot containing the dried remains of a plant. I walk over to it and, upon examining the brown stems, conclude that in its better days, it had been a fern. During the six weeks at the estate house when I tended to Elena Stepanovna Maximova's broken legs, I discovered how a fern's gracefulness can breathe life into a room. Tonight, as my finger pokes the dirt, it meets with unyielding resistance.

"This poor plant is dry as a bone. Would it be all right if I water it?"

"Umm, if you want to." Grisha is clearly perplexed that anyone would show interest in the expired plant. "You can use some of the water from the barrel in the kitchen."

I give the plant a drink, then return to stand beside Grisha's bar. I'm joined by Dunyasha.

"Those young ones are fast, aren't they?" she chirps as she springs onto a barstool.

"Without a doubt." I hope I sound credible.

Dunyasha's short legs swing back and forth like a child's. "Say, if your room is too crowded, you can put some of your things in Dunka's room. She's in room number 1. It has a little area that wraps under the stairs to the attic. Dunka hung a curtain to make a small closet. She lets all of us use it for storage. It's not much space, but you're welcome to stash a thing or two there."

"That's very kind of . . . "I trail off, unclear about who's actually making the offer—Dunka or Dunyasha.

A man enters through the vestibule. He hangs his muffler and shabby raccoon coat on the round, freestanding coatrack, revealing rings of sweat in his shirt's armpits.

Grisha beckons him over to the bar. "Perhaps a drink, sir, to warm you up?"

The middle-aged man shakes his head at the suggestion. His rotund torso combined with his thin arms and legs remind me of a beetle. Even his forehead is beetle-browed.

Grisha prods the man into conversation. "Frosty evening, isn't it?"

The man's yellowed fingernails comb his grizzly beard. "It'll get colder before it gets warmer," he hypothesizes as he looks first at me, then at Dunyasha, then back at me.

"That it will," Dunyasha peeps gaily.

He ignores Dunyasha as he scrutinizes me. I paste a smile on my face. *Say something*, I prod myself. *Say anything*. "But it's toasty warm in here."

His grunt is noncommittal.

The ensuing silence puts me further on edge. "Would you care to go upstairs?" I finally ask.

His subsequent grunt has a more positive lilt to it.

I clutch the skirt of my gown into a knot as I slip my arm around his and lead him up the stairs. The reek of his sweat wafts along with us. What will he want from me?

By the time he hauls his bulk to the second floor, his breath is labored. I'm nauseous as I imagine his sweat and flab spreading over me.

Customer by customer, I promise myself, week by week, I'll faithfully work to "end debt," to use Athena's words. Then I'll squirrel away every possible kopek so I can return home to Petrovo.

End debt. Save rubles. I silently repeat the words as the beetle-man unbuttons his trousers.

Nice women do this. To survive.

CHAPTER 13

December
1867

THE HOUSE IS silent while morning sunlight creeps around the heavy drapery. I lie in bed, calling to mind each of last night's customers.

First, the boy.

Second, the sweaty beetle-man.

I was back at the bar when the third pressed a couple of rubles into Grisha's hand. Sophia Mikhailovna appeared, seemingly from nowhere. "I'm afraid Pelageya is indisposed tonight."

He scowled. "She sick?"

"Just a little under the weather. However, I'd like you to meet Anna. She's new with us."

He eyeballed me from top to bottom while Sophia Mikhailovna continued. "Anna, this is Ermak Gerasimovich Pavlovich."

The jerk of his head indicated I should follow him.

After Pavlovich, Sophia Mikhailovna sent me to bed. "You look like death. Men don't come here to be with haggard women with dark circles under their eyes. Rest up for tomorrow night. And from now on, when you descend the stairs, use only one hand to hold together the folds of your gown. Using a hand to raise the dress on each side is unrefined."

This morning, I pull my coverlet high under my chin. That third customer left me sickened with shame. Ermak. It's my father's name. And worse, sooner or later I'll have a customer named Platon.

My one-room hut in Petrovo was home to an extended family of sixteen people, including aunts, uncles, and cousins. For the past two years, I've constantly ached to be with all of them, gathered on the benches around the table, devouring cabbage soup and salted cucumbers and maybe some fritters.

When my aunt died giving birth to Platon, I was seven years old. I delighted in showering the infant with all my boundless love that no one else in my practical, hard-laboring family seemed to appreciate.

As a toddler, my cousin was like a spring foal, chock-full of unbridled curiosity and high spirits. When the two of us visited the chickens in their nests, Platon's eyes turned somber as I explained that eggs are precious—that in fact, they are so difficult to make, a hen can muster only one a day, and sometimes needs an entire day to rest.

When we sauntered along Petrovo's rutted dirt road and past the earliest shoots of winter rye, Platon and I pondered the mysteries of how those fledgling plants would be transformed into next summer's dark, crusty bread. Platon's fingers reverently stroked the delicate leaves, then plunged into the revered black earth. He went home with mud stripes across his fat-as-dumplings cheeks.

He'd be a tall boy by now. I count my age on my fingers and toes, then subtract seven. My little Platon is ten years old.

Oh, Platon! Never be as foolish and immoral as I was!

HAVING GONE TO sleep hours before anyone else, I'm the first one downstairs this morning. My curiosity coaxes me to Sasha's cage. I remove the blanket and guardedly open the door.

"I hear you like to flutter about in the morning," I venture.

The bird and I exchange stares. His wing feathers are a medium gray, with pale gray scalloping along the edges. His breast and belly are light gray. He seems unwilling to emerge from the cage, and under no circumstances will I reach in and risk his treacherous beak. I leave him to his own free will.

In the kitchen, I make porridge. The familiar task offers me a comforting respite in these strange surroundings.

Sasha eventually toddles into the room. Using his bill as a third foot, he climbs to the top of a chair's back. He keeps a vigilant eye on the intruder in his house.

The first woman to join us introduces herself as Matryna. I remember her from last evening when she came downstairs to collect her "favorite friend" with no eyebrows. Devoid of makeup this morning, Matryna is plain of face with skin that's succumbing to the impulse to droop. She appears to be around Maria's age. Her dressing gown is faded with many washings, and her red hair is pulled into a disorderly twist at the back of her neck.

Matryna goes on at great length about my thoughtfulness for making the porridge. I take an immediate liking to her.

The next woman to enter the kitchen is a bird of an entirely different feather. Her beige dressing gown shimmers with beads and sequins. A patch of cherry red blankets each cheek, partially disguising the ravages of smallpox. She raises a painted eyebrow while she scrutinizes me.

As I ladle steaming porridge into Matryna's bowl, I introduce myself to the newcomer, adding, "Care for some porridge?"

"I suppose so." Her voice is deep—not sultry like Athena's, not judicious like Sophia Mikhailovna's, but gravelly and apathetic.

"Anna, this is Pelageya," Matryna offers.

"I hope you're feeling better today," I say.

Whether she would have responded or not, I'll never know, because at that moment Dunyasha bounces into the kitchen. Her sunburst voice addresses the painted woman. "Hey, Pelageya, one of your steady customers came in last night. I believe Anna took care of him." The pixie gives me a playful wink as she drops into the chair next to mine.

"Oh?" Pelageya's eyebrow arches again, this time higher. "Who was it?"

"Ermak Gerasimovich Pavlovich," I respond.

Pelageya's eyebrow rises to lofty heights as her spoon stops halfway to her mouth. "You're brand-new to this house, yet you feel free to steal your coworkers' customers?"

My thin skin bruised, I stammer, "I'm . . . I'm sorry, I didn't realize—"

"For Heaven's sake, Pelageya, ease up on the girl." Matryna quickly assumes the role of a mother hen protecting her weakest chick. "She just did what Sophia Mikhailovna told her to do. She's not trying to steal your steadies."

Pelageya dumps her spoonful of porridge into her mouth, then points the empty utensil at me. "Watch yourself. I've had young girls think they can step in and fill my shoes. Let me tell you, I have good repeat customers because I know my business. I was trained in St. Petersburg in a class establishment, not like these Moscow hovels."

I try to ingratiate myself with a smile. "Oh, you were in St. Petersburg?"

Sasha chooses that moment to get a closer look at me. He flies to Dunyasha's shoulder and pecks the tendrils of my hair.

"Careful," Dunyasha tells me. "Our little friend has been known to draw blood."

I'm not sure who presents the greatest danger—Sasha or Pelageya.

The cherry-cheeked woman fixes a wintry stare on me. "I was at Madame Jacqueline's. I dare say, she runs one of the most superb establishments on the continent. Champagne every night. Crackers with caviar. The finest linen in our boudoirs. There's none in Moscow that can compare. The capital, naturally, caters to a higher class. But I guess you wouldn't understand about working in places where avians don't shit on the breakfast table."

I'm not familiar with the word *avians*, but I assume it refers to Sasha, who is pecking precariously close to my ear.

Matryna's tone turns defensive. "You always say that about St. Petersburg, Pelageya, but I've traveled there. The slums I saw in the Spasskaia ward and Vyborg were worse than any in Moscow."

Pelageya trumpets a frigid laugh. "I'm referring to Nevsky Prospekt. The Winter Palace. The Mariinsky Theater."

Despite not finding the smallest bit of likeableness in Pelageya, I take another stab at comradery. "So you miss St. Petersburg?"

"Who wouldn't? Do you realize—probably you don't—that the capital has had French theater and Italian opera since the forties? Since the forties! St. Petersburg is a world apart from this overgrown village." She squints at me. "You know, lemon juice might bleach that mark on your face."

Matryna lets out an exasperated breath. "I need to be off to my medical examination. Anna, Sophia Mikhailovna said you'll go with me. Be sure to bring your passport. Do you have hidden pockets inside your coat? You'll want to conceal anything of value. How about you, Dunyasha? You and Dunka joining us?"

Dunyasha nods, and we three women and the parrot leave Pelageya to finish her porridge alone.

DURING THE TEN-BLOCK walk to the Women's Municipal Free Clinic, winter gusts cut through the knit shawl covering my head. A few paces ahead of Matryna and me, Dunka and Dunyasha walk arm in arm, their shoulders so close together you couldn't squeeze a thumb between them.

"Was I wrong to go with Pelageya's customer?" I ask Matryna.

"No. But it would be dreadfully wrong of you to be with Timofei Ivanov." Matryna winks at me, and her face lights up like the morning sky.

"He's someone special?"

"Definitely special! Don't be surprised when I marry him someday."

"How wonderful!"

Matryna lowers her voice, and I can barely hear it over the wind. "He has a wife, but they don't love each other. As soon as his business picks up, he'll be able to leave her and marry me."

"Hey, Matryna," Dunka calls over her shoulder. "Did you warn Anna what to expect at the medical-police? We don't want her running all the way back to her village."

With reluctance, Matryna leaves the topic of Timofei Ivanov to explain that the law requires brothel prostitutes to be examined twice a week for disease. If the physician finds evidence of venereal disease, the woman is whisked off to the syphilis hospital. "Disease is the worst thing that can happen to a working girl. The second worst is pregnancy."

As we near the medical clinic, bystanders fling taunts and heckling comments at us. Righteous women shriek, "Oozing evil!" Men call us everything from "honey" to "cunt." Young boys make moist smooching noises.

I clutch my shawl to cover more of my face. "Is this typical?" I ask Matryna, who is stomping out the butt of her cigarette.

"You'll get used to it." She leans close so I can hear her over the shouts. "It's against regulations for groups of us to appear in public. Yet the clinic is so crowded, sometimes we're forced to wait on the street in a long line. Rather duplicitous on the government's part, I would say."

Duplicitous. Another word I don't understand. Out of necessity during my first year in Moscow, I became familiar with city terms such as *neighborhood, lamppost, livery, footman, cab,* and various types of teas. But big words like *duplicitous*—I doubt I'll ever learn those.

Although today there's no line to get in the clinic, the waiting room is as crowded as an anthill. The few wooden benches along the wall are taken, and the remainder of the two dozen or so women stand or squat. Curses, arguments, and complaints echo off the grimy walls. The room is chilly and airless, and it smells of all manner of body odors, with an overlay of disinfectant.

"Watch your step," Matryna warns just in time for me to veer around a puddle of urine.

Next to a coal stove is a desk, at which sits a heavy-gutted, green-uniformed clerk, eyes closed and chin sunk onto his chest. Beside him on a flagpole hangs the imperial symbol of Russia: a green and gold double-headed eagle on a background of white.

The four of us are joined by a brightly painted woman with fiercely orange hair and a black eye. "Hello, girls," the woman shouts to be heard. "How's business?"

Matryna, Dunka, and Dunyasha clamor their greetings. "Feodora Filippovna, good to see you!"

"A customer give you that shiner?" Matryna asks.

"No. My madam." The woman removes a small pouch from her coat pocket and takes a pinch of tobacco.

"Blue is a good color on you," Dunka quips, referencing the strange sheen on Feodora Filippovna's skin.

"I hid the sores a long time from the quacks. You know, the usual dodges. Pinched out the pus before the exam. Covered them with my fingers when I spread myself. Concealed them with pastes. But eventually it got too painful, so I turned myself in." Feodora Filippovna shrugs at the inevitable. "Who's this?"

Matryna introduces me.

"At least you're not starting on a full moon. All the crazy customers come out in droves." Feodora looks closer at me. "You ain't the one who cut Shestov, are you?"

I nod mutely, astonished at the extent of my reputation.

Feodora grabs a passing woman by the arm and yanks her into our circle. "Hey, this is the one who knifed Shestov."

"That was you?" The woman's eyes bulge with admiration. "Next time, cut his liver out."

As the two women wander away from our group, I lean close to Matryna. "Why is Feodora Filippovna's face blue?"

"Courtesy of the mercury. It's used for treating syphilis."

Her explanation doesn't make sense to me, but now is not the time to ask further questions. Matryna has jumped to a more pressing topic. "When the doctor is examining you, keep anything of value clutched in your hand."

The physician's assistant sticks his head out the door, cups his hand around his mouth, and calls for the next group of women. Dunka manages to grab a newly unoccupied chair and pulls Dunyasha onto her lap.

Dunka, I decide, is a bulky version of the diminutive Dunyasha. Both have chestnut hair cropped in the new short, urban style. Both laugh at the same time, tossing their heads back with identical motions. But there are also some obvious differences. Whereas Dunyasha's voice is delicate, Dunka's is husky. Dunyasha's bones are as small and fragile as a chicken's, while Dunka's meaty hands look like they could completely encircle Dunyasha's tiny waist.

When at long last the assistant reappears, my head hurts from the noise and reek of the waiting room. My housemates and I are among a group of a dozen women who are called into the next room—a frigid, dank cubbyhole. I follow the lead of the other women as they remove their overcoats and various lower undergarments: heavy petticoats, drawers, bloomers, knickers. Skirts and blouses are left on. Purses, coats, and underwear are clutched to our chests.

We line up like horses being auctioned. I smile and nod at the woman standing next to me, but she regards me with dead eyes. The physician and his assistant, wearing jackets while we women shiver, inspect each of us—nose, mouth, and throat.

Lacking even the most elementary courtesy, the assistant then orders us to do an about-face, bend forward at the waist, hoist the back of our skirts, and, using our fingers, spread ourselves to give the physician easy access. In doing so, the dead-eyed woman falls face-first to the floor. The assistant drags her to one side of the room.

The physician thrusts a cold, metal instrument into one sex hole after another, taking a quick glimpse in each. In less than ten minutes, we're pulling on our coats.

The physician asks me if I've ever been inoculated against smallpox. Lacking any understanding of the question, I shake my head. He tells me to remove my blouse, then daubs a liquid onto my left arm. I flinch as the pointed end of his metal instrument scratches the substance into my skin. The assistant hands me a piece of paper and tells me to give it to the clerk in the waiting room.

Cold, degraded, and near tears, I push the paper across the clerk's desk. He doesn't bother to read it. "Passport." He holds out his hand.

I release my precious document to him. I'm seized with an almost overwhelming desire to snatch it back and run out the door, down the street, and all the way back to Petrovo.

The self-important blob of a man dips his pen into an inkwell and transfers the information to a yellow card, which he shoves across the desk. "Your identification card. Keep it with you at all times. Bring it with you every time you come here." A white piece of paper follows the yellow card. "Regulations. Read them." Never once does he raise his eyes to look at me.

I bite my lower lip and reach for the papers as if my bare hand is removing a boiling pot from the stove. My status is official. I'm a woman of loose morals, joining my fellow whores in their life of sin.

My cousin Platon's innocent face hovers in my mind, and I'm nauseous with shame. I elbow my way through the waiting women and back into the thin winter sunlight.

My eyes dart about until I see—*thank goodness!*—Dunka, Dunyasha, and Matryna.

I swallow back the bile that burns my throat. "I'm so glad you waited for me. I'm not sure I could find my way back to the house."

As we begin our return walk, Matryna stomps out the butt of her cigarette and asks what the white paper is. She laughs at my response. "Regulations! Now there's a good joke! They expect you to read it? Someone told me that only one-quarter of the women in Moscow can read, and that includes the hoity-toity ones. The bastards demand we follow their horrid regulations, but they won't bother to tell us what they are."

My forehead wrinkles. "What does 'one-quarter' mean?"

"It means of every four women, only one can read."

Goodness! I think of the entire village of Petrovo, where only three or four men could read—and not a single woman. "Can any of *our* women read?"

Dunka answers, "Sophia Mikhailovna can read everything. And my little Dunyasha has learned a few words, haven't you, dear?" She gives the pixie a quick kiss on top of her head.

I can't help but wonder how deep their affection is for one other.

The blustery wind makes conversation difficult, so we wend our way back to 903 Sviatoslavsky Prospekt in silence. Overhead, the bare tree limbs whack one another combatively, deepening my feeling of desolation.

WITH LONG SHADOWS falling over Moscow, I sit on my bed staring at the yellow card in my hand. My license to whore myself.

I toss it aside, disgusted that I can't decipher a single word on it. I must learn my letters if I'm to ever rid myself of the yellow ticket and the life it represents. I need to be the lucky one-of-four.

Please help me! I pray to God. *Since I left Petrovo, it's been one hellish moment after another!*

Shivering, I open my door wide to pull in heat from the hallway stove, then crawl under the blanket and bedspread.

It's dark when the jingling of the hallway bell wakes me. I've overslept. Panicking, I rush to get dressed. My left arm aches as I ineptly tidy my hair and apply my makeup. In the mirror, my face is a blotchy brick color.

Downstairs, Athena is chatting with Grisha at the bar. Irina is sitting on a divan, guffawing at the jokes of the man seated beside her and gleefully slapping his thigh. Sasha is jabbering nonsense inside his covered cage.

I drop into one of the Voltaire chairs. Maria descends the stairs and crosses the room to me.

"Sweetie, you're flushed." As she bends for a closer look, I'm taken aback by the number of wrinkles around her eyes and mouth. "I'm getting Sophia Mikhailovna."

Maria returns with both the madam and Athena. The three gather around me like a group of nanny goats appraising a new member of the herd. Sophia Mikhailovna places her cool palm against my forehead, just like Mamasha used to do. "You're on fire, girl. What happened to you?"

"I don't know. I felt fine this morning." My chest caves in. "I'm sorry to be such a bother."

"Is your stomach sick?"

"No, but my arm hurts."

Sophia Mikhailovna heaves an exasperated sigh that flings her face toward the ceiling. "Did they inoculate you this morning?" At my nod, she jabs her fist onto her hip. "They try to keep us healthy by making us sick. Go back upstairs. You're in full-blown fever and in no condition to entertain anyone."

Even though Sophia Mikhailovna's words are music to my ears, I protest. "But I can't. I promised you that I would work hard."

"Not tonight. And maybe not for a couple of days."

"I'll work hard as soon as I'm healthy. I swear I will, by all that is holy."

My third and fourth nights at 903 Sviatoslavsky Prospekt are spent shivering under my blankets and cursing the feverish sore on my arm. I've had only three customers so far. At this rate, I'll never end debt, as Athena advised. In fact, I wouldn't blame Sophia Mikhailovna if she fires me. And then what would become of me?

I press the pillow against my face to muffle my sobs.

CHAPTER 14

May

1868

NIGHTS MEAN WITHDRAWING into the private hermitage inside my head. While men rut on top of me, I ponder changing my hairstyle or imagine new wallpaper for my room.

Due to Sophia Mikhailovna's hefty fees, thankfully, most of my customers fall somewhere between respectable and well-heeled. Several have become steady patrons of mine.

Not only are the nighttime hours grueling, but they're completely inverted for a person whose days previously began at sunup. I awake each morning far closer to noon than to cockcrow and coax my achy muscles to drag me out of bed. Adding to the arduous nocturnal labor are daytime's ceaseless chores. And once the cooking, baking, laundry, and trips to the medical clinic and bathhouse are completed, my appearance needs to be preened and my mood bolstered so that I may be an engaging hostess. These seven-days-a-week demands sap the life from me.

I've been at the house five months when the first feathering of leaves on the maple and ash trees entice me to set aside my tasks in favor of an occasional afternoon walk beneath spring's precious morsels of sunshine. A few blocks to the north of Sviatoslavsky Prospekt is the Moskva River, the far side of which boasts the Kremlin's impervious red brick walls and Saint Basil's domes and turrets.

When I ramble south, bustling commercial streets give way to broad, sleepy avenues lined with the low-roof, closed-shutter houses of the Zamoskvorechye neighborhood. Here, members of the merchant class brighten their stoic homes with the jubilant faces of crocuses, jonquils, and daffodils. The flowers nod their greetings as I dawdle amid their splendor. Even in a city known for its gardens, the Zamoskvorechye district outshines all the rest.

Although Moscow's roses and lilacs burst with fragrance, its factories belch smoke and its streets are strewn with garbage. Every morning, I pray that someday I'll once again breathe sun-drenched country air rather than the city's sooty staleness.

Back home in Petrovo, everything happened in gentle, fluid motion: the caress of the breeze on the fields of rye, the horses seeking the most tender grass, the rhythmical swinging of the scythe. Petrovo's windswept pastures were vibrant with wildflowers and abounded with butterflies the size of sparrows—the handiwork of Mother Nature, not people.

Moscow's lines are straight and grim: streets, buildings, strangers' mouths. I feel trapped like a sardine in a can, when instead I should be splashing in the shimmering coolness of Petrovo's river.

But during those rare moments when I stop living in my memories, I grudgingly admit that Russia is far larger and more interesting than I ever imagined possible when I lived in a village with one church, one tavern, and fifty families. Although it's hard to concede that life in a brothel has its benefits, I acknowledge that my view of the world has widened. Customers often chat with Grisha and whichever girls happen to be in the Grand Salon. The gentlemen dissect newspaper articles, predict the success or failures of new business ventures, and pass judgment on the scoundrels in Moscow's government. I'm often stumped by the large words the men use, but that doesn't stop me from listening.

The women of the house also broaden my perspective in various and often surprising ways. For example, I went bug-eyed when I grasped the full extent of Dunka and Dunyasha's relationship. Dunka and Dunyasha are, of course, really two people, but I think of them as a single entity, like hair wound together in a braid. Dunka can be found wherever Dunyasha happens to be. Except when they're having a spat. Which is at least every other day.

Recently, Dunka, Dunyasha, Sasha, and I were having our noon meal when Sophia Mikhailovna sailed through the kitchen. She paused only long enough to tell Dunyasha to tidy up her room. "Need I remind you that I do not tolerate slovenly behavior."

After Sophia Mikhailovna left, Dunyasha lashed out at Dunka for not doing her fair share of laundering the sheets. "After all, we share the bed."

Dunka's fingers drummed the table. "Take into consideration that your bedding is not used solely for sleeping but also for money-making purposes that have nothing whatsoever to do with me. Tell me, Anna, who makes a bigger mess between the sheets, men or women?"

My response was an open-mouthed, wide-eyed stare.

Dunka turned back to Dunyasha. "I wash the sheets from *my* room, don't I?"

With the most severe expression her little-girl face could manage, Dunyasha snapped, "You're so boorish, I might as well be living with a man."

Such arguments are usually followed by the two of them storming to their respective rooms and slamming the doors. An hour or a day later, depending on the severity of the squabble, they can be found cooing and cuddling.

Irina is a horse of a completely different color. The raw-boned, gutter-mouthed woman strings oaths together like beads. And when I need a cure for my doldrums, I can count on Irina's salty jokes and riotous stories, such as the time she told me about biting off a customer's ear.

I cocked my head. "You bit off his ear?"

Irina shrugged her beefy shoulders. "Had to. He deserved it."

"Deserved it?"

"He was drunk and called me a cheap slut. So I told him he was full of mouse shit."

"Mouse shit?"

"That made him mad, and he smacked me. So I grabbed hold of his ear." Irina pulled her lips back, clamped her teeth together, and yanked like a wolf eviscerating a rabbit.

"You really bit it off?"

"Only half of it."

"What did you do with it?"

Irina scrunched her face in bafflement. "I didn't keep it as a souvenir, if that's what you mean."

In sharp contrast to Irina's indelicacy, Maria and Matryna are like the mother I lost. They hug me whenever I'm feeling down. Without ridicule, they answer all my ticklish questions. And they taught me that it isn't just handkerchiefs that should be embroidered, but undergarments as well.

With time, I realize that Maria and Matryna and Sophia Mikhailovna are right: The intimate garments I purchased during my first shopping spree are as provocative as my grandmama's nightshirt. A week ago, when I told Maria of my bold decision to buy new underclothes, my mentor announced, "It's such a fine day God sent. I'll go with you."

Inside the shop, although I ran my fingers along the tempting springtime pastel gowns, I stayed true to my plan of purchasing only one petticoat. Maria tried on a salmon-colored gown that lusciously complemented her chestnut hair, but left the shop empty-handed. On our way back to 903 Sviatoslavsky Prospekt, I asked her why she didn't purchase the dress. Maria replied that she needs to wear the dresses she has.

"Whatever do you mean? I can't imagine having too many dresses."

Maria's hazel eyes studied her protégé. "That's because you're young. My time for fine clothes is almost over. There's no point in squandering money I shall soon need."

Alarmed that her soft, maternal voice had suddenly taken on a hard edge, I admitted, "I don't understand."

"Remember your first morning at breakfast, when we met each other? I could tell from the look on your face that you wondered why an old woman like me was working in a whorehouse."

"Oh, Maria dear, my only thought was that you have the same gentle eyes as my mother." I slipped my arm through Maria's and squeezed.

"Nevertheless, my physical attributes have moved on, and soon I'll do the same."

"What will you do?"

"That's something I'd like to know myself." Maria pulled up the corners of her mouth in a dispirited smile. "Even if I had all the paint and powder in Moscow, I can't compete with young, pretty things like you. This business belongs to girls with slender waists and high breasts and heart-shaped mouths. We all have to leave sometime or other, my darling."

"But—"

"Oh, little Anna, listen to me. Find yourself a husband. Or respectable employment. This life you're living now won't last. Nothing's more pitiful than a prostitute who has tasted luxuries, only to find that in due course, she has become an old, used-up, painted whore in a gutter, like crazy old Aniska."

During the past week, Maria's words have haunted me. I picture the pitiful woman counting her fingers in the jail, and cold, silent foreboding slithers up my back.

CHILLY, DRIZZLY SKIES hover over Moscow during the last few days of May. Sasha sits atop the back of the kitchen chair next to mine while I pare an apple. In Petrovo, I was ridiculed for talking to dogs, cats, poultry, and livestock as if they understood me. Ha! Wouldn't my scoffing family be surprised to meet an animal that speaks back!

I cut off a tiny piece of apple for him.

"You'd better stop."

I jerk, and the knife grazes my skin. How can a man of Grisha's girth enter a room so silently?

"That bird's already overindulged. Don't spoil him worse." Grisha's eyes twinkle with mirth, and his cheeks balloon in a broad smile. I wonder if he, as a boy, had freckles to complement his red hair.

"Look at what that mean ogre made me do," I say in jest, showing Sasha the blood oozing from the tip of my thumb. I turn to Grisha. "Is there gauze? Or some bandaging?" I stick the finger in my mouth to stem the seeping.

"Bandaging? I'm not sure . . ." The line of thought seems unfamiliar to the gentle giant.

"Perhaps some old pillowcases that can be torn up?"

The big man settles in a chair and twirls his beard while he ploughs through the possibility. "Old pillowcases . . ."

Sophia Mikhailovna enters the kitchen. Even in a tatty old dressing gown, she creates a *swoosh* sensation as she glides about the room, coming to a stop behind my chair. Using both hands, she yanks back on my shoulders. "How many times do I have to remind you? And why are you sucking your thumb like a child?"

"She cut it," Grisha explains.

Sophia Mikhailovna doesn't respond as she begins pulling together a meal of bread, soft cheese, a boiled egg, and radishes.

I withdraw my thumb from between my lips. "I was wondering"—I pause until Sophia Mikhailovna swivels her eyes in my direction—"if perhaps there are any medical supplies in the house." I immediately pop the oozing finger back into my mouth.

"Medical supplies?" Sophia Mikhailovna bites a radish in half.

"Perhaps gauze? Or ointments?"

Sophia Mikhailovna crunches on the radish while she ponders the question. "We have a hot water bottle. For monthly cramps."

"Maybe, perhaps, could we put together a box of medical supplies?"

Sophia Mikhailovna swallows and turns full-face toward me. I, meanwhile, wish I had kept my mouth plugged with my thumb. "What are you inferring?" she asks.

"Sometimes, well . . . sometimes we've needed some things, such as . . . such as . . ." I curse myself for being so intimidated by the headstrong woman.

Sophia taps her foot. "Is your mouth full of flour or what? And look at the person to whom you are speaking."

Grisha comes to my rescue. "Such as when my finger got swollen with pus from that splinter."

"Yes, precisely," I quickly agree, looking Sophia directly in the eye. "I'd be happy to gather the supplies. Some balm for cuts. Mint lozenges for colds. Elixir for diarrhea. Nothing fancy."

I stop, hoping Sophia Mikhailovna will contribute to the conversation. But the madam continues leaning against the corner cupboard, her gaze cool, half a radish between her fingers.

I resume my attempt. "Just a small box. Keep it in the sideboard in the Grand Salon, so it's handy when we need it."

"Do you know what to buy?"

"Oh, yes. The young mademoiselle of our village's estate taught me very much about medicines and doctoring."

"All right. I know a place that sells such things. The owner will allow you to buy on my credit if I send my card with you."

Pleased beyond measure that Sophia Mikhailovna likes my idea, I build the courage to push my luck.

"Have you . . . ummm . . . " I draw a breath deep enough to make my belly pooch out. "I wondered if you've noticed how large the fern has grown." Under my tender administration of sunlight, rainwater, and used tea leaves, the once-forlorn brown stalk is not only stout and lush, but doubling its size every month.

Sophia Mikhailovna's nod is patronizing. "The area by the window looks almost tropical." She spreads the soft cheese on her bread.

I'm not sure how "tropical" looks, but I take the comment favorably. "I've seen them inside mansions—ferns just like that one. They can grow very large. And beautiful." I let the pent-up air out of my chest.

Sophia Mikhailovna holds the slice of bread in front of her mouth and looks squarely at me. "Are you attempting to make a point?"

My knees pull together and my feet fidget. "Well, I thought, perhaps . . . might it be a good idea if . . . I think the Grand Salon would look nice . . ."

"If there's a purpose to this conversation, I wish you'd get to it." Sophia Mikhailovna hides her amusement by biting into her bread.

I throw back my shoulders in faux confidence. "The fern is outgrowing its pot. If we got a larger pot, the fern could grow big and beautiful."

Practical Sophia Mikhailovna counters with "But it already has a pot. It seems like a waste of a good pot."

"Perhaps when we move the fern to a larger pot, we could put one of its babies in the old pot."

Grisha takes to the idea immediately. "Anna has a point. Two or three of those big plants would lend privacy to the divan area."

Hmmm reverberates behind Sophia Mikhailovna's pressed lips. She dabs her napkin at the corners of her mouth. "Yes. I suppose that makes good business sense. I'll give you two rubles, and not a kopek more. Find a pot that's chipped, and demand a discount." She picks up her small plate of egg and bread and heads toward her apartment.

"Thank you!" I'm floating on clouds. Sophia Mikhailovna listened to me—and respected my opinion!

"Make certain to get a good price." Grisha's words bring me back down to earth. "Sophia Mikhailovna won't be happy if you get jewed."

"Get jewed? What's that mean?"

"Jews always come out on top. They take a little more, give a little less."

I'm still perplexed. "Jews sell a lot of pots?"

"Naw. It's just a general expression." Grisha picks up the remains of my apple. "You're not going to finish this?" He sinks his teeth into the fruit. "It's in the Jews' blood to swindle and dupe. So if someone drives a hard bargain at another person's expense, that person *jewed* him."

The only thing I know about Jews is that they're in the Bible. And I don't remember the Holy Scriptures saying anything about swindling and duping. But a memory stirs. Athena said something about rich Jew bankers on my first day at 903 Sviatoslavsky Prospekt.

I suddenly see a way to use Grisha's guidance to my advantage. "I don't know much about these things. Perhaps you'll go with me? Would Kitay-Gorod be a good place to start?"

"Go shopping?" His lip curls. "I'd just as soon chew on broken glass."

"But I need protection from getting jewed. Plus, the pot is going to be very big. Bigger than I can carry."

"Then don't buy such a big pot." He bites off a fragment of the apple and offers it to spoilt Sasha, which is exactly what he told me *not* to do.

"But that's the point—to buy a big pot. My papa used to say, if you go in search of a rooster, you want to get a cockerel, not a bantam."

"So I'm your pack horse, is that it?" He appears to be joking, but I'm not sure.

A smile plays on my lips. "How about I make you a marzipan mazurka with almonds and honey?"

The lure hooks Grisha like a fish.

CHAPTER 15

May

1868

I RISE FROM my knees and brush the dirt off my hands. "I'll be right back with some water," I inform the fern.

Outside the rear door, I retrieve my bucket, which has been collecting rainwater cascading from the roof. My eyes dart toward a flash of movement among the drenched laundry hanging on the line. It's a girl, her rain-soaked dress clinging to her slight figure and protruding belly. She disappears around the corner of the building.

How did she get into the courtyard? Where's the good-for-nothing yardman?

I scamper back inside and give the fern a good dousing, then head toward my room to prepare for the evening. At the top of the stairway, I encounter a seething Pelageya, her talons shaking her skirt, sending a spray of water onto the hallway runner.

"My shoes are ruined! When will this damnable town get storm sewers like St. Petersburg?" Pelageya cocks her head back and scrutinizes the length of me. "You look like a drowned rat." She kicks the waterlogged hem of her skirt and stomps to her room, leaving vapors of perfume and wet wool.

The sheets of rain continue to fall for hours without stop, chasing the city's riffraff to the shelter of taverns and brothels. All my customers this evening, with the exception of one, are in various stages of inebriation. The sober one is so peculiar, he's an odd bird even without having imbibed alcohol tonight. He behaves like a twenty-year-old who has never outgrown being his mama's precious little darling.

While downstairs in the Grand Salon, the potato-shaped dunderhead brags about the size of his manhood, as though he were the boy who caught the largest frog in the pond. "You're such a sweet little treasure," he sing-songs to me in the style of a nursery rhyme, his grin displaying a broad expanse of gum. "But I'm far from a tiny tot. You'll have to open up wide."

As we mount the stairs, he's already fidgeting with the buttons on his trousers.

I pray this one goes quickly. And it does. Like a child who has wolfed down his piece of taffy, he whines for a second. I refuse, having learned during my months at 903 Sviatoslavsky Prospekt that imagination often carries a boy beyond the realities of his capability.

"But let's try something different this time." He lies on his back atop the mattress, his eyes aglow with what would be considered, under other circumstances, childlike enthusiasm. "Put me in your mouth."

"Let's look forward to it the next time," I propose with a practiced smile as I rise from the bed to pull on my clothes.

"Nowwwww." He mewls the word, stretching it into an entire sentence.

After smoothing my gown, I tap the toe of my shoe against the floorboards. "It's time to go."

He laces his hands atop his sunken chest and tucks his chin against his neck like a petulant child.

I extend my arm and wave him to come along.

He shifts to lie on his side to face me, his belly cascading like a formless sack of flour. "But your mouth is so pretty. And so is Yarik." He fondles his shriveled pod. "Don't you want to put your pretty lips around Yarik?"

Yarik? My arm falls to my side. *He named his cock Yarik?* "We'll do that when you come back. Perhaps next week?"

The guy rolls onto his back, kicks the sheet and bedspread into a jumbled heap at the foot of the bed, and bangs his fists against the mattress in a temper tantrum.

I fold my arms and move beyond the foot of the bed, as far from this brainsick kid as the cramped room will allow. "We had a nice evening, didn't we?" I try to cajole him. "Let's end it on a good note and look forward to the next time."

One of his eyebrows arches while the other falls in a low, straight line. The effect is unbalanced, like his mind. "That's how I want to end tonight—on a good note. With you kissing Yarik." He covers his face with the pillow.

My hand goes to my cocked hip. "You have to leave now, unless you want to go downstairs and pay for another visit."

"You don't like me," comes the muffled voice from under the pillow.

"Of course I like you. But you wouldn't want to get me fired, would you, for disobeying the rules? Then we'd never have any more fun together."

No response.

I snap my fingers twice as I imagine Sophia Mikhailovna would do. "Let's go."

The nutcase sits up, hurls the pillow toward the window and flops his hands up and down like a five-year-old frantic to get his toys back. "You've hurt my feelings. You can't . . . " He blinks several times in rapid succession. "You can't just go around hurting people's feelings."

I move toward the door. "I'm going to open the door now. You'd better get dressed." My leg reaches toward his pile of clothes on the floor. I manage to hook his shirt with my big toe and fling it toward him.

"No! You apologize to Yarik for hurting his feelings."

"I didn't mean to hurt your feelings or . . . or Yarik's feelings. Now get dressed."

"Not until you kiss Yarik and make us feel better."

I've had enough. Behind me, my free hand finds the doorknob, and I yank open the door. "Grisha!" I call over my shoulder.

This unravels the boy. He dives off the far side of the bed onto the floor, leaving only his head exposed above the mattress.

Fast, heavy footsteps ascend the stairs. "He hurt you?" Grisha asks me from the doorway while keeping the boy's head in his line of sight.

"No, but his time is up."

Grisha's thumb jerks backward over his shoulder. "Come on, pal, it's time to clear out."

"I'm not ready to leave," he snivels.

When Grisha makes a brawny fist, I raise a cautionary hand to stop him. "You have two choices," I tell the boy. "You can either put on your clothes and walk out of this house. Or this gentleman will throw you and your clothes onto the street in the rain." I turn away and tidy my hair in the mirror.

In the reflection, I watch the unstable kid jut his lip in a pout and, with painstaking slowness, gather up his clothes. Once dressed, he pauses just before going out the door. "Someday *your* feelings will get hurt."

Grisha follows one step behind him down the stairs.

I spend a few extra minutes in my room, calming my frayed nerves. This customer was harmless, but the next one might not be. Evenings should symbolize relaxation after the day's hard toil. Yet for me, apprehension rises as the sun sets.

During my last visit to the medical clinic, the scuttlebutt was that a customer had gone berserk at one of the houses and stabbed as many women as he could with a butcher knife. He kept screaming that God had sent him on a sacred mission to kill all prostitutes.

I utter a curse. Why do I have to live every moment in vigilance? When the last of the sun's rays stream through the window each day, why can't I be with Platon and the rest of my family, huddled around the table, dipping our spoons into the common soup pot while the night insects croon their songs? As soon as I end my debt, I'll save every ruble, every kopek, to pay for my return to Petrovo. Meanwhile, I'll purchase a second whistle so I have one under the bed and one at the dressing table.

When I finally go downstairs, I head to the bar, which is empty except for Grisha. I thank him for his help.

His index finger circles his temple.

"Yes, definitely cracked in the head." I lean forward and whisper, "He named his pecker Yarik."

"Yarik?" The bartender's grin plumps his cheeks into two apples.

Still feeling a little uneasy, I tell Grisha that I'd like a bit of brandy.

Grisha's ruddy face drops into a black scowl. "I'll get you some tea, like always."

"Why?" I lift my chin saucily.

"For one thing, Sophia Mikhailovna can and will ban you permanently from the house for drinking during working hours. Second, I keep a tab of all the liquor and wine you ladies drink during your off-hours, and Sophia Mikhailovna takes it out of your pay."

"Just a sip to see how it tastes. I want to see what's so good about it."

"That's the third problem. There's nothing good about it. Liquor has brought down many a hardworking girl."

A high-pitched screech sears the air beside me. It's Sasha, who drops into a panicky squawk, then howls again.

For the second time this evening, the beefy man bounds up the stairs two at time with the speed of a colt. Instinctively, I race behind him.

CHAPTER 16

May
1868

FROM PELAGEYA'S ROOM comes an ear-piercing shriek that puts Sasha's to shame. Matryna and I reach Pelageya's doorway on Grisha's heels. Pelageya is cowering naked in a corner. Grisha puts his boot to a stocky man curled on the floor.

"Get your clothes on." Kick. "Or leave naked." Kick. "Your choice."

The man has a generous covering of black body hair and appears strong enough and mean enough to bite through bone. He slowly rises and reaches for his shirt. He slips his arm through the sleeve, and as it emerges from the cuff, his fist lashes out and punches Grisha in the face.

The hit glances off Grisha's chin and does little harm there. However, it jolts his head to the left, and his temple slams into a wall sconce. Grisha steadies himself against the armoire as he shakes the fog from his head.

The hairy man, apparently steamed with alcohol, bends over at the waist and runs full force toward Grisha. He rams his shoulder into Grisha's midsection, pitching Grisha's broad shoulders against the wall.

As the louse staggers back a few steps, I grab the closest object—an umbrella. Using every bit of my strength, I wallop the umbrella's handle across the small of the man's back.

Beside me, Matryna raises Pelageya's water pitcher over her head and crashes it against the back of the intruder's skull.

I flip the umbrella so its tip points toward the man and drive the tip into the scoundrel's lower back, like I'm embedding a pitchfork into a pile of hay.

At the same instant, Grisha heaves himself from the wall. He grabs a shock of thick black hair, drags his opponent to a low chest of drawers, and pounds the man's face into its marble top. And again. When Grisha lets him go, the man stumbles a few steps and falls onto the mattress. The sheet quickly colors with blood and vomit.

Matryna hands a dressing gown to Pelageya, who is still crouched in the corner. I volunteer to get a bucket of water and some cleaning rags.

When I descend into the Grand Salon, Sasha is quiet. Sophia Mikhailovna is behind the bar. "Is everything all right up there?"

"Yes. Pelageya's customer hit Grisha, who hit him back. Then the guy vomited on the bed."

"I'd like to talk to you."

The gravity of Sophia Mikhailovna's voice makes me wary. As I approach the bar, I double-check that my spine is erect and my shoulders are back.

The madam levels her eyes at me. "I understand from Grisha that you had to call on him tonight."

Time and again, I'm stunned that Sophia Mikhailovna seems to know every-thing—truly *everything*—that happens, within moments of its occurrence.

"You did exactly the right thing," she continues. "In this business, we can't be frightened little bunny rabbits. But we can't take foolish chances, either. If you feel threatened, always get Grisha."

"Yes, I will."

"It will happen again. Do you understand what I'm saying? What happened tonight to you and to Pelageya was fairly minor. I want you to remember this—you must use your common sense when things heat up, as they surely will."

"Yes, ma'am."

"And another thing. I know you were trying to help, but you might have been of more use here, keeping an eye on the Grand Salon. It's risky to leave the room unattended. Is that understood?"

I give my third *yes*, adding, "I hadn't thought of that."

Grisha descends the stairs, carrying the naked, unconscious man across his shoulders. After heaving the drunken heap onto the sidewalk, he retrieves the fellow's overcoat from the rack and tosses it out the door.

I turn to fetch my rags and bucket but immediately swivel back toward the madam. "May I ask you a question?"

"Certainly."

"You weren't in the Grand Salon when the ruckus started with Pelageya. How did you know to come in here? And how did you know I left the room to go upstairs?"

With a bit of playfulness in her voice, Sophia Mikhailovna replies, "Sasha told me."

I initially think the madam is joking. Then I remember the blood-curdling screeches. "Are you saying that when he shrieks, it means something's wrong?"

"I think he hears certain sounds better than we humans. He can tell when someone is in distress." Sophia Mikhailovna lapses into a maudlin tone. "You know, when he was originally offered to me, I took him solely as a novelty. But he has more than paid for his keep." The madam's sentimentality disappears as quickly as it came on. "Anyway, I heard him screeching. And when I reached the Grand Salon, I saw your skirts flying up the stairs."

She gives a solitary nod of her head. It's obvious I'm dismissed—just as it's obvious the madam has no intention of going upstairs to check on Pelageya.

When I return with the bucket, Athena, whose customer skedaddled during the commotion, has joined Matryna in trying to soothe Pelageya. The vainglorious woman is sitting on the floor, her back against the wall and front draped by her dressing gown, whimpering into a clutched pillow.

On Pelageya's bed and rug, the blood is mixed with the vomit like smashed cherries stirred into curdled milk. I wipe the blood off the floor and pick up the shards of the water pitcher. Upon returning the umbrella to its usual spot, I notice some of its spines are broken.

When I haul the bucket of bloody water and a lit oil lamp out to the courtyard, the tiresome rain has faded into a cool drizzle. As I pitch the dirty water onto the cobbled ground, something catches my attention inside the remnants of an old henhouse. Something large and light colored.

The object moves.

I stiffen. Is it the crazy Yarik boy, waiting for me, wanting retaliation for his hurt feelings? Frozen in place, I squint though the misty, moonless night. Yes, it's a person. But not Yarik's owner.

I recognize the tattered dress. It's the pregnant girl I saw earlier in the day.

Silently, I approach the hen coop and shine my lamp in that direction. The girl is curled on her side. "Hello?" I say softly. "Are you sick?"

The girl bolts upright and scoots backward, pressing herself against the far wall of the coop, which is held together largely by habit. "I didn't do nothing. I swear. Nothing. I just fell asleep."

With the cautious speed of rising dough, I walk closer and squat before her, an arm's length away. My lamp's rays reflect the fright behind the stringy hair that curtains her face. I keep my voice hushed. "I saw you earlier today. Do you have nowhere to live?"

"I'll go now." Quivering from head to toe, she rises first to her hands and knees. Then, with considerable effort, she lifts her huge belly until she's standing, bowed, beneath the low roof of the coop. She's barefoot, and her garment looks more like a sack than a dress.

I oh-so-slowly rise to my feet. "When is your baby due?"

Hunch-shouldered, the girl crosses her arms and tucks a hand into each armpit.

"Soon?" I prod.

The girl remains mute.

The past nudges me. I can hear Mama scolding me as a child for having a spirit that was too gentle. Stouthearted peasants don't rescue drowning dragonflies or right upside-down beetles. Peasants grow robust by facing the harshness of life, by doing the Church's bidding, and by sweating out their strength drop by drop in the rye fields.

Despite Mamasha's reprimands, my heart remained soft and vulnerable. I couldn't turn a blind eye to those in need. Not in Petrovo. And not now.

"Would you like to sleep in our house tonight?"

A male voice bursts from across the courtyard. "Let her go!"

The girl jerks her head about, searching for the source of the voice.

"That's just Grisha. Don't be scared. He looks like a giant, but he's a good man, a kind man."

"I said," the kind man bellows, "leave her alone."

"How can I?" I call over my shoulder. "She has nowhere to live."

"You're asking for trouble from Sophia Mikhailovna."

I return my attention to the terrified creature. "My name is Anna. What's yours?"

She mumbles something imperceptible.

"Say it again."

"Felitsa."

"Well, Felitsa, it's warm and dry in the house. Why not come in for a meal?"

The girl hesitates long enough that I know I am winning the argument. I move to one side so she won't feel threatened.

"Anna, don't do it!" Grisha booms.

The girl, barefoot and hunched over, takes wary steps. One stride ahead, I guide her across the slick cobblestones.

The girl cowers as we pass Grisha, his arms crossed, his heavy head swinging back and forth. "There's no grief but the Devil sends it." He falls in line a few steps behind us.

When we reach the rear door, I go in first, followed by Felitsa. In the darkness, however, the girl misjudges the single step, stubs her toe, and stumbles, the weight of her belly throwing her off-balance.

Grisha intuitively grabs her shoulder and prevents her fall. The girl whirls around and, as quick as a cat swatting a mouse, lashes both hands at Grisha's face. No stranger to assault, he swiftly seizes her wrists and pins her arms to her sides.

I keep my voice unruffled. "Grisha was just trying to help you. No one is going to hurt you."

By the time the waif shambles to the kitchen, she's so weak, she's like a marionette attached to slack strings. Her legs and face freeze with fear when she sees Maria at the kitchen table, handing a cool towel to Pelageya to hold against her bruised cheek.

With red claw marks etched into his forehead and cheeks, Grisha barrels through the kitchen to the Grand Salon. I know where the barman's loyalty will lead him.

I place the girl in a chair and take the one next to her. I start to put a reassuring arm around the emaciated shoulders but stop abruptly when I catch sight of the girl's left eye. It's much smaller than the right one. Instead of an eyeball, the socket is filled with marbled shades of maroon. Its eyelids are rimmed in red, and the eyelashes are matted with a weepy yellow. Her other eye darts birdlike around the kitchen.

At a snail's pace, I proceed to clasp the girl's skeletal shoulder. "This girl has no home and it's raining, so she'll sleep here tonight," I announce to the two women at the table. "Maria, would you be a dear and get her a glass of tea from the samovar?"

As Maria leaves the kitchen, she crosses paths with the arriving Sophia Mikhailovna. To my surprise, the madam ladles up a bowl of soup and places it in front of the girl along with a slice of bread.

The benevolence ends there.

The madam locks eyes with me and jerks her head toward her apartment. I trail after her like an obedient, if reluctant, dog.

In her one-room apartment, Sophia Mikhailovna lowers herself onto the chair at her dressing table. She motions for me to sit on the bed, which I find to be remarkably softer than my own, She sedately lays a palm on her thigh, then covers it with her other hand. "So, what do you intend to do with her?"

I summon my courage with a deep breath. "She has nowhere to sleep, and she's cold and starving."

Silence hangs over the room as Sophia Mikhailovna tilts her head. "The question was: What do you intend to do with her?"

All of a sudden, I see myself at the edge of Petrovo's river. I'm six years old and walking toward my mother. My arms are extended straight in front of me, one hand cupped over the other.

Look, Mamasha. She was drowning, and I saved her.

I crack my hands apart ever so slightly. A ray of sunlight reflects off the iridescent wings of a dragonfly.

Mama asks, *And what do you plan to do with her?*

Now, at almost eighteen years of age, I wring my hands in my lap, wishing they held a dragonfly instead of a pregnant, destitute girl's future. "I thought she could sleep here tonight. It was kind of you to give her some soup. She's a walking skeleton. I know I'm overstepping my bounds, but can't we extend some kindness? Offer a helping hand, just this one time?"

Sophia Mikhailovna leans back, crosses her arms, and challenges, "And in the morning?"

I lower my eyes as the tips of my ears begin to burn. "I don't know. But I do know that when I found her in the courtyard, my Christian conscience demanded that I do something." I look up, searching for some indication that Sophia Mikhailovna is sympathetic. "When I needed help, you took me in."

"I took you in as a business deal. I don't run a charity. The streets are filled with women who have nowhere to turn. You can't bring home every stray in Moscow."

I stare at my wet shoes.

"Until tonight, you've shown a prudent mind, which is a valuable asset if you are to survive in this business. Tonight's behavior, well-intentioned though it may be, simply won't do. Is that understood?"

My head droops, and my shoulders curl inward.

"Look at me. Is that understood?"

I do as I'm told. "Yes."

Sophia Mikhailovna rubs the back of her hand across the furrows of her brow. "That useless yardman. He's not worth a fart in a whirlwind. I'm going outside to have a little talk with him. If I can find him. Meanwhile, I'll have Grisha hail a cab."

A cab? Panicked chills make me lightheaded. "Are you tossing me out?"

"If this happens again, yes, I will." She stands. "The cab is to take the girl to the Foundling Home. Or possibly to a charity hospital."

I remain seated, looking up at her. "At this hour? Do they accept people in the middle of the night?" Her delayed response implies she doesn't know the answer. Having never witnessed uncertainty in Sophia Mikhailovna, I seize the moment. "If those places are locked up for the night, then what? Have the cabbie bring her back here? You'll have spent double the cab fare and still have the girl under your roof."

Sophia Mikhailovna's lips thin. The silence is long before she directs, "You explain to Grisha that he'll be sharing the attic tonight with the waif. There's a cast-off mattress or two up there. Find an old sheet and one of the blankets that we keep around for rags. Then search her hair and body thoroughly for lice. And I mean thoroughly. Do not give her a pillow. Toss her clothes outside. Give her one of your old dresses."

One of my old dresses? That means giving up one of my two servant's dresses.

Sophia Mikhailovna isn't finished. "Tomorrow, tear up the sheet and blanket for rags, and wash them twice. In boiling water."

"I understand."

"See to it that she's out of this house by midmorning."

I swallow. Sophia Mikhailovna has placed the entire burden on me. Where, unfortunately—yet in all honesty—it belongs. "I understand."

"And you'd better pray she doesn't have that baby tonight."

Early the next morning, I wonder if the madam has missed her calling as a fortune-teller.

CHAPTER 17

May
1868

SHORTLY AFTER SUNUP, the household is awakened by a wail. Seven night-gowns cluster in the second-floor hallway while howls of pain filter through the ceiling. Athena, the only one of us who has given birth, volunteers to sit with Felitsa in the attic. While Irina, Dunyasha, and Matryna crawl back into their beds, Dunka, Maria, and I shuffle to the kitchen. Pelageya remains behind her closed door.

On the way, I pause to give Sasha his morning freedom. When I pull the blanket off his cage, his eyes are closed and he doesn't announce his usual greeting. His feathers are patchy, with many lying on the bottom of the cage and on the floor below. I open his door, but he merely hunkers down on his perch.

"Oh, Sasha, you're not sick, are you?" My finger strokes under his neck. "Please don't be sick. I have enough worries today." I pull back the drapes to give him a dose of sunshine.

Grisha stumbles into the Grand Salon and drops onto one of the divans for another few hours of sleep.

I join Maria at the kitchen table, while Dunka stirs the porridge on the stove. "What do you plan to do with her, Anna?" Maria asks.

I grimace. Everyone assumes—or Sophia Mikhailovna has spread the word—that the unfortunate wench is my personal responsibility. "She and the baby will have to go to the Foundling Home."

"Foundling Home!" At the mention of the huge government-run orphanage, Maria makes the sign of the cross. "May God keep her in His mercy."

Dunka's free hand goes to her hip. "Babies drop like flies at that pesthole."

"No one said life is fair." I'm startled to hear my mother's sharpness in my own voice. "I'm sorry. I didn't mean to sound cross. It's a saying my mother used." I lift my hands at my helplessness to solve Felitsa's dilemma. "Maybe one of you has a better idea."

Pelageya stomps into the kitchen, a cloth bandage wrapped under her chin and tied atop her head. She levels her eyes at me. "Don't you ever tire of wearing a halo?"

"What do you mean?"

"I mean, Mademoiselle Benevolence, that thanks to you, the yowling in the attic is making my tooth hurt even worse."

"What's wrong with your tooth?" Maria asks.

Pelageya's scarlet fingernails go to her swollen cheek. "That bastard broke it."

After pitching a cursory look at the pot of simmering porridge, Pelageya reaches for a loaf of bread. She smothers two slices in butter and the last of the honey—honey that I had intended to use for the marzipan mazurka I owe Grisha.

"Speaking of last night"—Pelageya tosses a look at me that's as brittle and sharp as an icicle—"what about my umbrella?"

"Your umbrella?"

"It's broken. Like my tooth."

I give a muted smile. "I guess I don't know my own strength."

"And I guess you'll be buying me a new one?"

"Pardon?"

"You'll be buying me a new one." Her voice is like a cat's snarl.

I blink in disbelief. Ice must flow through that woman's veins. "I'm sorry your umbrella is broken. I thought I was being helpful."

"I'm sure you thought you were. But I'm also sure Grisha could have handled the situation without your assistance. That's what he's paid to do."

My mouth hangs agape as I struggle to piece together a reply.

"Just as I'm sure Matryna owes me a new water pitcher." With sparks flashing in her eyes, Pelageya looks about the table for the missing culprit.

I feel as though the outcome of my good deed is the equivalent of lifting a rock and dropping it on my own foot. I decide to fight back. "What I did last night I did with the best of intentions for your safety. I see no reason I should buy you a new umbrella." My chair scrapes across the floorboards as I push away from the table and leave the kitchen behind me.

Damn that woman! She's like a poisonous cauldron that won't stop bubbling over.

WHEN DUNYASHA FINALLY rises from her bed, she bounds about the kitchen, clapping her hands like a child. "A baby! Oh, I can't wait!" she squeals in a spasm of delight. "Don't you just adore the smell of their little breath? And the way their teeny mouths curl up in a smile? Oooo, I'm so excited!"

Dunyasha's animated face falls when Dunka informs her that Felitsa and the baby will go to the Foundling Home.

"Assuming the baby makes it out all right," I add. "The girl's hips are so narrow."

"Only through the mercy of God and all the saints will she be able to have that baby," Maria predicts.

Athena walks into the kitchen, having spent several hours at Felitsa's bedside. "Votives. Need lots—everywhere in attic. Quick birth, just like that." She snaps her fingers.

"How many candles?" Dunka asks. "Would twelve or thirteen be enough?"

"Not thirteen." Dunyasha stomps her tiny foot. "An unlucky number."

"That's nothing but an old superstition," Dunka insists.

"Sometimes there's rats in the attic," Dunyasha frets. "They'll crawl on top of the baby and suck the life right out of it."

Dunka plants a hand on her cocked hip. "More twaddling nonsense! Why don't you join the nineteenth century?"

"We really should somehow separate Grisha's area from Felitsa's," I propose. Church bells chime the eleven o'clock hour.

"Let's get to work," Maria says. "Customers will be arriving in a few hours."

Irina gives a merry wink. "A woman screeching in labor—that will take the wind out of our customers' sails, won't it?"

The seven of us work together to string rope and drape old curtains to separate Felitsa's birthing room from Grisha's sleeping quarters. This is my first time in the attic, and I'm a little surprised by the sparse accommodations. But then again, this area is for sleeping; the rest of Grisha's time is spent downstairs.

Next, we devise a schedule so someone is always with Felitsa. Matryna volunteers to be the first.

Athena goes shopping for votive candles. "On the way home, I'll ask priest to bless them."

Maria insists that goat's milk is better for the soon-to-be mother than cow's milk and sets out to buy some.

Pelageya remains in her room, nursing her aching tooth.

Dunyasha and I go to the market to buy honey for the marzipan mazurka and grapes for the ailing Sasha—his favorite treat. On the way home, Dunyasha squeals, "There's little Sonia!"

Sonia is an affable, superbly mannered girl who just had her eleventh birthday.

A couple of years ago, her father was killed in a construction accident, leaving a family that now lives hand-to-mouth. Her mother takes in sewing and also bakes pies, tarts, pastries, and other delicacies in order to support her five children, each of whom contributes to the joint effort. One of Sonia's many home chores is the weekly delivery of her mother's ginger cakes to 903 Sviatoslavsky Prospekt. Sophia Mikhailovna indulges in the luxury as a kindness to the indigent mother.

Sonia, a wisp of a child, has bones the size of Sasha's and hair as fine as dandelion fluff. With freckles across her pug nose and cheeks rounded with mirth, she's like a little confection herself—always sweet and impossible to resist.

Dunyasha darts across the street to the tow-haired girl, grabs her shawl-draped shoulders, and jumps up and down. "Guess what! You'll never guess! You can guess all day, but you'll never guess!"

I cross the street to join them, thinking Dunyasha looks closer to Sonia's age than her own. Dunyasha is gushing forth details of the impending baby, making Little Sonia tremble with excitement. This, in turn, spurs Dunyasha to new heights of elation.

Once the story is completed and is in the process of being retold, I interrupt. "Sonia, do you have any suggestions from when your mother had your baby brother and sisters?"

The girl's cheeks puff out like a full moon. "Oh, yes. My aunt lives in the room next to ours, and she has three little babies. I helped birth them, too."

Using my fingers, I count ten people living in two rooms. Eleven, if the uncle is present. So very much like the huts in Petrovo.

"Most important is Saint Catherine the Martyr." Sonia overflows with adult wisdom. "The icon must be placed at the head of the bed."

Dunyasha and I question each other with our eyes. Neither of us has ever seen an icon of the patron saint of childbirth at the brothel.

"You don't have one?" Sonia's implication is that everyone of childbearing age surely keeps such an icon handy. "After I deliver these cakes, I'll run home and get ours. I'll bring it to your house in a jiffy. Then we can wash it and give the water to the mother to drink."

Dunyasha has the same peppering of freckles on her nose as Sonia, and right now they're bunched up in disgust. "You want her to drink dirty wash water?"

Sonia's nod is so emphatic, her blond braid slides up and down her back. "Chases away the evil eye."

"That's very kind of you, Sonia." Even as I say the words, the girl is backing away, itching to fetch Saint Catherine.

Dunyasha rises to the tips of her toes and calls to the girl, "Maybe we'll have a baby waiting for you!"

Sonia is an entire building away when she turns and shouts a bit more advice. "I just remembered. Aunt Lilya swallows vodka with soap in it. When she vomits"—the girl's sweeping arm mimics the act—"the unclean spirits all come out."

FELITSA DULY DRINKS the wash water from the on-loan icon. Countless priest-anointed votive candles cast fluttering shadows on the dusty cobwebs that lace the dark vaulted ceiling. All chests, wardrobes, cupboards, and interior doors throughout the entire house are flung open, a well-respected strategy to speed up the birthing process.

Athena's ebony eyes sparkle playfully as she says the baby had better be born before customers arrive. "Just think—bedroom doors open!"

Irina hoots and slaps her thigh. "All of you would be snooping around my door, trying to pick up a few pointers!"

Despite these interventions, plus Maria's prayers, Felitsa's baby makes no progress.

Midafternoon, I check on Sasha, who is still feeling under the weather. Then, with my lower lip pinched between my teeth, I reluctantly approach Sophia Mikhailovna. "I wonder if we should get a midwife." My toe prods the crimson pile of the carpet. "I'll pay for her."

Sophia Mikhailovna looks so softly into my eyes that I wonder if she might decline my offer and pull the rubles from her own pocket. Instead the madam replies, "Let's hold off a little while on summoning a midwife."

I nod, and the madam continues with "I'd like to help you out of this jam, but I'm not going to. There's a lesson to be learned. You can't dig your hole any deeper just to help strangers get out of theirs."

CHAPTER 18

May

1868

CUSTOMERS BEGIN ARRIVING. Although we close the doors to our rooms, Felitsa's outcries filter down through the attic floor. I bounce raucously on the mattress in hopes that the squeaking bedsprings will drown out the wails. None of my eight customers mention the shrieks. Either they don't hear them, or they think it's just the brothel's normal caterwauls.

Shortly before midnight, I fasten my dress for what I hope is the last time on this typically slow Tuesday evening. My eyes roll upward toward the attic as I appeal to the benevolent Saint Catherine the Martyr. "Our Lady, help Felitsa. And help poor Sasha." I sigh from the gut. "Help all of us."

Downstairs, the Grand Salon is empty except for Grisha. Sasha is quiet under his cage-blanket.

I climb onto a stool, prop my elbows on the bar, and rest my chin in my cupped hands. "Guess you'll be sleeping on the divan tonight," I mumble to Grisha.

He exhales a *humph.*

I glance at two men descending the stairway. As they cross the Grand Salon toward the vestibule, one thumps the other on his back. They both bellow like triumphant bulls.

As they leave, another customer enters. It's Matryna's favorite, Timofei Ivanov. Grisha tells him that Matryna is a little under the weather this evening.

Timofei Ivanov's fingers irritably stroke where his eyebrows would be, if he had any. "What about Dunyasha? She working tonight?"

Dunyasha? I question why the man who supposedly wants to marry Matryna would seek out another woman from the same brothel. It appears that Matryna is clinging to a very slippery fish.

"Yes, Dunyasha is working." Grisha consults the watch that hangs from his neck. "She'll be down shortly." His voice sounds flat when he asks Timofei Ivanov, "Care for something to drink?"

"No. I'll just wait."

Grisha nods as if expecting that cheapskate answer.

Timofei Ivanov flops onto a divan and cleans under his fingernails with a pocketknife until Dunyasha retrieves him. Grisha rolls his eyes at me. "The Devil is quite a charmer, at least in Matryna's eyes."

"I take it you're not fond of him." I keep my voice low, as does Grisha.

"I wish Matryna would wake up and realize that a promised horse won't pull a cart."

I grin sadly. "Are you saying his tongue is as forked as his beard?"

Just then another man passes through the Gentlemen's Entrance vestibule, removes his cap, and looks about the room as if getting his bearings. Grisha booms his greeting and offers the man a drink, which he declines.

I pull myself off the stool and put on a veneer of gaiety as I introduce myself. The customer is of short stature, probably around fifty years of age, with a flabby but not rotund middle. Although his head is bald on top, long, thin strands of hair hang over his ears and neck. Broken veins on his nose and bags under his eyes complete the picture of an aging man.

Typical of the lower classes is his red calico shirt and black vest. His wide velveteen trousers are tucked into black leather boots that are down-at-the-heels. But most important to me, he appears clean.

On the way up the stairs, he chatters about how hot the summer already is. I've grown tired of men making small talk. If they want to chat, they should stay downstairs with Grisha. Or at home with their wives.

But this particular evening, seeking a lively repartee to drown out the moans from the attic, I'm grateful for the man's blather. When he tells a joke that's been circulating around the city for months, I giggle wildly.

The man carefully places his gold-rimmed spectacles on the narrow chest of drawers. With his spectacles off, the bags under his eyes are more prominent.

He stiffly lowers himself onto the edge of the bed and removes his boots and socks. "I like to start here."

Here? Here where? "Pardon?"

"I like to start with a nice foot massage. With particular attention to my toes."

I've learned not to question a customer's quirks. After last evening's experience with Yarik's tender feelings, however, I'm a bit wary.

I curve my lips into a flirty smile. "Why don't you lean back against the pillow, put your feet in my lap, and tell me exactly what your toes like."

With his feet nestled in the folds of my dress and his back resting against the swirls of the iron headboard, he closes his eyelids like a contented cat about to sink into a nap. "Take your time down there. You have a nice touch," he murmurs, his speech slow and cordial. "I'm not a young stud, you know. My performance isn't what it used to be."

I'm accustomed to hearing this from grandfathers. "We can do whatever it takes."

"The old pecker doesn't respond to anything anymore except a hardy foot massage followed by an even hardier blow job."

This grandpa turns out to be an accommodating customer. Once I move upward from his toes, he finishes quickly, and my hair doesn't even get mussed.

His back still against the headboard, he says, "Since that didn't take up too much of your time, I believe I'm entitled to a few more minutes. So why don't you tell me what that noise is."

"I apologize for the distraction." Seated on the edge of the mattress, I explain how we came to be in possession of a woman having a baby. I close my story with "The mother is so poorly, I'm not sure she or the baby will live."

"If the baby dies, is it such a terrible thing?"

I'm taken aback by his response. "Why, yes. Of course. The death of any child is a tragedy."

"A dead child doesn't have to fight cold or disease or hunger the way its mother has to. Are you entirely sure the child's death, were it to occur, should be lamented?" I'm speechless, so he goes on. "What if they both live? What then?"

"They'll go to the Foundling Home."

The man places his stubby arm behind his head. "Ah, the Foundling Home, the heart-wrenching world of Russia's unwanted children. So basically, the mother has two choices—either place the baby in the uncaring care of the bungling government or try to raise the child by herself."

"I guess so. I mean, what else is to be done?"

"The accursed Russian question: *What is to be done?* The true character of Russian thought is tortured self-questioning. But I digress." He flings his hand as if backhanding a fly. "Returning to the woman upstairs—let's pretend for a moment that there is no Foundling Home. How will she support an infant when she can't even support herself? And what about a few years from now? Will she be able to afford the public school tuition of three rubles a year to see that her child is educated and isn't condemned to the same gruesome life she herself has suffered?"

My thumb runs pensively up and down the rickrack on my skirt. "She'll have a rough go of it, but I do believe she'll try to better her life."

He squints at me—for what reason, I don't know. Perhaps he thinks I'm an unsalvageable featherhead. Or perhaps he can't see clearly without his spectacles.

"Do you think the government will allow the mother to choose a better life?" he asks. "Do you believe it will offer her training, so she can earn a decent wage and educate her child? Ensuring a good future for our next generation should be a goal dear to the heart of every Russian."

I wonder what has happened to the docile little man who, just a short while ago, was telling stale jokes.

His legs swivel over the side of the bed, and he retrieves his spectacles. "What about you, Anna? Are you satisfied?"

"Satisfied? With what?"

"Everything in your life. Anything in your life. How well you ate as a child. Your level of education. Where you live. How society treats your friend upstairs." He raises his short arms out from his sides, palms upward, to indicate the whole of the earth and heavens.

"I suppose there are many things I'm not satisfied with."

He tucks the wire of his eyeglasses behind his ears and remains seated beside me on the edge of the bed. "And what are you doing about those 'many things'?"

"Well, I want to save rubles for the future. And learn to read."

"Learn to read? That's terrific! How's it coming along?" When I sheepishly look at the floor, he pushes his spectacles up his nose. "What I'm referring to is a society in which everyone has the opportunity to be literate. Only then can every individual recognize and develop his or her full potential. By 'every individual,' I mean that woman upstairs, her child, you, the family you left behind somewhere . . ."

I catch a glimmer of the man's meaning, but most is beyond my comprehension. "What you're saying is new to me. I can't quite understand everything."

The man pulls on his boots. "What I'm saying is that literacy shouldn't be bestowed only on those who were fortunate enough to be born well-to-do and male."

"Your desires sound very lofty, monsieur."

"My name is Yevgeny Ilyich Kruglov, not 'monsieur.'" His hand smooths down the few wisps of hair that remain on the top of his head. "And I believe you do understand what I'm saying. You just haven't thought about it long enough and hard enough to grasp that the problems you face are part of the larger miseries that confront this whole Empire."

The miseries of the whole Empire? I certainly have no intention of shouldering the burden of the entirety of Russia. My concerns right now are to end debt, make Sasha well, and get Felitsa and her baby to the Foundling Home.

I cock my head. What is that noise? Faint, but . . . yes! A baby crying! "The child is here! Please excuse me, I must go upstairs."

The man rises to his feet. "Yes, of course. I'll probably be back. Perhaps we can continue our conversation. That is, if you're interested."

I'm always interested in securing a new customer who is clean and safe, particularly one who doesn't demand I waste time undressing and redressing. This Yevgeny Ilyich is an odd but inoffensive fellow.

"Please come back, monsieur, so you can explain more to me." The man gives me a mock scowl, so I correct myself. "I mean, please come back, Yevgeny Ilyich."

I've never left a customer alone in my room, but I can't hold myself back from the attic. "Good evening to you."

As I race up the back stairs, he calls, "Be sure the baby learns to read."

CHAPTER 19

May–June
1868

THE DAY AFTER the baby's birth, Sophia Mikhailovna wastes no time securing a cab to take the mother and child across the river to the giant Imperial Foundling Home. As they depart, the women of 903 Sviatoslavsky Prospekt gather to kiss the baby's bald head. I promise the exhausted mother that I'll visit her.

I turn my attention to the ailing parrot. "What about you, little fellow? When will you be hale and hearty again?"

Eyes blinking and neck drawn against his breastbone, he has no greeting for me—neither the stretch of a wing nor a prance on his perch. Yesterday's food, including his grapes, hasn't been touched.

"How about some raisins?" I ask as I sweep up the copious feathers at the bottom of his cage. "Sound tempting?"

As I come through the kitchen door with a couple of raisins, I find Sophia Mikhailovna peering into the cage. "Are you feeling a little puny today?" she coos. "Handsome Sasha isn't so handsome right now, is he?"

So Sophia Mikhailovna isn't as frosty as she pretends to be. I clear my throat to make my presence known. "I brought Sasha some raisins."

Sophia Mikhailovna steps aside as I put my open hand inside the cage. When Sasha greedily gobbles the three raisins offered to him, I grin from ear to ear. "How wonderful! I thought he was too ill to eat."

"Ill? Is he ill?"

I turn puzzled eyes toward Sophia Mikhailovna. "I thought you noticed. He sleeps all the time, and he's losing his feathers."

"Oh, Anna, sometimes I think you actually look for sick and wounded creatures to take under your wing. Please tolerate the unintentional pun." Sophia Mikhailovna shakes her head in quiet amusement. Her smile is exquisite on those occasions, like now, when she allows it to surface. "Sasha's not ill. He's merely molting."

"Molting?"

"Every so often, his feathers drop out and he looks absolutely pathetic. And he gets moody. Or maybe he's just embarrassed by his appearance. But he snaps out of it in a few weeks."

"Molting? Oh, like our chickens did back home. But we never waited around to see if they got better. They went into the cook pot." I laugh at myself. "I was worried out of my mind about him all day yesterday. He and Felitsa both."

My smile fades. I bite my lower lip, wanting to bring up a question but afraid of the answer. "Speaking of Felitsa . . . I think she could be pretty once her cheeks fill out. I know that eye is ugly, but a patch would hide it. And I got the impression that she's experienced in—to use your expression—exchanging sex for pay. Perhaps maybe she could join the house someday?"

"Let's live one day at a time, shall we?" Sophia Mikhailovna's head drops to one side. "My dear, you can't save the whole world."

ONCE A WEEK, I pay a call on Felitsa and the baby. Both are filling out nicely. Over the course of my visits, Felitsa tells her story in fits and starts. She was born without an eyeball. As a baby, she was abandoned by her mother, left to be raised by her grandmother and great-uncle. Starting at age ten, Felitsa worked side by side with her grandmother as a laundress to keep the small family together, body and soul.

When she was fifteen, her uncle died. Felitsa and her grandmother slipped from poverty into destitution. For easy earnings, Felitsa began taking strolls.

She had two back-room abortions in less than a year. Meanwhile, hard work and poor nutrition took her grandmother's life. Felitsa was once again pregnant, this time without the resources to terminate it. She lost her laundry job and was thrown out of the one-room apartment. She wandered the streets until she showed up at 903 Sviatoslavsky Prospekt.

On the morning of my third visit, Felitsa is down in the mouth. Her milk is drying up, meaning she'll soon be without a place to live. "The Foundling Home isn't interested in feeding mothers who can't feed their own babies," she explains.

"And the baby?" I ask.

"The baby has to stay here."

I understand why tears are slipping down Felitsa's cheeks. Everyone knows that bottle-feeding a baby is the kiss of death.

As I leave the stone edifice and cross the river to Zamoskvorechye, I think about bringing Felitsa into the house and vow to broach the subject again with

Sophia Mikhailovna. I feel optimistic, perhaps because the weather was specially made for feeling hopeful. Soft as warm butter, the June day offers reassurance that the long winter is a thing of the past and the eve of summer is at hand.

Days this gorgeous cause a well of old memories to bubble up. The creak of wagon wheels as manure was hauled to the fallow fields for fertilizing. The scrape of the whetstone sharpening the scythe for hay cutting. The gritty, greasy feel of the wool as the sheep were sheared.

I leave the sunshine and the doves' doleful cooing and my memories outside as I reenter my real world. When I step into the Grand Salon, Maria and Sophia Mikhailovna are sitting in the Voltaire chairs, facing each other. Both women are stiffly poised on the edge of their seats.

The two simultaneously turn their faces toward me. I begin to toss a greeting to them but change my mind. Their faces are grim, their mouths unyielding. I climb the stairs with a hazy sense of foreboding.

CHAPTER 20

June
1868

LATER THAT AFTERNOON, I respond to Grisha's bell summons and find a man wearing a red calico shirt and wide trousers sitting at the bar, his arm raised in a toast. "To health!"

Grisha bellows, "Anna, Yevgeny Ilyich was just telling me it's his birthday."

"May you enjoy many, many more." I plant a kiss atop his bald head.

This is Yevgeny Ilyich's third visit, and he has become one of my favorites. He's a strange little man with extreme ideas, but those ideas, I'm discovering, challenge me to contemplate a world beyond myself.

"You're here early today," I observe.

"Yes, I am. This evening, I have several festivities to attend. All of them in my honor, I might add." He gives a jaunty wink and hoists his glass in a toast. "May my birth date pass this year without the misfortune that accompanied it last year."

I cock my head as I take the stool beside him. "What do you mean?"

"It's only because it happened on my forty-ninth birthday that I can place the hapless incident." He gives a gut-felt sigh and shakes his head sadly. "An incident that caused me enormous despair."

I tap an impatient foot against his shin. "Are you merely going to reminisce by yourself, or are you going to tell us what happened?"

Yevgeny Ilyich plunks his empty glass on the counter and melodramatically puts his hand over his heart. "That was the day the great Sovereign of all Russia—also known as the Tsar of Poland, and further referred to as the Grand Duke of Finland—escaped death at the hands of a would-be assassin."

"Oh? You mean the Paris incident?" Grisha asked.

Once again I'm amazed that our easygoing, semiliterate bartender is so well versed in current events.

"Paris." Yevgeny Ilyich jabs his upturned palm into the air in front of him. "That is precisely what I'm referring to." He notes the bewilderment on my face. "Our monarch was riding in an open carriage with the Emperor Napoleon III. A young Polish refugee fired two shots at Alexander. The callow simpleton missed his mark. Twice!"

"Poor Yevgeny Ilyich."

The heel of my hand makes circles of comfort across his shoulder blades. My hand halts for a speck of a moment as it encounters what feels like wagon wheel ruts crisscrossing his back. I keep my hand circling, pretending not to notice the chinks in Yevgeny Ilyich's back.

"If I remember your last visit correctly, you told me that the death of the tsar would be virtually meaningless, because there are always more Romanovs waiting in line."

From behind his gold-rimmed spectacles, Yevgeny Ilyich beams at Grisha. "She's a quick learner, isn't she? Brains and beauty both. What more could a man want?"

He reaches behind his back, lifts my hand from between his shoulders, and brings it to his lips, kissing it lightly. "Anna, my dearest, we've come to know each other intimately enough for you to refrain from using my patronymic. Simply refer to me as Yevgeny. Or possibly Yevgeny the Wise, if you feel that's more suitable." His forefinger taps the bar. "One more drink, please, before I take my quick-witted lady friend and her unabashed charms upstairs to her seduction chamber."

As he pours the drink, Grisha raises an eyebrow. "Are you a Nihilist?"

Yevgeny shakes his head. "The best description I can give of myself is a 'critical realist with revolutionary tendencies,' whatever that means." He tosses the vodka to the back of his throat, then nudges the empty glass across the counter toward Grisha. "Thank you for the conversation and the drink, sir, but I must bid you adieu. I can't spend the entire evening over a glass."

Once Yevgeny's toes and other parts are tended to, he and I sit side by side against the headboard for a bit of conversation, a pastime that's developing into an agreeable habit.

"What is a Nihilist?" I ask.

"A Nihilist is a person who rejects all authority and, in doing so, takes no principle for granted, however much that principle may be revered. Even the most basic of beliefs should be questioned. Here's an example: A Nihilist would ask why the man pays the woman for sex. Why isn't it the other way around? I'm personally in favor of the alternative."

I playfully slap his thigh.

"You don't care for that example? Here's another. In your profession, you must obey certain government regulations, regulations designed to give the customers illusory notions about the woman's health. But let's think about this. Male customers are exempted from medical examination. If you put a dam halfway across the river, does it stop the flow of water?"

"I have the same thoughts myself."

"But did you take those thoughts a step further, beyond the disease implications? It's clear to a Nihilist that those government regulations are nothing more than subliminal attempts to keep all women downtrodden."

"Downtrodden?"

"Yes, by maintaining the Russian tradition of patriarchal authority. Therefore, one can't help but conclude that medical examinations of ladies-of-the-night should be abolished."

"That sounds reasonable to me." I curve my mouth into a dimpled grin. "You didn't realize that I'm a covert Nihilist, did you?"

"Covert Nihilist! Just listen to her expansive vocabulary! I swear on the names of however many thousand saints that are revered by the Holy Russian Orthodox Church—you are too cute for your own good." He extends his arm behind my neck and drapes it across my shoulder. "So, you're telling me that, as a Nihilist, you believe the entire structure of the government and society must be questioned and detrimental ways abolished? And that, as a Nihilist, you'll join our efforts to use radical means to wipe out all that is stagnant and decrepit in aristocratic Russia?" Despite his whimsical tone, I can tell he's plagued by ambitious moods. "The old regime is dying. You'll join us in putting the final dagger in its chest?"

I try to quell the powerful tension I sense is building inside him. "And who exactly is the 'us' you're referring to?"

"Oh, my sweet, you have so much to learn. And I am just the person to open your mind to great thoughts." His fingers squeeze my shoulder. "The pot always boils from the bottom, does it not?"

He waits for my nod.

"Sixty million peasants will simmer until the pot finally explodes. Radical change must come *from* the people. It cannot be done *for* them or *to* them. And the change must be absolute. Nothing short of a revolution."

"The change will come from the peasants?" Platon and my brothers and the other village men will fight the tsar and his army? The thought isn't just bewildering—it's inconceivable.

He leans forward so he can look fully into my face. "I'd wager to say that in your former life, your family were serfs."

"However did you know that?"

"I'm getting to know you pretty well, wouldn't you say?" He runs a finger lightly down my nose. "You are so lusciously tempting. If I were a young buck of twenty, I'd have seconds. And, as already suggested by you Nihilists, you'd have to pay me rather than the reverse."

I purse my lips and sigh mock disgust through my nose. "Just answer my question. How did you know that my family were serfs?"

"Because I myself have had many former lives, each of which has given me a great deal of insight into people."

"As a former serf, I can assure you that no man in my village is silly enough to go to battle against the tsar. I don't know of a single gun in the whole village. Sometimes the villagers get angry with one another, but they don't kill each other. It's a peace-loving place."

"I would be happy to debate that particular topic with you, but not at this time. Right now, I need to get out of bed. My hemorrhoids are killing me." Yevgeny swings his legs over the edge of the mattress and looks over his shoulder at me. "As a former serf, you should realize that the emancipation was nothing more than a facade. How can peasants better their lot in life when they're strapped with more taxes and land payments than they could ever dream of paying? How can your former neighbors work for a brighter tomorrow when they don't have enough bread for their own children? And yet they are the very people who grow the rye and the wheat! Serfdom may be gone, but the poverty remains, with its mark stamped indelibly on the bodies of the peasants, just like the scars you felt on my back."

"How did you know that I felt—"

"Because I heard your delicate, feminine gasp downstairs."

"So where did you get—"

"In one of my former lives. But that's a story for another time." He stands and slips on his spectacles, then puts his hands on the red calico of his lower back and stretches. "Suffice it to say that the condition of my back makes me feel older than I am. Just as Tsar Alexander is causing me to age beyond my years."

Yevgeny walks to the edge of the heavy drape and pulls it back slightly from the wall. As he looks through the slit at the street below, his voice grows melancholy. "We were all so hopeful those first years of Alexander's reign." His head swivels toward me. "How old were you when he emancipated the serfs?"

"Ten."

"Without doubt, a noble action on his part. But even then, I believe he was losing his bearings." He turns again toward the outside world. "Tsar Liberator became Tsar Swindler. Perhaps the reality is that in a despotic country, even the best intentions are doomed to fail."

"But he meant to do the right thing, didn't he, when he freed us serfs?"

"My astute political insights tell me that the Romanovs have lived off the fat of others for so long, they have no idea what Russia's true needs are."

He lets the drape fall and turns toward me, his lips a thin, unyielding line. "What you said downstairs is correct. Shooting one person won't solve anything." The back of one hand strikes the open palm of his other. "We must take direct action against the entire regime, right down to its very roots. Western winds are blowing. Eventually those winds will blow revolution right into Russia."

The cold certainty of his words sends a shiver through my belly, and I find my back pressing hard against the headboard's iron bars.

His face softens as he peers over the top of his glasses. "You have the wide-eyed look of a frightened doe. Fear not, Anna. I won't start a revolution from your boudoir. But mark my words: Russia will be summoned to arms. I'm as sure of that fact as I am that you have the bluest eyes of any woman in the world." He sweeps his arm in a low curve. "I'd give you a gentlemanly bow, but my back won't allow it. Until next time, my dear."

After the door closes, I place the back of my wrist across my forehead, where too many confusing thoughts are tumbling about.

If Alexander were killed, who would be the next tsar?

Peasants will change Russia down to its very roots? I myself was a peasant, and as Sophia Mikhailovna recently pointed out, I can't save the whole world.

Russia will be summoned to arms. What does Yevgeny mean by that? Will the citizens of St. Petersburg storm the Winter Palace? Or does he mean all of Russia? If so, would my sweet little cousin Platon bear arms? Who would he fight? The nobility, such as Mademoiselle Elena and her family?

And what about Yevgeny's former lives? Who is he really? Why is his back so battered?

I don't know what to make of it. Not any of it.

———

WHEN I FINALLY push myself from the bed, I head toward the back stairway. I need a slice of bread from the kitchen to settle my stomach. As I pass Maria's darkened room, the door is slightly ajar.

With two fingertips, I gingerly push open the door. The bed is made. All her personal belongings are missing.

Maria's words swirl in my mind. *My time for fine clothes is almost over.*

My forehead wrinkles as my thoughts harken back to this afternoon's somber scene with Maria and Sophia Mikhailovna seated across from one another in the Grand Salon.

I now find Sophia Mikhailovna perched on the same chair, immersed in discussion with a man. As I approach, her cherry-red lips curl up gleefully. "Here's our Anna. Anna, this is Monsieur Thibodeau. He is visiting from Paris."

Following a dimpled smile directed toward the gentleman, I request, "Madame, may I speak with you a moment, please?"

Sophia Mikhailovna casts an anxious side-glance at the customer. "Can it wait, dear? We have company."

"I'd like to talk to you now."

Sophia Mikhailovna's eyebrows drop precariously, but she replies with a spirited "Of course." She calls to Grisha, "Please get Monsieur Thibodeau a glass of champagne, on the house, while I speak briefly with Anna."

Sophia Mikhailovna hurries me to the kitchen. "What is it?" Her foot taps. "You have a gentleman waiting."

"Maria's room is empty. Where is she?" I neither stammer nor chew my lip.

"Maria is gone."

"Gone where?"

"I don't know."

"Why would she leave now?"

An angry red creeps up Sophia Mikhailovna's neck. "You seem to have forgotten your obligations. You have a customer waiting for you. We'll discuss this later."

I throw my shoulders back. "Did you send her away?"

"Don't use that querulous tone with me. I assure you, she left of her own accord. She knew it was time to go."

I level my eyes at the madam, wanting desperately to believe her. But a twinge of doubt keeps poking me in the ribs.

As if reading my mind, Sophia Mikhailovna says, "Believe what you want. But you might be interested in knowing that Maria's empty room means Felitsa can join the house. I should think that would make you happy."

"Felitsa?"

"I stopped by the Foundling Home this afternoon on my way home from visiting my sister. The girl will make a good addition to the house. Now get back to work." Sophia Mikhailovna turns on her heel and strides from the kitchen.

I lean against the table and sort through the possibilities. Where would Maria go? She has no employment skills. No prospects for a husband. What will become of her? True, Maria had told me, *I can't compete with young, pretty things like you.* Which means she had been planning to leave the house. But had Sophia Mikhailovna sped up her departure?

Felitsa can join the house. I should think that would make you happy. Sophia Mikhailovna's words smother me with guilt. If I had never brought Felitsa into the house that rainy evening, might Maria still be here? But then, where would Felitsa be?

More of the madam's words resonate within me: *You can't save the whole world.*

CHAPTER 21

June
1868

IN THE GRAND Salon the following afternoon, Irina, Pelageya, Dunka, Dunyasha, Athena, and I give the recent turn of events a thorough hashing. Every so often, Sasha joins in.

"Maria left so suddenly."

"Any idea where she went?"

"At least her room won't be empty for long."

"Felitsa's deserting her baby?"

"Her milk dried up."

"She'll need to go shopping for clothes for the Count's party."

"Yes, sirree!" Sasha agrees, swinging upside down with suicidal abandon on the iron curtain rod. His moody molting is but a memory.

The Count's party, as it was explained to me, is an annual private affair hosted by Sophia Mikhailovna's old friend, Count Kochubev, a wealthy businessman who owns a large sugar beet refinery in Kiev. His acquaintance with Sophia Mikhailovna stretches back to their younger days, before she moved to Moscow.

The Count and a few of his top employees come to Moscow on business each summer, and he spends considerable time with his longtime friend. He also throws an incredible party at 903 Sviatoslavsky Prospekt. According to Dunyasha's fanciful description, "The night just slips away."

This year's party will take place in two weeks. Most of the women purchased new gowns. The exceptions are Athena and me. Athena, prudently saving money for her return to Greece, is in the process of sewing gold lace onto an old gown to revitalize it. And I simply can't justify spending precious rubles on another dress when my gowns are practically new.

Dunka, with pins between her lips, is shortening Dunyasha's new taffeta dress as well as tightening the seams around the elfin waist. Despite Dunyasha having bought the smallest size she could find, it still swallows her teeny figure.

Dunyasha orders, "Don't pin the dress too tight, or I won't have room for the sturgeon."

"Last year," Irina explains to me, "the Count had a monstrously large sturgeon brought up from Astrakhan on post-horses."

Pelageya looks up from her fingernails, which she is softening with rose oil. "Who cares about a fish? It's the champagne and the brandy that make the evening. The Count has epicurean tastes and purchases only the most exquisite brands."

Epicurean means nothing to me, but I certainly won't ask Pelageya to clarify.

Dunka adds, "And it's the only night of the year Sophia Mikhailovna allows us to tip a few glasses."

"But only three at most," Athena says.

"Unless we sneak a few on the sly." It's the first time I've heard Pelageya contribute a bit of comradery to our gab sessions.

"Remember the trays of apricots, figs, and candied fruit, all imported from who knows where?" Irina asks. "And those green nuts—what were they called?"

"Pistachios," Dunka mutters through the pins tucked between her lips.

Sasha, apparently feeling left out of the group, sails down from the curtain rod to my shoulder. He bends his neck forward and fluffs his feathers, soliciting the attention he feels he is due. I oblige by rubbing his belly.

"And that's not all," Dunyasha continues, rehashing last year's party. "The Count brought all of us blancmange from the confectioner's shop. Scrumptious!"

I look at Sasha and he at me, neither of us having any idea what the foreign-sounding *blancmange* is.

"Let's not get too carried away, girls," Irina says. "Despite the music and the mountains of food and the wealthy, attractive men, each of us ends up in the wee morning hours, flat on our backs, underneath one of those men."

"Thanks for being a killjoy." Dunka's hands stab her hips.

"I simply want Anna to have realistic expectations, that's all."

Dunyasha suddenly flaps her arms up and down. "Oh, Anna, you should have seen what the Count bought for Sophia Mikhailovna last year! A stunning fur stole and muff, the most ravishing in the whole of Russia!"

Dunka admonishes, "Stand still, for Heaven's sake, or I'll turn you into a pin cushion. Besides, if you're going to tell the story, tell the complete story." She explains to me that the fur was sable.

Pelageya adds, "It was from Pavel Sorokoumovsky and Sons."

I'm familiar with the firm's reputation for fine furs. Nikolai Osipovich Shelgunov once purchased a fur for his wife from there.

"The crux of the matter is, Anna," Irina opines, "Sophia Mikhailovna is in love with the man."

Pelageya says, "Who wouldn't be in love with a man who gives you plush furs and takes you to posh restaurants?"

Irina expands on her original statement. "And we believe he's in love with her."

"Such a gentleman," Athena gushes. "He kiss her hand so elegant."

In a lusty whisper, Irina discloses, "There's just this one sticky little complication. His wife."

The conversation is squelched as Sophia Mikhailovna's quick steps cross the kitchen. She enters the Grand Salon and announces that she has instructed the cleaning girl to give Maria's empty room a thorough scrubbing. "Felitsa can have your room, and Grisha will help you move your things into Maria's former room. Let him know if you want any of the furniture rearranged."

I look up from stroking Sasha's belly to find Sophia Mikhailovna looking directly at me.

"You're addressing me, aren't you?" Pelageya kinks a penciled eyebrow.

"I'm speaking to Anna."

"What!" Pelageya squawks like a chicken.

Sasha shoots to his cage.

Sophia Mikhailovna's eyes narrow dangerously. "I believe you heard me."

"I've been here longer than her!" Pelageya's face is beet-red. "I deserve the bigger room. Felitsa can take mine!"

"No. It would be best for Anna to move. You will stay where you are." Sophia Mikhailovna's civility is ebbing.

"Her?" Pelageya throws me a stormy glower. "With her frumpy clothes and her flat chest and that thing on her face—"

Sophia Mikhailovna cuts her short. "There's no reason for you to be in a huff toward Anna."

"I'm tired of being treated like an old shoe. I've brought scores of good customers into this house." Pelageya's chest heaves. "That room is rightfully mine."

"Actually, that room is mine. And I've decided to put Anna in it." Sophia Mikhailovna's lips tighten like a purse string.

Oh, Holy Mother. I shudder. There's going to be hell to pay for this.

Mutinous anger disfigures Pelageya's face. "And you expect me to put up with such an insult?"

Sophia Mikhailovna's simmer rises to a full boil. "What I expect from you is good work and to treat your housemates with respect. And I suggest you curb that bitter tongue of yours. Is that understood?"

Bug-eyed with fury, Pelageya storms out of the salon. Three days later, she stomps out of the house, taking her possessions and unbridled self-absorption with her.

THE MORNING OF the party, all the women except Matryna are gathered in the kitchen when Athena announces, "Wait until all of you see Felitsa's gown for party." Yesterday, Athena took the new girl shopping. "She look like goddess!"

Felitsa's single eye is as bright as a harvest moon. "Never in my life did I think I'd wear anything so beautiful." To complement her new working dresses, Felitsa purchased eye patches in a variety of colors, complete with faux gems: emeralds, diamonds, rubies.

Dunyasha, standing at the stove as she stirs butter into the porridge, twinkles at Felitsa. "You'll let Dunka and me fix your hair, won't you? *Pleeeease?* We have some diamond combs that you'll just adore." The quixotic pixie bounces up and down on her toes, which are tucked into white satin shoes purchased specially for tonight's occasion.

"Why are you wearing your new shoes?" Dunka demands to know.

"To break them in for this evening."

"You should have done that last week. You'll have blisters tonight."

Irina preempts the bickering with "Hope you have a hearty appetite, Felitsa. Breast of turkey. Pâté with truffles. Caviar. Smoked salmon. We feast for days afterward!"

The air snaps as Sophia Mikhailovna enters the kitchen, her sleeves rolled up to her elbows. Both hands knuckle onto her hips. "Damnation! Where is that slothful girl? I told her to be here early today." She looks from face to face around the table, as if the cleaning girl might have melded in with her ladies. "I have a good mind to fire her! After she cleans today, that is."

She removes a slipper and swats the air. "Damn flies!" Her eyes seek out more invaders to clobber. "Even if the worthless girl shows up this very minute, she won't be able to get everything in order before the champagne is uncorked!"

The madam drops to her hands and knees. Like a swift and nimble feline, she extends her arm in a broad swipe under the cupboard and nabs a dust ball. Rising to her feet, she asks in a feverish pitch, "What am I going to do?" Without waiting for an answer, she whirls about and leaves the room, the dust ball clenched in one hand and her slipper in the other.

Following the slam of her apartment door, we cup our hands over our mouths to mute our giggles. By now I've learned it's a standing joke that during the

Count's annual visit to Moscow, Sophia Mikhailovna acts like a young maiden infatuated with her first love. One minute, she's attacking the silver candlesticks with a polishing cloth, determined to bring out that extra bit of sheen. The next minute, she's preening in the mirror as if going to her first ball.

Yesterday, when Sophia Mikhailovna thought she was alone, I caught her tarrying in front of the large gilded mirror at the head of the stairs. She laid the heels of her hands on her temples and tightened the skin over her cheeks. Following a scowl and a curl of her upper lip, she placed the back of her hand under her chin and pressed upward, tilting her head back slightly. With a heavy sigh and numerous forehead furrows, she scrutinized her neck.

I tiptoed back into my room, never making my presence known. It was a private moment for Sophia Mikhailovna—a time of examining the irreversible departure from youth.

This morning we're still silently giggling when Matryna prances into the kitchen, humming a merry tune.

"You certainly slept in," Irina says, taking a jab at her friend.

"My last visitor stayed quite late." Matryna's mischievous grin roves to each woman in turn. "Timofei Ivanov." In a girlish gesture, she raises her shoulders almost to her ears. "Guess what. He said he would divorce his wife and the two of us would move away from Moscow as soon as his last child leaves home. He said he'd swear on a Bible, if I had one." She giggles.

The ensuing congratulations are bland. Timofei Ivanov's string of broken promises have cost him his credibility with everyone except Matryna.

Love is definitely blind—or so I surmise, coaxing the last sprinkling of tea leaves from the bottom of the tin. I'm sorely tempted to tell the lovesick woman that Timofei Ivanov has nothing going for him, including his missing eyebrows.

Before I can butt into business that is none of my concern, I'm rescued by the arrival of little Sonia. "Here's your ginger cakes," calls the sunny, freckle-faced girl. "Five instead of just three. Plus rose-petal candies. You must be having a special day."

Down the hallway, Sophia Mikhailovna's door slams again.

My teeth stroke my lower lip as I hurriedly think through the idea that just popped into my head. The benefits are obvious, and I hope against hope that Sophia Mikhailovna approves.

"We're having a party tonight. Sonia, do you have lots of errands and tasks to do for your mother this afternoon?"

Sonia stands tall with expectation. "Not too many."

"I bet you're a good housekeeper. Would you like to take an extra ruble home to your mother?"

The sweet little lamb and I work in a feverish scramble to make the house gleam before the Count and his men arrive. All the other women, however, seem to have other things to do besides standing in for the missing cleaning girl.

Felitsa, accompanied by Irina as her mentor, goes to the medical-police to register her new employment at 903 Sviatoslavsky Prospekt.

As Dunka predicted, Dunyasha's new shoes caused a blister on her heel, so Dunka helps her soak her feet in warm salt water while admonishing, "I told you so."

Athena bakes her fabulous honey-walnut Greek pastry, which, she insists, the Count absolutely adores.

Matryna sweeps a little of the upstairs hallway, when she isn't busy gazing out the window, lost in fanciful musings about her future life with Timofei Ivanov.

Sweeping. Dusting. Mopping. Scouring. Polishing. As the afternoon progresses, the Grand Salon teems with caterers and musicians and florists. But still only two cleaners. When the last mirror is streak-free, when the last oil lamp is filled, when the last spent candle is replaced, I drop like a rag doll onto one of the Voltaire chairs. And to think I still have an entire night of gaiety ahead of me.

CHAPTER 22

June

1870

ON A MUGGY afternoon two years after Pelageya left the house, she returns. Irina and I arrive home from our medical examinations to find our former housemate pacing the salon, half demanding, half begging her former madam to take her back.

"My final answer is no," Sophia Mikhailovna says.

"And I'm telling you it would be worth your while to kick out one of the girls," Pelageya insists. "When I return, so will my customers."

"Your customers never left," Sophia Mikhailovna replies coolly.

"You can't expect me to believe that."

As in the old days, Pelageya is highly costumed. But today, I note the sinews of her neck, her gaunt shoulders, the sagging corners of her mouth. She looks exactly like what she is—a bony, late-life prostitute.

"Besides, during my past two years in St. Petersburg, I met countless wealthy men from Moscow who were visiting the capital for business purposes. I'd bring them with me to this house." Her eyes swivel about the room. "At least, I think they'd follow me here. This place has really gone to the dogs." Pelageya's insolence is almost humorous—like a hare trying to intimidate a fox.

"This conversation is over. You'd best leave."

"How dare you thumb your nose at me!" A sneer spreads across Pelageya's face. "If you turn down my offer, you're not nearly the businesswoman you think you are."

"I didn't like your attitude before," Sophia Mikhailovna counters, "and I don't like it now."

"*My* attitude!" Pelageya's menacing eyes narrow like a viper's. "Take a look at yourself. A cold-as-a-fish, used-up old whore."

Irina tosses her reticule onto the bar and barrels across the Grand Salon. "Enough of your bluster! No one wants you here." The big woman seizes Pelageya's arm.

Pelageya wrenches free. "This discussion doesn't involve you."

"You think you're the most sought-after nocturnal butterfly in all of Russia. I say you've missed the mark."

"I'll handle this, Irina." Sophia Mikhailovna remains calm and poised. "Leave, Pelageya, or I'll—"

"You'll what? Call your big oaf of a lover to throw me out?" Pelageya's laugh is wicked as her head swivels about the room. "Where is ol' carrot-top Grisha?"

"You haughty bitch!" Irina shoves Pelageya. "There's the door. Make use of it!"

The shove catches Pelageya off-balance, and she stumbles. Barely has she righted herself when Irina gives her another good prod.

Pelageya pushes back. "You fat cow!"

Irina ramrods her bulky shoulder into Pelageya's corseted waistline. Pelageya topples against the sideboard. Her flailing arms send the samovar careening sideways onto Irina.

Irina wails in anguish as her upper body is pelted with both hot coals and steaming water. Like a maddened bull, she knocks Pelageya to the floor.

Burning coals on the Oriental carpet! I bolt to the kitchen and return with a bucket of water. The wool carpet is starting to smoke. I jerk open the drawer of the sideboard where my clean rags are kept with my medical supplies. I plunge the rags into the bucket and strew the dripping cloths atop the scattered coals. As the coals hiss, I spread a second layer of wet rags for good measure.

I'm aware of Irina and Sophia Mikhailovna behind me, one on each side of Pelageya, hauling her by the arms to the door. They shove her out and lock the door.

Irina is wearing a short-sleeved, scoop-necked dress, and her neck and arms are bright red and starting to blister. While I doctor her with ointment infused with mint and chamomile, Sophia Mikhailovna tells us about the rumors she heard—that upon returning to St. Petersburg, Pelageya had discovered her aged charms weren't in high demand. Living hand-to-mouth for two years had led her to circle back to Moscow and 903 Sviatoslavsky Prospekt.

Irina shook her head. "You'd think she'd realize that she's rung her last peal and it's time to get off the bell tower."

Using the toe of her shoe, Sophia Mikhailovna lifts the wet rags from the floor. The carpet is seared black.

The Count is due to arrive in ten days for his annual visit and party, a deadline that doesn't allow time to have the carpet repaired. Sophia Mikhailovna improvises by placing a throw rug in front of the sideboard to hide the charred wool.

———

ON MY FOURTH day of changing Irina's bandages, Sophia Mikhailovna sends me to purchase the Count's favorite tea, a strong black blend from Kiakhta. Actually, I volunteer for the errand, as I love visiting the little shop, situated only a few blocks away on a dead-end lane too narrow for wagons and carriages. The result is a charming pedestrian plaza that's a half block in length. It's flanked by two-story brick buildings that, except at midday, block the sun's hot summer rays. Mossy, uneven cobblestones turn the hushed alley into a soothing retreat from Moscow's congested streets.

The proprietor of the tea store is a Chinaman who's no bigger than young Sonia and almost as cute. His smiling face is full of thousand-year-old wrinkles. His wardrobe seems limited to a loose-fitting red shirt, its bottom hem falling over his baggy black trousers. His Russian is abysmal, but he makes amends for it with courteous bows.

Today I sail past the silver and bronze samovars from Tula so I can linger over the tiny Oriental cups and delicate teapots adorned with exotic images. Iron-red chrysanthemums. Metallic gold dragons. Black Chinese lettering that means nothing more to me than Mother Russia's Cyrillic letters do.

After paying for the tea, I glance behind the counter at shelves lined with glass jars. Although I'm aware that the pigtailed man sells Chinese herbs, I've never paid any attention to them until now. I'm intrigued by the jars of powders, dried leaves, insects, and animal parts, their colors as vivid as the tea sets.

An idea flares. Irina's burns have used up almost all the mint-chamomile ointment. But why go elsewhere to purchase more ointment?

While the shopkeeper fingers the extraordinarily long, wispy ends of his graying moustache, I point to the jars behind him and pantomime my request by placing my forearm on one of his samovars. "Ouch!" I pull back, blow on my supposedly scalded spot, then fan it with my other hand.

His face pleats into an immense smile. Sandals scuffing to and from the rear shelves, he brings forth three metal canisters, each the size of a large spittoon.

I scrutinize the viscid contents. Except for their varying colors, all three resemble the paste the tradesmen used when they wallpapered the upstairs hallway last year. I select the blue ointment because it puts off the least offensive smell. The Chinese tea importer/apothecary runs a spatula around the edge of the thick blue-gray paste and plunks it into a tin jar.

He taps the side of the jar. "Bring back. Refill." He smiles as his head bobs frenetically.

When I return to 903 Sviatoslavsky Prospekt, Sophia Mikhailovna intercepts me in the Grand Salon. Her back, normally as straight as a broomstick, slumps like a top-heavy sunflower. "Wait in the kitchen. I'm calling a meeting of all the women."

CHAPTER 23

June

1870

SOPHIA MIKHAILOVNA YANKS Grisha's bellpull and keeps yanking until all the women are assembled. "Come to the kitchen with me."

Once we're seated at the table, a cautious quiet descends on the room. Everyone's attention focuses on the man seated at the head of the table next to Sophia Mikhailovna.

Truth be told, however, it's hard to regard him as a man. He's obviously a grown adult, but his face has the softness of a child. His bulk is like a mound of raised bread dough, its edges sagging over the sides of the chair. His hair is sheared to the scalp. His heavy-lidded eyes move to each woman in turn while his lower lip hangs slack.

There's no mistaking that he's an imbecile.

Sophia Mikhailovna's tongue flicks over her upper lip. Then she clears her throat. These are the only signs of nervousness I've ever detected in her.

"I've just come from my sister's, offering her what little succor I could." Words catch in her throat. "She has cholera and will probably die." Her head nods in acknowledgement of our exclamations of sympathy. "Needless to say, I am deeply distressed by this turn of events, and I appreciate your condolences. I accept that I will not see her again. As we speak, a sanitary cordon is being placed around the building where she lives."

Murmurs crisscross the table. Cholera! There were rumored cases of the savage disease in St. Petersburg and Nizhny Novgorod. And now it's here in Moscow!

Sophia Mikhailovna pulls a soggy handkerchief from her pocket and wipes her eyes and nose. "My sister had a visitor three days ago. Somehow Pelageya found out where she lives and went there to plead her case. She wanted my sister to convince me to accept Pelageya back into the house. Pelageya didn't look well when she arrived at my sister's, and during the visit, she grew so weak that my sister allowed her to rest on the sofa. We've all heard stories about how suddenly cholera will claim a life. It's true. Pelageya died that very evening. But not before sharing the contagion with my sister."

Only Irina attempts words. "I'm . . . we're . . . "

"I know. I'm stunned also. But I cannot alter God's will." Sophia Mikhailovna lays a hand on the man's arm. "My main concern now is for my brother."

"Your brother?"

"Your brother!"

"Your . . . brother?"

The women look as though they could be knocked over with one of Sasha's feathers.

"This is Fyedka," Sophia Mikhailovna says. "Fyedka, say hello to these nice ladies."

"Hello." The word is a thickened slur, as if his tongue is glued to the roof of his mouth. His smile is as broad as the little Chinaman's, and he waves his hand side to side like a child saying goodbye to his favorite aunt.

Never has this busy kitchen been filled with such a deafening silence. "I owe you a complete account, because I have to rely on your generosity to help me with him. What I am about to tell you I learned from the doctors in Kiev who tried unsuccessfully to give Fyedka a normal life. Fyedka is nine years my junior and twelve years younger than our sister. He was born perfectly normal and was a whiz in school. Life changed for him when he was ten years old."

Fyedka rests his folded arms across his great expanse of stomach, still looking about the table at us women.

Sophia Mikhailovna inhales and places her fingertips against the base of her throat. "My sister and I had already moved out of my parents' home in Kiev when we had a particularly cold winter with a wet, foggy spring. Coincidentally, our family fell on hard times, forcing my parents and Fyedka to switch from wheat bread to rye."

A bit of spilt salt on the table catches Fyedka's attention. Using one finger, he pushes the little pile back and forth across the table in front of him.

Sophia Mikhailovna continues. "Fyedka has always been a big boy with a hearty appetite. The summer following that bad winter, he became ill. So did a lot of other people that year, and many of them died. The rye crop was tainted with a certain corruption, you see, and it eventually turned up in the bread. But the corruption had no taste, so there was no way of knowing it was there. Fyedka was sick to his stomach, and his head hurt so badly he couldn't sleep. He suffered from hallucinations."

"Is there a name for this sickness?" Matryna asks.

"It's called 'evil writhing.' His brain was so affected, it seemed broken. He's been in this condition ever since." Sophia Mikhailovna pauses again to dry her eyes.

Fyedka spreads his salt pile into a thin layer so he can draw lines through it. I'm sure that at any moment, I'll wake up from this dream and have a good laugh. I toss my head to chase away what must be an apparition, but the image of a grown man playing with salt still confronts me.

The madam returns to her story. "I need to back up in time so that you understand everything. Behind our parents' dry goods store in Kiev was a one-room apartment where a man and his wife and son lived. The husband and wife were supposed to help my father run the store, but they were clerks in name only. Their true profession was drinking. For them, sobriety was an unnatural condition."

Emotion strangles her voice.

"Most days, they simply lay around the house in a stupor, sending their son to play with Fyedka. The two boys were the same age." She pauses. "The boy is Grisha."

It seems the silence around the table will never end. We women glance at one another, each wanting someone else to ask the inevitable question. Finally, Dunyasha whispers, "*Our* Grisha?"

Sophia Mikhailovna gives a single nod.

Fyedka looks up from his salt drawing, his eyes alive with expectation. "Grisha?" He scans the room.

"Grisha will be here soon." Sophia Mikhailovna pats Fyedka's thigh. "When it became clear that Fyedka would never get better, my mother's anxiety grew, and she began spending her days with Grisha's parents. Within three years, she had killed herself with drink." Her tone grows increasingly callous with each sentence. "During that time, my father cut back on the store's hours so he could take care of an imbecile son and a confused neighbor boy. He had to hire a woman to keep house and help with Fyedka and Grisha. He fell into arrears with his creditors."

Her voice turns to ice. "The bankers were ruthless. They shut down his store. Shortly thereafter, my father put a pistol to his head. My sister and I have taken care of Fyedka ever since. And we took in Grisha and raised him as our own brother." Sophia Mikhailovna's voice cracks. "He has repaid me a thousand times."

I break the ensuing silence. "We'll do anything we can to help you. And Fyedka. Tell us what you need."

Several others chime in with similar sentiments.

"I'm very glad to hear that," Sophia Mikhailovna says, before dropping the next thunderbolt. "Because for the time being, Fyedka will have to live here. I don't—"

Irina interjects, "But that's against regulations."

Sophia Mikhailovna replies with cool confidence. "I'll handle the police, as long as I can count on all of you to keep Fyedka's presence confidential. Not a word can leak out to your customers or the women at other houses."

Heads nod around the table.

"He'll share my apartment. Treat him as you would any four-year-old. He can change his own clothes, if he's reminded to do so. He'll let you know when he has to go to the outhouse, but he'll need to be walked there and back so he doesn't wander off."

"Of course," several women affirm, although they sound anything but certain.

"What else do you need to know?" Sophia Mikhailovna rubs her temples. "Oh, yes. He has a tendency to lock himself in his room. I'll hang a spare key to my apartment behind the kitchen door." Sophia looks each woman in the eye. "Thank you, all of you. Come along, Fyedka. Let's go to your new room. Say goodbye."

"Bye-bye." The pudgy hand waves side to side.

As I watch the madam gently lead the lumbering man down the hallway, I call to mind that fateful night when Sophia Mikhailovna swooshed into the jail and commanded the jailer's deference. Today's haggard step portrays an entirely different woman.

My housemates trudge upstairs to prepare for the evening's business, but I remain at the table, my hands in my lap, my eyes fixed blindly upon the pile of salt. Many things are becoming clear to me.

First, no wonder Sophia Mikhailovna has absolute trust in Grisha. She raised him.

Second, it's now obvious why both Sophia Mikhailovna and Grisha disdain alcohol.

Third, it's also evident why Sophia Mikhailovna takes in girls with deformities and those who are down on their luck. Birthmark. Missing eye. Women who love other women. Scared peasant girls who'd been accosted. If Sophia Mikhailovna is helpless to make Fyedka better, then she gives what opportunities she can to someone else—a sort of surrogate benevolence.

I also realize that over the years, Sophia Mikhailovna's sister shouldered the bulk of the burden of looking after Fyedka. Perhaps Sophia Mikhailovna feels guilty.

Upon second glance, though, it seems very possible that the arrangement wasn't as lopsided as it seems. I reason that Sophia Mikhailovna makes a good income off the brothel. Yet except for her working clothes and jewelry, her spending appears modest. The extra rubles probably supported her sister and brother.

My elbow goes onto the table and my chin into the cup of my hand. How amazing that no one knew anything about Grisha's past, yet not one of us women inquired. Do we all take him so much for granted that no one cared about his background?

My thoughts are interrupted by Fyedka plodding into the kitchen. He fixes me with a daft stare. "I have to pee."

I respond with a weak smile. My mother's words hit me full force. *No one said life was fair.*

GRISHA READS ALOUD to us the newspaper reports that travel is banned to and from St. Petersburg due to the cholera outbreak. Moscow, however, has only a few cases, and its outbreaks have been "effectively extinguished through the prompt action of the medical authorities."

A week following Fyedka's arrival, Sophia Mikhailovna is granted permission to enter her sister's apartment. By law, all items—food, furniture, clothing—have been burned. Yet Sophia Mikhailovna, who excels at bribery, was able to obtain a beautiful mahogany case clock that stands taller even than Grisha.

She hires carters to deliver the clock to the second-floor hallway. After the mechanism is replaced, an assemblage of spectators—me, Grisha, Irina, Sophia Mikhailovna, and Fyedka, with Sasha on his shoulder—watch the heavy pendulum hypnotically swing back and forth. We're joined by little Sonia, who takes a break from her cleaning chores.

A year ago, when I was adding a few kopeks to my coveted savings, I was dismayed to discover I was five rubles short of what I thought I had stashed away. Soon thereafter, the cleaning girl was caught pocketing one of Matryna's necklaces. Sophia Mikhailovna promptly fired the girl and, much to my delight, replaced her with dependable little Sonia. The little elf moves about the house as quiet as a shadow, diligently performing her tasks.

The clock notes the hour by erupting with two deep, soporific bongs. I find the heavy chimes soothing. Sasha, however, regards the new noise as intolerable and squawks a tirade. Sophia instructs her brother to take the bird downstairs, then emphatically tells the rest of us, "The chime must be turned off during business hours."

Nodding their understanding, Grisha and Irina go their separate ways. "Today's mail," Sonia says as she hands her employer a single envelope, then scoots off to continue her housework.

Sophia Mikhailovna is sliding her finger under the envelope's sealing wax as I go downstairs to fetch vinegar and rags to clean the glass of the clock's case. When I return, the madam's back sags against the wall as if lacking the strength to support her. The hand holding the open letter is hidden among the folds of her skirt.

"It's from the Count," Sophia Mikhailovna volunteers. "Cholera has struck Kiev. The sanitary cordons have closed the city down. He canceled his trip to Moscow."

As my rag disperses the vinegar over the glass, I inquire, "Perhaps he'll merely postpone the trip until the fall?"

"Perhaps." She heaves a weary sigh as she flings her head back and glares at the ceiling. "Damn that bloodthirsty disease! Oh, Anna, I'm so very tired of life's cruel tricks."

It hurts me to look at her. Sophia Mikhailovna always slices through life's problems so effortlessly. But not today.

CHAPTER 24

June

1870

I PEEK UNDER the towel beside the warm stove. Proud that the dough has risen superbly, I slip the concoction into the oven. A special delicacy is in order. Tomorrow would have been the Count's party, leaving everyone a little down in the mouth. Although the decadently rich cake—with its ten eggs, pint of milk, pound of butter, and three teacups of sugar—is a poor substitute for a banquet of gourmet food, I think the ladies will appreciate the gesture. Especially Sophia Mikhailovna.

Next, I warm some beer and mix a smidgeon of milk into it. I sponge the mixture onto my burgundy gown to deepen the silk's dulled color, splashing the mixture onto my apron and my one remaining servant's dress, left over from my employment with the Shelgunovs—a threadbare garment whose days are numbered.

As I hang the gown to dry, the rear door slams. Pounding steps in the hallway rattle the dishes on the shelves.

"You!" Irina roars like an angry bear. After a string of gutter curses, she concludes with "You're the one!"

"Which one?" I ask in true innocence.

"The one who almost caused me to get hauled off to the hospital!"

My head pulls back in confusion. Irina sounds serious, but the accusation is ludicrous.

Irina holds the back of her substantial hand against the tip of my nose. "What do you see?"

My mouth twitches as I repress a sassy response: *Fingernails. Wrinkled skin over the joints. A couple of freckles.*

Irina withdraws the hand and points to her blistered forearm. "Is this the normal color of skin?" Her finger moves to her throat. "Is this the normal color of skin?"

"N-n-no."

"What color is it?" Irina's eyes flare.

"Well . . . blue."

"Blue like what?"

"Blue like the color of your burn ointment."

"Blue like what else?" she hisses like a snake.

I lift my eyebrows and my shoulders at the same time.

"Blue like mercury, perhaps?"

The air creeps from my chest in a lengthy *Oooooohhhhh*.

Red patches of fiery emotion spread over Irina's face, which is the only exposed part of her body that isn't stained with the Chinese ointment. "That blundering police-doctor accused me of treating myself for syphilis!"

My hand flies to my mouth. "Oh, no."

"I told the old bugger, 'The ointment's for burns, not the pox.' Then I spread my legs and said, 'Look for yourself. You won't find any sores.'"

"Then what happened?"

"He said, 'We need to get women like you off the streets.' So I said, 'The Devil take you! I work in one of the most reputable houses in all of Moscow.'"

I cringe. No wonder Irina is furious.

"He said that he wasn't impressed. Called the clerk to have me carted off to the hospital."

"Oh, Irina, how horrible!"

"I fought off the clerk. Nailed his cream-puff ass to the floor."

Ah. That explains why Irina's hair looks like a display of corkscrews.

"I pressed my arm against the physician's nose until it was flat against his face. I asked him, 'Does this smell like mercury?' He said, 'You stink like dead fish.'"

I nod my concurrence. "So he let you go?"

"Told me to come back at the end of the week so he could check me again." Irina goes on to demonstrate her elegant command of vulgarities, concluding with one invective just for me: "Never again put your putrid Chinese goop on me!"

Still feeling feisty from her scuffle with the physician and the clerk, Irina slips her hand into the open bin of flour. With a speedy *swish*, she sends a flurry flying toward me. Like wind-carried snowflakes, the flour powders my apron and gray servant's dress. I try to backhand it off, but it clings to the splotches of milky beer.

Seizing a handful of flour, I return the favor. Irina, an experienced brawler, retaliates by pitching the next handful at my head.

Astonished that I'm having such a devilishly good time, I pick up the bowl containing the remains of the beer-milk. I rear back to fling the mixture at Irina.

"Don't!" Irina blocks the bowl with her hands. "I don't know what's in there, but I'm wearing a good dress."

I drop my eyebrows to let Irina know that I'm aware she would never wear a good dress to her medical exam. But Irina, an adept opponent, uses the pause to slip her hand under the bowl and flick it backward at me.

My mouth hangs open as I watch the milky rivulets soak into the gray material. Irina erupts in lusty belly laughs, grasping the back of a chair to keep her balance. After a moment, I join her with tear-provoking laughter.

"A lesson for you, Anna Vorontsova," Irina sputters between whoops. "Never try to get the better of me."

I double over at the waist, trying to catch my breath. "Oh, Irina, I wish . . . I wish I had been there to see you wrestle that slothful clerk!" When the howling finally subsides, I wipe the moisture from my eyes. I feel a slurry form as the tears mix with the flour dust on my cheeks.

Chest still heaving, Irina announces she's going to the bathhouse to scrub off the blue gunk. "Considering the slop on your face, you'd be wise to do the same." She chortles her way out the back door, leaving me to clean up our mess.

I grin as I begin the chore. How fortunate I am to have a madcap friend like Irina! Certainly there's none like her in Petrovo.

The kitchen is almost back in order when I remove the cake from the oven and place it on a wire rack to cool. I congratulate myself on how beautifully browned it is. Hearing Grisha's voice in the Grand Salon, I cover a plate with an embroidered towel and place the rich dessert in the center of it. With a flourish, I carry my accomplishment to the Grand Salon to present to the barkeeper.

I freeze in midstride. A man is seated on one of the divans. A customer? Damn! I had no idea the time was so late.

"Excuse me," I mumble as I bow my head, lower the platter, and back toward the kitchen.

Grisha, seated on a Voltaire chair, waves me over. "Anna, what smells so delicious?"

I hoist the plate as I continue my reverse steps. "Just a cake I made."

"Let's have a look. Perhaps Monsieur Segalovich would like a bite."

With great reluctance but with shoulders properly thrown back, I advance toward the divans. I position the plate next to the man's glass of tea on the low table between the divans. "Would either of you care for a slice? I'll get saucers and forks."

Both men decline, though Grisha says it looks scrumptious and he'll have some later. "What in Heaven's name was the ruckus in the kitchen?"

The flush that had been crawling up my neck makes a mad dash to my cheeks. There it lingers beneath the smears of flour, milk, and beer. "Irina is disgruntled because the ointment I put on her burns turned her skin blue."

The man, who appears to be in the latter part of his twenties, crinkles his dark eyes in merriment. "Blue skin? I can understand why she'd be upset."

"Anna is our resident doctor," Grisha says. "And a top-notch one, at that."

The man gives an impressed tilt of his head. "A chef *and* a doctor." His wide smile reveals teeth as white as a string of pearls.

I push aside beads of sweat from my forehead. "Grisha is just letting his mouth run on again. I'm not really a doctor."

Could I have said anything stupider than that? Of course I'm not a doctor. This refined man is well aware that I'm a prostitute, a harlot, a public woman. Unless, of course, he presumes I'm the servant I appear to be.

The man rises from the divan and holds out his hand Western-style. "I'm Abram Abramovich Segalovich."

I eyeball the proffered hand and its immaculate fingernails. In my entire life, no man has requested to shake my hand. Shaking hands is limited to men and maybe cosmopolitan women of a certain status, but certainly does not apply to me.

"My name is Anna." *Why do I keep saying dumb things?* Grisha already called me by name. Twice. As I place my hand in Abram Abramovich Segalovich's, I realize the afternoon's chores have shriveled it like a prune.

"It's my pleasure to meet you, Anna."

While my fingers brush aside the strands of hair that trail across my cheek, I wonder what he's doing here. Waiting for one of the girls? Men don't visit brothels just to drink tea.

"Is there anything . . . "My voice squeaks. I clear my throat. "Is there anything I can do for you?"

My bare toes grip the crimson rug in embarrassment. Of course, there isn't anything I can do for him. I'm in slovenly disarray while he's stylishly turned out.

Well-cut gray business suit, complete with waistcoat.

Starched shirt, its cuffs embellished with gold links.

White silk handkerchief in an upper coat pocket.

Gold pocket watch and chain.

Blinding shine on black boots.

"Actually, I'm just enjoying chatting with Grisha." The man's full lips smile. "You see, my younger brother is getting married this week. Our cousins are planning a surprise bachelor party for him later this evening and asked me to divert him for a couple of hours while they get his apartment ready. I reasoned, why not keep him occupied here?"

Grisha gives a full-throated laugh as his palm slaps the arm of his chair. He rises and reaches for Segalovich's empty glass. "Care for another glass of the Chinese herb?"

The man replies, "Yes, I would. Perhaps Anna will join us."

I'm thrown into a tizzy. On one hand, I'm oddly drawn by this fellow's dark eyes that are locked onto mine. But I also need to clean up before more customers arrive.

I justify my decision to stay by rationalizing that Abram Abramovich Segalovich could develop into a regular customer. Which, of course, is complete nonsense, considering my current appearance.

As I lower myself onto the divan opposite the man, the reek of beer wafts from my spattered dress. I hide my bare feet under the low table that sits between the two divans.

While Grisha is at the bar, I take swift measure of the black-eyed man. He's not handsome, but he is dangerously appealing. His build, while solid, isn't particularly powerful. His brow is a little too broad, and his nose is rather large. His heavy-lidded eyes are just a tad too close together. His complexion is slightly on the dark side. Yet for some reason, all the slightly flawed pieces fit together to create a very nice whole.

"This is a slow time of day for you?" Abram Abramovich asks.

The peculiar question throws me off-balance, but at least he acknowledged what I am, which certainly isn't a doctor. "Yes. Our business starts when the other businesses close, but it doesn't really pick up until nine or ten o'clock."

"That's the advantage of this job," Grisha chimes in as he returns with two glasses of tea. "You get to sleep until noon every day!" He gives a playful wink.

Abram Abramovich Segalovich chuckles and glances around the empty room. "I assume Monday isn't one of your busier nights?"

Such a strange slant to this conversation! I cock my head and stare at the stranger until I realize he's actually waiting for an answer. "I'm sorry." I give a slight shimmy of my head, as if to reengage it. "It's not often that men care which days are slow."

Again he brandishes his winter-white teeth. "Yes, I imagine that's true. Please forgive me. You see, I'm a banker. So I am forever analyzing what makes businesses successful, including when their peaks and valleys occur. It's an unbreakable habit I've acquired." He has a smooth voice, the sort that makes me want to close my eyes and simply listen to it.

Grisha exclaims, "If you want to see busy, then you should come here on any holiday. There's a waiting line out the door. Our house has the best reputation in all of Moscow."

I come close to sliding off my chair and crawling up the stairs. Although I normally enjoy the barkeeper's unsophisticated humor, I find it humiliating in the presence of this impeccably mannered banker. I take refuge in sipping my tea.

"But Mondays tend to be slow?" Abram Abramovich asks again.

Why is he so persistent with that question? "Yes. Mondays and Tuesdays are very slow compared with Friday and Saturday nights."

"I'm afraid you won't get my brother's business on Friday night. It's the Sabbath."

My eyebrows come together. "The Sabbath?"

"Yes. We're Jewish."

The vestibule door opens, and in walks a man with a delivery of liquor. Grisha rises and meets him at the bar, and the two enter into a discussion about rising liquor costs. I have Abram Abramovich all to myself, a situation that delights and scares me.

"Jewish? I don't know anything about being Jewish. I mean, about Jewish customs. Such as the Sabbath, I mean." I tap my naked foot on the carpet, vexed with myself for stumbling over my words. "There weren't any Jews in my village."

"Well, now you've met me. I'm happy to tell you anything you'd like to know."

I lower my eyes over a long sip of tea, garnering time to organize my thoughts. "Your Sabbath is on Friday? Is that similar to our Divine Liturgy on Sunday?"

"In a manner of sorts, except that Sabbath is more than attending a worship service. Sabbath is a full twenty-four hours devoted to rest and peace, beginning at sunset on Friday and lasting until sunset on Saturday."

"Your holy day starts at night?"

"Exactly. And at its conclusion, everyone says '*Shavua tov*,' which is Hebrew for 'Have a good week.'"

I practice the words. "Shavua tov. Shavua tov. I like the sound of that. Is it all right for me to use Hebrew words?"

"I wouldn't know why not."

Memories skirt through my mind of the dreary, joyless church services of my youth—services that I've skipped during my four and a half years in Moscow. "Surely you're not in church for twenty-four hours?"

"Synagogue, which is our church, occupies part of the time. The remainder is reserved for family and home. It's based on the part of Scripture that says, 'God blessed the seventh day and made it holy, because on it, God rested from all the work of creation.'"

I give him a look of exaggerated disbelief that includes squinted eyes, a furrowed forehead, a raised shoulder, and a half smile. "You truly do no work for a full night and a full day? And you do this every week?" Continuously faced with an endless list of chores, I can't imagine devoting that much time to resting.

"Yes, and therein lies the problem. Some of the bank's customers prefer to conduct business on Saturday. But Jewish law strictly forbids such transactions on the Sabbath. As a result, some of our customers became quite disgruntled. But, being Jewish, I'm used to being regarded as . . . different. To put it mildly."

"What do you mean, 'different'?" I take a sip of tea and glance toward the bar. I'm grateful to find Grisha and the deliveryman are in a deep discussion about new flavors of brandy.

"Although we call ourselves the 'Chosen People,' others prefer the term 'Christ killers.'" Even as he says the harsh words, Abram Abramovich's countenance remains placid and full of equanimity.

"Certainly people don't treat you that rudely?"

"Rarely did I encounter such enmity while growing up in Kiev, because Jews were such a large segment of the city's population. However, Moscow is a different story." Abram Abramovich leans forward and rests his forearms on his thighs. His words assume an undertone of privacy. "They're the model of politeness when they come into the bank needing a source of credit. But have no doubt—I, my wife, and my entire family are barred from their gentile world."

Wife. An unexpected and absurd pinprick tenses my shoulders. "You make it sound as though you're an outcast."

"To certain people, I am." Abram Abramovich's smile seems a tad self-conscious. "Forgive me. How boorish of me to prattle on with answers that veer so drastically from your question about the Sabbath."

"Not at all." I shake my head so fiercely, motes of flour flutter from my hair. One more embarrassment. "I understand what you mean about being treated as an outcast. I've often felt that way."

"Because of your occupation?" The question is asked affably, without condemnation.

"You mean as a doctor? Or as a pastry chef?" I laugh, hoping to sidetrack him from the topic. I never let my guard down with any man except Yevgeny. But something about the openness of Abram Abramovich's face bids me to continue. "I've felt like an outcast because of my birthmark."

I swivel my head so he has full view of the crimson blotch on my cheek.

"When I was born, the people in my village thought it was the stain of the Devil. They advised my mother to kill me. They said as I grew older, I would become more and more wicked." I run a nervous finger around the neck of my servant's dress. "Sometimes I wonder if perhaps in some ways they were right."

He looks at me with the utmost fixedness. "How can you even consider such a notion? You, who doctor the sick and the injured?" His black eyes curve into whimsical crescents.

I grin and sheepishly draw my neck into my shoulders.

As his smile slackens, he leans forward. His voice is earnest. "The two of us must never let the petty opinions of others make us feel any less worthy as human beings."

My goodness, that's a weighty statement, far removed from the empty chatter that ordinarily occurs in the Grand Salon. Momentarily thrown off-balance, I dimple my cheeks—something I do these days as a matter of course around men. Somehow I'd forgotten to do so during this conversation with Abram Abramovich Segalovich.

"Now I'm the one who needs to apologize for prattling on too long about myself." I stand and pick up the cake platter. "I really should tidy up—both the kitchen and myself."

He rises from the divan. "Thank you for the conversation. I thoroughly enjoyed it."

My voice is unsteady as I say, "Shavua tov, Abram Abramovich."

"Shavua tov, Anna."

I try to look as dignified as possible as my bare feet drag my faded, smelly, floured servant's dress into the kitchen. I wonder if he's watching me. A faint tingle skitters up my neck at the thought that he might be.

CHAPTER 25

June
1870

"YOU SHOULD HAVE seen Sophia Mikhailovna's face when I came down-stairs during working hours with my birthmark in all its glory," I tell Athena as we slice cucumbers.

I suggested pickling cucumbers to take Athena's mind off her disappointment. She finally saved enough money to return to her village as a prosperous woman. However, she received a terrible blow when she found she couldn't obtain the necessary passport.

Years ago, Athena journeyed to Russia with a band of Greek gypsies. A member of the caravan died en route, so Athena, having no documents herself, handed the medical-police the Greek documents of the deceased woman.

Now, with only a yellow ticket (which merely labels her as a prostitute) and no male family member to vouch for her identity, she has no way of obtaining the Russian passport required for every traveler. She considered leaving the same clandestine way she had arrived. However, with age comes wisdom, and she found the potential consequences to be more than she was willing to risk.

The dream that has kept her going through five years of hard work and scrimping has been ripped from her, and it's clear she's hollowed out by the defeat.

Earlier today, I glanced in Athena's bedroom and found her sitting in the center of her bed, arms clasped around her knees, staring out the window at a pewter sky that had spit and sputtered all morning. The Grecian beauty seemed to have melted into a puddle of sorrow. So I dragged her to the kitchen for an afternoon of pickling.

I keep the chatter lively, laughing at how our madam's eyes and mouth became circles of shock at the sight of the scarlet stain blazing on my cheek, free from the mask of makeup. The moment was short-lived, however. Sophia Mikhailovna merely rendered her acknowledgment with a small nod of her bejeweled head, then glided across the room to chat with a customer.

I'd been toying with the idea for some time. Applying and reapplying the heavy makeup every evening had become a soulless chore. Plus, extra laundering was needed to keep my pillowcases clean. Not to mention, I have a steady clientele who I assume wouldn't be deterred by the birthmark. In fact, most of them are well aware of its existence.

A week ago, after I bid Abram Abramovich Segalovich *shavua tov,* I rushed around in my room preparing for the evening. My nerves were still inexplicably taut from my encounter with the banker. As I prepared to don my makeup, I stared at the strawberry-hued blotch reflected in the mirror and informed it, "I'm not wasting any more time on you."

This afternoon in the kitchen, I wink at Athena. "I'm certain Sophia Mikhailovna is watching my receipts to see if there's a change in income."

"I no blame you," Athena says as her knife edges the cucumber slices off the cutting board and into the pickling jar. "When first I come here, I worry customers no like my poor Russian. But I make good money." With those words, her mouth sags. Now that her dreams have been shattered, she has no real need of those rubles.

An impassioned knocking comes from the side entrance. "I'll get it," I say, glad for a short reprieve from Athena's doldrums. "Grisha said to expect the chimney sweep."

Rather than finding a chimney sweep, I encounter a woman who appears as though she's been grubbing around inside a chimney. A filth-spattered dress, damp with the day's drizzle, clings to her bony frame. Alongside her is a scrawny, pale girl who's staring at her bare feet, her face veiled by stringy brown hair.

"I'm looking for Sophia Mikhailovna Ovsianikova." The woman's voice is as husky as a man's.

"Madame Ovsianikova is not home."

The woman's crusted eyes narrow with distrust as she lisps through a nearly toothless mouth. "I'll wait for her."

"No. She has strict rules about visitors."

"But I must see her. I was told she wants my daughter."

I come very close to calling the woman a damn liar. Instead, I say, "You may wait on the street if you'd like, but I don't expect her home for several hours. Besides, we don't have any openings right now."

"Listen to me. She wants my daughter." The woman yanks on the grimy hair that clings to the back of the girl's neck.

The child's head jerks up. She looks twelve or thirteen years of age, with no breasts evident beneath her frayed shirt. Revulsion ripples through me.

"This thing will make a fine whore. She hasn't had her first bleeding. Men pay extra for a fresh hole. A lot extra." The miserable woman's face is twisted with vileness: yellow corruption in the corners of her eyes, a hairy upper lip, a weeping sore on her chin.

I try to close the door, but she wedges her shoulders between it and its frame. A stench, as bad as any at the medical-police, floats across the threshold.

I straight-arm the woman out of the way, whip the door closed, and bolt it. As I stare at the doorknob, a foul taste contaminates my mouth, as if the woman has spread some of her corruption onto me. How despicably awful the contemptible creature treats her own daughter! A *thing*. A *hole*. That poor child is doomed to the existence of a destitute street prostitute—until syphilis or alcohol or a man takes her life.

I return to the kitchen to find Athena emptying the final dregs from the salt-box. "Supposed keep full. No pickle without salt."

I volunteer to go to the market and buy some. I describe the awful woman and tell Athena not to answer the door while I'm gone.

I knock on the door to Sophia Mikhailovna's apartment to ask Fyedka if he wants to go with me. No answer. "Fyedka? Fyedka?" Receiving no response, I try to open the door. It's locked.

"Fyedka!" My voice is shrill with impatience. "How many times have you been told? Don't lock the door."

I reach for the key hanging beside the kitchen door but grab only empty space. Why can't people return the key to its rightful place? I don't have time for this nonsense today.

I go upstairs to retrieve a hatpin. When it became evident that Fyedka was dead set on locking himself in the room, Grisha taught me how to pick the lock. A hatpin, a nail, a fingernail file—over time, I've mastered all the techniques.

As the door swings open, I shake a fierce finger at Fyedka. "I was going to ask you to go for a walk with me, but I've changed my mind. You make me very angry when you do things you know are wrong."

His bottom lip juts out.

"You stay home with Athena."

His lip protrudes further, but it does not dissuade me.

"Do we have enough garlic and everything else?" I ask Athena as I lace up my ankle boots. At this rate, we'll still be pickling when customers arrive.

Once outside, I glance anxiously at the clouds stuffed with rain, then bend like a sickle into the wind, my skirt buffeting around my calves. I shiver, wishing I'd worn more than a muslin day dress and a shawl. My pinned hair is soon flying about, intent on wrapping itself across my face. When I reach a cross street, a wagon douses my skirt with muddy water from a puddle. I clench my jaw, regretting that I ever suggested those damn pickles.

I'll have to ask Sophia Mikhailovna—yet again—to lay down the law among the women about keeping the cupboards stocked. *Why can't they act like responsible—*

I stop short. Is someone calling my name? Over the sound of the wind and the slashing of my skirt, I can't be sure. Yes, there's a man across the street, hands cupped around his mouth.

When the fellow lowers his hands, my eyes blink in disbelief.

Abram Abramovich Segalovich crosses the street toward me, looking as flawless as he did last week—tailored raincoat, sturdy boots, disarming smile. I pull my lower lip between my teeth. Why isn't he muddy and disheveled like I am?

"Anna. Such a coincidence to encounter you again." His smile widens.

"A pleasant surprise to see you here, Abram Abramovich. Perhaps another bachelor party?"

His laugh is robust. "No, not another party." His teeth shine even on this dreariest of days. "I was in the neighborhood for another reason and thought I'd stop by to see you or Grisha."

Me or Grisha? Huh?

"I'm in need of directions."

"Directions?" My right hand fights to keep my recalcitrant skirt under control. Meanwhile, my left hand shields my eyes from my whipping tendrils of hair, allowing every opportunity for my reticule on that wrist to repeatedly bash my face.

"My uncle has a special occasion coming up soon, and I'd like to give him his favorite tobacco. It's from Turkey and difficult to find." He removes a small square of paper from his breast pocket and shows it to me. "I've heard about an outstanding tobacconist in this neighborhood. Are you acquainted with this shop?"

I bend close to him and pretend to read the three words written on the thrashing paper. The nearness of him flings my heart into a wild Tropak dance.

Although I haven't a clue as to the meaning of the written words, I'm familiar with the tobacco shop. It's located in the cobblestone alley, next door to the Chinese tea and medicine shop.

"It's only a couple of streets from here. Go to the next corner and turn right, then walk three blocks. No, I think it's only two blocks. Then turn right again at a large wooden building. Not the wooden building with stone on the first floor, but the one that's entirely wood."

Not only is the wind whisking away half my words, but my rattled thoughts are finding it impossible to lay out concise directions. I keep getting lost in Abram Abramovich's dark eyes.

"Just past that building is a short little street. Well, actually, it's more of an alleyway. It dead-ends near the shop you're seeking." I can tell from his blank face that my instructions are useless. Why am I so featherheaded around this man?

"It might be easier simply to take you there," I say. "I'm headed that direction anyway."

"I'd appreciate it, if you have the time."

I'm fully aware that I don't have the time, but that's not going to stop me. Remembering my birthmark, I slip to his left side so the blotch is hidden from him.

"I told Grisha last week that I've always liked this section of town," he says as we begin to walk. "The older buildings have a grace that's lacking in the newer neighborhoods. I'm seldom in this part of the city, even though my office is just across the river. I'll have to visit more often."

I stare straight ahead, not daring to interpret the meaning of his last sentence. I'm taken aback by the effect his presence continues to have on me. How incredible that, considering all the men I've lain with, here's one merely walking beside me, yet my every fiber is alive to his being. I'm aware of his every footfall, every swing of his arm, every rustle of his trousers.

When we reach the cobblestone alleyway, the proximity of the buildings buffers the wind. I summon the courage to say, "I've never visited this shop. Perhaps I'll go in to see what it's all about."

The bell jingles as Abram Abramovich pushes open the door. I step into a masculine world filled with the earthy scent of unburnt tobacco, so unlike the Grand Salon's chronic stench of stale smoke. I fill my lungs with the heady, gratifying mixture of aromas.

While Abram Abramovich speaks with the shopkeeper, I wander about the small store trying to smooth the riot the wind made of my hair. As in the Chinese shop, sundry jars line the shelves, but here, the jars contain loose tobacco rather than herbs and dead lizards. Also on display are snuffboxes that cater to the extremes of taste, from simple papier-mâché to carved ivory festooned with jewels.

I'm drawn to a display of decorative cigar boxes, mesmerized by the beauty of the woodwork. Each box is a unique tapestry of inlaid wood grains and hues. I ease open a polished lid and brush the tip of my finger along the velvet lining of the deepest maroon.

In addition to his uncle's pipe tobacco, Abram Abramovich purchased three cigars for himself, which he's placing in his breast pocket as he walks up beside me. "They're pieces of art, aren't they?" he asks as his fingertips glide over the sleek smoothness of a cedar box, unadorned except for the silver braces in the corners and a silver key.

The nape of my neck tingles as if his fingers were gliding there.

"They're so . . . so strikingly beautiful!" I stammer.

"Only a true master could craft this." Abram Abramovich points to an Oriental black-lacquered box embellished with gold leaf. An inlay of mother-of-pearl portrays a sword-wielding figure that's half man, half tiger.

"And this one!" I exclaim. "The wood looks just like marble. And this one—the etching is so detailed." I feel Abram's gaze on me as surely as I had felt the downy lining of the cigar box. I'm behaving like a wide-eyed child. I quickly assume the Sophia-stance: head up, shoulders back.

"Ready to go?" He lightly touches the elbow of my dress. Prickles course to both ends of my arm. This man is dangerous, and I'd be wise to bid him a fond farewell.

As we retrace our steps down the narrow lane, late-afternoon sunbeams wedge between the buildings. Customers will soon be arriving. Athena has probably given up on the salt and the pickling.

"I'm indebted to you," Abram Abramovich says. "I would never have found this out-of-the-way street on my own."

"I'm glad for the opportunity to visit that shop. The craftsmanship is stunning." We reach the point where the alley intersects with the street—and its wind. "Well, I'd best get on with my errands."

"I hope I didn't keep you from anything pressing." He stops walking. "Anna . . ."

I swivel toward him and am immediately snared by his eyes, as soft and long-lashed as a milk cow's.

He swallows as if to make room in his throat for his words. "Is Monday really the slowest day?"

"Yes, Monsieur Banker, it is."

He grins at my feeble jest. "What I meant is, Monday's the best day for this banker to see you?"

How did my legs suddenly fill with champagne bubbles? "You're referring to seeing me at the house? As opposed to shopping together for cigars?"

"You're teasing me."

I want so badly to nibble insecurely on my lip. Or maybe it's *his* lip I want to nibble. I curb my unexpected flight of imagination by tossing my mop of disheveled hair. "I'm definitely teasing you."

"I would like to see you next Monday. The same time as last week." His words are proper, like he's conducting a business transaction. Which, I remind myself, he is. Nevertheless, my world has gone topsy-turvy.

"I'm surprised," I reply. "I'm always such an eyesore when we meet. Hardly what men find appealing."

For a long, sweet moment, he gazes at me. His hand slowly rises, and his forefinger nudges a recalcitrant curl away from my cheek. It then moves down to lift my chin. "If I may borrow your own words, you're more 'strikingly beautiful' than any of those elegant boxes. Certainly you realize that."

My heart gives a lurch unlike any I've ever felt. I grasp for a response that is bright and carefree. "Now *you're* teasing *me*."

"Not in the least."

I think I give the slightest shake of my head, but I'm not sure. In truth, I'm not sure if any of this is really happening, so strangely affected am I by this man's words and touch.

"I'll see you next Monday," he says. "Shavua tov."

In the midst of my marrow-melting confusion, I sputter, "Shavua tov."

Having completely abandoned my pursuit of salt, I turn toward 903 Sviatoslavsky Prospekt, my heart tripping over itself.

Get your head out of the clouds, I chide myself. He'll be a paying customer, nothing more. I won't let myself be lured into hoping that the incredible past half hour was the beginning of something promising.

Keep your dreams buried, where they belong.

CHAPTER 26

July
1870

IT'S BEEN TWO and a half years since I've awoken early enough to witness the eastern sky as it welcomes the sun. I pull the coverlet over my head to fend off a pesky mosquito, then allow my thoughts to wander leisurely through fanciful musings about this afternoon's customer.

During the past week, memories of his dark eyes tugged constantly at me. Echoes of his voice chased me like a shadow. I mulled over his words, both at face value and their every possible implication. My imagination summoned the aroma of the tobacco shop and the touch of his finger under my chin.

Strikingly beautiful. Had he actually said that?

How will his long-fingered hands feel, sliding down the curve of my spine? And what will his late-afternoon beard feel like against my neck?

But this morning's enchanting fantasies are knocked aside by rock-bottom truth, just as they are every day. I've taken leave of my senses if I believe Abram Abramovich wants anything more than merely to cavort in my bed.

Facts are facts.

First fact: He's married. Therefore, I mean nothing more to him than a sexual bauble.

Second fact: I'm an illiterate peasant-turned-prostitute. The only reason I'm not starving is that my flesh can be bought. I abuse my body in ways no decent woman would dream of doing. Meanwhile, he's an esteemed businessman who wears a suit with a waistcoat and a pocket watch.

Final fact: He's Jewish. I'm Russian Orthodox. The two could never mix. His faith certainly wouldn't allow it. And just imagine what my family would think. A snort escapes me. *Ha!* If only they knew what my life is like now, with or without a Jewish lover!

I throw off the coverlet and swing my legs out of bed. The mosquito instantly homes in on me. I curse the hungry little insect. "You'd better be either gone or dead by the time he arrives this afternoon."

After putting clean linens on the bed, I remove the cornflower-blue taffeta dress from my armoire. Over the past few days, I spent a great deal of time—more than I want to admit, even to myself—selecting this evening's gown. The blue dress is unadorned except for the ribbon around the neckline and waist. Sophia Mikhailovna says it has the sex appeal of a peasant's bast sandals. But every time I wear it, someone remarks how nicely it complements my eyes.

I lay the gown on the bed and top it with silk stockings, a white taffeta slip, and my faux pearl earrings and necklace.

Barefoot and in my dressing gown, I pause halfway down the staircase. I look down on the Grand Salon and nod my approval of my own work. For the past week, I sought respite from my restless agitation through a frenzy of cleaning. *A busy body precludes a fretful mind.* I'd heard the saying often enough. I decided to put it to the test.

I started in my own room, which hadn't enjoyed a thorough scrubbing the entire time I've occupied it. I hauled the bedspread and drapes outside and beat the dust from them. While they were airing in the sun, I made the windows sparkle with vinegar and water, then dusted the woodwork.

After Maria left, I gained possession of a heavy steamer trunk—a godsend for extra storage. As part of my cleaning frenzy, I pulled the wooden trunk from its location under the stairwell leading to the attic and gathered up the colony of dust bunnies that had propagated there. I oiled the trunk's parched wood and was rewarded by a long-forgotten luster.

I then applied my energies to the Grand Salon, the stairway, and the upper and lower hallways, where my feather duster assaulted the baseboards and the chandeliers' prisms and everything in between. I put the cushions and decorative pillows outside for a much-needed airing. I polished all the doorknobs, both upstairs and down, with brick-dust and vinegar.

On Saturday—the Jewish Sabbath, the day of supposed rest—I enlisted the help of Grisha and little Sonia to move all the furniture and rugs, even the massive Oriental carpet. Then, on my hands and knees, I scrubbed and waxed the floors.

On Sunday, I did my laundry and replanted a couple of ferns. I asked Grisha to haul my mattress to the courtyard so it could air.

"Why don't we just turn the whole house inside out?" the big man grumbled. I kept him going with my usual bribe of a marzipan mazurka.

Today—Monday—my vigor abandons me. I'm irritable and sluggish, without the ambition to accomplish anything worthwhile.

Not only did the week's labor physically deplete me, but I'm also emotion-
ally exhausted thanks to my internal tug-of-war. Do I really want to see Abram
Abramovich Segalovich? Do I hope he'll vanish from my life? Or do I long to be
held in his arms? The answer changes from minute to minute.

I release Sasha from his cage and discover he's out of food and almost out of
water. I grumble, "Don't any of these brothel Fräuleins pay the slightest attention
to what goes on around here?"

In the kitchen, I find that my fellow occupants haven't left so much as a piece
of bread to eat. Why won't people do their fair share of the work?

It's almost noon when Irina, Dunka, Dunyasha, and I head to our medical-police examinations. A couple of blocks from our destination, three teenage boys
approach us. I know from their cocky strut that they're looking for trouble and
are destined to find it.

The ruffians stop in front of us, blocking our way. The three talk over one
another.

"Look what we have here."

"Hey, sweetheart, got any to give away?"

"Which one of you got the freshest stuff?"

Irina's quick temper kicks in. "Step aside, pipsqueak."

The largest boy feigns hurt feelings. "Aw, come on, honey! Is that any way to
treat a potential customer?"

Dunyasha tugs at Irina's arm. "Let's just walk past them."

Irina isn't about to be sidetracked. "Customer? You snotty-nosed runt! No
doubt you're as worthless as a melted candle. Besides, it's obvious you can't afford
quality services."

"Quality? You call yourself a quality fuck? You old cunt."

I hiss to Irina, "Ignore them and they'll go away."

Instead, Irina curses the boys in spirited terms.

Another boy sneers, "You're just as brazen as your profession, aren't you?"

Dunka's eyes and my own exchange an unspoken agreement. We each grab
one of Irina's arms and drag her down the sidewalk. Irina spews a torrent of
curses at us.

"Stop it!" I retort with a ferocity that shocks the three women. "I should think
you'd be used to being badgered after all these years. Besides, they're just young
whippersnappers. You're the adult. Have some self-restraint."

I'm already in a dark mood as we enter the stifling waiting room at the medical clinic, where women jostle each other like piglets in a pen. Next to me, a drunken woman upchucks.

Irina, her blood still boiling from her row with the young riffraff, bellows, "Go outside if you're going to puke up your guts."

The toothless woman wipes the spittle on her sleeve. "Well, well, well, if it isn't the bitches from Sophia Mikhailovna's dump. You house-whores think you're so much better than us odinochki. Let me tell you something." She sways as her finger pokes Irina's breastbone. "I heard that your customers are going elsewhere. Something about lice and bedbugs and dog-faced women."

"Shut that ugly beak of yours, you old sow, before I shove it in that pile of puke you just upchucked."

The woman snorts. "If you want to shove something, shove your high-minded-ness up your ass."

Irina, not given to idle threats, lunges at the woman. They both land on the floor, hair-pulling and kicking less than an arm's length from the puddle of vomit. The fray is broken up by a couple of guards, who hustle the women to opposite corners of the room.

"One more brawl, Irina, and you'll find yourself in jail," warns one of the guards.

With her hair spilling from its pins, Irina grins at the familiar face. "Vadim, you know someone else always starts these little tussles."

Beside me, a woman coughs. Her hacks seem to start deep in her feet and work their way up through her chest.

I close my eyes to shut out the wreckage of human beings swarming about this room. The smell of the nearby vomit, which no one has bothered to mop up, is making my stomach queasy. Eyes closed, I try to conjure up the comforting aroma of the tobacco shop, but I can't get past the waiting room's stench.

"Hey, I heard you're the one who knifed Shestov."

I drag my eyelids open and see a woman with yellow hair bunched up like a swallow's nest. Her teeth are the same color, except where they're missing.

I close my eyes and lean my head against the grimy wall. "That was a long time ago."

I LINGER AT the bathhouse, slapping the birch branches against my skin and steaming my pores until I've scoured off every trace of the clinic's muck.

When I return to Sviatoslavsky Prospekt, I'm at loose ends about how to occupy my time. I try to nap, but I'm too fidgety, as though a line of ants were crawling up my back.

I look about the room that serves as my home and torture chamber. How many men have I been with over the past two and a half years? And how many still loom in my future? When, oh when, will I be able to save enough rubles to get back to Petrovo? And when I arrive, will I be welcome?

I pick up my old lace-up ankle boots and set about polishing them with wax. And so it is that one day passes into another day, another month, another year. How many more years can I endure this life? Or perhaps a more accurate question would be: How many more years before I end up as a casualty of the profession—a victim of disease or violence?

I heave an enormous sigh that empties my chest.

In the next room, Dunka's and Dunyasha's voices rise in argument. My nerves are as brittle as dried rye stalks. I'm so very tired of it all. The senseless bickering of the two women. The never-ending stream of men. The unnatural hours I keep. Constant anxieties about my future. Living with eight other women and a barkeeper instead of a family. The shame of merely walking down the street while proper women gather their cloaks of respectability around themselves.

And now I'm allowing a rich Jew banker to trifle with my emotions. To him, I'm sure I'm nothing but a plaything in a parlor game, a pretty doll to enjoy and then toss away, a frolicsome diversion. Little does he know or care how breakable I am.

As I buff my boots with excessive ardor, I swear I'll keep my head this evening, regardless of his hypnotic eyes.

It's three o'clock when I descend the steps, dressed in blue taffeta, painstakingly coiffed, and breath freshened with mint leaves. What time did he arrive that first Monday? Around four o'clock?

I organize the disarray of medicines and bandaging in the sideboard. I try to memorize what supplies need replenishing, but the unrelenting tick of the tall clock's pendulum frays my mangled nerves to distraction. My inability to write even a simple list once again sticks in my craw.

I tidy Sasha's cage, then sit on a divan and begin to mend a camisole. Anticipation and foreboding twist my gut in equal measure.

At the kitchen table, Grisha is sharpening knives. Through the open door streams the repetitive rasp of cold steel as the knife courses across the honing stone. Back and forth, the whine of the knife scratches into my brain. Back and forth, as steady as the ticking clock.

What if Abram Abramovich doesn't come, I fret for the hundredth time—or is it the thousandth?

I glance about the room and recall how lavish it initially appeared to my gullible eyes. When did it become garish and tawdry? The decor is nothing but tinsel and glitter—a pitiful pretense of luxury, like rouge applied too thick.

The gigantic paintings of the half-naked women and dancing gnomes are tasteless, and the gold leaf on their frames is flaking. The heavy drapes are faded. The seats of the upholstered furniture are worn into hollows. I drop my head closer to my mending, embarrassed to be part of the ostentatious furnishings that unmistakably scream *bordello.*

Grisha's rhythmical grinding pulsates in my head. First one side of the blade, then the other, each stroke louder than the previous one. My fever of impatience reaches a crescendo that threatens to be my snapping point.

"Fyedka, I'm sorry." Sophia Mikhailovna enters the Grand Salon, trailed by her brother. "No flute concert. Not today."

I look up. "Flute concert?" Every so often, I hear him tooting disjointed notes on a toy flute, but this is the first I've heard of a concert.

Seeing my quizzical expression, Sophia Mikhailovna explains, "Fyedka occasionally held concerts for my sister and me. All day he's been nagging to have one."

"Then let's do it." The silly distraction would speed up my wait. Before Sophia Mikhailovna can object, I say, "I'll gather the others. Grisha, come in here and rearrange these chairs, please, and bring in some from the kitchen. We're having a concert."

Despite a few grumbles, Grisha and most of the women agree to attend the performance. Even little Sonia takes a break from her cleaning and settles into a seat among the semicircle of chairs positioned in front of the fireplace.

Unfortunately, the star performer is in tears. He has misplaced his flute. An impassioned search is conducted in all corners of the house, before the instrument is located in the pot of one of the ferns.

Finally, Sasha is placed on the fireplace mantel at Fyedka's left shoulder, and the two begin their earsplitting recital. Fyedka pours his soul into his music, his inwardly turned toes tapping without regard to cadence. His head swings back and forth in a rhythm that's in sync with neither his feet nor the melody.

Other than a sporadic *whrrrrp,* Sasha doesn't contribute much in the way of music. He's a masterful conductor, however, his head bobbing up and down independently of Fyedka's improvised music, toe tapping, or head swaying. It's difficult to distinguish where one song ends and the wailing notes of another begin. Rather than letting things go on interminably, the ragtag audience periodically interrupts with a round of applause.

The resulting smile on Fyedka's face is worth all the inconvenience. It's the type of smile one rarely sees on an adult—a smile that radiates delight in the moment at hand. After the third round of applause, Fyedka mercifully ends the concert by lowering his flute to his side. He grins over our heads, in the direction of the Gentlemen's Entrance, and waves his free hand back and forth in greeting.

My head swirls about.

CHAPTER 27

July

1870

I POP OFF my chair like a jack-in-the-box. "Monsieur Segalovich, I didn't hear you come in." My cheeks flame with embarrassment, while tingling shivers chase each other down my limbs.

Hat in hand, Abram Abramovich is, like Fyedka, all smiles. "It wasn't my intent to interrupt such a talented and well-received performance. My compliments to the musicians." He walks around the semicircle of chairs and shakes Fyedka's hand. "Your concert was stunning."

Fyedka's pride is palpable. As is Sasha's.

My knees are weak as dishwater as I move toward my customer. I notice his startled eyes following young Sonia into the kitchen.

"She's the cleaning girl," I explain.

"Ahhh," he nods.

As my coworkers return their chairs to their proper locations, they smile greetings at Abram Abramovich. Then they scurry upstairs.

Sophia Mikhailovna glides toward him. Warmth exudes from her every pore as she extends a graceful hand, palm down. "Good day. Grisha told me that you are Monsieur Segalovich." Her voice overflows with that habitual sultry creaminess. "I'm Sophia Mikhailovna, the owner of this establishment."

Abram Abramovich takes her fingers in his and bows slightly. "My timing today couldn't have been more fortuitous."

"This was our first concert, and"—Sophia Mikhailovna's red fingernails massage her earlobe as she chortles—"possibly our last."

After allowing them time to enjoy a mutual chuckle, I say, "The two of you have something in common." I had rehearsed the line, knowing the opportunity to use it would arise. "You're both from Kiev."

"Is that so?" Sophia Mikhailovna seems delighted to no end.

"Yes," Abram Abramovich replies, "but I left there to attend the university and never returned."

"And what is it you do now?"

"I'm a banker."

Abram Abramovich Segalovich might as well have said he's the Antichrist. Sophia Mikhailovna's smile disintegrates into a thin, white line. Her body stiffens as though about to enter a seizure. She stops breathing, and her eyes canvass every fragment of his face.

Dumbstruck by the madam's response, I grasp for something to say that will break the cumbersome silence. But Sophia Mikhailovna, her face hard and tight, saves me the trouble.

"Anshel Iosifovich Segalovich?"

"My uncle. A few years ago, he left his employment in Kiev to open a bank in Moscow."

The muscles in Sophia Mikhailovna's neck twitch. "Then I must insist that you leave. You are not welcome here."

"What!" The floor sways beneath me.

Abram Abramovich peers at the woman as if she has taken leave of her senses.

"Leave and do not return." The creamy voice has turned vicious.

I stare at her. Has the madam's mind gone astray? Or is she making a bad joke? Apparently neither. Her body is erect, her tone is calm, and her eyes bore into Abram Abramovich's.

"Sophia Mikhailovna, whatever is the matter?" I ask. "Some mistake, perhaps?"

"Perhaps not. Anshel Iosifovich Segalovich's abuse of power was insufferable. He's the banker who destroyed my father. Neither that scoundrel nor his cronies nor his kinfolk shall ever step foot in my house."

"Although Anshel Iosifovich Segalovich is my uncle, I assure you I am *not* him." Abram Abramovich's voice remains composed. "I further assure you I had no involvement in whatever unfortunate incident transpired."

His reply doesn't sway her. "Monsieur Segalovich, I do not intend to repeat myself."

Grisha, returning from placing Sasha in his cage, positions his bulk beside his employer. "I'll show you to the door."

"No!" I command.

Abram Abramovich offers the madam a deferential tilt of his head and a placating smile. "Please, let's discuss this civilly. I'm sure we can resolve our differences and put the past where it belongs—behind us."

"I regard it as 'tending to unfinished business.'" Sophia Mikhailovna turns to the ever-faithful Grisha, gives him a *Take care of this* nod, and strides with the utmost regal bearing toward the kitchen.

"No!" I repeat to the departing figure. I grapple for more words, but my chest has collapsed on itself. I turn, gape-mouthed, to face stunned Abram Abramovich.

Grisha's thick arm gestures toward the door. "This way, monsieur."

I place a hand on Grisha's extended arm. "Please. Wait. Perhaps we can talk with her, make her see this thing logically."

"Her mind is set, Anna." Using his thumb and forefinger, Grisha gently lifts my hand from his forearm.

My teeth clamp down on my lower lip as I turn to Abram Abramovich. He holds up his hands as if powerless to win, or even fight, a battle with an absent opponent.

"I'm . . . I'm . . ." I don't know what I am. Aghast. Dismayed. Mortified. Livid. Sorry.

"Perhaps our paths will cross in the future," he says, presenting a shallow bow.

I'm dumbstruck as I watch Grisha usher Abram Abramovich Segalovich to the door. Like the first snowflakes of the season landing on the still-warm ground, in an instant all my daydreams for this evening—and all my illusions of evenings to come—vanish.

CHAPTER 28

July

1870

I LOOK DOWN at my carefully selected blue taffeta dress and pearl necklace. Then I glance about the Grand Salon—the dust-free baseboards, the chandelier's sparkling prisms, the fresh-smelling cushions, the shiny doorknobs, the waxed-to-perfection floor. All that work I did! All that time I devoted! All the wear and tear on my body, all the anxiety that gnawed at me the entire week— every bit of it wasted! All because of Sophia Mikhailovna's outlandish and misplaced grudge over something that happened two decades ago.

"To blazes with you!" I spew savage vengeance at the wall of Sophia Mikhailovna's apartment as I slam down the back hallway toward the rear door.

My throat feels thick with tears that are rising to my eyes. I stomp across the cobblestones and enter the outhouse, not only to tend to business, but also for privacy. I don't want the others to see me sniveling.

I know I'm overdramatizing. After all, what's there to be upset about? Abram Abramovich Segalovich means nothing to me, and I mean nothing to him. Our business relationship simply didn't materialize.

"But that bitch is unreasonable!" My words bounce off the walls of my cramped quarters.

Even as my fists pummel my thighs, I realize there's no reason for my excessive reaction—other than the mistake I had made by allowing the sloe-eyed banker to burrow into my fanciful daydreams and take root there.

Yes, I acknowledge, my reaction is excessive and inappropriate. But so is Sophia Mikhailovna's pigheaded behavior.

My temples throb with howling rage as I swear I won't see any customers this evening. *Ha!* Abram Abramovich Segalovich might have developed into a good-paying, long-term customer. Instead, Sophia Mikhailovna won't earn a kopek from my labors tonight.

Or maybe ever.

Maybe I'll quit this place altogether.

My retaliatory thoughts are cut off. Something burns. Why does it sting when I'm peeing? My heart clutches in fear. My head swirls, and I feel nauseous.

I tiptoe up the back stairs to the second floor and dash to my room. My hand mirror reveals the ludicrousness of my hysterics. Every color of my makeup—the black of eyeliner, the jade of eye shadow, the rose of rouge—is smeared, from forehead to chin.

Sitting on the edge of the bed, I lower the mirror to examine between my legs. Is it my imagination, or is something there? I put my finger on it to determine whether it's real or merely the result of my tear-blurred vision.

The mirror falls from my hand. The room heaves first one way, then the other.

Oh, precious Savior!

Two and a half years without a sore.

Please, not now!

NEEDING TO TALK to someone cool-headed, I catch Irina between customers and ask her to stop by my room after closing. At one o'clock, the springs creak as Irina drops cross-legged onto my bed. "Why didn't you tell me about that Jew banker?"

I wave away the topic. Instead, I blurt out my discovery.

Irina inhales deeply. "Who else knows?"

"No one."

"We were just at the medical clinic today! How the hell did that quack doctor miss it?"

The terrified little girl inside me emerges. "I don't know what to do."

"Well, the bright part is that once you've had it, you probably won't get it again. But that's not true for everyone. My husband had it twice."

"Your husband? I didn't know you used to be married."

"Still am, as far as I know." Irina shrugs with complete apathy. "He couldn't keep his little worm inside his pants. After he got the pox a second time, I left him and found work at a glass factory. The boss offered me increased pay if I'd let him screw me. I called it 'the wages of sin.'" Irina smirks. "By that time, I knew I had the pox, so I made certain that randy old goat got his just deserts."

"Then you got treatment?"

"The doctor cured me right up. Never got the pox again, praise God." Irina shakes her head at the incredulity of it all. "A person tries to live a good, clean life, and she gets diseased. She makes her living through fornication, and she stays healthy. Hardly fair, is it?"

No one said life is fair. "What about the old woman in the jail? Aniska. Isn't the pox why she's crazy?"

Irina gives a dismissive shoulder-shrug. "Who knows why she's crazy."

"Do you think Sophia Mikhailovna will keep my room open for me to come back?"

Irina doesn't respond except to avert her eyes. The sour feeling in my stomach rises to my throat.

I lie awake the rest of the night. Intertwined with anguish over my disease is fury at myself for screaming obscenities through the wall of Sophia Mikhailovna's apartment. That outburst sealed my fate. The madam will immediately and permanently turn me out once she learns about the pox. And without this house, I have nothing. No job. No place to live. Not enough rubles to get back to Petrovo. No assurance that I'm even welcome there.

Don't spit in the well—you might want to drink from it. How many times I heard the expression as a child! Why didn't I take its meaning to heart tonight?

When I leave the syphilis hospital, I'll have no choice but to seek work in another brothel. And I've heard such horrid stories about other madams.

My stomach twists into so many knots, I fear I might upchuck.

THE FOLLOWING MORNING, I stare at the closed door of Sophia's Mikhailovna's apartment, biting my lip until it hurts. Finally, I knock. "It's Anna."

"Come in."

Sophia Mikhailovna, still in her dressing gown, takes the news stoically, as I knew she would. "I'll figure up your wages for this week."

"I guess I should I take my clothes and other things with me?"

"Or if you'd prefer, we'll store your belongings in the attic. You can pick them up when you leave the hospital."

"In that case, could I ask you a favor?" My throat tightens as I feel my world crash in around me. "I've been able to save a few rubles. Would you keep them for me? I trust you." From my skirt's pocket, I pull a roll of paper rubles tied with a string.

Ever true to her straight-backed character, the madam replies, "Be assured, they'll be here when you want them."

My gaze falls to the floor, and I watch a tear spatter on my shoe. "Well. Goodbye. Would you wish everyone well for me?"

The woman lightly touches my upper arm. "Of course."

I nod and leave the apartment, feeling as though a fireplace poker is impaled in my chest. As I pass through the Grand Salon, I wonder what will become of the ferns. They now number five. Who will pick off the broken fronds? Who will open the drapes for them every day? Who will collect rainwater for them to drink?

No one.

A movement across the room catches my attention. Sasha, with his awkward waddle, is maneuvering along the back of one of the divans.

"Oh, Sasha, I'm so scared."

CHAPTER 29

July
1870

I'M BONE-TIRED, AND my mind is a pandemonium of fear and dread. I sit on the edge of a thin mattress in a ward that houses seventeen other women, most of whom seem more dead than alive as they lie curled in a ball on their metal-frame beds. Nauseated by the stench, I take quick, shallow breaths.

My fingertips rub my forehead. The pox. The inevitable finally caught up with me. The words of my grandmother chastise me. *If you chop down enough trees, you're bound to cut your finger.*

A sandy-haired man strides over to my bed and towers over me. "Are you"—he glances at the paper in his hand—"Anna Vorontsova? I'm Doctor Burylin, the physician in charge of your medical treatment. I understand you admitted yourself. That's a very noble thing to do. Most women of your class have no scruples about infecting others."

He reads a series of questions from his paper. I confirm that, for all practical purposes, I have no permanent address and no next of kin.

"First, I'll examine you. Then I'll describe your medical treatment. Then you may ask questions." His no-nonsense style is so similar to Sophia Mikhailovna's, I half expect him to conclude with *Is that understood?*

He conducts a head-to-thigh examination—my legs and feet hold no interest for him. I guess him to be in his early forties. He has an enthusiastic growth of eyebrows, and his handlebar moustache stretches almost from ear to ear.

He sits beside me on the edge of the mattress. "We'll start in the morning with daily injections of mercury. After a while, we'll switch you to drinking liquid calomel, which is also mercury. The side effects include drooling and abdominal discomfort. There's a chamber pot—"

"You goddamned liar!" The acid remark comes from the next bed. "Why not tell the poor girl the truth? It rots your guts, that's what it does." She doesn't bother to roll over, but shouts with the back of her gray hospital gown toward us. Her words are thick, as if slurred with vodka.

"Galina, shut up. Just because you're having a particularly bad time of it doesn't mean you have to scare every woman entering this hospital."

The doctor receives a foul response.

He rolls his eyes and brings his attention back to me. "We occasionally give you a little 'vacation' from the treatments"—the corners of his mouth curl at his own levity—"by putting ointment on your skin that contains mercury mixed in a base of suet and lard. Most women don't care for the blue-gray sheen it bestows on the skin."

Galina snorts. "We also don't like the gruesome sores it causes. And it stinks."

Doctor Burylin ignores the interruption this time. "Any questions?" His caterpillar-like eyebrows tent above his nose. He seems fearful I might waste his time by asking something.

"How long will I be here?"

"Depends on how well you respond to treatment. Could be anywhere from six weeks to six months. Your stay could get cut short if we get too crowded."

"But I will be cured when I leave, won't I?" My voice pleads with him.

"We do our best to ensure that every woman who leaves Miasnitskaia Hospital will not infect others with her disease." He rises from the mattress and strokes one of his handlebars.

I sense that I've used up my allotted time. "May I go outside?"

The chuckle from the next bed sounds like a gurgle from Hell. "Honey, you won't feel like going nowhere."

The physician retorts, "Galina, you're testing the limits of my patience." He turns back to me. "The Charitable Society of Miasnitskaia Hospital has set up a lovely courtyard for the patients. The Society also furnishes a lounge for relaxing. On the days you feel well enough, you'll eat in the dining room. I suggest you eat a good meal tonight. You may not have an appetite tomorrow."

After he leaves, I thank Galina for filling in the details that Doctor Burylin neglected to mention.

"There's plenty more the good doctor omitted—minor details like, oh, the injections burn like hellfire. And the mercury can sometimes kill you."

Her comments introduce mayhem to my already nauseating fears.

Galina continues to speak with her back toward me, her words so garbled that I barely understand them. "Eat while you can, before the treatment makes your teeth fall out. Breakfast is at nine o'clock. Bread and tea. At midday, some kind of soup with milk or roasted meat. At half past six, porridge. Never varies. Always the same, every day. Unless it's a goddamned meatless holy day."

"How long have you been here?"

"Almost a month. Every day is misery."

"Is it that awful?"

The woman rolls toward me. A gag seizes my throat as Galina mutters, "Look at me and tell me if it's awful."

Gathering thunderheads have dulled the windows' light, but even in the shadows, I can see Galina's swollen tongue protruding between her cracked lips. Her thin hair exposes substantial patches of scalp. Her skin is tinted blue, while her eyes are rimmed with red. The woman tucks a towel under her cheek to catch the saliva that streams from the corner of her mouth.

"Does everyone look . . . I mean, does the treatment affect everyone the same way?"

"As our good doctor said, I'm having a particularly bad time. But you can expect much the same." She coughs and spits rotted parts of her mouth onto her towel. Her rancid breath settles on me like one of the thunderheads.

"By the way, my name is Anna."

"Pleased to meet you, Anna." Galina reaches for a clean towel from her nightstand and tosses the saliva-drenched one under the bed. "Welcome to Hell."

CHAPTER 30

July–August

1870

PAIN. NAUSEA. EXHAUSTION. A haze of misery.

That's my life. Every morning, Doctor Burylin administers his torture. I cry in agony as he plunges the needle to the hilt and the caustic liquid sears the deep flesh of my thigh.

Soon after the injection, I feel as though a ram has caught his horn in my belly and is thrashing to get it loose. I curl on my side, knees drawn to my chest, unraveling only to bring back up the little bit of bread and tea I managed to swallow at breakfast. Then empty, agonizing gags take over.

By the fourth morning, my parched lips and painful gums refuse to accept food. Stringy, bloody drool pours from my mouth and drenches the towels I laid over my pillow. My mouth can't close around my enormous tongue. Whenever I roll from one side to the other, the inside of my head pitches about like a leaf hurled by waves. With strangled words, I implore Burylin to switch from injections to ointment.

"I'll switch when your bowels can't tolerate it anymore." The physician stabs his needle into my buttock now that my thighs are too bruised to accept any more punishment.

At the end of a week, Doctor Burylin changes my medication to the ointment. The salve covers every bit of my skin and fouls my clothes and bedding. I silently pledge to never again be a patient in this hospital. I'll bathe in purple potassium permanganate if I need to!

After three days away from the injections, I'm capable of eating and walking, though not very much of either. I find the lounge that Doctor Burylin mentioned when I first arrived. The room contains a few ladder-back chairs, an equal number of rocking chairs, and a window that allows us to view a smidgeon of the outside world.

I listen to the prattle of the other women who are on ointment, hoping the idle gossip will lead me to a good house when I'm discharged. But good houses are few and far between. The women refer to their madams as "snakes" and "old buzzards." Their houses are dank basements beneath shops.

To abate the scourge of boredom as well as put a few kopeks in their pockets, patients are given the opportunity to sew the gray hospital gowns. As soon as I feel well enough, I speak with Madame Martynova, who volunteers with the Charitable Society of Miasnitskaia Hospital. The matronly woman shows me where the cloth and sewing notions are kept.

She explains that the Charitable Society was founded by Princess Olga A. Golitsyna with the dual purpose of making the women's stays more pleasant and helping them find ways to forever cast off the evil of prostitution. "The Society has a garden in the courtyard, both flowers and vegetables," Madame Martynova tells me. "If you have a penchant for such things, I'll show you where the hoes are kept."

I do indeed have a penchant for such things. The following day, I weed and hoe while the July sun bears down on my neck. The buildings block any breeze that might have blown away the flies. But after years of night work, being outdoors acts like a balm on my spirits. The hoe's handle feels like a dear old friend from Petrovo, and my muscles fall easily into their former rhythm.

The courtyard supplies a reprieve from the stark ugliness of the sick wards. But more than that, the tiny patch of dirt resonates with the sweetness of my youth. Might my mother be hoeing her kitchen garden at this very moment? Or perhaps she's cutting hay. Or maybe weeding the flax. The rye should be almost ready to harvest.

I turn my face skyward and let the sun crimson my cheeks. Wouldn't it be glorious to recline atop one of the soft white clouds and float away to Petrovo! I smile at the memory of little cousin Platon insisting that someday he'd hitch a ride on a cloud and see what the world looks like to the birds.

I leave the garden only when my arms give out and my soft hands begin to blister. It's true what they say: A peasant always and forever belongs to Mother Earth.

The unaccustomed exercise should have lulled me into an early sleep. Instead, I toss about on my mattress, the windows alive with the play of sunshine on summer's white nights. As I scrunch the pillow under my head, I think how the rubles I'll make sewing hospital gowns will put me that much closer to returning to Petrovo.

Following breakfast and my daily application of ointment, I return to my bed and doze, only to be awakened by angry words.

"What the hell are you talking about, *get dressed*? I'm not well enough to leave!"

Through drowsy eyes I see Galina, her legs hanging over the side of her bed, defiantly glaring at Doctor Burylin.

"You've been here six weeks. That's sufficient. Besides, we need your bed."

"Need my bed? So it's goodbye to Galina, whether she's cured or not?"

Burylin strokes his handlebars. "Your treatment has succeeded in accordance with God's will."

"Listen here. If I find out I still got the pox, I swear I'll come back here and yank out that moustache of yours whisker by whisker!"

Galina's spot is immediately filled by a skeletal young woman in her late teens who seems to be sleepwalking as the orderly leads her by the arm to her bed. As soon as the orderly leaves, she strips off her hospital gown and, glaring at me with raw disdain, pitches the gown onto my bed. Then she lies face up on the mattress, completely naked, staring at the cracked ceiling.

When Doctor Burylin arrives for her examination, he sits her upright and slips the gray gown back on. He snaps his fingers in front of her face, but she does nothing more than blink. He turns to me, lowers his exuberant eyebrows, and shakes his head. "You'd better sleep while you can."

I open my mouth to request further explanation, but he's already moved on to the next patient.

I nap a bit more but am awakened by the young woman thrashing in her bed. She flips from one side to another, then back again. At one point she bolts up, swings her legs over the edge of the mattress, and calls me a bitch. Then she flings herself back onto the mattress and resumes thrashing.

When my nerves grow taut from the ceaseless creaking of bedsprings, I head to the lounge to do some sewing. My buttocks are bruised where the injections left lumps the size of walnuts, so I take my pillow with me to pad the chair's seat. I gently lower myself onto a rocking chair next to the tall window.

A spider puts the finishing touches on its web on the outer window frame.

A kerchiefed grandmother, moving on stiff knees, climbs the steps to the Church of Saint Nicholas.

A young woman pushes a baby pram.

A harness bell jingles as a cart hauls its goods to the Friday market.

One day, I'll step out of this hospital. Which direction will I start walking? Where will I sleep the first night—in a defunct chicken coop as Felitsa did? Where will I find a meal? What will I look like? Will I have any teeth? Any hair?

A gentle rain begins to fall, washing the grime off the buildings and the leaves of the trees. Its fresh scent creeps around the wooden frame of the closed window, taking my mind back to another drizzly day, a day when I was told I was strikingly beautiful.

I lift my feet onto the rocker's seat and rest my forehead on my knees.

The pox.

Well, Abram Abramovich Segalovich, Heaven certainly favored you two weeks ago. You seem like a nice man. Probably your wife is also a good person. You should thank your Jewish God that Sophia Mikhailovna refused you service.

At the sound of footsteps in the doorway, my head flies up.

"Good morning. Already hard at work?" asks Madame Martynova of the Charitable Society.

"I want to get as much sewing done as I can before the injections start again." I hastily replace my feet on the floor and thread my needle.

"I noticed you were in the garden quite a long while yesterday."

"Being outside felt so wonderful," I confide. "For a moment, I almost believed I was back home in my village."

"Is that what you want, Anna? To go home to your village?"

"Oh, yes. More than anything."

"What awaits you in your village?"

"My family."

"And what else?" The woman's dove-gray eyes remain soft, but behind them lies a hard challenge.

And what else?

I mull over the question. A snug hut. A snug hut that houses a dozen people, probably two dozen, now that my brothers have wives and children.

What else awaits me in Petrovo? Not a few merry hours of hoeing in a garden, but backbreaking fieldwork that melts the flesh off one's body. Blistering days of toil that last from sunup until sunset. Years when drought shrivels the soil, and the peasants survive by eating nettles and bark.

But Petrovo holds many good and wonderful things. Why are they eluding me right now?

My hesitation prompts Martynova to question, "Are you sure, Anna, are you absolutely sure the city doesn't offer you more opportunities than your village does?"

"But I must go home. Other than my . . . my . . . previous work, I have no skills, no way to earn a living."

"Would you like to be able to earn a living?"

"Why, of course!"

"Then perhaps there's help for you. Have you heard of the Shelter of Saint Mary Magdalene? The organization helps redeem prostitutes. Some patients who leave here go directly to the Shelter. There they learn skills that enable them to find respectable employment."

"Would they teach me to read and write?"

"Yes, among other things."

I inhale sharply. Suddenly, life glows with potential.

"You appear to be diligent, clean, and hardworking. If you'd like, I'll make some inquiries."

"Oh, Madame Martynova, that would be absolutely wonderful! I won't disappoint you or the Shelter." I cross myself. "You have my sacred promise." Finally, the answer I've been praying for has arrived! I'll break free of the chains of ignorance and prostitution!

AFTER THE NOON meal, the young woman in the next bed is drenched with perspiration as she shivers, curled in a tight ball. Her moans are low, as though she's having a bad dream. When Doctor Burylin arrives, I ask him what's wrong with her.

"Your neighbor is an opium fiend."

The words *opium fiend* mean nothing to me, but his next sentence resounds with a familiar theme: "She's fighting to free herself from it."

"Do you mean, like someone who has been drinking vodka a long time and suddenly stops?"

"Yes, but worse. Opium is a potent medicant. Once the body tastes opium, it can't get enough." His caterpillar eyebrows come together in a scowl. "Before she's freed from it, she'll be praying for death. Fortunately, we don't see many like her in this city. We have laws."

"What's her name?"

"Tatiana. But don't expect her to answer to it." He tugs on one of his handlebars, his signal for a change of subject. "Soon I'll switch you from ointment to oral calomel. That will give your thighs a little more time to heal before we return to injections."

As the day goes on, Tatiana perspires so profusely, sweat can be wrung from her sheets. Then, oddly enough, she begins to yawn, sometimes with such fierceness her jaw looks in danger of becoming unhitched.

I try to speak to her, but she doesn't respond. Several times that night, she shrieks like a small, terrified animal, her howls ricocheting off the long wall of the ward.

First thing the following morning, while my thoughts are still misty dreams, Tatiana vomits on herself. When she finishes retching, she looks at me with uncomprehending eyes, the blacks of which are the size of my thumbnail. Water streams from her nose and eyes. Her bowels erupt with violence.

Two attendants remove her gown and place a towel between her legs, securing it on both sides of her hips. They don't bother replacing her hospital gown. When Tatiana lies back down, the surface of her belly moves as if a tangle of snakes are fighting beneath its surface. She repeats the same words over and over: "Candy. I need candy."

I distance myself by spending the day in the lounge. The tortured soul provides an unsurpassed source of gossip. Listening to the other women helps me to better understand opium. The wicked substance comes from China and is used in the painkiller laudanum. Because of its potential dangers, laws require that physicians dispense laudanum only to those whose medical conditions warrant it.

But opium is increasingly infiltrating the prostitutes' world, providing a euphoric escape from the women's dismal lives. *Opium-eaters,* they're called. One woman, who saw her sister cleanse herself of opium, says that Tatiana's private hell is just beginning.

That night, I grow angry. Now that I'm not receiving injections, I feel good enough to sleep through the entire night. But I can't because of the ceaseless moans from the next bed.

Despite my natural instincts to feel compassion for those weaker than me, I draw the line at this revolting vermin. As I toss and turn on my mattress, I reason that Tatiana must be a fool to have taken such a poison. And now others are paying the price.

The following day, Tatiana says she's cold and demands the attendants bring blankets and candy. A mountain of blankets is piled atop her. Still her teeth chatter. She makes more demands. The attendants' frustration snowballs, and I hear mutterings of *the lunatic asylum.*

Meanwhile, I keep my hopes pinned on hearing good news about the Shelter of Saint Mary Magdalene. At last, on the third day, Madame Martynova appears in the doorway of the lounge. She greets the women, then her finger motions me into the hallway. Heart pounding with hope, I follow her to the empty dining hall. We take seats on opposite sides of a long table.

Madame Martynova announces, "The Shelter's administrators say that you sound very favorable. They are interested in meeting you." Her smile radiates with her innate goodness.

My heart somersaults with joy.

The smile loses a smidgeon of its vitality. "Anna, I need to ask you one question. How old are you?"

Unless I've lost count, I turned twenty last month. When I tell Madame Martynova this, her face loses its sparkle. "Oh, my. So unfortunate. The Shelter only accepts girls under the age of twenty."

My limbs go cold. "Isn't there some way around this? I've no passport. In fact, I may be mistaken about my age. Perhaps we could pretend . . ."

Madame Martynova shakes her head sadly, as I knew she would. "I can't deceive the good people at the Shelter."

I look down at my clenched blue fists lying in the lap of my gray gown. One more hope shattered. *What does God have against me?*

Madame Martynova puts her index finger across her upper lip for a long moment before speaking. "I have another proposition for you. Would you like to learn arithmetic?"

I crinkle my forehead. Arithmetic? What good is counting beyond one's fingers and toes? So I can add up the number of men I've lain with? So I can calculate the number of times I've fornicated? No. I want to learn a useful skill, like how to run a fancy dress shop or be a copyist in a government office.

"The hospital is always short-staffed," she continues. "You could take on duties that are falling by the wayside. I'll teach you how to keep track of the number of gowns each woman sews and how much is owed to her. Likewise, we must have a daily record of how many women are in the hospital. At the end of each week, we need to know how many sheets and blankets were used, how much medicine was administered, how many pounds of food were eaten. Do you see the importance of this?"

I gnaw on my lower lip as I give a slight shake of my head. Learning to read seems far more important.

"Numbers are everything. They're used everywhere." Madame Martynova lays her forearms on the table and leans toward me. "Every good merchant tallies his books. Each government office reports numbers to a higher office. Banks figure the interest owed by the people who borrow money."

I flinch at the unbidden vision of a dark-eyed banker figuring interest. I replace the image with one of Sophia Mikhailovna counting the money her girls bring in, then subtracting the amount they owe her.

"You think I can learn?"

"Of course," Madame Martynova exclaims with great certainty. "A person who can add and multiply can find work just like that." She snaps her fingers.

"But keeping books—doesn't that involve reading and writing?"

"Let's just start with numbers. We'll add letters and words as we go along."

STARTING THE NEXT day, I take a daily elixir of mercury that leaves me drooling and puts my bowels in an uproar. But I refuse to allow my physical misery to interfere with my instruction from Madame Martynova. I'm grateful not merely for the training, but also for an excuse to be away from Tatiana.

The young woman is constantly befouled with vomit and feces. Although the attendants are able to get her to swallow a couple of spoonfuls of soup each day, her stomach soon expels the nourishment.

Tatiana has been in the ward six days when, at dawn, she lands on the floor between her bed and mine. Every muscle in her body seems to be pulsating, and the air is filled with cries of agony. The young woman's sunken, pleading eyes turn toward me. "Help me. Please. Help me."

For the first time, I see a frightened child rather than an opium-eater. My heart softens. She's a mere remnant of a human being.

Although Tatiana is too weak to be of much assistance, she and I work together to get her emaciated body back onto the bed. The girl coils up under her blankets like a ringlet of hair. *Thank you,* she mouths.

As the days go forth, Tatiana spends her time sleeping. Eventually she begins to walk about the hospital, at which time Doctor Burylin starts her mercury treatments.

I see very little of her because my time is occupied with sewing to earn rubles, gardening in the courtyard, and learning to count over one hundred, and then over one thousand. Then I labor with Madame Martynova to learn the principles of addition and subtraction.

My tutoring takes a hiatus when the doctor pronounces that I'm fit enough to return to injections. The mercury resumes its quest to wreak havoc on my body. My vomit contains blood and pieces of rot that I assume are part of my stomach.

My gums are raw and bleeding, and my face is so swollen that opening my mouth is agony. The headaches never cease.

Ten days into this round of injection treatment, Burylin says the words I long to hear: "Your bowels can't take any more." He switches me back to ointment.

Three days later, although I'm still frail and hurting, I return to the lounge and resume sewing. I glance in the small mirror on the wall. My skin is the color of a copper roof's patina. My hair is so thin, it makes Yevgeny's meager gray strands seem luxurious.

The click of high heels crosses the plank floor. I know without looking that Valya has entered the lounge.

Valya worked in a high-class brothel. At Miasnitskaia Hospital, she continues to keep up appearances by sewing lace on her drab gray gown, strutting about in French heels, and putting bows in her hair, which is the color of a rooster's comb. It's my opinion that her masquerades help her maintain some semblance, however pitiful, of the esteem she enjoyed in the outside world, even though she occupied the bottom rung of society's ladder.

I keep my attention on my needle until I hear a woman shout, "Snooty brothel bitch!" I look up to see the room's other occupant, a big-boned blonde, towering over the seated Valya.

Valya's nostrils flare. "Shut up, you odinochka tramp!"

The customary insults of *you ugly she-dog* and *dog-fart* and *maggot-shit* are exchanged. Then the two women set about trying to scratch out each other's eyes. Scuffles are as common as sunrise, but this scrap turns nastier than usual when the blonde attacks Valya with a pair of scissors. A hospital attendant breaks up the brawl and sends the two women back to their beds.

I lean back and close my heavy eyelids, lulled into torpor by the steady *clip-clop* of hooves on the cobblestones below. My stomach rumbles—not from the usual nausea, but from hunger. I'm incredibly weary of eating the same food every day, week after week.

My mouth waters with recollections of the Count's annual parties and my stomach stuffed with grapes as large as pigeon eggs. I grin at the thought of the special treat at the previous year's party—sherbet drenched in liqueur and set afire. I can hear Irina asking for seconds. Then thirds.

Wait! It is Irina's voice! Her actual voice!

CHAPTER 31

August
1870

I SHRIEK AND fly to the doorway of the lounge. Behind Irina is Dunyasha, who squeals her greeting. With Dunyasha is, of course, Dunka.

After much hugging, I gather four chairs into a close circle. How fine the three women look compared to the sickly horde I live with now! Their cheeks are rosy. Their hair is shiny. I feel a prick of self-pity at how nonchalantly each woman carries her purse, a small symbol of the outside world.

"How did you manage to get in?" I ask. "Visitors aren't allowed."

"Greased palm." Irina keeps her explanation concise. "Wish we had gotten here a few minutes earlier. Sounds like we just missed a helluva cat fight."

Dunyasha flaps her hands beside her head with the delight of a child on her name day. "Show Anna what we brought her!" To me, she chirps, "You'll be ever so surprised!"

Dunka hands me a package secured with string. Inside I find a winter muffler of mauve yarn. "How very lovely," I say as I unfold the scarf. And unfold it further. And yet further. All told, it's twice as long as I am tall.

"Guess who made it." Dunyasha swings legs too short to reach the floor. "You'll never guess."

"Give her a chance," Dunka tells her.

"She'll never guess," Dunyasha insists.

"You're right. I can't guess," I admit as I wrap the beautifully crafted scarf around and around and around my neck.

"Fyedka!" Dunyasha scrunches her shoulders to her ears and clasps her petite hands in front of her chin as though the world's best-kept secret just slipped from between her lips. "Matryna taught him how to knit!"

I ask the women to take the scarf home with them. "I'll pick it up after I leave the hospital. I fear it would get dirty or stolen here."

Irina hands me a round tin. "This gift is from all of us. Plus little Sonia."

"Guess what it is!" Dunyasha chirps.

"I think I can guess this one." I bring the tin to my nose.

But the nimble elf is unable to resist. "Ginger cake!"

Her unbounded joy is contagious, and I find myself beaming like carefree Fyedka. "Tell me, how's everyone getting on?"

"Everyone's fine," Dunka says.

"Not everyone," Dunyasha corrects her. "Sasha misses you so much that he's molting again."

Dunka rolls her eyes. "Everyone is fine except Sasha."

"That's not exactly true, either." Dunyasha gives a small grimace. "Anna, the ferns—they're a bit peaked. I must ask you: How much should I be watering them?"

"Except for Sasha and the ferns, everyone is in fine spirits," Dunka states with finality.

"That's still not entirely true," Dunyasha admonishes her.

Irina falls, exasperated, against the back of her chair, but I merely laugh. It's just like old times.

"Yevgeny misses you terribly," Dunyasha informs me. "He came here to visit you, but male visitors aren't allowed, even with bribes."

"Yevgeny came here? How thoughtful." I miss him too. His wispy, scattered hairs. His seamed face. His impassioned discussions.

"I think he's a queer old bird." Irina doesn't mince words. "Always ranting about revolution."

I rise to Yevgeny's defense. "He's just an old rebel looking for someone to listen to him."

Dunka seconds Irina's opinion. "Seems like a cantankerous old mule."

"He's a little eccentric, that's all." A thought occurs to me. "Is he . . . is he . . . did he switch to one of the other girls?" How odd that I should feel a pang of jealousy.

"Naw," Irina says. "He stops by now and then for a drink with Grisha, but that's the extent of it."

"Who . . . who . . . " The words catch in my throat. "Who took my place?"

Dunka answers, "Sophia Mikhailovna brought home another stray. She's a real sullen thing. A peasant, straight from the village."

Dunyasha expands the story. "She was driven from her in-laws' hut when her husband went into the military."

Dunka huffs. "She'll be out on her ear in no time. The girl's consumptive."

"You don't know that for sure." The reprimand comes from Dunyasha.

"Yeah, just like you don't know for sure that I'm not the Tsar's daughter." Dunka rolls her eyes, then turns to me. "You should see her handkerchief after she hacks in it. Blood."

Irina declares, "I know Sophia Mikhailovna like I know the back of my hand. Trust me, Dunka's right—that girl's days are numbered."

The three women suddenly fall silent as the grave while they peer at me. As their joint stare bores into me, I ask, "What?"

Dunka eyeballs me as if the mercury has destroyed my brain. "Think about what we're saying."

I look quizzically at the women.

Dunka nudges Dunyasha, "Tell her. Oh, never mind. I'll tell her." She takes a deep breath. "Consumptive. Medical-police. Regulations. Sophia Mikhailovna gets rid of the girl. So that means . . . " Dunka holds out her upturned palm for me to finish the sentence.

An empty room! My mouth opens, but it takes me a moment to gather the breath to whisper the question. "Do you think Sophia Mikhailovna might . . . ?" I don't dare put my hopes into words, for fear of putting a hex on them.

Dunyasha bounces up and down on her chair. "Of course! I know she wants you back."

Irina wags her forefinger at all of us. "I bet you anything that crafty Sophia Mikhailovna hired the girl assuming she wouldn't last. And she put her in Anna's room, hoping that Anna would return."

The women chatter for a while longer, but I keep losing the thread of the conversation. I ache for that poor peasant girl, fresh from her village. I know the loneliness and confusion she feels. Not to mention the horror of facing certain death from consumption. Yet I can't stop my heart from singing with the joy of hoping that I'll soon be back in my old room.

After some time, the ladies gather their purses. I walk with them down the hall.

"We wish the best for you with your treatments," Dunka says.

Irina gives me a brisk slap on the back. "She'll be fine! She's tough. She's the one who knifed Shestov, remember?"

"Oh, Anna, darling," Dunyasha pleads, "please hurry home. Fyedka is planning a flute concert for you."

A flute concert. My blood pools in my feet. I quickly banish the image of those haunting dark eyes. It's pointless to lick that wound.

I switch topics. "It means so much that you visited me. I can't wait to get back with all of you, my dearest of friends!"

After squeezing each woman goodbye, I return to the lounge, but I'm too excited to resume sewing. I offer silent gratitude to Sophia Mikhailovna. And to God. And to the Blessed Virgin. And even to the medical-police—and anyone else who may have a role in my return to the house, to the people who care about me.

"Anna, may I talk to you?" Tatiana stands in the doorway.

"Of course," I say, wondering what the devil the opium-eater could want.

Like a skittish bird, Tatiana takes a seat opposite me. "Please forgive me. I didn't mean to eavesdrop. But I passed you and your friends in the hall as they were leaving. It sounds as if you'll be going back to your old house."

"Yes. It's a miracle."

Tatiana swallows. "I don't suppose your house would have a spot for me?"

I break away from my own happiness to examine Tatiana's forlorn face. I know full well Sophia Mikhailovna's disdain of drunks; she would never tolerate an opium-eater. "You don't have a house to go back to?"

"I won't go back. It's an evil place."

"What do you mean?"

"The madam cheats the girls. She demands that we buy new dresses and jewelry on credit, then charges us interest that is horribly high. She beats girls who don't make good money every night, even when they're sick or it's their monthly time."

"But it's against regulations for madams to beat their girls."

"She uses wet towels. They leave no marks."

"How awful! How did it happen that you joined her house?"

"I was working as a servant. My employer was a very busy person, a civic leader. One night, about a year ago, I was delivering papers for him. To the Moscow Literary Society. A man caught me by the arm, said I'd lose my job if I didn't give him what he wanted."

"Don't you think your employer would have defended you?"

Tatiana shakes her head. "You see, this man who grabbed me—he's a policeman."

A bone-rattling chill courses through my body. Is Moscow really that small of a place? "And this policeman, he had a scar on his cheek?"

Tatiana nods. "I heard your friend mention his name." She peers out the window. "The second time Shestov made his demand, he told me he knew a nice place where I could work and make lots of rubles. He took me for a visit. When I saw it was a whorehouse, I wanted nothing to do with it. But he said that in no time, I'd get rich working there." Her eyes return to mine. "I'd been so very poor and hungry my whole life."

"You were scared and alone. I understand those feelings."

A tear slips down her delicate, pallid cheek. "The brothel keeper showed me a room and said it would be all mine. I'd never had a room to myself. Then Shestov placed a glass in my hand and made a toast to my new life. I wasn't sure what was in the glass, so I took just a sip. It tasted like licorice." Tatiana gives a little-girl smile. "I love licorice." Her voice purrs with touching simplicity.

"I drank the whole glass, and then another. The next morning I had another. Shestov joked about it, called it 'candy.' The drug was already affecting my mind. I stayed at the brothel. I simply couldn't get enough. It was laudanum."

"What did it feel like when you drank the 'candy'?'"

"It's like you're bundled up in a warm coat made from the softest wool, and you're free from all pain." She twirls a limp strand of hair around her finger. "Anna, you seem like a good person. I apologize for anything I might have said or done when I first arrived. I don't remember anything about that first week here, but I think I may have been horrible."

"Your actions were under the control of something other than yourself." All of my hostile feelings evaporate, and I'm moved to pity. "But I'm curious—how did you continue to get the laudanum? I thought there were laws."

"All I had to do was ask Shestov, and he'd give me a few days' worth of candy. Of course, he didn't really *give* it to me. It was deducted from my wages. Most of the girls in the house are on opium. Some, like me, are content with laudanum. Others take it as a powder. Or smoke it. But it always comes from Shestov."

"I'm confused. What is Shestov's relationship with the brothel?"

"I think he gets a portion of the rubles that pass through the house. And all the opium rubles."

I've heard various women call Officer Shestov the foulest of names. But none of those names are sufficiently vile to describe what he has done to Tatiana.

CHAPTER 32

September

1870

JOY SHIMMERS AS I step back inside 903 Sviatoslavsky Prospekt.

My room. My fingertips blissfully run over the armoire. Over the water basin. The iron headboard. The old steamer trunk tucked under the stairway to the attic. If my furnishings are sparse, the decorations are even more so—wall sconces, a landscape picture, two books sitting atop a lace doily (never mind that I'm unable to read them). Yet to me, the room is as beautiful and as welcome a sight as Heaven's pearly gates.

I walk to the window and find solace in the humble view. A breeze pulls down the earliest of the orange and yellow leaves from the courtyard's sole tree and sends them scampering across the mossy pavers. Even the grayed boards of the dilapidated chicken coop are comforting in their familiarity.

I move from the window to the vanity's mirror. In the midst of these well-known surroundings, an unrecognizable face stares back at me.

Gone are the waves of flaxen hair that once fell across my shoulders. They've been replaced by brittle wisps the texture of straw and the color of pickled cabbage, which I cover with a scarf. Several women at the hospital told me that perfumed bear's grease promotes hair growth, but it's expensive. Perhaps I should bob my hair short like Dunka's and Dunyasha's.

The skin around my fatigued eyes is dark. My once rosy, dimpled cheeks are now flaccid and pale, a dismal yellow with an overlay of blue-gray sheen. The blue-gray supposedly wears off with time, and—I assume—so will the bilious cast, which also stains the whites of my eyes and the flesh beneath my fingernails.

I pull my lips back like I'm an old nag being inspected for auction. My gums are tinged with the same yellow. However, I must give Doctor Burylin credit. He pushed my body as far as he could, but he stopped before any teeth fell out.

At a knock on the doorframe, I swirl around. There stand Dunyasha and little Sonia.

"I just wanted to say welcome back." Sonia bashfully tucks the toe of one foot behind the heel of the other. She looks adorable in the white cap and apron Sophia Mikhailovna bought for her. I give her a bear hug.

Dunyasha, meanwhile, wrings her hands, her expression fretful. "I'm so sorry about how awful the ferns look. I did my best. I'm just not as clever as you."

"Did I ever tell you the secret," I ask, "of occasionally adding used tea leaves to their rainwater?" When the tiny woman shakes her head, I exclaim, "Well, there you have it! You were missing a crucial piece of information. If the ferns are a little peaked, it's entirely my fault."

The guilt lifts from the pixie, and she flits like a butterfly down the hallway. Suddenly she stops and swivels about on the ball of one foot. "Oh, by the way, you have a visitor downstairs."

When I peer down the stairs, I see a red calico shirt. "Yevgeny!" I rush into his open arms.

"So, my dear, why are you wearing your grandmother's babushka?"

My cheeks grow hot with embarrassment. "It's not a babushka. It's just a little scarf. My hair didn't care for the hospital's treatment. I think . . . I think I'll cut it short like Dunka's and Dunyasha's."

"Grand idea! Let's do it now," he proposes.

"Don't be silly." I give him three kisses on alternating cheeks. "I missed you and want to hear who's been tending to your feet while I've been gone. Besides, you don't know a thing about cutting hair."

"I'll have you know that I'm an experienced barber. It's a glorious September day. We can talk and cut hair outside. Get a chair, comb, and scissors."

Once seated in the back courtyard, he immediately takes to snipping. I look down, dismayed to see my long locks, sparse though they are, lying on the cobblestones.

"A barber," I laugh. "You told me you were a bookseller. You're a fibber, that's what you are!"

"Every word you've heard pass my lips is truthful. My mother had a Pekingese lapdog when I was a child. I was forever snipping burrs from its uselessly long hair."

"I know the hospital treatments made me look dreadful, but you're saying I look like a dog?"

He ignores my wordplay. "It's also true that I work in a small, out-of-the-way bookstore. Of course, we have to keep it low-key or else the Third Section will be paying us a visit."

"You must sell some very extraordinary books if the tsar's secret police find you interesting."

"Hold still. Or I'll have you as bald as me."

"Your occupation sounds rather dangerous."

"I've lived with danger so much of my life, it no longer holds any fear for me." He's quiet for a moment as his scissors work close to my ear. "My back is testimony to that."

I recognize that the tone of the conversation has turned completely about. "You've never told me how those scars happened."

"It was decades ago. I was young and full of idealistic notions."

"I'd like to hear the story—if you're willing to tell it."

He sighs. "Bear in mind, memory is very malleable. My recollection of my youth may be somewhat skewed from reality."

He steps directly in front of me, combs some hair forward, and begins to cut bangs. "I'll tell you the story, but don't you dare start yawning, understand? Because the 1840s, when I was a university student in St. Petersburg, was an unbearably boring time. Society was sheltered and intimidated. A few thousand boorish landowners. Forty million utterly ignorant peasants. And a few tiny circles of intelligentsia who were socially and psychologically isolated from the rest of the population.

"One of my fellow students was named Petrashevsky. He and I and a handful of unbridled youths formed a tight little band, held together by our joint alienation from the government."

"So you've always been a renegade."

"I've always been a renegade *and* a fool, but they both become me, don't you agree? Anyway, the special qualities of adolescence, combined with our privileged position as university students, convinced us that we were destined for grand accomplishments. After graduation, both Petrashevsky and I stayed in St. Petersburg. I worked as a translator in the Asiatic Department of the Ministry of the Interior."

"Certainly I misheard! You worked for the government?"

"My dear girl, I am revealing this to you as part of the true story of my life, most assuredly not because I'm proud of it. In fact, I was driven dangerously close to insanity, watching my fellow bureaucrats seek refuge in complex procedures and ritualized routines to the point they become incapable of making the simplest decision. Few people realize the special traits required to be a successful bureaucrat, such as an incapacity for independent thought and an unparalleled ability to mark time."

"Get back to the story." I'm determined to wheedle Yevgeny's past from him.

"Well, in the midforties, a small group of us started dropping in at Petrashevsky's house every Friday evening. There were usually fifteen or twenty of us at any one meeting. Over the years, I suppose more than two hundred people attended at one time or another. Many of us were of gentry background and—"

"Gentry?" I'm dumbfounded. "You never told me your family was among the gentry."

"I never had occasion to. Now, may we finish one story at a time, please? We were sincere, educated idealists who felt Russia was socially and politically unjust and repressive. We wanted change. But in hindsight, I now see that none of us had any idea of the monstrous size of the task we had laid out before us."

"And what task was that?"

"To create an open society in which all men and women would attain the full development of their attributes plus the complete satisfaction of their needs." His mouth creeps into a wry twist. "Obviously, we didn't enjoy a great deal of success."

"And how were you going to effect that change?"

"What got into you at that hospital? Usually I'm the one who's full of queries. You've turned the tables on me." He tugs on my earlobe. "That very question was a source of much heated contention in our circle. But we all believed that reform was essential for the agencies of legislation and regulation."

"So you talked and argued every Friday night?"

"We didn't argue—we debated. And we listened to speeches. And read articles." He grins down at me. "And yes, I suppose we argued. But overall, we were a good-natured, fraternal organization. Several of us went on to lofty heights. Fyodor Mikhailovich Dostoevsky, for one." Yevgeny snickers. "Petrashevsky and Dostoevsky always had a stormy relationship, but it made for good entertainment. Mikhail Saltykov-Shchedrin was also part of our circle."

Yevgeny is obviously enjoying his reminiscing. I chuckle inwardly at the decades upon decades that he has been railing against the government.

"Anyway, it doesn't matter who attended the meetings. Suffice it to say, we had some brilliant minds present, and we believed ourselves to be young apostles of progress. Fortunately or unfortunately, at the height of our activities, I was called home to my family's estate in Kaluga because of the death of both of my parents."

"Ahhh. Now we're getting to the gentry part of the story."

He continues as if I hadn't spoken. "For two interminable years, I watched my siblings and neighbors spend hours of idle time in complacent self-satisfaction—drinking, nodding before the fire, playing cards, and visiting relations, then gossiping about them."

"Sounds ideal to me."

He gives a protracted sigh, whether at my comment or at his memories, I'm not sure. "Finally, when I could no longer vegetate in the countryside, I sold my part of the holdings to my siblings and moved back to St. Petersburg.

"While I was gone from the city, the tsar caught wind of the Petrashevsky Circle, reputed by that time to be a focus of civil ferment. Nicholas's secret police convinced him that we were a conspiratorial society dedicated to the forceful overthrow of the regime. Nothing could have been further from reality. Nonetheless, all the members of our group were arrested. When I went to Petrashevsky's house in May, fresh from the country, the police were waiting to pick up stragglers, and they nabbed me."

"But they let you go, didn't they? You weren't part of the Circle at that time."

"Eventually they let me go, but only after they gave me this." Yevgeny motions toward his back.

"May I see?"

Yevgeny removes his red calico shirt and turns his back toward me. From his shoulders to his waist, the skin is hard and grotesquely misshapen. Lacerated skin and muscles had knitted themselves together long ago, creating craters in the flesh.

When he pulls his shirt back on, he leaves it unbuttoned. He musses my short hair with his fingers and circles around me for a final look at his artistry. "Splendid job, if I do say so myself."

"Then I have a suggestion." I rise and button the shirt of this little man of iron. "Rather than sitting here, downwind of the outhouse, let's go for a walk before the last of summer's warmth disappears." I nibble my lip. "Unless . . . unless you'd rather go upstairs."

"Believe it or not, I came here with only one intention: to make certain the hospital hadn't done you in." He takes my hand and slips it around his bent elbow. "A walk sounds delightful."

"Continue the story," I insist as we round the front of the house.

"For weeks, the Investigating Commission took our testimonies, during which time I behaved like an obnoxious, egocentric schoolboy." His Adam's apple rises and falls before he continues. "We were kept in solitary confinement in the Fortress of Peter and Paul. That's where the flogging took place. Among other things."

Yevgeny's pause is lengthy. We walk along in silence until I ask in a soft voice, "What other things?"

"Scurvy, for one thing. But worst of all was the lack of light and sound. The small window grate was so high, I had to stand on the stool to see out of it. The only view was the outer wall of the fortress. Nothing penetrated that cell. Not the heat of the sun. Not sounds from the Neva. Just the damp, dead silence of a grave. I walked back and forth across my tiny room three hundred times every morning, hoping to keep my body and mind fit. I took comfort in befriending the pigeons, who landed on the bars of the window every morning and afternoon to receive the moldy bread I threw to them. Time ceased to move forward. The monotony destroyed my soul."

His steps slow, as if the memories are draining him. "I developed fantasies, fainting spells, hallucinations. When I was released, even my friends didn't recognize me."

In sympathy, I rest the side of my head on his shoulder.

"In retrospect, the physical abuse was the lesser of the two evils, though the beatings certainly did their damage. One young guard in particular was a sadist who derived demonic pleasure from other people's suffering. Beat me like I was a mangy cur. Before my wounds were healed, he'd whip me again." His hand rubs the back of his neck. "I'll never forget that little bastard Shestov."

My breath catches, and my steps halt in midstride. Could it possibly be the same Shestov? How much damage has that son-of-Satan policeman done in his lifetime?

Yevgeny stops beside me. "What is it? You look as though someone just dashed you with ice water."

"I'll tell you later." I tug on his arm to resume walking. "Please, go on with the rest of the story."

"All right, but you must explain why you took such a fright. The rest of the story is short. Because I had been in Kaluga for the previous two years and was no longer part of the Circle, I was pardoned at last. They put me under police surveillance for what they termed 'suspicion of political unreliability.' For a couple of years, the tsar's watchdogs recorded my daily travels, who sent me mail, who stayed in my apartment, who I visited, the newspapers I read."

I squeeze his arm. "How unjust! All you did was meet in someone's home and discuss ideas."

"Ideas aren't allowed in Russia, Anna." His voice is as hollow as a bell without a clapper. "And there you have it—my life as a member of the rural gentry and as an enemy of the tsar. But enough of me. Tell me about your stay at the hospital."

"I learned numbers," I answer nonchalantly.

"Numbers?"

"Oh, you know." My hand flutters airily. "Addition. Subtraction."

He pushes his spectacles higher. "I'm not at all certain I like this Anna-of-the-Short-Hair. Her wisecracks are as difficult to sort out as mine."

I bestow him with the smug look of a cat flaunting its latest catch. "It's true. I was hoping to learn multiplication, but I ran out of time."

"Bravo! Good for you!"

I break loose with a jubilant smile.

By now, we're on the bridge, leaning against the railing. I observe a flat-bottomed boat loaded with firewood while I plan my words. I drop my arm from his, and my voice becomes solemn. "I think there's something else you should know. The young guard you mentioned—Shestov. He's here in Moscow."

Yevgeny seizes my shoulders and turns me to face him. He stares at me, motionless, his eyes probing mine.

"I've seen him. We've all seen him. He preys on young girls and prostitutes." I recount that cold night almost three years ago when I was introduced to the world of prostitution.

Yevgeny runs his fingers though his smattering of hairs. He is surprised to learn that Shestov is now part of Moscow's police force. But he's thoroughly dumbfounded that no one has killed the miscreant somewhere along the way.

I take a deep breath and recount Tatiana's tale, starting with how Shestov duped her into addiction and prostitution. I pour out the details of her hospital stay—the stupor, the incapacitation, the wrenching howls for help—and of Shestov's opium scheme in the brothels of Moscow.

Yevgeny's eyes become as hard as clenched fists, and his voice fills with venom. "My God, the man is evil incarnate. May that heinous predator wind up in the blackest depths of Hell."

YEVGENY AND I part ways—he walks north to his apartment, and I return to Sviatoslavsky Prospekt.

When I enter through the back hallway, Sophia Mikhailovna emerges from her apartment. She scans my new coiffure. Then she moves directly to the point. "I want you to talk with the woman waiting in the Grand Salon. Her name is Madame Karelina." Offering no further information, she steps back into her apartment.

A silver-haired woman sits on one of the divans. As I enter the salon, she places her glass of tea on the side table.

"Please don't think me a crazy old woman," she begins as I lower myself beside her on the divan. "I want you to understand that I'm here today because I love my son very much, and I want his life to be as fulfilling as possible. It's only normal for a mother to want that for her child."

"Be assured, I don't think you're foolish," I reply. "However, I'm not clear on the purpose of your visit."

"I lived near Sophia Mikhailovna's sister before she died. I was hoping to find the same caliber of woman in Sophia Mikhailovna."

"You can expect the utmost integrity from the owner of this house."

Madame Karelina dips her head in a slight nod. "I'm looking for an understanding soul. Sophia Mikhailovna directed me to you." Her hand quivers as she picks up the metal handle and sips from the glass of tea. "You see, my only child, Peter, has been in a wheelchair since he was a boy. He's been an invalid for twenty-two years. As a child, he was never able to play with the other boys or make chums."

"My heart goes out to you. And to your son."

"Fortunately, my late husband left me a generous inheritance, so Peter was able to attend the university. He has a good job as an actuary at an insurance office. He keeps a cheerful disposition and never complains. And he does what he can around the house to help me."

She pauses for another sip of tea.

"Peter and I go to the theater every so often. And he plays cards with some of the men he works with. He'll play chess with anyone who will take him on. But he needs something else, something that's lacking in his life." She runs her finger around the lip of her tea glass.

"Of course. I understand."

"He needs the assurance that he is a man, in the strictest sense of the word. Please, don't think I'm daft."

Before me is a face engraved with life's sorrows. I place my yellow fingers over the blue-veined hand in Madame Karelina's lap. "I don't think you're at all daft. I would be proud to meet your son. Thank you for selecting me."

"You're a very nice girl. I used to pray that Peter would find a wife as kind as you." Madame Karelina straightens her back. "Now for the practicalities. My carriage will drop him off. The driver will assist getting him into the building." Her forehead wrinkles as she surveys the long stairway. "I guess . . . I guess everything happens upstairs?"

"Yes, I'm afraid so. However, Grisha will help him. Grisha is our . . . our . . . " What is Grisha? Barman? Handyman? Guardian? Friend to all who live here? "Grisha is built like an ox. He will carry Peter up the stairs and do whatever is needed to make your son's visit pleasant."

"I'd be very much obliged if Peter didn't have to face ridicule from the other men here."

"If he comes early, perhaps four o'clock, there's usually no one here. Especially on Mondays and Tuesdays."

"Then we'll plan on Tuesdays. And there's one more thing. I'm a mother, you understand, so it's my duty to worry." Her eyebrows tent above her nose. "What about disease? You do take precautions, don't you?" Her pale eyes implore mine.

"Oh, yes. I'll explain all of that to Peter when he arrives." I don't think this kindhearted lady wants a detailed description of how the purple solution is used. "Have no worries, Madame Karelina. Grisha and I will make certain everything goes smoothly."

I accompany Madame Karelina through the vestibule door and to the front of the house. I'm flooded with tenderness as I watch the coachman help her into the carriage. How difficult it must have been for her to come here, not knowing the type of reception she or her son would receive.

Life can be so damn unfair!

Stomach rumbling, I head to the kitchen. To my surprise, Sophia Mikhailovna is seated alone at the table. Both the table and her hands are empty. I suspect she was eavesdropping.

I begin with "Madame Karelina wanted—"

She cuts me off. "You're a very kind person, Anna."

The soft caress in Sophia Mikhailovna's voice gives me pause to study her. Am I mistaken, or are the madam's eyes misty? *Of course*, I realize. She's thinking of Fyedka's cruel lot in life.

"I'll tell Grisha to expect Peter on Tuesdays," Sophia Mikhailovna says, her no-nonsense voice resurfacing. "By the way, while you were in the hospital, you started slouching again."

CHAPTER 33

February
1871

WHEN I MET Peter, my initial instinct was to pity him. The unfortunate guy is trapped in a cumbersome wheelchair, disregarded and overlooked by most others. But I soon discovered his agile mind, self-assured sense of bearing, and devilish sense of humor. Our initial awkwardness gave way to easy laughter, and Peter turned out to be a favorite, albeit atypical, customer.

When I asked him what an actuary is, he explained that he examines life and death in terms of numbers. For instance, I, having survived the hazardous years of childhood, could reasonably live to age fifty-five. However, my occupation might shorten that expectation.

Peter and I grew to be on such good terms that I now meet privately with him at his home. Every Saturday, I hand back his Tuesday night fee, less Sophia Mikhailovna's fifty percent. In exchange, the actuary devotes an hour to teaching me how to multiply, divide, and calculate interest.

Those skills, combined with my ability to add and subtract, prompt me to open a small side-business. I supply a monthly tally for six prostitutes scattered among three brothels. By comparing their income against the debt they owe their madams, I find several errors that, not surprisingly, favor the madam. At such moments, I allow myself to dream that as word circulates about my service saving the women more money than it costs them, my business will soar. Meanwhile, I garner a couple of rubles of income each month.

Every now and then, I look down at my ledger's lines and numbers and am amazed that in Petrovo, I couldn't count beyond fifty.

On the Tuesday just prior to the start of Lent, I'm alone in the house with Fyedka. Although Grisha is home, he's in his bed in the attic, laid up after twisting his back while chipping ice off the doorstep.

Except for the whistling of the north wind, the house is quiet. I take advantage of the peacefulness to spread my accounts over the kitchen table and work on my bookkeeping. But Sasha and Fyedka have other plans.

Sasha struts about the table, pecking at my papers. Now and again, he demands attention by wrapping a claw around my pencil.

"Enough of your tomfoolery!" I scold. But as disruptive as the parrot is, he's less aggravating than the man.

Fyedka has been bored and cranky all the past week, having been kept indoors by the bone-snapping cold. Today, although the clouds are thick, the weather is a touch milder, hovering just below freezing. "Let's go for a walk," Fyedka pleads for the eighth time in the past hour.

My patience is quickly evaporating. "See all this work? As soon as I'm finished, we can go for a walk. You can help me deliver the papers."

"Now." His fist slams the table.

I slap my pencil full-length against the tabletop. "Later. When I'm finished."

"How long?"

"An hour. When the clock chimes two times. Until then, stop nagging."

He sinks into a bitter sulk, clomps to his room, and slams the door. The lock clicks. *Up to his old tricks*, I fume, clenching my teeth.

Sasha climbs onto my shoulder and bestows me with an ear kiss. "Enough!" I put the bird in his cage.

I finish the accounts for the six women before tackling my own. My spirits always sag when I tally up how much money I've earned versus how much has seeped through my frugal fingers. Clothes are the biggest expense, my profession being hard on garments. Lace and buttons can be replaced only so many times before the cloth will no longer hold the stitches. And there's a limit on how many appliqués can be added to cover red wine stains on a gown.

There are also the other tools of my trade, such as a new pot of rouge and, now that my hair has regrown, a box of hairpins. Not to mention the five rubles the cleaning girl swiped from me a year and a half ago. And then, during a recent medical-police examination, someone stole the woolen coat Elena gave me six years ago. Purchasing a replacement put quite a hole in my savings.

Even trivial items exact their toll, such as the mirror I bought Sasha so he could admire himself in his cage. Plus, there's the expense of almonds for the marzipans that are occasionally necessary as friendly bribes for Grisha.

After gathering my papers into a neat stack and closing the ledger, I knock on Sophia Mikhailovna's door to retrieve Fyedka. "Ready for that walk?" Receiving no response, I picture him on his bed, mired in a disconsolate pout. I reach behind the kitchen door for the spare key. Missing again.

Exasperated, I fumble with a hatpin until the lock gives way. But the room is empty. And freezing cold. The window is open.

My throat plummets into my belly. I thrust my head out the window and holler, "Fyedka!" The narrow walkway between the two buildings is empty.

I slam the window closed, dash out the back door, and scour the courtyard. Then I sprint around to the front of the building and ask the yardman if he has seen Fyedka. He shakes his head.

I scan the street in both directions. The wind has turned mean, and the day is as gray as a corpse.

When I dash back inside for my coat and gloves, I also grab the colossal mauve muffler Fyedka knitted for me while I was hospitalized. Perhaps he'd recognize it from afar.

If I don't find Fyedka before Sophia Mikhailovna returns, she'll surely fire me on the spot. I tremble as if doused with a freezing rain.

Plus, I need to find him before the police do.

It's against regulations for family members to live in a brothel. The police could take away Sophia Mikhailovna's license. Thus far, they've been content to accept the madam's hush money. But it would be difficult for the neighborhood constable to explain to his superiors why an imbecile from the local whorehouse is wandering the streets and alleyways.

As I lock the door, I order myself to think. Which direction does Fyedka like to walk? Sometimes over the bridge. At other times, in the opposite direction.

I fly like a bird on the wing to the bridge. Stopping halfway across, I shift from one cold foot to the other as I scour both banks for his bulky physique and his telltale, bumbling amble.

I dash back to the south side of the river. My pace slows to a trot as my hand presses against the knifelike stitch in my side. Up one street, down another. Past livery stables, blacksmiths, and pawnshops. I peer through every store window, between buildings, and behind snowbanks. My hopes pale.

My undergarments are drenched with sweat, but my bare cheeks tell me the air is getting colder. He'll catch his death out here!

As the bells toll the three o'clock hour, the first snowflakes land on my face. I decide to return to the house. Probably Fyedka is warming himself beside the fire at this very moment.

"HOW THE DEVIL did this happen!" Sophia Mikhailovna enters a towering rage. A gust rattles the shutters, adding intensity to the moment.

I squeak, "I'm sorry," a dozen times as I tell the story.

"Don't stand there like a post." Sophia Mikhailovna pushes me toward the door, her mouth pinched tight. "Go find him. I'll send the others out, too."

Reeling from the barbs of the madam's tongue, I return to the streets, where the snow is falling thick and fast, and the wind is as sharp as broken glass. I hasten to the church where Fyedka likes to linger on our walks. I lean against a hitching post while I catch my breath. Low clouds obscure the church's cupolas. Winter's early darkness will be closing in. I need to move faster.

With haggard breath, I question yardmen, doormen, street peddlers, shop owners, taxi drivers, tramps, and lamplighters. Eyes watering from the cold, I peer down alleyways, behind fences, inside parked wagons, within churches. I pick my way around steaming horse dung and slop from chamber pots. My toes are numb, and pain stabs my chest as it pitches in and out. Still, I keep my legs moving.

My imagination conjures up fearsome images. Childlike Fyedka plodding about, lost and confused. Guileless Fyedka falling into cruel, daunting hands. Innocent Fyedka being questioned by the police.

All at once, my feet freeze to the wooden sidewalk. Everything around me keeps moving—creaking carts, droshkies, horses covered with blankets, drivers shouting for right-of-way. Scurrying pedestrians come from behind me and part like a stream around a boulder.

At the corner just ahead, a man in a gray cloak is stepping down from an open carriage. I squint through the whirlwind of blowing snow. Can it be? My legs suddenly feel as stable as soggy noodles.

When both his feet are planted on the ground, his dark eyes spot me. His head pulls back, and a startled expression flows like a wave across his face. Then comes that pleasant smile that has haunted me the past half year.

CHAPTER 34

February

1871

FOREARM PRESSING AGAINST my aching ribs, I puff white plumes of frost.

"Anna, where are you bound?" Beneath his fur turban, Abram Abramovich's face darkens. "Whatever's the matter?"

"I know, I look a fright." My voice is weak as my heaving chest sucks in cold air. "Fyedka. The flute player. He's gone missing."

Vertical lines form between his eyebrows. "Missing?"

"Several hours."

His gloved hand opens toward his carriage. "Can I be of help to you?"

Tongue-tied, I stare at him.

"The owner of that little tobacco shop you and I visited—he's become a client of the bank," he elaborates. "I was just about to pay a call on him, but it can wait. My carriage, my driver, and I are at your disposal."

A wind gust peels my muffler back from my head. I yank the overgrown scarf into place over my hair, which surely must look like a haystack that's been trampled by cows.

"Just tell the driver where you want to go."

Am I really climbing into Abram Abramovich Segalovich's carriage? With a complete lack of finesse, I half lurch, half slither to the far side of the seat, grateful the unfolded hood blocks some of the snow and wind.

My muffler's boundless ends trail over his half of the seat. With hurried, bungling motions, I gather the free-roaming tassels. "Fyedka made this scarf. That's why I wore it."

He hoists himself on the seat and positions his lap blanket across our legs. My breath, which had been coming in steaming pants only moments ago, now comes to a standstill.

I instruct the driver to go into a working-class neighborhood that is thickly studded with cobblers, tallow makers, woodworkers, harness crafters, and metal workers. The unpaved streets are buried beneath manure, dingy snow, and frozen garbage. Soiled straw spills out of stables. Children toss snowballs and obscenities at each other. The driver pulls the horse to a slow walk as we peer into squatty brick warehouses, dingy sweatshops, tawdry bottle shops, and crumbling boardinghouses.

In the half-light of late afternoon, I'm forced to give up the search. Abram directs the driver to turn toward Sviatoslavsky Prospekt.

My eyes continue to squint through the blowing snow.

What's that?

A round figure is sitting on the sill of a shop's plate glass window. A knitted muffler wraps round and round his head, obscuring most of his face. His hands are deep in the pockets of his overcoat.

"Stop here!" I shout.

"Shall I go with you?" Abram Abramovich asks as the driver reins in the horse.

My teeth rake over my lower lip. *Think hard!* I command myself. There must be a way to make some good come from this unfortunate incident.

Fyedka isn't going anywhere, so I close my eyes and piece together a plan. It's a tad dishonest, but the end justifies the means.

"Is something wrong?" Abram Abramovich asks.

My eyes flutter open. "No, not at all. I'm just wondering the best way to approach him." In a penitent gesture, I tuck in my chin against my collar. "You see, Fyedka and I had a falling-out earlier this afternoon. It was quite a clash, actually. I think that's why he ran away."

My tongue feels thick, reluctant to tell even the slightest exaggeration.

"Maybe . . . maybe it would be best for you to walk up to him. Act surprised, and be glad to see him. If you say the words 'flute concert,' he'll remember you straight away. Then, when he's in good spirits, I'll casually wander up. I hate to impose upon you, but if he's still angry with me, he might run off."

Abram Abramovich believes my story, which is profoundly close to the truth.

In no time at all, Fyedka lowers his muffler and begins to chat away, as if he and Abram Abramovich are old friends. His cheeks are rosy from cold and excitement, and steam puffs from his nostrils.

I stroll up to them. "Why, Fyedka, hello! I see you and Monsieur Segalovich are having a wonderful conversation. How lovely for all of us. It's so cold. Shall we go home?"

When Fyedka rises from the sill, I turn to Abram Abramovich. "I'm grateful to you beyond words." I glance about. "We're so close to Sviatoslavsky Prospekt, Fyedka and I can walk from here."

"But it's almost dark. He's half-frozen, and so are you. You must take my carriage," he replies, as I assumed he would.

"But we've already inconvenienced you."

"Nonsense."

Sitting three abreast on the carriage's two-person bench is a tight squeeze, especially with Fyedka's girth. I'm not the least bothered, however, to have my entire left side tightly pressed against Abram Abramovich.

When we arrive at the house, I insist that Abram Abramovich come inside. Understandably, he balks and reminds me that he's not welcome.

"And I'll tell you the same thing you just told me: nonsense. I want Sophia Mikhailovna to know what a fine person you are and how badly she misbehaved the last time she saw you."

His face screws up with skepticism.

"Trust me." I summon the courage to lay a hand on his forearm. How can his arm send prickles all the way through his shirt, his cloak, my glove, and up my arm? "I know that woman as well as I know myself. She'll be so relieved to see her brother, she'll welcome you like a prince."

Abram Abramovich's mouth drops into an oval. "Fyedka's her brother?"

Time runs out for both conversation and hesitation as Fyedka vaults from the carriage and pumps his heavy legs to the door. Abram Abramovich tells the driver to wait, and we follow Fyedka's footsteps in the fresh snow.

In the Grand Salon, Sophia Mikhailovna is wrapped in Fyedka's embrace, her arms pinned to her sides, leaving her with no choice but to sway with him as he rocks from side to side. Eventually she breaks loose and grabs her brother by the shoulders. "Fyedka, darling, where have you been?"

"Had fun walk. But got cold. Then monsieur gave me a ride home."

The corners of my mouth curve slightly upward. My plan is working beautifully.

Sophia Mikhailovna's head swivels toward the man standing just inside the door, his hat in his hand. The joy in her eyes dissipates. Her mouth tightens. Her shoulders pull back. She asks Fyedka, "Is that so?"

"Yes, it is," I intercede, as melted snow runs down my cheeks and off my chin. "Monsieur Segalovich lent me the use of his carriage, enabling us to cover so much territory. That's how we were able to find him." I can hear the challenge in my voice, and as I see from the scowl lines that form between Sophia Mikhailovna's eyebrows, so does she.

"Fyedka." The madam's voice is taut. "Say hello to everyone while I thank Monsieur"—his family name sticks in her throat—"Segalovich."

Fyedka's bear hug engulfs Irina, then Athena, Dunka, and Dunyasha. When he reaches for Grisha, the burly man shakes his head. "Hurt back. But I'm glad you're home." He gives Fyedka a manly cuff to the chin.

Finally Fyedka hugs Peter in his wheelchair. I grimace. In the chaos, I'd forgotten Peter's standing Tuesday appointment.

After Fyedka has bestowed his greetings, Sophia Mikhailovna squares her chin and strides over to Abram Abramovich Segalovich. I watch the madam labor to conduct herself with her normal decorum.

"I owe you my deepest gratitude. I hope you will accept it." The edges of Sophia Mikhailovna's mouth twitch like mouse whiskers. "Please know that you are always and forever welcome in this house."

While my heart leaps about the room with joy, Abram Abramovich's head drops forward in a chivalrous bow. "I thank you for your offer and will avail myself of it."

The reconciliation is cut short by a commotion in the second-floor hallway. "Get out, you yellow-bellied coward!" Something hits a wall with a dull thud. "You self-centered lout!"

Timofei Ivanov appears at the top of the stairs, pulling on his coat while sputtering words of explanation. Matryna, directly behind him, hoists her skirt and gives his hind end a solid kick. "For six years I've taken in your promises the way a cat laps up cream. But your word isn't worth an empty eggshell. I've had my fill of your lies! Layers upon layers of lies!"

Matryna runs out of insults to hurl at him. The void is filled by Sasha, who bestows Timofei Ivanov with the most blustery of admonishments.

At the bottom of the staircase, the man-with-no-eyebrows skirts around the gaping onlookers, head-down, and makes a beeline for the vestibule. Matryna is on his heels. She yanks an umbrella from the tin stand and throws it like a spear at his retreating back. "Take your tall tales and never return!" Then she trudges back up the stairs, engaged in a long spate of sniffling and tear wiping.

Abram Abramovich blinks a couple of times, then replaces his hat. "I'd best be leaving also."

Dunyasha declares, "But you must stay for our celebration!"

"Celebration?" Dunka questions.

"Fyedka's homecoming!" The elf bounces on her tiptoes. "What day is it?" She answers her own question. "Shrove Tuesday! Pancakes! So you must stay. Both of you must stay. Her head pulses up and down, first at Abram Abramovich, then at Peter, who has been sitting silently in his wheelchair, taking in both Matryna's and Fyedka's melodramas.

Everyone turns as the vestibule door swings open. A man enters, his gloved hand dusting the snow off his shoulders.

"And you too, Yevgeny!" Dunyasha shrieks, outdoing the screeching wind. "We have oodles of butter and sour cream and honey and three kinds of jam. What fun!"

The three befuddled men shift their eyes from one woman to the next. We women in turn pivot our questioning eyes toward Sophia Mikhailovna.

"Well," she thinks aloud while her forefinger twirls her dangling faux-diamond earring, "the storm threatens to be a bad one, so business will be slow." Her eyes roll toward the second floor, where Matryna is wailing like Mary Magdalene. "That one will be worthless this evening."

"I'm going upstairs to lie down," Grisha interjects. "My back feels like one of Fyedka's knitting needles is rammed through it."

"So we don't have a barman," Sophia Mikhailovna continues.

"Felitsa is holed up in her room for the evening with a hot water bottle," Irina adds.

Sophia Mikhailovna continues her inventory of employees. "We still have a room empty."

"I like to go Mass on Holy Day," Athena says.

Dunka looks at the Greek woman like she's lost her mind. "You're going out in this weather?"

Athena nods her head of lavish black hair. "Short walk."

"Pancakes!" Fyedka exclaims from across the room, where Sasha is gleefully swinging upside down on his pal's forefinger.

After a few moments of contemplation, Sophia Mikhailovna lifts her hands from her sides in resignation. "Oh, why not? We'll just close up shop this evening."

"Hoorah!" squeals Dunyasha, her toes bobbing.

Dunka drops her chin to her collarbone, rolling her perturbed eyes toward Dunyasha. "Must you always indulge yourself in your tendency to get carried away?"

I turn to face Abram Abramovich. "Will you stay?" I brace for a polite refusal.

"I'll tell the driver to return in an hour."

CHAPTER 35

February

1871

FYEDKA INSISTS ON sitting next to his new friend, Monsieur Segalovich. Yevgeny and Peter sit at one end of the table, and Dunka and Dunyasha occupy the other end. I distribute the plates, silverware, and glasses, chagrined at how thoroughly mismatched the tableware is. Then I take the chair between Irina and Sophia Mikhailovna, which affords an outstanding view of Fyedka's new friend seated directly across the table.

"Grand idea to bolt the door," Dunyasha asserts. "Lent is always such a slow time anyway."

Dunka is incapable of allowing even a superficial blunder by Dunyasha to pass without comment. "Lent doesn't start until tomorrow." Her tongue captures a dribble of butter escaping from the corner of her mouth. "But nonetheless, it is a good idea. We certainly can't lock the door after Lent and risk losing a customer. Everyone knows if you lose a customer on the Monday after Easter, the entire year will be a disaster."

"Aren't you a banker?" Irina asks Abram Abramovich as she plunks down a bottle of vodka in the middle of the table. "You must know a lot about business. Do you think it's true that the first day after Easter can make or break a business?"

Abram Abramovich dabs his mouth with his napkin. "I admit I'm a poor one to ask. You see, Jews don't celebrate Easter. I'm afraid the holiday slips right by me."

Silence swathes the table. Irina, Dunka, and Dunyasha exchange quick glances of concern that we're celebrating the beginning of the highest of holy days with a nonbeliever. Sophia Mikhailovna purses her lips as she looks down at her plate. Yevgeny's smirk implies he's pleased beyond words to share a meal with an infidel. Peter appears unruffled. And Fyedka, having ploughed through his first helping, looks about for his second.

"Putting aside Easter's alleged ability to forecast prosperity or ruin," Peter says to Abram Abramovich, "how do you feel about Moscow's current financial situation? Is this slowdown the prelude to something greater?"

"I hate to be an alarmist, but if manufacturing continues to slacken, the consequences will ripple throughout the city."

"Possibly a recession?" asks Peter.

"What's a recession?" The question comes simultaneously from Dunka and Dunyasha.

Abram Abramovich explains that when the demand for a product or service decreases, the people employed in that industry lose their jobs. They in turn buy fewer goods and services. He likens the economy to a spiral. When started in one direction or the other, it feeds off itself and intensifies.

"Moscow is particularly vulnerable because of its extensive textile industry. When people don't have money, rather than purchase new clothes, they make do with the clothes they have." He turns to his hostess. "In a downturn, I would think your business would be particularly susceptible."

"Yes, my sentiments fall along that line also." Sophia Mikhailovna's mouth presses into a grim line, perhaps because she's worried about future income—or maybe due to her resentment that a Segalovich banker is sitting at her table.

"What about banks?" I ask Abram Abramovich. "Do recessions affect them?"

"Not as much as one might think. First of all, banks keep as much of their money as possible in silver rubles, which hold their value better than paper. Second, in a recession, people are short of cash, so they go to banks for loans, which is, of course, the business banks are in. Third, most banks speculate heavily."

Taking note of the confused looks on most of the faces around the table, Abram Abramovich elaborates.

"We've all experienced how the price of items, such as grain or wool, goes up and down. A bank will gamble, so to speak, on the direction it feels those prices might move. So, even in a recession, when prices go down, a bank can make money by having guessed correctly."

Irina reaches for the vodka bottle. "If it's just a matter of guessing, why don't we all play that game?"

"Because it's a risky game," Peter interjects. "Thousands of rubles can be lost in a single day."

"Peter's an actuary, which is a special type of accountant," I explain to the group. "He knows all about numbers."

"Where did you attend university, Monsieur Segalovich?" Yevgeny asks as the platter of paper-thin pancakes makes another round of the table.

"Please, let's not be so formal over pancakes. 'Abram' is fine. I took my degree here in Moscow."

Yevgeny turns to Peter. "And you, sir?"

"St. Petersburg."

Yevgeny nods. "Myself also, although I dare say I was there a few years prior to you. I went to the city from Kaluga and never had any desire to return to my family's country home."

"Is that so?" Peter asked. "I've always been envious of the provincial life. Seems so healthful for one's spirit."

Yevgeny snorts as he passes the vodka to Peter. "The meaningless daily repetition of country living saps the enthusiasm of even the most spirited youth."

"But living close to the soil seems so honorable, so wholesome."

Yevgeny leans close to Peter. "Unless you want to dally along life's primrose path day after endless day, be enormously grateful for your access to cosmopolitan benefits."

"You're saying that life is stagnant only in the country?" I dimple my smile at him. "The rhetoric I've heard you use is that everything in Russia—charities, universities, professional associations, literature—is oppressive and stunted."

Yevgeny sets down his fork, looks woefully at Peter, then at Abram, and finishes his display of heartache with an exaggerated sigh. "Witness the treatment I receive in exchange for opening her mind to new ideas." He gives a conciliatory nod of his head toward me. "I was referring to the opportunities presented to a man in the city, thereby affording him the prospect that he might attain his full potential."

My eyes open wide in mock dismay. "Only men?"

Yevgeny says as an aside to Peter, "Can you believe how cheeky she is? She presumes that because she has intellectual capacity, she should be allowed to use it." He pivots toward me. "No offense was intended, dear Anna, and I hope none was taken. I have no quarrel with including the term 'woman' in my statement."

I slowly close, then reopen my eyelids to acknowledge his concession.

Yevgeny addresses Abram. "She believes that by merely batting those blue eyes, she's entitled to have her way in every regard. But notwithstanding her eyes or her intellect, wouldn't you hate to be in her shoes? And I'm entirely serious about this. Wouldn't you hate not only to be a woman in patriarchal Russia, but to be of peasant background, living in bondage, without rights and without education?"

No one offers an answer, so Yevgeny barges on.

"Then top that off by becoming a member of the scarlet profession, which incontrovertibly implies that she's considered a menace to morality and a dangerous fount of disease. The result? She is monitored and controlled every day of her life." The airy flutter of his hand encompasses all the women present. "Just like the other femmes fatales at this hallowed repast."

Around the table, jaws drop in astonishment. My colleagues are not accustomed to Yevgeny's brand of humor, and I must make amends. "Satire is Yevgeny's way of making a political statement. He's not serious about us being a menace to morality."

Clenching her fork upright, Irina slams her fist against the table's wooden boards. "I completely agree with what he said. Women have no status and no opportunities."

"Here, here!" Dunka toasts her glass of vodka in agreement. Dunyasha follows suit, as does Fyedka with his glass of kvass.

Irina, Dunka, Dunyasha, Yevgeny, and Peter have drained the first vodka bottle, so Irina retrieves another from the bar. Dunyasha brings to the table what little is left of the ginger cake baked by Sonia's mother, offering it to the men first.

"Thank you, but I must pass." Yevgeny pats his round tummy. "Sweets and flatulence. As you get older, you'll understand."

"I'd like to revisit our discussion, if you don't mind." The request comes from Peter. "If you want to talk about bigoted laws, you need look no further than the ones that protect decent citizenry like ourselves from filthy, blood-sucking Jews like Abram Abramovich Segalovich."

I whirl toward normally benign Peter, aghast at his crass words. Yevgeny, his expression amused, shifts in his chair to admire the young man. Abram's broad forehead is a mishmash of shocked wrinkles.

Then Peter's smile stretches the width of his face. "Well, that's the rhetoric used by our hidebound bureaucrats. Tell me, does this man of impeccable manners look even remotely filthy? Or as though he enjoys meals of blood? Narrow minds can't accept that some of their fellow men prefer to wear skullcaps and have penises that look different from a so-called true Russian's." His tone is playful. "And yes, Anna, I am purposely excluding women from this discussion of skullcaps and penises."

All the women howl with laughter. All, that is, except Sophia Mikhailovna, who undoubtedly continues to regard all Segaloviches as filthy and bloodsucking. To her credit, however, she has kept her veneer of gentility intact thus far.

Yevgeny clasps young Peter's shoulder. "How fortunate to be seated next to a fellow malcontent! So, you agree with me that the huge, stagnant behemoth known as the Russian government mercilessly tries to suppress every human thought?"

Peter nods. "I must admit to occasionally having similar sentiments. But I've never been around anyone who had the courage to express them."

Yevgeny places his arm on the back of Peter's chair. "Well, my son, you have just befriended one."

While Yevgeny and Peter put their heads together and spout phrases such as "a thousand injustices" and "extreme failings call for extreme remedies," the rest of the table turns to Moscow gossip. Soon, peals of laughter echo through the kitchen as two or three conversations take place simultaneously.

But I'm having trouble joining any of the discussions due to the overlapping distractions.

The hodgepodge fragments of conversation.

Guffaws at one end of the table and disgruntlement at the other.

The clink of silverware against plates.

The smear of jam on Fyedka's chin as he wolfs down yet another helping.

The wailing wind and the moaning seams of the house.

But the sum total of the commotion doesn't rattle my brain as much as the singular peculiarity of the situation. How did four such diverse men come to be eating Shrove pancakes with a houseful of whores?

By far my greatest distraction, however, is the proximity of my knees to those of the cordial man seated across the table. The closeness ignites my skin, as if I had just received a hundred slaps with a birch switch in the bathhouse. And tugging at my curiosity is the question of what Abram's Jewish penis looks like.

Finally, the talk becomes muted as everyone settles back in deference to their overstuffed bellies. When the second bottle of vodka is emptied, Dunka wags the bottle by its neck for Irina to get another. But Sophia Mikhailovna shakes her head in a definite *no*.

Peter consults his pocket watch and offers Yevgeny a ride home so they can continue their discourse about the need for a representative government. "But I'm afraid I'll have to ask you gentlemen to help me to my carriage."

"Of course," Yevgeny and Abram reply simultaneously.

Abram rises and addresses the entire group. "Please, all of you"—his head bows specifically to Sophia Mikhailovna—"accept my gratitude for the splendid pancakes and stimulating conversation."

I sense the hostess's nod is one of resignation.

He slides his chair beneath the table. "And how fortuitous that we chanced upon one another this afternoon, Fyedka."

Fyedka's eyes light up. "Will you be at my next flute concert?"

"When will that be?"

"This weekend," Fyedka asserts as if plans are already in place.

Abram shakes his head. "I'm afraid I can't attend this weekend. But possibly the concert after that."

I trail after the three men to the Grand Salon and lift their outerwear from the coatrack. While Yevgeny and Peter shrug on their overcoats, they discuss getting together for a game of chess.

Abram Abramovich faces me as he buttons his cape.

I keep my voice soft and private. "Please don't mention to anyone that Fyedka lives here. It's somewhat frowned upon by the authorities."

He nods. "I understand."

"I truly thank you for your assistance this afternoon."

"I'm gratified that I was able to help." He gives a dip of his head. "Until next Monday. Shavua tov."

After the men depart, I cradle myself in my arms. My lips silently form the words *shavua tov*.

CHAPTER 36

February–June
1871

WHEN I WAS a sprouting girl, I gave credence to the expression that love finds its beginning in the eyes. I cast aside that callow notion long ago. Yet I can't deny that Abram Abramovich Segalovich's dark eyes reach to the bottom of my soul. They are so intense, sometimes they're scary. But when he smiles, oh, how they sparkle!

He's in my bed every Monday, arriving between four and half past the hour, and staying one hour. At first, I worried that Grisha would burst into the room when the standard thirty minutes had lapsed. But for some unspoken reason, Grisha never appeared.

During Abram's first visit, I discovered raw desire and what it meant to be sated. From that day on, I have shamelessly allowed my body to unfold, greedy for the taste of his hungry kisses and the provocative wanderings of his hands.

Sometimes our lovemaking begins with deep passion, and other times with frisky nibbling. It always ends in frolicsome disarray, often with our feet where our heads should be. We chuckle about how many different positions we can fit into an hour. Every so often, we eschew the bed altogether, finding an intriguing substitute atop the huge steamer trunk in the alcove beneath the attic stairway.

I'm certain Dunyasha in the next room can hear our antics, but it bothers me not one bit. Goodness knows how many hours over the years I've been forced to listen to her rollicking exploits with Dunka.

Being with Abram is happiness itself, whether tumbling about the mattress or, afterward, drenched in bliss in the crook of his arm, absorbing the gentle timbre of his voice. If I could purr, I certainly would.

As the months pass and our pillow talk grows more personal, I admit to him that I'm homesick, especially for my cousin Platon—his misadventures and well-endowed imagination. I recount a phase Platon went through, in which he was convinced that people would be better off if they were worms.

Abram props himself on his elbow and looks down at me, his eyes crinkling with mirth. "Worms?"

"He said having a baby in the mother's stomach is too cumbersome and giving birth is too painful. It would be quicker and easier to be cut in two."

Abram chuckles. "That's taking practicality to an extreme."

"His mind was never still. He was forever asking questions: How does the sun make the rainbow? Why don't people's brains spill out their ears?"

With each of Abram's visits, I piece together bits of his life. I learn that he's grateful to God and his parents that he was blessed with an extraordinarily retentive memory; otherwise, he never would have been able to obtain his degree at the university. He spent too few hours with his nose in his books and too many rabble-rousing with classmates.

He chats openly about his career, unaffectedly telling me that he's already been promoted several times. He radiates a resoluteness of character and purpose that I find in very few men. He places a high value on honesty and integrity, if not marital fidelity.

His eyes shine brighter and warmer than a fireplace when he speaks of his children, five-year-old Isaak and three-year-old Sarah. He rarely mentions his wife, but I commit every word to memory. Leah, apparently, is the embodiment of the Jewish woman of valor. Her many virtues include generosity, wisdom, cheerfulness, kindness, and family devotion. I don't ask, but I suspect the woman's attributes include beauty.

EXCEPT FOR MY very existence being turned upside down by Abram Abramovich Segalovich, life at the brothel ambles routinely along. By April, the ferns in the Grand Salon have multiplied with such carefree abandon that the women offer them as gifts to their best customers. The men have no interest in the plants, but a couple of them have the wisdom to take them home as Easter gifts to their wives.

In late May, Sophia Mikhailovna bails Irina out of jail. I recall the madam's vow to oust Irina should she ever again be arrested for fighting. But she either has forgotten that long-ago threat or, more likely, chooses to ignore the transgression because of Irina's commendable behavior the previous week.

Irina had been tidying herself between customers when she heard Matryna's muffled scream. It took both Irina and Grisha to overpower the burly man who was too drunk to feel pain. After all the commotion was said and done, Irina and Grisha sported matching black eyes.

Not long thereafter, Matryna makes an announcement at the breakfast table.

"I'll be leaving at the end of the week. Evgraf Parfenevich Khludov asked me to marry him, and I accepted."

The table goes silent. Everyone knows Matryna neither likes nor respects Evgraf Parfenevich, a customer who's a low-class drinker and gambler.

Sophia Mikhailovna is the first to speak. "Are you certain about your decision? There's no rush for you to leave."

"Yes, Sophia, there is."

We women collectively suck in our breaths. Did Matryna actually address the madam without including her patronymic?

Matryna continues, "Everyone knows there's no place in a brothel for old whores."

"But you still have plenty of good customers," I wail.

Matryna irritably stubs out her cigarette. "If I don't leave now, I might never get another chance."

"But you won't be happy," Dunyasha snivels with childlike innocence.

"What of it?" Matryna's desperate eyes flash from face to face. "How many of you are happy? How many of you like waking up in a whorehouse, looking forward to another night of abusing your bodies? How many of you want to end up an old hag, fucking with cockroaches and worms in the gutters?"

On Athena's shoulder, Sasha gives a nervous twitter.

Matryna composes herself, though her features cry out her weariness. "Each and every one of you will have to leave sometime. Do it before you become a useless, used-up piece of wreckage."

Her departure begins a parade of new girls, each with her own hard-luck story. The first is Gayla, who is replaced by Irma, who is followed by Anisia, who succeeds Lucya. Or did Anisia come before Irma? I've lost track.

THE LAST WEEK in May, Abram informs me that the following Monday, he might arrive a little later than usual. I reply that he should expect the Grand Salon to be decorated. "An out-of-town friend is visiting Sophia Mikhailovna. The door will probably be locked, with a 'Private Party' sign on it. If you knock, Grisha will let you in."

As usual, the house swirls with excitement over the Count's upcoming party. The porcelain china is brought out. Silverware and doorknobs are polished until they're blinding. Vases and garlands of flowers are delivered.

At five o'clock, I begin pacing the Grand Salon, wondering how late Abram will be. I'm far from alone in the room. Little Sonia is topping off the water in the splendid arrays of white lilies and long-stemmed red roses. The caterer is creating pyramids of fresh fruit and lighting the candles beneath the silver chafing dishes. The quintet is tuning their instruments.

Another quarter hour passes.

My patience grows to edginess, and I decide to warn the madam that I might be late for the Count's party.

When my knock on the closed door of Sophia Mikhailovna's one-room apartment is answered with "Come in," I'm taken aback by the statuesque woman seated at the dressing table, anointing her throat with lavender cologne.

Since the night I first saw Sophia Mikhailovna at the police station, I've always viewed her as an elegant jewel, emanating boundless grace, maturity, and self-confidence. But on the nights Sophia Mikhailovna is with the Count, she truly glows. Tonight's radiance isn't due to the flawless cut of her burgundy gown or the sparkle of her earrings. It's as if, for three or four days a year, she's truly happy.

"I'm sorry to interrupt you, but I wanted you to know that I might be a bit late arriving at the party. And I also wanted to see how Fyedka is doing." I feel sad that he'll be left out of all the fun this evening.

Fyedka is sitting on a stool at the edge of Sophia Mikhailovna's dressing table, lining up her assortment of perfume bottles, one behind the other. "Railroad train," Fyedka explains. He points to the three-tiered jewelry box. "Locomotive."

"That's a very special locomotive!" I exclaim and bend closer to examine the honeycomb of little drawers. "It's a gorgeous case," I tell Sophia Mikhailovna.

"Thank you. It was a gift from the Count many years ago." She places a velvet choker with a cameo around her long neck. "Would you mind?" In the mirror, her eyes turn to me for assistance.

To be at eye level with the clasp, I sit on the edge of the bed. As I fasten the necklace, I notice threads of gray in her chestnut hair. I lift my eyes to meet Sophia Mikhailovna's serene, indecipherable gaze in the mirror. "No wonder the Count keeps coming back year after year. You're so beautiful."

"How kind of you to say that, Anna. Yet what I wouldn't give to once again have my youthful charms, the beauty that you now enjoy."

"Obviously the Count finds you irresistible."

"The Count and I have known each other for many years." She runs a powder puff down her nose. "His mind probably still sees me as I was when we first met in Kiev."

"He treats you with such respect, holding your chair for you, taking you to dinner almost every evening he's in town." I don't know the purpose of my statement, only that I feel some ill-defined need to keep the woman talking.

"He's the inveterate gentleman." She pulls on white gloves that reach almost to her elbows.

"Was marriage ever considered?" I scissor my legs forward and back, like a child who knows she's taken her questions a step too far.

Sophia Mikhailovna swivels from the mirror to look directly at me. "He was already married." She rests her gloved hands in the folds of her skirt. "I'll satisfy your curiosity, Anna, and I'll trust that you won't turn our conversation into gossip at tomorrow's breakfast table. Denis and I fell in love when we were young. Like all loyal mistresses, I prayed he would leave his wife. But typical of unfaithful husbands, he didn't. Over the years, I learned to be content with the small moments of happiness that were offered to me." A pause fills the room. "You may have to learn to do the same."

Those last few words ramrod my chest. My legs stop swinging. "Do you . . . do you ever wonder what she looks like? The Count's wife, I mean."

"I used to agonize over it all the time. But I don't anymore. She's dead." The statement exudes Sophia Mikhailovna's usual placidity.

My head jolts back as if a fist has whopped me between the eyes. "She's dead?"

"Seven years ago. It's only since then that the Count and I go to public places together. Dinner and such. Prior to her death, I was kept safely tucked away, like the jewelry in that locomotive."

"Do you . . . do you mind if I ask, why didn't you get married after she died?"

Sophia Mikhailovna gives a wistful sigh. "We spent too many years living at arm's length from one another. The moments we stole weren't real. They were dreams and desires, not reality. We both felt it was best to leave the relationship as it was, rather than testing it with the unvarnished truth of day-to-day living." Her voice takes on a maternal undertone. "I'm sure it's difficult for you to understand why we chose that path."

As if Sophia Mikhailovna's statement was his cue, Abram calls my name. I excuse myself and scramble to my feet, kissing Fyedka's cheek and promising to visit him later in the evening.

In the Grand Salon, I have to chuckle at the astonished look on Abram's face. "You call this a party? It looks more like the tsar's coronation banquet!" He opens his arms wide, encompassing the caviar, the oboe, the dahlias, and everything in between.

I sense an undercurrent of jealousy, which, I smirk inwardly, isn't necessarily a bad thing. I slip my arm through his. "The host is a cherished friend of Sophia Mikhailovna's."

As we climb the stairs, he asks that I forgive his tardiness. "Pressures at work. Besides, I had to pick up your gift on my way over here."

"Gift?"

As soon as my door is latched, Abram hands me a brown sack with loop handles of starched twine and a flat bottom strengthened with an inner layer of corrugated paper.

I lift my eyes to his. "You want me to open this?"

"Of course. It's for you." He laughs as I eyeball the package the way Sasha sizes up a new toy.

As cautiously as if I'm grabbing a wasp's nest, I remove a rectangular item loosely wrapped in cream-colored paper. I lift a corner of the paper.

A cigar box!

Richly inlaid with several types of wood, it's polished to an exquisite luster. I open the lid and put my nose to the velvety lining. Even though the box is empty, an earthy, masculine smell enfolds me like a warm quilt.

Misty-eyed, I look up at him. "This is so beautiful. So much more than beautiful! Why in Heaven's name . . . ?"

He lightly kisses me. "It was one year ago this week that I first laid eyes upon you."

"How ever did you remember the date?"

"Simple. I asked my brother when his wedding anniversary is." His eyes crinkle with delight. "I know giving a lady a cigar box is rather unusual, but I thought perhaps you could use it as a jewelry box. Or maybe keep your handkerchiefs in it."

"And think of you whenever I look at it." I picture Sophia Mikhailovna's elaborate jewelry case. This one is far more elegant, at least in my mind. "Such a kind and thoughtful gift."

Our lovemaking is most tender, and afterward, as we lie in each other's arms, I whisper, "The last time I received a gift, I was fifteen years old. It came from Mademoiselle Elena, the daughter of the estate owner."

"Why would the daughter give you a gift?"

I raise my head to gaze at his sensitive, intelligent face. "That sounds strange, doesn't it?"

I explain that I assisted Mademoiselle Elena for six weeks while she was in a wheelchair. I describe how the twenty-one-year-old and I would sit in the mansion's study while she taught me to read. My voice grows wistful. "I'll never forget the room's aroma of leather and wax."

I replace my cheek against his shoulder and lighten my tone. "When Elena could walk again, she thanked me by giving me a whole trunk full of her old clothes and a potted plant and a canoe."

"A canoe?" His chest vibrates in a long, sincere chuckle. "Your stories always have such a funny twist."

I pause for a heartbeat. My childhood hadn't seemed the least bit funny at the time.

I give a wicked giggle. "Then you'll really enjoy hearing about this. When I first met you"—I snicker again, letting the suspense build—"you reminded me of Malinka, Elena's milk cow."

"I beg your pardon?"

I plant a quick kiss on his chest. "Don't take offense. It's a compliment. Your eyes are big and brown and gentle and long-lashed, like Malinka's."

Male laughter fueled by alcohol filters up from the first floor.

I sigh. Where has the hour gone?

We untwine ourselves from each other, and Abram gets dressed. Then he bids me goodbye. "Shavua tov, my darling."

As I hurriedly pull my appearance together, I reflect on his words: *my darling.* Did he really mean *darling* in the same way that I feel about him? Or was he merely using the term as so many people do, in a casual, careless sort of way? Does he call his wife "darling"?

I'm jolted to reality by a heavy pounding on my door.

"Anna, it's me." Without waiting for me to answer, Abram bolts into the room. He whips the door shut and stares at his hand on the doorknob.

"Did you forget something?" I ask.

He glances at me but doesn't respond. His face is as white as the lilies in the Grand Salon. He paces about the room, fiddling with a cufflink. "I don't quite know how to tell you this, but I'm trapped here. Those men downstairs . . . they're from Kiev."

"I never thought to mention it. Sophia Mikhailovna's friend is from Kiev. Denis Kochubev."

"Ah, yes. Made a fortune in sugar beets." He moves to me and takes my hands in his. "I don't want to hurt your feelings by what I am about to say. Please understand that." He brings my hands to his chest. "I know several of those men. Some are close business associates of my family in Kiev." His eyes flick toward the door. "They mustn't see me here. If it gets back to my family, to Leah . . . It's a devilish situation."

His words cut through me like the north wind. I withdraw my hands from his. "I see."

Beads of perspiration glisten on his broad forehead. "I can't go down those stairs."

"Yes, of course, definitely a ticklish problem." My voice is thin and brittle. He looks so distressed, I know he'd appreciate an understanding smile from me, but I can't summon one. My fingernails dig into my palms. "You can go down the back stairs and out the courtyard door. I'll show you the way."

He pinches the bridge of his nose between his thumb and index finger. "It's not just tonight. Every time I come here, I take a chance."

I step back as if he had struck me. "Are you saying you're not coming here again?"

"No, nothing of the sort. What I'm saying is, ummm . . . it would be much safer if I could just come in the back way. Please understand. The last thing I want is to hurt your feelings."

No, the last thing you want is to put yourself in harm's way.

I keep those words to myself.

He reaches for my hand, but I jerk it away. A red cloud of anger descends on me. He wants to sneak in the back door to see his whore, lacking the gumption to come in through the front entrance.

My thoughts are eclipsed by words I heard just an hour ago. *I was kept safely tucked away, like the jewelry in that locomotive.*

I'm about to tell Abram that he can use his fancy cigar/jewelry/handkerchief box as a spittoon for all I care, but my fury is cut to pieces by another of Sophia Mikhailovna's comments.

I learned to be content with the small moments of happiness that were offered to me. You may have to learn to do the same.

"I'll talk to Sophia Mikhailovna," I say. "I'm certain she'll understand." But my words taste bad, like a mouthful of bitter soap.

CHAPTER 37

November

1871

AFTER WIPING SLEEP'S debris from my puffy eyes, I entwine my fingers and slide them under my head. A contented sigh flutters from between my lips as I gaze at the cheerful autumn chrysanthemums. My heart fills to bursting.

For days after Abram decided he needs to creep up the back stairs, I hauled hurt and anger with me everywhere. But my rational side gained control in the end, allowing me to understand his predicament.

When he arrived for his visit the week following the Count's party, Abram brought me a vase of irises, and now he refills the etched glass container with flowers at least once a month. His bouquets aren't the large sprays of exotic hothouse plants that fill the Grand Salon during the Count's parties. Rather, Abram brings me clusters of daisies or roses or other local flowers from a street peddler, which adds a much-appreciated splash of color to my bland room.

This morning, I check the chrysanthemums for water, then open the drawer below them. I lift the lid on a cheap wooden box decorated with seashells that I purchased at the Palm Sunday bazaar a couple of years ago. Typically, my spirits are lifted at the sight of the banknotes' warm colors. I'll soon have enough for passage to Petrovo.

Lately, however, I've been burdened with the question: *Do I have the gumption to leave?* I'm not at all sure I could tear myself from Abram. For ten months, my life has been built around one hour each week. Not once has he given the slightest hint that the two of us have a future together. But I continue to hope.

To complicate matters, my mind clings to Madame Martynova's question at the hospital: Are you absolutely sure the city doesn't offer you more opportunities than your village does?

Is life truly better in Petrovo than in Moscow? The recent welt on Athena's face, given to her by a customer, struck a long-ignored chord in me. I was quite familiar with the back of my father's hand. More familiar than I prefer to remember.

I swallow hard at the memory of my father's swift temper. Then I swallow again, hoping the scratchiness in my throat is my imagination. But it's real.

I've fallen victim to the influenza that is steadily working its way through Moscow. Felitsa is already laid low by a clogged nose, a rattling chest, and a sweaty fever. Knowing the grippe will eventually march through the entire house, Sophia Mikhailovna directs me to obtain medicine.

At the apothecary's recommendation, I purchase two remedies. One is an elixir that contains a substance known as codeine, which supposedly works wonders for coughs. The second is a white powder called salicylic acid, which eases the fevers and aches of the flu.

For the next three days, I shiver in bed. In addition to the apothecary's new medicines, I stick with the time-honored remedies of garlic soup three times a day, plus lemon and honey in warm water. And I inhale steam from boiling apple cider vinegar diluted with water.

For supper, Dunyasha brings a soup of noodles and chicken broth to my bedside. "Works better than garlic soup," the elf insists.

"That's nothing but drivel," Dunka calls as she strides by my open bedroom door. "Garlic soup is far better."

On Friday, sleet pummels Moscow intermittently throughout the day. Irina, Athena, and Sophia Mikhailovna are added to the sick list. I sit on my rumpled bed, the cold damp seeping into my bones, and scowl at my dresses though the open door of my armoire. Should I work tonight or not? The sweating has stopped, and the tight pressure in my head has eased somewhat.

Even as I cough up yellow phlegm into my handkerchief, I know I'm capable of working—I simply don't want to. But we all are anxious about the downturn in business, which Abram fears will worsen. Deciding that I need to make what rubles I can, I push myself off the bed and get dressed.

Downstairs, my first stop is the sideboard, where I swallow a generous dose of the codeine cough elixir. I take a second swallow for good measure.

I drop onto a divan. My mind feels as soft and formless as a dollop of porridge. My head falls forward in half sleep as I wait for the first customer.

An hour later, I'm back downstairs, waiting for my second customer and wondering if I'm a fool for trying to work while I'm still sick. A spasm seizes my chest. I take another hefty gulp of cough medicine.

I lower myself into a Voltaire chair and rest my drowsy eyelids, feeling as though I have only half my wits about me. Moments later, three men in their early twenties strut through the door. They stomp their feet, flinging bits of ice from their boots and onto the Oriental carpet. One of the men attempts to hang his caftan on the rack. He misses the hook, watches the garment fall to the floor, scratches his crotch like it has bugs, then lurches away. Already in their cups, they bump into each other as they swagger toward the bar. They remind me of a gaggle of fattened geese, ricocheting off one another in their mass attempt to move forward.

Grisha rings the upstairs bell twice to call down two more women. He doesn't offer the men anything to drink.

Before I go to the bar, I try to blow my nose, but the congestion won't loosen. I try again but succeed only in making popping noises in my ears.

"Hello, gentlemen." My raw throat has me sounding like a hoarse bullfrog.

The three men bestow me with liquored-up grins. One guy boasts a mouthful of tobacco-stained teeth with white patches on his gums. The second man has greasy hair tied back with a string and a face like a warty toad. The third man, shaped like a keg, has a wolfish smile, lips that glisten with spittle, and the abrasive stubble of a two-day beard.

"This sweet little treasure is mine, boys." The keg guy steps so close to me, the toes of his boots are under my skirt. "You two can have what's left over." Vaporized alcohol rolls from his mouth.

I take a step backward.

The clod tries to focus on my face, one eyebrow raised while the other droops over a squinting eye. "My trouser mouse needs warming up real quick." He fondles his crotch.

The other two whoop at their friend's nimble wit.

He drapes his arm around my shoulders. "Come along. I've been waiting for this a long time." He leads the way up the stairs and turns toward the front rooms.

"Back this way." I shuffle down the hallway to my rear room. Standing at the foot of my bed, I croak, "Perhaps you'd like to clean up before we start. I have some sweet-smelling solution." My words flip back and forth, from frail to strident.

A mocking smile shows more gum than teeth. "Clean up? I thought that was what you were for—to polish my knob."

"I'm told the solution heightens a man's pleasure," I fib.

"Shut up and pull up your skirt. You'll have to open wide to fit my friend in." He puffs up like a rooster.

I steady my eyes to keep them from rolling. How many times over the years have I heard a similar line?

Without warning, he shoves me onto my back atop the bed. My congested head whirls. He climbs onto the mattress and straddles my neck with his knees.

He pulls his limp penis out of his trousers and holds it in the palm of his hand as if presenting me with a present. "Say hello," he tells me.

"Hello," I rasp, disappointed it's not already enlarged. Events would have moved along more quickly.

A deep freeze enters his voice as he mutters, "Pull down those drawers so Yarik can have a look at you."

> Yarik!
> The uneven eyebrows.
> The gummy smile.
> Turning toward my old room along the front hallway.
> *I've been waiting for this a long time.*

Why didn't I recognize him! My chest tightens with apprehension. Is he still the off-balance boy from three years ago? Or has he matured into a madman?

CHAPTER 38

November

1871

THE YARIK GUY'S hand lashes out for my necklace. He pulls it tight around my neck, digging its metal chain into my skin. "I said, take those drawers off."

I lift my hips and do as I'm told. His red-rimmed eyes continue to roll off-kilter, one large with a raised eyebrow and one narrowed in pure aggression. He lets go of the necklace.

He seems content to fiddle with himself, running his limp penis across my cheeks and lips. "Last time, Yarik was very disappointed." His chin juts forward. "You won't hurt Yarik's feelings again, will you?"

When I don't answer fast enough, he slaps my face with his free hand. Cold fear sweeps through my feverish body. I must keep my wits about me.

His hand claps over my mouth. "If you scream, this hand will be around your neck. Understand?"

Grappling for air through my plugged nose, I nod.

His hand drops from my mouth, and he belches. "Where were we?" His eyes have a glaze of lunacy. "I believe you were admiring Yarik." His flaccid member snakes about my face again. "Kiss Yarik."

I run my lips along the shaft.

"Deep. Give Yarik a deep kiss."

As I work on the man, I gulp breath through the side of my mouth. Minutes go by, and they lengthen into an eternity. He's no closer to finishing the job, and he's growing increasingly agitated.

How can I escape from the room? My thoughts flounder in a foggy blur. Perhaps it's the cough elixir. Or maybe I'm weak from being sick. It's as if my mind has quit me. I know all I have to do is scream, but I'm not sure my feeble voice will carry downstairs or even to the next room. And what will this maniac do to me in the time it takes Grisha to rush up the stairs?

Livid over the lack of progress, his nostrils flare as he growls obscenities at me. I wish he'd yell at me, alerting Grisha and Sasha. But he keeps his voice low.

"You're going to have to do better than that." He leans forward and wedges his forearm against my throat. He presses harder until my windpipe feels as if it might collapse.

My arms flail as I writhe for a single gulp of air. Gripped by wild terror, I roll my eyes toward the door. It wavers like a heat image, retreating farther and farther away. There's a ringing in my head.

"You give Yarik what he's been waiting for all these years! You hear me?"

I nod as best I can.

He lifts his arm from my neck. Blessed air flows into my chest.

As my chest heaves, an image comes to me. Sophia Mikhailovna's whistle!

"I'd like . . . "I gasp another deep breath. "I'd like to kneel before Yarik, tell him I'm sorry. Honor him like he deserves. Please, may I show you?"

The madman's lopsided gaze reveals his struggle to comprehend.

"You sit here." My palm rubs circles on the edge of the mattress as my breathing slows. "And I'll kneel in front of you and give Yarik the admiration he's due."

As I slide onto the floor, my left fingers stroke his shriveled shaft while my right hand searches the floor under the bed. *Where is it? It's been here since the very first day!*

At last my fingers brush the whistle. While I position it in the palm of my hand, I stretch my neck toward his penis and begin licking it.

He grabs a fistful of my hair in each hand and crams my face deep into his crotch. "Show Yarik you're sorry about the way you treated him!"

I press my eyelids tight to keep his pubic bristle out of my eyes. Thick snot rolls from my nose. I breathe in small puffs of air around his penis.

Still clutching my hair, he pulls my head up. Pain sears as hair tears from my scalp. "You worthless, yellow-haired bitch." His hands plunge to my shoulders and shake them savagely. "Yarik wants to hear an apology from you." He slaps my face, and I taste blood in my mouth.

"Of course," I squeak. I gently put my free hand around Yarik. "I owe you an apology."

My hand catapults down and clamps, with all its strength, on one of his balls. Simultaneously, my other hand brings the whistle to my mouth, and I blow with all my strength.

He yells and kicks me in the ribs. I knuckle over in pain. He hits the back of my head with something solid. Blue sparks explode against a background of black.

CHAPTER 39

November

1871

THROUGH A VEIL of eyelashes, I glimpse three people sitting in chairs beside my bed. The sliver of light streaks through my head like a thunderbolt, leaving a trail of white pain. I snap my eyes shut.

Someone squeezes my hand. A nose is blown. Voices try to cut through the fog. I sink back into oblivion.

The next time my eyelids part, the window's sunlight churns up waves of nausea. I guess it to be late afternoon.

I hear a light tread approaching my door. I don't rotate my head to look. My neck bones feel so tortured, I fear they might break.

Felitsa creeps into the room and sits on the edge of my bed. The slight shift of the mattress skewers my back like a hot fireplace poker.

Eyes closed, I hear the concern in Felitsa's voice. "We were so worried about you. Grisha almost killed that bastard. Literally almost killed him. Sophia Mikhailovna was in bed with the grippe when she heard the whistle. She raced up the back stairs. Grisha was already here, throwing the guy around the room. She jumped on Grisha's back to stop him." Felitsa giggles. "In her nightgown, no less."

I want to speak, but my tongue lies dead. The best I can do is a soft grunt.

Felitsa continues, "Do you want something to eat? Perhaps some tea?"

"Tea," I breathe, "and flu powder."

"You want some of the white flu powder? But you're almost over the flu. Honey, are you aware of what happened to you? You got beat up."

My eyes still closed, I give a single, tiny nod. If the salicylic acid can soothe the aches of the flu, then it might lessen some of my misery now.

After I swallow the powder, I sleep for the better part of two days, giving my body the chance to begin mending.

———

MONDAY MORNING MY pain has lessened, but I still feel half-dead. I lie in a milky consciousness, listening to the household awaken. One by one, the women who aren't bedridden with influenza come to my room, each of them praising Grisha for his swift action. They say Sasha has never made such a commotion as when he heard me scream. I don't remember screaming, but nor do I question the accuracy of their account.

Throughout the day, the women bring me flu powder, tea, soup, and a ginger cake sent specifically to me by Sonia's mother. With moistened rags, they wipe off the dried blood where the madman pulled out my hair.

By midafternoon, I can't put it off any longer. After taking a healthy dose of white powder, I slowly stand up, gripping the headboard for support. No new pains jolt me—just the now-familiar throb in my neck and lower back. The stuffiness in my head is gone, but my nose refuses to stop leaking. I cram the corner of a handkerchief up my left nostril and leave it there.

I cautiously shuffle to the armoire, look in the mirror, and gasp.

My swollen cheek is purple. Dark circles drag at my eyes. Swelling and a scab mark where my teeth cut my lower lip. My nose is raw from its incessant dripping.

My scalp behind my left ear is sore, and there's a scabby patch on the top of my head where hair is missing. On the back of my skull is a tender knot the size of my thumb.

I have a necklace of bruises. I turn sidewise in the mirror and lower the shoulder on my nightgown. Each of that son-of-a-bitch's fingers left a yellow and purple memento.

My strength runs out of me like water, and I sink onto the edge of the bed. My chin drops, and warm tears soak through my nightgown. Every night we put ourselves at risk with strangers—men so drunk they vomit on the bed, men with evil tempers, men devoid of scruples. Living here is like roasting in a slow fire.

What will Abram think when he sees me? "Strikingly beautiful," he called me a year and a half ago. Would he still consider me strikingly beautiful with my head jammed into that lunatic's crotch? Will today's bruises open his eyes to what I really am? Perhaps he'll realize that I'm a public woman, to be used and abused by men from all levels of society. Perhaps he'll leave and never return. And perhaps that would be best for all concerned.

I wake from my nap when the hallway clock chimes three times. I give myself an agonizing sponge bath, then slip the faded teal-blue dressing gown over my flannel nightgown. I tie my oily hair with a ribbon. After haphazardly straightening the sheet and coverlet, I prop the pillows against the headboard, slump against them, and pull the covers to my waist.

CHAPTER 40

November

1871

THE SOUND OF the back door opening and closing filters up the rear stairs, followed by the muffled voices of Abram and Sophia Mikhailovna. When Abram begins taking the stairs two at a time, I quickly wipe the drip from my nose.

He bursts through the open doorway, then stops as if hitting an invisible wall. His mouth tightens and his fists clench. His eyes are as wide and black as I've ever seen them. With slow precision, he closes the door behind him.

"Oh, Anna!" he breathes. "How could this have happened to you?"

I realize his rhetorical question is an expression of his concern. Nevertheless, I have to fight the urge to throw a sarcastic response back at him. *Yes, indeed, how could such a thing happen to a harlot?*

He tosses his overcoat and hat onto the vanity's chair and haltingly moves toward the bed. I force my lips into a meager smile and lift my arms to him. He gingerly lowers himself onto the edge of the mattress, and my arms reach around his neck. He clasps me to him, which unleashes new thunderbolts of pain. I sink back onto the cushion of pillows.

Both his hands take hold of one of mine, and he lifts it to his lips. "My God!" His head shakes in disbelief, a knot between his eyebrows. "What kind of beast would do a thing like this?"

Again, I have an acerbic response, but I hold my tongue. My body may be beaten and bruised and my head crammed with enraged thoughts, but that doesn't give me the right to throw harsh words at this kindhearted man.

He strokes my hand. "Tell me what happened."

My slight shoulder-lift courses pain up my neck. "A man was drunk."

"Do you know who he is? I'll find him. The louse needs to be held accountable for this."

"Please, Abram, try not to dwell on it. Things like this happen." My handkerchief swipes my raw nose.

"Where was Grisha while all this was happening?" He immediately slides his lips to one side, probably realizing the absurdity of his question. "Where are you hurt?" As I list my injuries, his jaw muscles tighten and retighten like he's chewing his cud. "You must get out of here!"

I level my eyes at the man before me. I'm sick. I'm in pain. I hate my life. And I'm without hope. Abram and his well-meaning but pointless suggestions can go to the Devil!

Convinced of the wisdom of his recommendation, he grips my hand tighter. "Do you understand me? You must leave this place."

In a moment of frozen silence, I squeeze my eyes shut and slowly withdraw my hand from his. My hurts can't be soothed away with his caresses. In fact, the touch of his hand right now incites a searing anger. Biting words erupt one at a time. "And just where the hell do you propose I go?"

My eyelids spring open just in time to see his head jolt back as if slapped. "But you can't stay here."

My insides scream with violent fury. "Don't you think I'd leave if I could?"

His mouth moves, but no sound comes forth.

I continue to fling savage words at him. "Or do you think I enjoy the merry life of a prostitute? Tell me, Monsieur Segalovich, how in God's name would I support myself?"

He reaches for my hand, but I slide it under the covers.

Like a breath that's been held too long, all my frustration demands release. "Do you suppose the thought of leaving never occurred to me? How dimwitted do you think your little whore is?"

Abram swallows, then slowly bends a knee, lifting one leg onto the mattress so his arm can cross over me. "Anna, please, I didn't mean to imply you're dimwitted. Seeing you hurt like this sickens me."

I give my head a small fling, which I instantly regret as sharp pain encircles my neck. "Is that so? If you're so concerned, why is it you never suggested I leave before? It's been rather convenient for you, hasn't it, to take a little walk after work once a week for a quick tryst? A nice diversion from the pressures of making money."

He looks at me as if I'd cut him with a knife. "I never meant to hurt you, by any word or deed." His eyes plead with me, but I give him nothing in return. "You must know how much I care for you. Tell me that you do."

My lips tighten as I glare at him. I intend to keep him on tenterhooks a while longer. Possibly forever.

As if backing away from a scorching fire, he straightens his back. Deep lines frame his mouth. He places an open palm on each of his thighs. "Ever since I started visiting you, the worry has gnawed at me that you are in danger."

One side of my mouth curls with mockery. "In danger? Well, you're right. Only I haven't thought about that possibility for a few months. I've thought about it for four years."

He gropes for words. "Couldn't you get a job in . . . in a clothing shop or an office? True, factories are cutting back right now, but government offices, insurance companies, even banks need women who can assist with paperwork."

My fury lashes out at him. "And how am I supposed to do that if I can't read? I have to be realistic when I look at my future, Abram. I suggest you do the same."

With open-faced bewilderment, he gapes at me. "You can't read?"

Now it's my turn to be puzzled. Why would he think I can read? My tone softens when I reply, "No. Of course not."

"But you have a couple of books on your vanity."

My head droops forward, which provokes my nose to run. I wipe the dribble. "Those are just for decoration."

"And you told me that the daughter of Petrovo's owner taught you to read."

I look up at him, my anger spent. "She taught me a few words, nothing more. Besides, that was so long ago, I don't remember any of it." My voice cracks and my lower lip quivers. I fight the tears, but they brim over anyway.

"If you can't read, how do you keep accounts for other women?"

"I can do basic arithmetic. And I draw pictures."

"Pictures?"

"At the top of each page, I draw a picture of the woman whose account it is. Down the columns, if the expense is a new dress, I draw a dress. If it's a pair of new shoes, I draw—surely you get the idea."

Slowly he maneuvers until he's shoulder to shoulder with me, his back against the headboard. He lifts an arm behind my shoulders and softly draws me to him. My dark temper melts away like wax before a flame. I put my head on his chest, and he softly strokes my back.

Tears of despair gather strength until my entire body convulses. Every time I think I can pull myself together, I break down again. It's not until the front of his shirt is drenched that I'm too exhausted to cry anymore.

"Anna, I want you to listen carefully to me. Are you listening?"

I hiccup a nod.

"You must learn to read. I will teach you."

"You can't do that."

His arm gently tightens around my shoulders. "What do you mean, I can't?

Are you saying you're too simple-minded to learn, or that I'm too thick-headed to teach you?"

I pat his chest. "Stop joking."

"You must learn to read. And who better than me to teach you? I'll bring some of Sarah's books. No, I have a better idea. I'll bring newspapers and journals. We'll read them together. If you're going to read, there's no point in reading children's fairy tales. You might as well learn something about the world in the process."

I can hear the ardor in his voice, and his enthusiasm is contagious. Literacy would open so many doors!

"Are you willing to try?" he asks. "Because I know if you try, you'll succeed."

My wary nature takes control. "But you're only here for an hour a week. By the time we . . . we . . . then it's almost time for you to leave."

"I'll begin staying an hour and a half. Is that an acceptable arrangement?"

"Well, yes, but . . . " I chew my lower lip. The opportunity might never present itself again. "I really would like to learn. But Sophia Mikhailovna will expect compensation for that extra time."

"I'll see that she gets her rubles."

I silently vow to disappoint neither myself nor this kind and wonderful man.

CHAPTER 41

August
1872

WITH UNPARALLELED DILIGENCE, Abram teaches me first the alphabet and then how to put letters together to form words. By the following summer, I can read shop window signs and newspaper articles. At last I can make lists for myself and spell out simple words for my accounting business.

Toward summer's end, Abram delivers a message I knew had to arrive sooner or later. He will miss several visits in a row. The annual Great Fair at Nizhny Novgorod is a lucrative source of revenue for his uncle's bank. When both bank employees attending this year's Fair came down with typhoid fever, his uncle's finger tapped Abram to finish out the season.

My heart slows like a clock that needs winding. A full month without him!

During the ensuing week, my whole world seems out of balance. I keep imagining Abram's tongue flicking across my neck, my shoulders, my breasts. I spend a ridiculous amount of time hugging my pillow and wondering what his beard feels like in the mornings when he wakes up, or when it's freshly shaved. Countless times a day, my mind slips into some ill-defined future where Abram comes home to me daily.

When the first Monday of his absence rolls around, I drag open my drapes only to be greeted by a morning deep with melancholy. Rain flows like tears down the windowpanes.

The murky light falls on Abram's cut-glass vase of last week's bluebells and lilies of the valley. The faded blooms torment my lonely soul. I open my precious cigar box and inhale. More than a full year has passed, but its aroma still lingers.

"Oh, Abram," I whisper to the desolate room. "I so desperately want to be in your life—your real life, not a Monday fantasy."

I trudge downstairs and greet little Sonia, who's tidying the kitchen. I poke around, looking for something to eat, but nothing appeals to me. In the end, I flop into a chair at the table with some tea and a small plate of leftover boiled ham and potatoes.

The snippet of a girl stands beside the table, shifting her weight from one foot to the other. Obviously, the child has something on her mind.

"Would you help me finish this?" I ask, pointing to the ham and potatoes. "I'm not very hungry."

"No, thank you. I had plenty to eat at home this morning."

Considering her matchstick arms and legs, I doubt that's true. Then again, based on the little breasts poking against the thin dress, perhaps she's merely going through a spindly adolescent stage.

Sonia slips onto the chair next to me. As I push the food around the plate, I sense a pair of large brown eyes on me. "Is everything going well with you?" I figure the sooner the girl comes out with it, the better.

"Anna, are you happy with my work?" Sonia's reedy voice begs for reassurance.

"Why, yes, of course. Completely happy. Why do you ask?"

"Because Olga yelled at me yesterday."

Olga joined the house a couple of months ago. She's a loner who rarely joins our hen sessions.

"What did Olga yell at you about?"

"She said the sheets were as dingy after I wash them as before I wash them. She said she's going to complain to Sophia Mikhailovna." Sonia's slim shoulders droop like the petals of a plucked flower. "I try hard to do good work. My mother can't afford for me to lose this job. The problem is, the water's brown. I scrub and scrub, but without clean water, I don't know what else to do."

My heart brims with pity. I've been told that Sonia was nine years old when she first showed up at 903 Sviatoslavsky Prospekt, desperate to find buyers for her mother's baked goods. She first eased her way into the house on a part-time basis four years ago when she pitched in to clean in preparation for the Count's annual party. When Fyedka moved in, Sophia Mikhailovna made a deal: if the women would help look after him, she'd hire Sonia to take over some of the cooking and other chores that belonged to us, including laundering the sheets. The girl is as quiet as a mouse and so dependable that everyone takes her for granted.

"I think you do fine work," I assure her. "Don't let Olga make you glum. Sometimes her liver gets out of order."

"Her liver gets out of order?"

"Just an expression. It means she tends to be peevish."

"Peevish?"

"Grumpy."

Sonia scrunches her face. "You know lots of big words."

I cock my head. *Lots of big words?* Such an odd thing to hear. It wasn't long ago that I was the one awed by big words. I offer Sonia a little fib. "I love how my sheets smell after you wash them."

"Truly?"

"Truly. I think you're the best housekeeper we've had. And I think your employer feels the same way."

Sonia's smile blossoms more beautifully than any of the resplendent bouquets the Count ever lavished upon Sophia Mikhailovna.

I slide my ham and potatoes in front of Sonia. "I'm not going to finish this."

The girl's wrists poise on the edge of the table. "If you're sure . . . "

"I'm sure."

The girl attacks the food like a famished wolf. As I finish my tea, Dunka and Dunyasha enter the kitchen, wearing facial masks of mashed cucumbers and honey. Dunyasha, the portrait of dejection, is complaining that Dunka isn't any fun anymore.

"If you don't like the fun we have," Dunka goads, "why don't you find yourself a man?"

Dunyasha bleats like a lost lamb. "Stop being mean." With a sigh of inconsolable gloom, she slumps onto a chair.

"Why don't you both leave off quarreling for once?" I bark. Usually I'm amused by their little tiffs. But today, a Monday without Abram, I find no pleasure in anything.

Both women swivel their heads to give me a level look.

"You're a crabby old hen this morning," Dunka admonishes.

"Don't you ever get tired of scraping like a couple of alley cats? You two act like worst enemies instead of"—I glance at the girl who is scooping up the last of her potatoes, unsure how to finish my statement—"instead of best friends."

I sigh at what is undoubtedly my wasted effort at shielding little Sonia from the full story. Tiptoeing around this particular mare's nest is probably unnecessary. Sonia is far from stupid and has probably figured out the particulars on her own.

"Anna, guess what's coming to town this weekend!" Dunyasha, of course, can't wait for an answer. "The circus! I want to go so badly. But sourpuss won't go with me. What do you say? Want to go?"

I shake my head, but Dunyasha is as relentless as a hound on a fresh scent. "It would be so fun. When was the last time you went to a circus? Not since you were little, right? Pleeeeeeease!"

The truth is, I've never been to a circus. It might be interesting to see what it's about. Plus, it would occupy my lonely mind.

"You win. I'll go."

Dunyasha claps her hands as delight spreads across her face. I've never understood how a grown woman can be so adorable when she behaves like an eight-year-old.

I catch Dunyasha's eye and purposefully motion my head toward the girl who is cleaning her dirty plate in the washtub. Dunyasha's confused eyebrows come together. I roll my eyes toward Sonia. Dunyasha silently mouths, *What?*

Vexation gnaws at my stomach. Am I the only person in this house who cares a whit about the girl? "Maybe Sonia would like to go with us."

Sonia whirls about, her eyes as wide as saucers.

With her tendency toward the dramatic, Dunyasha squeals, "That's the most marvelous, wonderful suggestion in the whole entire world!"

"Oh, no." Sonia shakes her head emphatically. "I haven't any money."

I offer to pay her way.

For the second time today, I'm rewarded with Sonia's smile. It's actually a darling smile. And her face, though thin, is engaging. She'd be attractive if she had some meat on her bones.

"There, that's settled," I affirm. "But Dunyasha, I know someone else who would like to go."

Dunyasha ponders this for an eternity before comprehension dawns. "Do you think Sophia Mikhailovna will allow it?"

Dunyasha's qualms are justified. Taking Fyedka into a crowd of people has its perils. "Perhaps we can talk Grisha into going with us for added safety."

Later, after Grisha makes it clear that he will not be cajoled into going to any circus, I set to work on Irina. I'm finally able to persuade the big woman to be our bodyguard, but only because I have the persistence of a ram in rut.

THE CHOSEN DAY boasts a gloriously blue sky and tolerable humidity. A keyed-up Sonia arrives at the house with her face scrubbed pink and her eyes as bright as stars. I'm certain the dress she's wearing is her best, even if it is a tad small.

Knowing Fyedka can't walk the whole distance to the far north side of the city, Sophia Mikhailovna gives me money to hire a cab. As we climb into the carriage, Sonia's eyes are round with expectation. Fyedka sports an open-mouthed grin. Dunyasha's open hands flap up and down with giddy excitement, and Irina complains it's too early to be out of bed. I, meanwhile, feel trepidation about traveling to a strange part of town accompanied by a guileless child, a retarded man, and a woman who's as flighty as a colt.

The circus greets us with an extravaganza of motion. Colors vibrate wildly. Children, parents, and lovers, all dressed in their best and brightest clothes, meander through the grounds. Hordes of boys in long blue caftans swoop like ravens around the pedestrians in their attempts to peddle their paltry wares. Fyedka spots the food vendors and wants to sample everything: nuts, kvass, apples, sausage, pig's tripe, pickled herring, juicy strawberries.

We ignore the hawkers promoting clowns who climb on greasy poles, a stage performance of the glorious Battle of Sinope, an acrobatics display, and a performing dog. We want to spend our kopeks on Petrushka, the grandest puppet of all time.

"Please come in! Petrushka will soon begin!" the barker trumpets from a booth beside the opening of a low, white, unimpressive tent. "Ladies and gents, come watch our show! It's three tons of fun!"

Inside the musty tent, a blaring drumroll and a clash of cymbals cue the curtains to open. The audience breaks into thundering applause as up pops the infamously ugly Petrushka wearing his ever-present pointed red cap.

Through nine acts, laughter rocks the benches as the hunchback, with his long nose, beady eyes, and useless, swinging legs, meets with a steady stream of other characters: the Policeman in a uniform, the Gypsy carrying a whip, the Doctor wearing all black.

I laugh along with the others, delighted to see Fyedka's big belly jiggling with glee. During the show's final scene, Petrushka portrays a new character with a heavy accent.

> *I'm an honest little Jew*
> *Known well to you,*
> *How I love gold,*
> *To have and to hold.*

I lean back on the bench, as if to put more distance between me and the hurtful words.

> *All I hold dear*
> *Is gold, gold, you hear?*
> *With gold, even in Hell*
> *Jews can live very well.*

While the audience stands and claps in time with the final music, I remain seated, my veins on fire with rage. Why do people feel better about themselves when they toss ridicule at someone who's different from them? And why do they so commonly select Jews to be the unjustified target of their scorn?

I'm still fuming as we file from the tent, shielding our eyes against the bright sunlight. I summon Peter's words at Shrovetide: *Narrow minds can't accept that some of their fellow men prefer to wear skullcaps and have penises that look different.*

I scold myself that it's senseless to stew over people's bigotry. I'm helpless to change it. Besides, I don't want to think about Jewish penises right now.

Fyedka pulls me by the arm toward a hawker who wants to guess his weight. I give the greedy little man three kopeks. Fyedka hands Sonia his well-licked lollypop and lumbers up the steps onto the stage. The man, twirling his goatee, circles Fyedka and scrutinizes him from head to toe. After completing his third go-round, he pronounces Fyedka to weigh 195 pounds. The man invites Fyedka to step on the scale. Its arrow points to 224 pounds.

With great fanfare, the hawker admits he underestimated Fyedka's manly size and offers him a choice of prizes. Jowls happily puffed, Fyedka debates between a whirligig and a red balloon. When he finally selects the balloon, Irina ties its string around his wrist before we continue our journey through this make-believe world.

Sonia and Dunyasha are skipping side by side like young lambs when Sonia suddenly stops and begins waving both arms over her head. From the throngs of milling people emerges an outrageously handsome young man in his midtwenties. He hugs Sonia, kissing both her cheeks. She introduces the dark-haired fellow as her cousin Gavril. Upon discovering that he came to the circus alone, we invite him to join our troop.

By the time we enter the big tent, seats are scarce. We're forced to separate, with Sonia, Gavril, and Dunyasha seated several rows above Irina, Fyedka, and me. I keep reminding Fyedka to keep his balloon in his lap so the people behind can see the performers.

The crowd thrills to the high-wire act, the bareback riders in short skirts, the trapeze artists, and the fearless sharpshooters. A man in a red jacket and tight black britches enters a cage with a ferocious tiger, cracks his whip, and bids the tiger to do various tricks in exchange for raw meat.

I glance behind me at Sonia and Dunyasha. Gavril is crammed between them, and all three are clapping whole-heartedly. Gavril shares Sonia's wide, easy smile.

Following the performance's grand finale, Fyedka fusses when we tell him it's time to leave. With a little cajoling and a fried pirozhki to eat on the way home, he settles into a quiet pout.

After the carriage drops off Gavril, I tell Sonia that her cousin seems like an exceptionally pleasant fellow.

Sonia nods, her chin nearly crashing against her collarbone. "He is my most favorite cousin. And I have thirty-four of them."

THE EXCURSION WAS a tonic for everyone, and when I reach my room, I am completely unprepared for what ensues on the other side of the wall.

"You slut!"

"You don't own me! Whose fault is it, anyway, that I went to the circus without you?"

"You empty-headed two-timer! A man, of all things!"

Downstairs, Sasha adds his own shrieking.

Something is very wrong. The two women have had so many rows that at times it seems they spend their lives squabbling. But this afternoon isn't merely spirited bickering. They're turning their full wrath on one another.

On the heels of the blaring commotion of the circus, the ceaseless yelling leaves me with a headache. I flop onto the bed and cover my head with the pillow. I ache for the serenity of home, of sitting beneath Petrovo's misshapen willow tree on a sunlit day while the murmuring river dawdles past.

The torrential hollering persists the remainder of the afternoon. As I leave my room to begin the evening. Sophia Mikhailovna is standing in Dunyasha's doorway, shaking her finger. "You two finish this in the morning. Now get dressed." When Dunyasha tries to present her side of the story, Sophia Mikhailovna cuts her short. "I don't give a damn what happened. Both of you—downstairs in ten minutes. Is that understood?"

By noon the following day, the story has trickled throughout the brothel. Dunka had reconsidered her belligerent stance and showed up at the circus after all. She was greeted by the sight of her lover giggling and, according to her, "cavorting with a man" inside the big tent. Dunyasha, hurt over Dunka's initial refusal to go to the circus—and resentful that Dunka had taken her possessiveness a step too far—allowed Dunka to believe the misperception that she had been flirting with the man.

The sparks fly as Dunka removes her belongings from Dunyasha's room. The two women have shared their lives for so long that ownership of most of their possessions is difficult to determine. Jewelry, scarves, hairbrushes, icons, even a chamber pot had been jointly purchased while the women were walking arm in arm through markets and shops.

Not content merely to face off over who has claim to the spray perfume bottle, Dunyasha elevates the dispute by alleging she's trapped inside a whorehouse with a yellow ticket all because of Dunka. Dunyasha had been engaged to an apprentice printer when she first met Dunka. Too young to know any better, she complied with Dunka's entreaties to break off her engagement and cohabitate with Dunka at 903 Sviatoslavsky Prospekt, "a decision I've come to regret deeply."

Dunka's comeback is that Dunyasha would have ended up sleeping in a factory barracks or under a sewing machine. "No man would have put up with your flat chest and narrow hips, not to mention your infantile behavior."

Dunka's mockery cuts Dunyasha to the bone. A weeklong silence ensues as the two women sulk in their respective rooms.

As the standoff enters its second week, I happen to enter my own room while Sonia is putting fresh sheets on the bed. I pitch in to help, and when the task is completed, Sonia's tongue drifts across her upper lip. "Can I ask you a question?"

"Of course."

Rather than look at me, Sonia fluffs the pillows. In a tone of utmost gravity, the girl reveals that her bleeding has begun. Although her mother has explained that every woman is plagued with this monthly curse, she refuses to speak further on the subject. "What do I do with the . . . the mess?" Sonia's freckled cheeks turn the color of cherries.

I take a deep breath and explain how to place rags inside her underwear. Sonia replies she doesn't own any underwear. My heart fissures, and pity flows from it. I hand her a few kopeks to purchase underwear. "Until then, wrap the linens around you like a diaper."

Sonia fusses and fidgets with a lock of hair that crosses her cheek, finally asking whether it's normal to have a stomachache. I assure her that it's quite typical and that a hot water bottle offers some relief. "Sophia Mikhailovna keeps one in this house, and I'm certain she'll allow you to use it."

From the next room comes a strange sound, like a puppy begging for the food that its master holds temptingly over its head. Then on the other side of the wall is the sound of weeping. As it continues, I realize it's the two women sobbing in unison.

Knowing what is sure to happen next, I give Sonia's arm a quick squeeze and tell her to come back if she has any more questions. I hand the girl the dirty sheets from the bed and guide her from the room.

The sobs evolve into low moans and, ultimately, cries of delight. The storm has run its course. Dunka and Dunyasha are back together.

TWO WEEKS AFTER the circus, a Friday night drizzle cleans the air of dust and presents an azure morning sky. Still missing Abram beyond words, I put on a freshly purchased secondhand bonnet and walk across the bridge. I hope to push aside my loneliness by trying something new—a shopping excursion to the chic stores of the upper-class Moscovites.

Amid the joyful ringing of church bells, I head toward Petrovka Street, a glorious boulevard lined with elegant boutiques, apartments, and hotels situated in tall brick and stone buildings, which are a far, far cry from the log-and-mud huts of Petrovo. Bubbling with awe, I window-shop at jewelers, florists, and pastry shops.

But I also find myself increasingly disquieted. The sidewalks teem with women adorned with enormous hats trimmed with ribbons and feathers. Some ladies push baby strollers, parasols perched on their shoulders. Others have their gloved hands tucked around a dapper man's elbow. More times than not, a silver-handled walking stick is hooked over the man's other arm. These people reap the benefits of lives that are completely inaccessible to me, and I wind up feeling so awkward and noticeably out of place that I begin walking with my shoulders slumped and my head down.

At last! The object of my search! A store that sells writing materials.

As I step through the heavy oak door, I enter a world softened by plush carpet runners between aisles of books. Silent, well-heeled customers have their noses poked inside weighty tomes. Some of them stand and read amid the wooden shelves, perhaps trying to decide which is truly the right book for them. Others encase themselves in leather reading chairs at small square tables situated alongside the plate glass window.

I chuckle silently. I am completely and unmistakably certain this posh store is the exact opposite of the "small, out-of-the-way, low-key" bookstore where Yevgeny works.

Trying to portray a confidence I don't feel, I wander the aisles, thumbing an occasional book for the sheer pleasure of feeling the pages glide through my fingers. It gladdens my heart to realize I can read more than half the words on the pages.

Reminding myself why I came into this store, I browse the writing supplies and select a box of pale-yellow sheets bound together with a festive lemon-colored ribbon. If only I can summon the courage to put the blank pages to use. My plan is to write a letter to my family.

On the way to the counter, I spot a table piled helter-skelter with books. Its sign advertises *Discount*.

I pick up a book entitled *Russian Poets and Their Verse, 1825–1850*. The book randomly falls open. I haltingly unravel the words.

DARK EYES
By Yevgeny Grebenka

Oh, your dark eyes, eyes so passionate,
Eyes that burn through me, eyes so beautiful.
How I love you, and I fear you so.
When I saw you first, was my fatal hour!

Oh, your eyes are darker than the sea's darkest depths!
Within them I see my dear soul's demise.
In them I can see the flame of defeat,
It's been burned into my poor suffering heart.

But I am not sad, and I feel no grief,
I draw comfort from my own destiny:
Everything fine in life that God gave to us,
I have sacrificed to your fiery eyes.

My blood sinks to my toes, leaving me lightheaded. As my lips silently reread the lines, I begin to hear the rhythm of the wording. My body tingles. To think that the first poetry I ever read would give such breathtakingly beautiful voice to my own feelings! Regardless of the book's cost, I have no choice but to own it.

CHAPTER 42

August
1872

FINALLY! THE REAR door slams, and boots leap up the back stairs, two at a time.

To my unbounded delight, Abram sweeps me into his arms. His lips cover every bit of my face and neck as his foot nudges the door closed. "My precious Anna."

We run our fingers across each other's lips, eyebrows, chin, neck. The feel of him, the scent of him—they're like a long-awaited salve.

We unburden ourselves of clothing. When he pulls back momentarily to gaze into my eyes, I see a hunger that wants to devour me. But much to my bewilderment, he releases me instead and retrieves a box next to his leather attaché case beside the door.

I reach for my old teal dressing gown, draped over the headboard. However, he grabs my wrist, forcing me to drop the faded garment. Eyes crinkling merrily, he shakes his head.

"From the Fair," he says, and hands me a white box embedded with silver swirls.

I lower myself onto the edge of the mattress and have barely begun to untie the silver ribbon when he blurts, "I knew the moment I saw it, you had to have it. Because of your eyes."

The silky nightgown is of the palest blue, accompanied by a matching pair of delicate satin slippers. Also in the box is a robe of a complementary cobalt blue, adorned from top to bottom with gold brocade.

I run the plush fabric through my fingers. "I've never owned anything so lovely."

"From Persia," he says.

Rising from the bed, I slip on the robe and tie its sash. The material feels like water flowing over me.

Abram walks to the alcove under the angle of the attic stairwell and lowers himself onto the lid of the steamer trunk. With a raised forefinger, he makes a leisurely circle in the air.

I twirl slowly. As his gaze pours over me, my breath comes fast and strong.

"Luscious," he whispers. "Now come to me."

I do his bidding, and as I stand before him, he slowly unties the sash. His hands slide between the sleek material and my body. His lips go to my belly. Then he pulls me onto his lap.

Once the steamer trunk has served its carnal purpose, we sit unclothed at opposite ends of the chest, facing each other with our backs against the opposing walls of the alcove. Our bent knees place our feet at each other's hips.

"I missed you more than I could ever have believed possible." His voice is deep and rich and sincere.

I take in his words hungrily, praying for more. *Say it, Abram, say it. Tell me you can't live without me any longer.*

But those words aren't spoken.

"So," I quip when the silence verges on cumbersome, "what is it you did at the Fair, besides pine for me?"

"I made money for the bank. Which means a nice paycheck for me, so I could afford to buy stunning Persian garments for a beautiful Russian woman. Plus two more presents."

My eyes grow as large as an inquisitive kitten's. "Two more?"

"You greedy little hedonist!"

We rise from the chest, and Abram pulls on his trousers while I slip on my new robe. He moves his valise next to the bed, where we sit beside one another, our backs against the headboard as usual.

"The next two presents are related to your new reading skills. But I warn you, the final present is a test." He winks. "And you won't get the first of the two presents until next week. And it's not just for you. You have to share it with Athena and Irina and Dunka and Dunyasha and Felitsa and—"

"Share?" I playfully punch his arm, my curiosity piqued. "What are you talking about?"

"I'm saying your second gift is a subscription to *The Grainfield*. What better gift for a houseful of women? Recipes galore. Decorating ideas. All the latest froth and bubble of fashion tips. Not to mention some fairly decent stories."

I contemplate those wonderful black-satin eyes. "How kind of you to think of the others."

His face turns serious. "You must promise me, Anna, that you'll read it aloud. Particularly to Sonia. You said you wanted to teach her to read. Well, now you're ready to do just that."

"You have my word." My smile flares. "And I'll teach Sasha also."

His eyes roll at my joke. "And now for the third and final present." With a flourish, he retrieves a flat, rectangular package from his valise.

As I remove the ribbon and unwrap the waxed paper, I'm greeted with the divine smell of rich chocolate. Inside a tin box are a dozen or so pieces of candy, each with a different shape and nestled in its own little paper wrapper.

"These look scrumptious!" Chocolate is a rare and luxurious treat. The only times I taste it are when the Count brings some to Sophia Mikhailovna. "Let's have one now!"

But Abram's eyes have sobered. "You missed the reason I bought them for you. Remember, this is a test of your new skills."

A test of my reading skills? I replace the lid and labor with the unfamiliar words. "Assorted Bonbons. Made by the loving hands of the Holy Trinity Women's Community, village of P . . . P . . .'" I focus on the word, sounding out the letters. "'Village of Petrovo, in the province of'"—a band tightens around my throat—"'province of Tambov.'"

Petrovo! This box came from Petrovo! I lift it over my head to search its underside, as though a blade of rye or a bit of yarn may have somehow traveled the distance along with the chocolates. But, of course, there's no such thing.

I continue to clutch the box, aware of nothing except its magical feel in my hands.

A spiderweb of bittersweet images drapes over me. The monastery at the edge of town. The village road with its wheel ruts. The Maximov mansion on the hill.

So vivid is my recollection, I can smell the heady fragrance of new-mown hay, the smoke from the chimneys, the manure as it's worked into the garden. I feel the penetrating heat of the massive stove in our hut. The security of my mother's arms as she rocks me back and forth. Little Platon's thin arms around my neck.

Realizing that Abram is patiently waiting, I blink my moist eyes. "Thank you."

"Good, you're back. For a moment, I thought I'd lost you."

"I'm sorry, I couldn't help but think of the village. And my family. It doesn't seem possible that Platon is fifteen now." I inhale deeply as I look at the generous man sitting beside me. "But enough of that! I can't look backward while you're here with me." I plant a large, noisy smooch on his cheek. "You bought the candies at the Fair?"

He nods. "A boutique selling expensive sweets set some out as samples. I popped one in my mouth and found it to be sinfully rich. When I looked at the label and saw the word 'Petrovo,' how could I help but buy a box for you?"

I swallow, hoping my voice will hold steady. "This means a tremendous amount to me. It's not the rubles you spent, but the thoughtfulness you've shown." I pick up a bonbon and feed it to Abram, his lips and tongue sampling my fingers.

"Speaking of rubles," he says, "you'd be amazed at the cost of these little sweets. You'd think those nuns sprinkled them with diamonds instead of nuts. But that doesn't seem to stop people from buying them."

How odd! It appears tumbledown Petrovo has found a potential source of prosperity: a dainty delicacy that appeals to Russia's high society.

AFTER THE LAST customer leaves, I open the drapes in the Grand Salon and peer between the louvres of the shutters. It's half past two in the morning. A cat saunters in the otherwise unruffled stillness of the street. The silence is broken only by the steady *tick* of the tall clock upstairs.

I climb atop a barstool. In the flicker of a single oil lamp, I sink into pensive melancholy, my thoughts a jumbled patchwork. The bonbons from Petrovo evoked a cascade of emotions. As with a seasoned stew, the individual flavors are difficult to recognize.

Resentment at being banished to Moscow.

The heart-ripping need to be part of a family.

Sympathy for the villagers' poverty and backwardness.

Nostalgia for what once was, but can never be again.

During my early years in the city, I lived day by day in my recollections of Petrovo. But as time went by, I began to see only shadow-dappled memories—memories so lacking in substance that I had difficulty clinging to them. Tonight, however, the bonbons churned my emotions like a pot of my mother's soup on the big clay stove.

My intention is to pen a short letter telling my family that I chanced upon the nuns' delicious candies, which prompted me to write this note. I'll give them a brief description of the hustle and bustle of Moscow, followed by my hope that all is fine with them. In closing, I'll include my address, should they desire to write me back.

But as I put the pen to my new yellow stationery, the words are awkward and impersonal. Earlier this evening I was in Petrovo, walking its road, hearing the crow of its roosters, listening to the chatter of gossip at the village well. But those sensations are already fading like a morning mist. The flat, unbroken horizon of grainfields is a long way behind me, and those memories, once colorfully vivid, have become dim. The longing to return to Petrovo is falling away like a dry, crumbling piecrust. Perhaps I've drifted too far from home to ever go back.

THE FOLLOWING AFTERNOON, I'm heading out the door to post the letter when Sophia Mikhailovna summons me to the kitchen. With slow deliberation, she pulls a chair from the table and motions me to sit across from her.

My muscles tense.

Sophia Mikhailovna leaps into her subject. "I know you're fond of little Sonia, but surely you've noticed she's not so little anymore."

I nod. "She does good work, hard work—work that grown women would find difficult."

"That's exactly my point." The madam looks directly into my eyes. "She does excellent work. She's dependable. And she understands the rules of this house."

I wait for more, but Sophia Mikhailovna sits deathly still. Suddenly my heart gives a terrified lurch. "No!" My head wags back and forth. "No, you can't!"

The slight cock of her head seems to challenge me with *Who says I can't?*

"Tell me I'm wrong! Tell me she's not joining the house!"

"I know you have tender feelings for the girl—"

My open palm slams the tabletop. "That's precisely the correct word. *Girl.* She's still a child. You can't expect her to do that type of work."

"Her mother expects it."

Heat surges up my neck as I recall the odious creature with the sour eyes who came to the door with her pitiful daughter two years ago. *Men pay extra for a fresh hole. A lot extra.* "Sonia's mother is surrendering her own daughter for money?"

"She's surrendering her for food for the empty bellies of her other children. The woman is desperate. She's on the verge of having her teeth pulled out and selling them." Sophia Mikhailovna pauses to let that sink in.

I fold my arms and press them against my chest in tight opposition.

"Upstairs, Sonia can make ten times the amount I pay her for cleaning. And she wants to continue doing the baking to earn extra money."

"Are you saying you've already finalized this?"

"That's correct."

"She's barely a woman!"

"But the point remains—she *is* a woman." Sophia Mikhailovna's eyes bore into mine while her fingers slowly drum the table. "Be realistic, Anna. We haven't had a dependable girl in Matryna's room since she left. And you know that competition in the sex market is vicious. Plus, Abram Abramovich told me he expects Moscow's economic slowdown to worsen. If we are to survive, we need dependable employees who can bring in new customers."

"By selling schoolgirls? You don't care one whit about her, do you?" I lift my open palm beneath my chin. "Look at me. Look at all of us. Beatings. Disease. That's the life you're condemning that child to!"

Sophia Mikhailovna fixes me with a stare that's as immobile as a block of ice. "Perhaps you have other options for Sonia and her mother?" When I don't respond, she continues. "Perhaps Sonia can take her body out on the streets and see what she can dredge up there?"

I'm livid—at Sophia Mikhailovna's callousness, at myself for the lack of an alternative plan, at society for abusing innocent girls. I change tactics. "You can't hire her. Not legally. She's not old enough for a yellow ticket."

"Eight months from now she will be. Until then, she'll work here and live at home. As far as the medical-police are concerned, she's still just our housekeeper."

It doesn't matter a smidgeon what I say. The deal has already been struck.

My shoulders go back, and my chin goes up. My voice is cool. "I guess I put misplaced faith in your integrity." I stand and push my chair back with such force, it topples backward. Leaving it lying on the floor, I stalk from the kitchen.

Damn Sophia Mikhailovna and her impenetrable wall of reserve! How can she be so heartless as to sentence a sweet child like Sonia to a life of prostitution? How old will the poor thing be when she gets the pox? Or pregnant? Or beat up?

Tears sting my eyes. My despair is as much for myself as for Sonia. Once you accept a yellow ticket, your future is as dark and treacherous as a moonless night that lasts forever.

I glare at the envelope clutched in my hand. Why in God's name did I choose *yellow* stationery?

As I stomp through the Grand Salon, I spot Grisha arranging freshly cleaned glasses behind the bar. I toss my letter on the countertop and hoist myself onto a stool. Plunking my elbows on the counter, I drop my chin onto my closed fists and glower at him. "I want a glass of red wine."

He looks at me from under shaggy eyebrows and slowly pours a third of a glass.

I stare at the wine, eventually lifting my eyes, but not my head, to look at him. "I'm sure you already know."

He gives a single nod.

"Do you approve?"

He hunches his shoulders in a deep shrug. "It's not for me to approve or disapprove."

I take a sip of wine, relishing the warmth in my throat. I run my thumb around the rim of the glass. "How can she be so hard-hearted?"

His fingers comb his red beard. "It's her defense in a hostile world."

I study the chubby-cheeked face and the bull-like shoulders. This is one of those moments when Grisha shows the keen insight that lies beneath his brawn and jolly humor.

He continues philosophizing. "It's much the same as Irina's jokes and swift temper. We all need weapons in order to survive."

CHAPTER 43

December
1872

DEEP IN DECEMBER, on the shortest day of 1872, Sophia Mikhailovna calls a meeting at the kitchen table. Most of the women are present, plus Fyedka and Sasha, when she starts with "I am afraid we've attended the last of Count Kochubev's parties."

After the murmurings of disappointment die down, the madam clears her throat and continues. "Unfortunately, the Count suffered a stroke last month. His mind is fine, but he's having difficulty moving his right arm and leg. Most of the time, he's in a wheelchair."

"The Count in a wheelchair!"

"But he's always so vibrant."

"I can't imagine."

When the hailstorm of condolences subsides, Sophia Mikhailovna's chin tilts upward. "He has requested that I move to Kiev to oversee his care."

Everyone seems to stop breathing. At long last Dunyasha squeaks, "You're not going, are you?" Her face is drained of color, as if she might faint dead away.

"I will join him in mid-January. I was fortunate to find a purchaser for the business. Her name is Madame Olesya Vasilevna Kurygina." She fidgets with an earring. "Madame Kurygina ran a house in Yaroslavl, but when the textile mill shut down, her business fell off and she moved to Moscow."

Irina's head drops backward, and she stares at the ceiling.

Sophia Mikhailovna isn't finished. "Grisha will also be leaving. He's taking a position at the Count's sugar beet mill as an apprentice machinist. With his intelligence and determination, he's sure to do well."

A poisonous miasma plunges everyone into depression. A couple of women mumble their best wishes. Then, with seemingly nothing left to say, we excuse ourselves from the table.

Irina's door is open. My friend is lying crosswise at the foot of her bed, hands behind her head, staring at the ceiling.

I assume the same position at the head of the mattress. "What are we going to do?"

"Now that you can read and cipher numbers, I know what *you're* going to do. Hell if I know what *I'm* going to do."

"Will you stay here? Or move to another house?"

Irina snorts. "I think I've lost the bloom of youth, wouldn't you agree?"

"So you'll find other work?"

"Where? In a factory sixteen hours a day, not paid enough to support myself?" Irina withdraws her hands from behind her head and slams both fists into the mattress beside her hips. "Damn it all!"

I ponder what effect the recession had on Sophia Mikhailovna's decision. More than once, I saw concern pinch the madam's face as she gazed about a Grand Salon that was half-empty, even on Saturday nights. Of my six bookkeeping clients, two of them can no longer afford my services.

Dunka shambles into the room. Behind her trails Dunyasha, looking like a porcelain doll that could shatter at any moment. The two women flop onto the floor and rest their backs against the mattress—Dunka on one side of the bed, between Irina's and my heads, and Dunyasha on the other side, between our feet.

"Don't hesitate to come on in, girls." Irina's voice is humorless. "My room is your room. Just help yourselves."

"I can't believe she's leaving," Dunyasha wails.

"What's there not to believe?" Irina's reply is tart. "Sophia's getting a little long in the tooth to be earning a living in a brothel, wouldn't you say?"

"Although I'm sad about what happened to the Count, this is probably the best thing that could happen to her," I assert. "She has to be approaching the legal age limit for madams, if she hasn't passed it already."

"Plus, she needs to get Fyedka out of here before the police lose patience," Dunka proposes. "I'm dumbfounded he lasted this long."

"Where's the Count's wife?" Dunyasha asks. "Surely she's not going to allow his mistress into the house."

When no one else answers, I do. "She's been dead for a number of years."

Dunka asks, "How do you know that?"

I shrug my shoulders, not caring that, with Irina looking at the ceiling and Dunka and Dunyasha staring at opposite walls, not one of them can see my response.

"If his wife has been dead a long time," Dunka questions further, "why didn't he marry Sophia before now?"

"I didn't hear her say they were getting married," I respond. I find it curious that, with the madam's forthcoming departure, the women suddenly refer to her merely as Sophia, without her patronymic, as if they're all the best of friends.

"I wonder if the Count can still get it up," Dunka muses. "I mean, if a person's arm and leg are paralyzed, doesn't it stand to reason that the parts in between also don't work?"

"Both of Peter's legs are paralyzed," I point out, "but the part in between works."

"What if this Olesya Vasilevna Kurygina doesn't accept that Dunka and I are . . . the way we are?" Dunyasha squeaks.

"We're illegal, you know." Dunka's tone is dour.

This sets me reeling. The relationship between Dunka and Dunyasha is accepted as commonplace by everyone in the house. I never realized that their variety of love is a crime.

"She could turn us in to the police, and we'd be exiled to Siberia." Dunyasha's troubled voice rises to a fevered pitch.

"If she's unhappy with the way we are, we'll just leave," Dunka states with finality. "We'll find another house and take our customers with us."

Without speaking a word, Dunka and Dunyasha rise in unison and leave the room.

For several minutes, all I hear is the pendulum in the hallway. Eventually Irina pronounces, "Mark my words. Things will never be the same."

My thoughts mirror Irina's. With the departure of Sophia Mikhailovna and Grisha, the fabric that held the house together will surely unravel.

CHAPTER 44

January

1873

SOPHIA MIKHAILOVNA'S ANNOUNCEMENT hangs like a pall over the house. I try not to dwell upon her departure, but it tinges my every thought. How did five years of nights slide past? What will this house be like without her? Without Grisha? I should leave, but where would I go? Fears whirl chaotically within me.

The night before Sophia Mikhailovna, Grisha, and Fyedka are scheduled to depart, after the last customer has gone, we women host a farewell party. Grisha opens several bottles of champagne. Athena serves her savory Greek stew with its mouthwatering aroma of cinnamon and cloves.

The party starts off with carefree laughter as the women recall our madam's adages.

> *Sex is an instrument of barter.*
> *Honest service in exchange for honest rubles.*
> *It is our firm desire to please you in every way.*
> *It's all in the wrapping.*
> *Is that understood?*

And our favorite:

> *Get it out, get it up, get it off.*

Our howling laughter comes so hard and so frequently, I lapse into a fit of hiccups. I tell the group, "I'll never forget—*hic*—what she said to that policeman the night—*hic*—she rescued me from the jail." Despite my words, my memory fails me. "What was that little peacock's name?"

Sophia Mikhailovna responds, "Chizhov."

"Yes. Chizhov. Sophia Mikhailovna put her face right in Chizhov's and told him that Shestov was lower than an earthworm, harmful to the interests of civil society, and a mockery of the law."

Irina sighs. "It was a beautiful sight to behold."

Numerous stories are rehashed, until eventually a dull silence settles over the women. The party breaks up when Dunyasha melts into tears.

Grisha rises from his barstool, and I give my stalwart guardian a lingering hug. He climbs the back stairs to lie down on his bed in the attic for the last time.

I ascend the main staircase and stop halfway up. My eyes roam over the Grand Salon. The new madam came by the house last week to measure the downstairs rooms. After giving the furniture a long, appraising look, she announced she would bring her own furniture with her.

Olesya Vasilevna Kurygina is thin, but not willowy like Athena or petite like Dunyasha. Rather, she's gaunt and bony. Her motions are quick and foxlike. When she smiled, which was only once during her visit, her eyes remained small and hard. Jewelry adorned her arms, fingers, neck, hair, yet it did not create the impression of refinement. Although she's younger than Sophia Mikhailovna by a good ten years, the older madam, even with her settled contours of maturity, is by far the more alluring.

I continue up the stairs, their creaks portraying weariness from the many footfalls that have tread upon them. I pause to regard the impassive face of the tall clock. "Goodbye, faithful timekeeper. I'll miss you." With a clarity I've rarely experienced, I finally and fully understand the impossibility of turning back the hands of time.

When I reach my room, I freeze at the sight of a moonlit outline of someone in my bed.

"Anna?" It's Fyedka. "Can I sleep with you?"

I walk across the dark room and fumble to find his chubby hand. "Why do you want to do that?"

"We're leaving. We're going to live in a big house far away."

"Won't it be nice to live in a big house?"

"*This* is a big house."

"Your new house is even bigger than this house."

"But I don't want to leave my friends." His thick voice blends sorrow and apprehension. "I don't want to leave Sasha."

Fyedka entered a fit of gloom when Sophia Mikhailovna stood firm that the bird would not accompany them. I don't understand why the madam was so adamant about it. After all, the parrot would ease the transition for Fyedka. Plus, there would be servants to clean his birdcage. I wonder if the parrot is simply a too-poignant reminder of brothel life.

"We'll take good care of Sasha. He likes living here. Besides, if you took Sasha, then not only would we be unable to see you and your sister and Grisha, but we would miss Sasha, too. And our hearts would break to lose *all* of you."

"But what if no one likes me at the new house?" Fyedka continues to fret. "Anna, I want to sleep in your bed tonight."

I'm not sure of the wisdom of such an arrangement. Despite his childlike ways, he is, after all, a grown man—and probably subject to the urges of grown men.

"Why don't we do something special on your last night?" I suggest. "Let's sleep in the Grand Salon with Sasha. You can sleep on one divan, and I'll sleep on the other one. And we can watch the fire in the fireplace."

Downstairs, the fire's dying embers bathe the red walls with a warm glow. Fyedka promptly begins to snore. Meanwhile, I can't stop the swirling thoughts in my head. With Sophia Mikhailovna gone, it's inevitable that the house will change. And probably not for the best.

Truth be told, I'm the one who needs to change. I live in a whorehouse, and I'm hopelessly in love with a married man.

Not only do I need to move on, but I have to make certain little Sonia has the means to leave this place. I must, starting immediately, teach her to read and do numbers. Maybe twice a week I can tutor her. Another possibility is Madame Martynova from the hospital. She may have suggestions that can help Sonia.

My focus must remain steadfast. Sonia and I will establish new lives.

I'm nodding off at last when someone kneels beside me.

"Anna?" Sophia Mikhailovna whispers. "Anna, what's going on? Why are you and Fyedka in the Grand Salon?"

"Fyedka came to my room, unable to sleep. So I suggested we do something special for his last night here."

Sophia Mikhailovna nods and shifts her weight as if getting ready to rise. I put out a hand to stop her. We'll never have another chance to talk.

"I hope the Count is healthy enough to appreciate what he is finally getting. You've both waited a long time to be together."

Sophia Mikhailovna rests her weight on her heels and her tone turns maudlin. "A bittersweet twist to a love affair that has lasted almost a quarter of a century."

"I want to thank you for the chance you took—"

Sophia Mikhailovna cuts me short, speaking softly. "Coming into this house was a good opportunity for you at the time. It turned into a beneficial arrangement for both of us. But now that you know how to read and do mathematics, you must move on. You must find a job that will allow you to advance in your pay. You must. Because when you leave here, you'll be alone."

The last sentence chills me as if a frost has crept across my skin. Does she mean that when I move out, I'll be losing the support and solace of women who have meant so much to me over the years? Or does she mean that Abram will never marry me?

Apparently, it's the latter, because her next statement is "Tell Abram if he's visiting his family in Kiev, he's always welcome to attend a flute concert. He knows where Denis lives."

I don't try to hide the tears in my voice. "I'll miss you."

"And I shall miss you. God grant you happiness."

CHAPTER 45

January–February
1873

ON HER FIRST day at 903 Sviatoslavsky Prospekt, Olesya Vasilevna Kurygina informs us that we should refer to her as "Madame Kurygina" whenever guests are present.

"Therefore," she continues in her raven-like voice, "you might as well reference me by that name all the time. It will be less confusing for you."

The following morning, the new madam enters the kitchen with brisk, purposeful steps, her armload of bracelets jangling. Several women are eating or smoking while they listen to me read a serial story from *The Grainfield*. Kurygina purses her bloodless lips and glares at Sasha with barefaced disgust. Her ring-festooned hands go to her hips.

"That bird has to go," she trills. "Surely one of your customers wants a parrot?"

In the face of clamorous opposition, she relents. "Well, he certainly can't continue to flit about the house. He'll have to stay in his cage."

"But he's lonely in his cage," Dunyasha protests. "He wants to be with us."

"Nonsense. Birds don't have emotions." Kurygina's high pitch makes my marrow shiver. "To think, bird shit in the kitchen."

Sonia timidly ventures, "Perhaps he could stay in the Grand Salon and not come into the kitchen."

"And what would you suggest men tell their wives when they go home with feathers on their clothes?"

Sonia's head hangs low.

Kurygina's hand goes to her hip. "I asked you a question. Do you have a tongue? Answer me, girl."

Sonia's head droops farther. Felitsa dumps the remains of her porridge back into the pot and stomps from the kitchen. Athena follows suit.

"By the way, Anna"—a bony, bejeweled forefinger points at my cheek—"have you ever considered covering that mark with makeup? There are some very good products that are capable of hiding blemishes even worse than yours." The old bat pinches her face into something that is supposed to resemble a smile.

I avert my eyes to *The Grainfield* and bite back the question: *Have you ever considered taking all the rings off your fingers and thumbs, the bracelets off your arms, the two necklaces off your neck, and the brooch off your chest? All that jewelry doesn't do a thing to hide* your *blemishes.*

I vow to begin my search for employment in earnest. In the back of my mind, I hear Viktorya Borisovna Vialtseva, all those years ago, laying down the conditions of her employment. I agreed to Vialtseva's terms because I had no alternative. But now I have options. And I intend to make the most of them.

PETER, EVER THE actuary, gives me the names of three insurance companies that might be hiring. Abram rehearses with me what I should say and how to conduct myself. I purchase a two-piece cotton muslin outfit. The dark-gray fitted bodice has long sleeves and a high neck and flares over a skirt of the same color. I must say, the garment does indeed lend me a professional appearance.

I apply a mask of makeup to cover the stain on my cheek, pin my hair in a matronly chignon at the back of my neck, and head across the bridge. My breath comes in short, nervous bursts as I enter the insurance building.

"I'd like to see the person in charge of employment, please."

"We're not hiring now."

"May I leave my name? You could send me a letter when you are hiring again."

"Check again next month."

Despite a similar response at the second company, I pluck up enough courage to visit the third.

"I'd like to see the person in charge of employment, please."

The woman's pin-sharp eyes look over her wire-rimmed glasses. "Your name?"

"Anna Vorontsova. I don't have an appointment." Abram and I went over all the variations of possible questions that could be asked.

"Wait here." The woman's voice is as brittle as thin ice.

She returns with a man no older than me, his moustache waxed to a point. "I understand you're looking for employment. What are your skills?"

"I can read very well, including legal documents. I can perform arithmetic, including percentages. I have excellent penmanship. And I'm a fast learner."

"Come to my office."

In my stomach, butterflies slam against one another. I trail the young man down the hallway and into an office that's smaller than the kitchen larder at 903

Sviatoslavsky Prospekt. He indicates that I should take the sole chair in front of his desk, which he squeezes around to get to his own chair.

I take a breath deep into my chest and hold it. I remind myself to sit up straight with ankles crossed and keep my hands sedately folded in my lap.

"Where are you working now?"

"I'm currently unemployed."

"Then where did you acquire these skills?"

"In my hometown in Tambov province. I worked for a solicitor there."

He hands me a piece of paper the size of my hand and tells me to read what it says.

I exhale my relief as I easily read the words aloud.

> 10:00—meet with Arkady
>
> Noon—lunch with Marusya
>
> 3:00—review estimates with Popov

The man leans back and lays his forearms on the wooden arms of his chair. "We might have an opening for a person like you, if you can actually do the things you say. When could you start?"

I tremble with hope. "As soon as you'd like."

"Come back in the morning, nine o'clock sharp. We'll give you a try." His smile is meager. "You said you're from Tambov?"

"Correct."

"Bring your passport with you."

"I'm afraid my passport is lost. You see, while I was traveling to Moscow, the carriage overturned, and my trunks slid into the creek." I clench one hand with the other to keep them from fluttering about. "I lost all my important papers. In fact, most of my good clothes are being laundered right now." I smile, hoping my dimples imply *Goodness me, these sorts of things happen. We simply have to pick up the pieces and go on.*

"Do you have any document that proves you're who you say you are?"

"I regret that everything was lost."

"Then I can't hire you." He rises, maneuvers around his desk, and stands by the door.

My prospects are unraveling, like a ball of yarn dropped on the floor. "But I'm a good worker." As I rise, my blood pools in my feet. "You wouldn't be disappointed."

He places his hand on the edge of the door, prodding me to move a little faster.

"You said you would give me a try. Let's proceed with that. Then, after I get my new passport from Tambov, we'll make it all neat and legal." I'm clutching at straws, but I'm desperate. I had gotten so close, so very close.

"Rules are rules. Good day."

As I head back to the house, I promise myself that tomorrow morning I'll visit two more potential employers. But I feel as if I'm stumbling blindly through a blizzard, fully expecting defeat as I take my first steps.

At the plush department store Muir and Merrilees, I receive a cold "We're not hiring."

At my second stop, the Botkin tea firm, the man seems interested. Knees shaking, I tell him that I'm a recent widow living in Moscow. He says he'll have to see some form of identification, such as a church record of my marriage.

Head hanging low, I drag myself back to Sviatoslavsky Prospekt. I glare at the brick building I've called home for far too long. I feel like a bird trapped in a cage. Is there no possible way out?

The following Monday, I tell Abram, "No one will hire me without a passport."

Furrows form across his broad brow. "Where's your passport?"

I stare dumbfounded at his well-meaning face. Then it dawns on me that, of course, he has no reason to know that I don't possess one. "Do you understand what it means to have a yellow ticket?"

Abram nods. "I understand what a yellow ticket is."

I get out of bed, pull on my blue Persian robe, and remove my yellow card from the bottom drawer of my vanity. "This is a yellow ticket." I hold it an arm's length from his face. "When they give you this, they take away your passport."

His eyes rise from the card and meet mine. His cheeks are rounded with air, which he slowly lets out through pursed lips. "I see."

"When you accept a yellow ticket, you place yourself beyond the pale of acceptable society." I replace the despised slip of paper in the drawer.

His forefinger and thumb press the bridge of his nose. "So what you're saying is that you need to turn in your yellow ticket before you can reclaim your passport."

"And if I turn in my yellow ticket, I can't work here anymore, so I don't have a place to live," I explain with an air of frustrated tedium. "And no reputable landlord will rent to someone without a passport."

He rises from the bed and tenderly kisses my forehead. "Look at it this way. You had two companies interested in hiring you. Two out of five. That's excellent."

"Do you really think so? Because if I leave here, I have only enough rubles saved to live a month or two without employment."

"With your skills and impeccable character, some business or government office will snap you right up."

"In that case, on Friday, I'll ask the medical-police how I go about turning in my yellow ticket and getting my passport back. Once I have my passport in hand, I'll find a place to live and begin looking for employment."

Abram's head jerks back. "Are you saying, if you get your passport on Friday, you might not be here next Monday?"

"I'm saying that when I regain my passport, I'll lose my yellow ticket. As soon as Kurygina finds out, she'll kick me out of the house."

"But how will I find you?" The alarm in his voice has grown to panic.

I look coolly at him. "I always assumed our relationship would end once I left this place."

"End? You'll simply leave one day, and I'll never see you again?" The muscles of his face twitch. "You'll just . . . disappear from my life?"

"Do you have any alternatives for me?" I bait him. The conversation has taken an unforeseen twist, and I intend to use it to my advantage.

Abram stands as if carved of stone. He stares at me for what seems like three years before he slowly pulls on his trousers.

I sit down on the steamer trunk in the alcove, knowing better than to rush him. I've given him an emotional ultimatum. This is the closest I've ever been to hearing the words I crave.

After he finishes dressing, he lowers himself next to me on the trunk. I see the answer to my question in the sorrow that clouds his eyes.

He places his hand on my thigh, clutching and unclutching it like a cat sharpening its claws. "I've always known that someday you'd move on, Anna. And I want you to find a better life. I truly do. But selfishly, I can't imagine my life without you."

His fingers keep grasping and releasing my leg as if he's tormented by some inner demon. I lay my hand lightly on his forearm.

At my touch, he appears to lose what little strength he possesses. Staring across the room, he murmurs words that seem to be formed of emotion rather than reasoning. "Sometimes I ask God why He worked things out the way he did. Why I was born Jewish. Why I married Leah when I was I too young to understand the meaning of such a commitment. Why I can have you only two hours a week." He looks up at the ceiling, then at me. "I've never lied to you. I never implied there could be any other ending."

"No, you never did," I respond softly, my eyes level with his. "But I always had hope."

"I must allow you to go on with your life. I can't expect you to reserve a portion of it for me when I can offer nothing more than I give you now."

It's the answer I anticipated, but it crushes me nonetheless. I reach deep within to find a steady voice. "I promise, regardless of what happens at the medical-police on Friday, I'll be here next Monday."

FOR ALL THE years I've been going to the medical-police station, the same laggard clerk has been sitting in the same dingy corner with his mouth hanging slack, doing the same dreary thing, which is essentially nothing.

On Friday, the dunderhead blinks. "You gave up your passport five years ago, and you want us to find it?" He blinks again. The guy has the mental acuity of a sheep.

Irina, standing beside me, doesn't give me a chance to answer. "No, you little rat-face. You *took* her passport from her five years ago, and now she wants back what's rightfully hers."

The clerk points his index finger at Irina. "Don't get smart with me, Irina. Your new madam isn't going to bail you out of trouble like your old one did."

"I thought you were a civil servant," Irina retorts. "Perhaps you should start serving the public, of which Anna is one."

Knowing that it doesn't pay to be rude to an opponent, I ask, "How long do you think it will take to find my passport?"

The clerk shrugs. "Maybe a couple of days. Maybe never. I'll fill out a work order. The registrar will go through the files. Ask me again next Friday."

"Next Friday?" Irina sputters. "Why can't you have an answer for her when we come in for our regular visit to this pigsty?"

The clerk retorts, "I see no reason for undue haste. After all, the document was relinquished five years ago. Keep in mind the expression: 'More hurry, more folly.'"

On my way out the door, I notice a faded sign that has undoubtedly hung on the wall for years. When I first started coming here, I couldn't read it. Even after I could read it, I never bothered to.

Do not spit on the floor.

I render an embittered snort. The floor of the medical-police building is coated with every foulness imaginable—vomit, urine, blood, squished cockroaches—but by all means, let's keep it free of spittle.

On the way back to the house, Irina and I encounter Felitsa. The weather is bitter, and I intend to merely toss her a friendly nod as we scurry past each other. But instead I stop. Below Felitsa's fur turban is a face slack with hopelessness.

"That bitch made it clear that my days at the house are numbered."

"What?" Irina shouts.

"What did she say?" I ask.

"She didn't say anything specifically," Felitsa replies in disgust, "but she implied that a woman without flaws would earn more than one with flaws."

"What of it?" Irina asks. "I thought the old crone was referring to Anna's birthmark when she said stupid things like that. What does it have to do with you?"

"What does it have to do with me?" Felitsa's sarcasm cracks the cold air. She shoves her face closer to ours, both her mouth and her single eye gaping open.

I quickly apologize. "We know you so well, we no longer see the eyepatch. What's important is that you do your share of the work. And you bring in good customers."

"Not only does that woman have a heart of stone, but she's also full of horseshit," Irina vents. "The color of the cat doesn't matter as long as it catches mice."

The two of us watch Felitsa shamble away, her shoulders burdened with a heavy weight. Irina growls, "Shit. We're being winnowed out, one by one."

I nod silently. Kurygina seems dead set on dismantling the house.

THE FOLLOWING FRIDAY, the gray-faced clerk tells me that the registrar at the headquarters building was sick all week and therefore will look for my passport next week. But the clerk, for reasons known only to him, decides to be generous with his information. "I doubt he'll find it. The document is only valid for a year at the longest. They're usually thrown away after that, to make room for the next ones."

"Why didn't you tell me that the last time I was here?" My fist wallops the top of his desk.

The man clicks his tongue with indifference. "It's *your* passport. I figured you knew how long it was good for."

"How do I get a new passport?"

"Not difficult. All you need is your father or husband or whoever is the male head of your household to vouch for you. That you are who you say you are, that you have his permission to be in Moscow, and that you are not a threat to society. Your town's assembly will then issue the document."

Not difficult. All you need is the male head of your household.

My cheeks are frozen with tears when I reach Sviatoslavsky Prospekt. My family cut all ties with me when they banished me from Petrovo. And I never received a reply to the letter I sent last August.

CHAPTER 46

March

1873

"SO, MY ENCHANTRESS, tell me about your quest for gainful employment." Yevgeny pulls off his boots and wiggles his toes. "When you leave here, my ten little friends will miss you terribly. Not to mention, Peter and I will have to break in a new courtesan." Ever since the Shrovetide pancakes, Yevgeny and Peter not only play chess weekly, but they've become staunch allies, rabidly devoted to "a new Russia."

"If I were you, I wouldn't worry too much about my leaving," I respond dolefully to his jests. "Every time I turn around, another door slams in my face."

"A genteel, literate woman skilled at numbers, not to mention blessed with graceful penmanship, can't convince someone to hire her?"

"There's the sticky issue of a passport."

Yevgeny removes his spectacles but deviates from his normal routine of putting them on the table beside the bed. Instead, he blows on the lenses, polishes them with his red calico shirt, and replaces them on his nose. He pats the spot on the mattress beside him. "Anna, sit down. I want to talk to you."

I'm taken aback by his tone. What has become of my sassy quipster?

"You realize, of course, that Peter and I talk endlessly about you behind your back. Almost always in favorable terms." His shoulder taps mine in jest. "We wondered if perhaps the documentation might present a problem for you."

"You're correct. As usual."

Yevgeny takes my hand in his and holds it in his lap. "I have an opportunity for you. But I must emphasize, it's not without risk. Whether you accept or not, I expect what I'm about to tell you will not be repeated to anyone. No one. Not even that banker who's insanely smitten with you."

I nod.

"The circle that runs our little bookstore is in need of a proprietor. Someone who can keep accounts, manage inventory, wait on customers. Someone who is aware that something transpires behind the scenes but isn't involved in it.

Someone to be the upstanding front for our subversive little organization. The window dressing, so to speak."

"I see the risk you're referring to."

"That's only part of the risk. But let's approach one danger at a time. We've been relying on volunteers from our group to run the bookstore, but none of them have their heart set on being a capitalistic entrepreneur. The volunteer bookkeeper recently fell ill, leaving the accounts in an indecipherable tangle." Yevgeny runs his free hand through the wisps of his hair. "Creditors unpaid. Inventory in disarray."

"So it would be like starting from scratch?"

"Precisely. In more ways than one. You see, we have no money to pay you."

"No money?" I bring the tip of an impatient forefinger to my chin, begging the question: *Then why are we discussing this?*

"However, the store has a small back room that can be cleaned up and painted for your use as a bedroom and kitchen. Plus, we have a strategy to obtain rubles."

"Is this where the second risk comes in?"

"The second of three." He pauses. "Are you familiar with a Chinese tea shop a few blocks from here?"

"Also sells Chinese medicine? An adorable little shopkeeper with a pigtail? Doesn't speak much Russian?"

"Oh, don't be fooled by that wolf-in-sheep's-pelt. The little Asiatic shyster speaks Russian very well. The pidgin talk is just his version of 'window dressing.'"

"And how does this Oriental conniver fit into your plan?"

"A member of our circle lived for a time in the Far East and is quite learned in Chinese culture. You've seen the Chinaman's shelves of dusty old teapots and samovars? Our comrade is quite certain that one of those teapots is from the early Qing Dynasty. Unbeknownst to the pigtailed proprietor, it's two hundred years old and worth hundreds of rubles. Is the picture becoming clearer to you?"

"Still murky."

"Think of yourself as a beautiful but naïve shopper. You dicker with the Chinaman for the teapot. Buy it for a couple of rubles. Our organization takes care of reselling it. Part of the proceeds goes toward your paycheck for the next year."

"And part of the proceeds goes to your organization's underground operations?"

"It's precisely that astute mind that our group needs." He gives me a peck on the cheek.

"And the third risk?"

"The Chinaman doesn't make his living by selling tea and medicinal herbs."

"That's also 'window dressing,'" I announce with boastful flamboyance.

"I see your expanded vocabulary has bestowed you with inflated self-admiration." He squints an eye at me. "Behind the window dressing lie a couple of covert pursuits. Along with his tea, your adorable pigtailed Chinaman imports opium. He also deals in counterfeit documents, such as passports. His side-businesses are part of a superbly organized labyrinth of crime, headed up by a notorious crook by the name of Fedchenko. One of Fedchenko's lackeys is someone you and I have crossed paths with."

The tombstone timbre of Yevgeny's voice tells me the "someone" is Shestov. "The risks keep getting riskier," I murmur.

Yevgeny gives a single dip of his head. "Our bookstore has managed to avoid any semblance of misbehavior. However, the tsar's police keep an eye on us, watching for 'undesirable tendencies.' If we hire a proprietor, the person will need to be above reproach. That means when the Third Section comes checking, her documents must be in order."

"Including a passport."

"Including a passport. Using your wiles, when you're in the store purchasing the innocuous teapot, you'll also pick up a handful of the passports."

"Pick up a handful of counterfeit passports! You make it sound like I'm picking up some zhulan tea."

Yevgeny appears blasé as he languidly stretches his puckered back.

"Where are the passports?" I ask. "Surely the Chinaman keeps them well hidden under lock and key."

"We don't know precisely where they are, but we're certain they're in that store."

"If I succeed, I'll have the passport that I require to work at the bookstore. What do you and your comrades intend to do with the remainder of the illegal documents? Sell them to raise money for your cause?"

"No! Nothing so vulgar as that!" His flippancy suddenly turns solemn. "Anna, I don't want to involve you any further than what I've already disclosed. The ultimate utility of the documents doesn't concern you. We're merely looking for someone to oversee our little bookshop."

"You have a hidden motive."

He held up a hand. "That matters not at all as far as you are concerned. Suffice to say that our group considers it a travesty that a man hired to uphold public morality uses his power to trample the rights of others."

"But if I'm involved, I have a right to know."

"Knowledge can be dangerous. I won't have you putting your head in a noose. As you know, I'm a stubborn old mule. Try as you might, you won't pry any further disclosures from me."

I suspect Yevgeny and his cohorts are in pursuit of not just simple revenge, but complete reparation. I remind him, "The Lord said, 'Vengeance is mine.'"

"He's welcome to join us if He so desires."

WHEN THE NIGHT'S work is finished, I take a final look in my mirror. Dull eyes. Limp hair. Sunken cheeks. My youth is vanishing. Or perhaps I'm simply losing all hope. I recall the expression that guides prostitutes' lives. *Today in satin and velvet; tomorrow sweeping the streets.*

I lie on my bed, hands laced behind my head, watching the oil lamp's shadows play on the ceiling. Yevgeny's proposal buzzes through my thoughts like a bee ready to sting. It's fraught with danger, just as he said. Images flash in my mind, of getting caught and ending up back where I started—in a jail cell.

But it's also intriguing and unlike anything I've ever done. Yevgeny's work has a purpose. So I play with the possibilities, letting desire spar with pragmatism.

> Purchasing the teapot at a fraction of its cost.
> The danger of finding, then stealing the passports.
> The consequences of getting caught.
> Becoming a shopkeeper.
> And continuing to bring in rubles from my ladies'
>   bookkeeping accounts.
> Don't do it.
> Do it.
> You don't have the pluck to do it.
> Why can't you be brave? You've done scary things before.
> You'll wind up back in jail. Or Siberia.

As my thoughts rage in battle among themselves, I roll onto my side and scrunch the pillow beneath my cheek. Fears, hopes, and possibilities attack me mercilessly. How do I sort through it all?

I'm usually so wary, always scampering from danger like a bunny rabbit. So why is such a dangerous proposition haunting me this way?

The answer is obvious: I've been trapped in a dark tunnel for too long. I have no choice but to try to escape. Regardless of the risk, I must salvage my future. I can't end up . . . how did Matryna describe it?

An old hag, fucking with cockroaches and worms in the gutters.

A useless, used-up piece of wreckage.

CHAPTER 47

March

1873

AS I RINSE my face in the washbasin, I can't stop myself from humming. I'm up early, eager for this wonderful day to begin, knowing it will lead to an absolutely glorious night.

Last Monday, Abram told me that Leah and the two children would be visiting Kiev for a couple of weeks to attend her cousin's wedding. He wondered: Could he expand his next weekly visit to include the whole night?

An entire night!

"Yes, yes, of course!" But I warned him that he'd have to make arrangements with Kurygina, and the old shrew would charge him outrageously.

How I wish he had asked to spend all three Monday nights with me! But I understand the risk involved for him, so I admonish myself to be content with whatever he can offer.

As I descend the stairs in the gauzy morning light, I envision us having all the time in the world to make love and talk and make love again. Just imagine—stirring during the night and being able to touch him, to cuddle against him! And waking up to the daylight in his arms! Perhaps afterward, Abram might feel the need to spend a lifetime of nights with me.

Knowing it's too early for Kurygina to be up, I decide to take the risk of briefly allowing Sasha to flutter about. I lift Fyedka's hand-knitted blanket off the cage.

His little body lies motionless.

Blood roars in my ears, and guilt consumes me. Why hadn't I noticed how sick he was? He'd been moody over the past few days. And finicky about eating. I'd assumed he was merely molting. I'd been too busy with my own self-interests to pay attention to him.

Through bleary eyes, I spot a gray wing feather on the floor. I lift it by its quill and delicately tuck it into my pocket.

Little Sasha had been a friend to all of us. No, more than a friend—he had been our protector. I fall to my knees and crumple in half.

I cry until my handkerchief will hold no more tears. Once I gather my emotions, I consider the feelings of the other women. I don't want them to find Sasha like I did. Fyedka had knitted both a dark green blanket and a gray one to cover Sasha's cage. I wrap the former around the little bird and put it on the bottom of the cage. Then I cover the entire cage with the gray blanket.

Leaving the drapes closed and the room dim, I sit on a stool at the bar and rest my cheek on its cool surface.

When I hear footsteps, I raise my head to see Felitsa and Athena coming down the stairs. After I tell them about Sasha, the three of us sit side by side on a divan in a silent vigil.

Dunka and Dunyasha descend the staircase next. Following on their heels is little Sonia. Upon hearing about Sasha, Dunyasha begins sobbing, which prompts Sonia to do likewise. The two cling to each other in mutual grief over the death of a beloved friend.

Irina tromps down the stairs. "What's going on? Why is it so dark in here? And what are those two boohooing about?" She opens the drapes, then lifts an edge of the blanket covering the cage.

"Oh, shit." Irina sits down with the rest of us.

Dunyasha sobs, "We . . . we . . . we need to bury him."

"The ground is still frozen," Dunka reminds her.

"We can thaw it with boiling water," Felitsa proposes.

Irina offers to dig the hole.

I suggest doing it right now. "What's the point in waiting? Are we missing anyone? Where's what's-her-name? The new girl."

Sonia speaks up. "Anna, I have a different suggestion. Today's Monday."

"Yes?"

When no one seems to grasp the implications of Sonia's statement, she explains, "Abram Abramovich always enjoyed talking with Sasha. Perhaps he would be willing to conduct a burial service. Being a man, he's better able to do these things."

Stunned, I wait for the others to voice their opinions. They are in favor of the idea.

"I'm sure he'll be honored." Although I speak with conviction, I'm uncertain how Abram will feel about holding a funeral for a bird. Not to mention how it might impinge on the romantic evening I had planned.

Suddenly Irina blurts out, "That cold-blooded bitch killed him."

"Shush!" Felitsa cautions. "The walls have ears."

"Irina's right," Dunka says. "Kurygina poisoned him."

"Hush, both of you!" Felitsa's single eye roves in the direction of Kurygina's apartment.

"Besides, you can't prove your accusation," I point out. "Sasha was well into old age."

Dunka retorts, "I don't give a spit about what that bitch hears or doesn't hear. Or what we can prove and can't prove. You see"—she gulps back tears—"it doesn't matter anymore."

"What do you mean?" Sonia asks.

"We're looking for another house to work in." Dunka reaches for Dunyasha's hand. "Last night, Kurygina made it clear to us that we're not welcome here."

THAT AFTERNOON, I draft a letter to Kiev. I'll ask Abram to check the spelling this evening.

> Dearest Fyedka, Grisha, and Sophia Mikhailovna,
>
> Everyone here sends their warmest regards. We wanted you to know that we buried Sasha in the courtyard. I do not know why he died. Abram conducted a funeral service, and nearly all of us attended. We wrapped Sasha in his blankets that Fyedka knitted, along with his bell and his mirror. We thought you'd want to know. Dunka and Dunyasha will leave the house soon, as will Felitsa. We pray all of you and the Count are well.
>
> Your sincere friends at 903 Sviatoslavsky Prospekt

At four o'clock, all the women of the household, except the new girl and Madame Kurygina, are sitting at the kitchen table in our separate silences when a man's boots cross the back threshold.

"I'm in the kitchen," I call.

Abram's stride stops short when he sees seven gloomy women.

Dunyasha begins sniffling. She pulls a handkerchief from the sleeve of her dress and whimpers, "Sasha's dead!"

Abram slowly sets his valise on the floor. The women fall over one another in their attempts to describe how I found him this morning.

I interrupt with a solemn voice. "Abram, Sonia has something she'd like to ask you."

Tenderhearted Sonia swallows back her sniffles. "We decided he should be buried in the courtyard. We'd like you to conduct a service."

Abram places his open hand on his breastbone and asks a silent, *Me?*

Sonia nods. "If you don't mind, that is. Jews have funerals for their dead, don't they?"

"Well, yes, but . . . " His eyes reach out to me for guidance, but I sit with my hands folded in my lap and my eyes moist, my face neither frowning nor encouraging. He lightly runs his tongue over his upper lip. "Jews consider it both an honor and a duty to help bury the dead. It would be a privilege to contribute what I can."

We gather in the courtyard, and Sonia lines the bottom of the little grave with the folded gray blanket. Dunyasha places the green bundle atop the blanket. The women stare down at the cobblestones as we wait for Abram to begin.

He clears his throat and grasps his hands behind his back. "Some people would ridicule a funeral for a parrot, but such attitudes are merely a reflection of their arrogance. This little bird was very dear to us, so it is entirely fitting that we come together to say goodbye to Sasha. An important part of a Jewish funeral service is the *hesped*, in which we look back at the life and achievements of the deceased. This is my hesped for Sasha."

He bows his head, apparently collecting his thoughts, and then looks around at the small assembly.

"All of us want to thank Sasha for the joy he brought into this house. There's not a one of us who didn't find delight in his acrobatics on the drapery rod. All of us will remember how he savored having his neck rubbed and how much pleasure we took in doing that for him. At this gathering, we are bound together by the common scar he gave each of us when he sat on our shoulders and playfully nipped our earlobes."

Soft laughter ripples through the assembly.

"All of us who had the honor of listening to a flute-and-whistle concert will value the experience to the end of our lives." He removes his hands from behind his back and takes my hand. "Most of us have been the subject of his tirades at one time or another. There was never any doubt that Sasha had a temper second only to Irina's." Following a muffled chortle by the group, he asks, "Does anyone have something they would like to contribute?"

Athena speaks up. "I thank Sasha for alert Grisha when we in trouble."

The women all nod their agreement.

Abram turns his head to look quizzically at me. I never told him about Sasha's role as our bodyguard. He continues, "Would anyone else like to add something?" No one speaks, so he concludes with "Let us use Sasha's death as a reminder that we live and die at God's behest."

CHAPTER 48

March

1873

ON THE THURSDAY following Sasha's burial, a brunette woman pushes Peter's wheelchair down the knobby cobblestone lane and through the doorway of the Chinese tea importer. Makeup conceals my birthmark. Wire-rimmed glasses rest on my nose. Nauseating fear lodges in my belly.

The Chinaman bestows me with a beaming smile and a low bow. "How I help you?"

"Help me?" My eyebrows fly to the top of my brow. "Help me?" I march around the wheelchair and up to the counter. "I sincerely hope you *can* help me. *This* time."

The elliptical fissures of his eyes pop into circles of alarm.

"I'm absolutely beside myself over this!" Hand in my muff, I swing open an arm toward Peter. "Look at my brother and tell me what you see."

The proprietor's ebony eyes shift from the raging woman to the seated man, both of whom are slight of build with hair a matching shade of brown, courtesy of an auburn rinse. Their skin tones, however, are strikingly dissimilar. Whereas the woman's is creamy, the man's is tinged an odd blue.

"Do you remember selling me an ointment?" I will my gaze to stay unflinching, which isn't that difficult since the Chinaman is a blur, courtesy of Yevgeny's spectacles. "Smells like fish?"

The Chinaman thoughtfully strokes the lengthy threads of his moustache.

"My brother"—I sniffle, as though on the verge of tears—"my baby brother has led a hard life, as you can see. He's intelligent, educated, morally upright, but . . . but . . . oh, my goodness, I can barely tell the story." My free hand wraps around my forehead.

Peter comes to his "sister's" aid, bitterness spilling forth with every word of the sad tale. "No one will hire a cripple. No matter how many positions I apply for. No matter what my credentials are. I'm turned away at every door."

My distraught hand drops from my forehead to the base of my throat. With my thumb on one side and four fingers on the other, my voice is strangled. "Finally . . . finally, last week, someone offered him a job. Good-paying office work with a bright future. He was to start work yesterday." My head drops forward.

Peter continues the saga. "But do you know what my new employer thought when I turned up with blue skin? Can you guess? Can you?"

The shopkeeper's head quivers back and forth like a plucked string on a balalaika.

I pick up the storyline. "They thought he was taking mercury treatment for . . . "I lean in close to the counter and whisper. "For the pox."

The flat of the Chinaman's hand goes to his chest. "I so sorry."

"As you should be!" I rear back, my spine arrow-straight. "Why didn't you warn us? Now my little brother's one chance at a good career has been ruined. Completely ruined." I inject two deep sniffles into our charade. "We have only each other to lean on, and money is scarce."

"Shouldn't you have told us about this unfortunate side effect?" Peter demands.

"Should have tell you about blue," the little man agrees.

"Yes, you should have," Peter said. "And our attorney thinks so too."

"Attorney?"

I give a solitary, contemptuous nod. "Yes, attorney. Solicitor. Counselor. Lawyer. You're familiar with the term?" During this bluster, I keep an image of Sophia Mikhailovna in my mind, her erect carriage exuding confidence.

The shopkeeper's Adam's apple travels up and down between the long tails of his moustache. "My apologies. How I make up to you? Perhaps other ointment? Or maybe beautiful gift?" His open-handed wave indicates the whole of the store.

I flick my eyes around the cluttered shop. I note that other than the entrance, there's only one door—an interior door. Closed.

The shopkeeper pursues his bribe. "You like tea? Have wide assortment. I share you."

I saunter toward the shelves and tables strewn with tea accessories, discreetly lowering my spectacles to clearly see over them. "Yes, we like tea very much. But that is neither here nor there." I run my finger down the shiny brass of a large, ornate samovar while eyeballing the other items.

"You like samovar? We make fair agreement." The proprietor's face wrinkles into a smile.

There it is! Exactly as Yevgeny described it. A round pot the size of a spittoon. White porcelain and decorated with indigo peonies. Metal handle. The knob atop the lid is a small upright rabbit.

I pick up the teapot. "This is pretty. And just the right size for the two of us." I hold it out so my "brother" can view it. "Perhaps this will compensate."

"Oh, no. In China, very expensive. I pay much for it. No give away free."

"How much would you sell it for?"

"Twenty-five rubles. Rabbit is silver."

"Twenty-five!" Peter and I exclaim simultaneously.

"Our attorney would never accept such a paltry amount," Peter adds.

I replace the pot back on the shelf.

"But for you, fifteen."

I give a long, disconsolate look at Peter. "That hardly makes up for the loss of wages and the humiliation my brother has suffered."

"For brother, ten rubles."

I blow the dust off it. "It's been sitting here quite a while. No one seems to want it."

"Eight rubles."

I turn to Peter. "What do you think of it?"

"It reminds of me of Grandmother Filosofova's teapot." Peter's voice is melancholic. "Before she died."

I return to the counter and place my muff and reticule on it. Loosening the drawstring, I cast about the purse's dark interior and eventually bring forth a paper ruble. I fumble around and find a second. Groping deeper yet, I come up with a third. Thrashing about yet some more, I find a fifty-kopek coin. Then a five-kopek piece.

As I search, I pull items from the purse and place them on the counter, one by one. A folded handkerchief. An empty coin purse. A tiny bottle of cologne. A glove without its match.

"Oh. I've been looking for this."

Another handkerchief (this one dirty). A parrot's gray feather. Another couple of five-kopek coins. A skeleton key.

The Chinaman gives a pained sigh.

Three hair combs, each with different ornamentation. Another couple of coins. Half a shoelace.

When I've finally relieved the purse of its contents, I carefully add the total, then hand the paper rubles and coins to Peter, who takes pains to check my addition. The Chinaman shifts from one sandaled foot to the other.

"Five rubles," I announce as I began reloading items into my reticule. "In exchange for the teapot."

Once again, he plays with the flimsy wisps of his moustache that rest against his chest. "You. Me. Total even up."

Palms planted on the counter, I lean forward until I'm almost nose-to-nose with the man. Bringing to bear fortitude I didn't know I possessed, I whisper, "Not quite."

The Oriental eyes narrow to the size of sesame seeds.

I step back from the counter and bend at the waist, so my head is beside Peter's. "Misha, why don't you go to the carriage? By the time you get settled in, I'll be finished here."

After holding the door open for Peter, I take a breath that fills my chest. *If you botch this, instead of a bookstore, you'll see a jail cell.*

I stride back to the counter. Sighing deeply, I widen my blue eyes. "I'll be honest with you, sir. Misha has the opportunity to interview for an exceptional position in Smolensk. The trouble is . . . " For the first time in my life, I purposefully gnaw on my lower lip. "In Misha's younger days, he was a bit imprudent. I believe his real problem was deep-rooted anger over being crippled."

I squeeze my eyes tight for a moment while heaving a heartfelt sigh.

"His rebelliousness landed him in a bit of trouble with the Third Section. Nothing serious, you understand. Even though he's now the most loyal of citizens, he's still blacklisted from receiving a passport."

The Chinaman stands motionless, face vapid, hands clasped in front of his hips.

"Perhaps you can help me."

"You have teapot."

I throw back my shoulders and lengthen my neck. "You wanted twenty-five rubles for the teapot, which we both know was overpriced. I'll give you five. That's a difference of twenty rubles. Which also happens to be what Misha would have made at his new job in a single week. That is, if his skin hadn't turned blue. So you see, you've compensated us for one week. What about the rest of his life?"

The little man raises his hands and eyebrows in helplessness.

"Our attorney won't accept the samovar as fair compensation." I pause to let those words sink in. "Might I add, it was my attorney who suggested I ask you about a passport. He said that if you won't compensate us, Misha and I should discuss this with a gentleman named Fedchenko."

The shopkeeper's lips tighten like Fyedka's when he plays his flute, and I know I've struck gold.

"In exchange for one piece of paper, Misha and I will disappear from Moscow and from your life. Forever."

Shrewd black eyes study mine. "Just one?"

"Just one," I say as lightly as if selecting a single jelly bean.

"Wait here."

The shopkeeper's sandals shuffle to the interior door. He withdraws a key from his pocket, unlocks the door, and enters the adjoining room. He closes the door, but only partway.

I silently move to the end of the counter, where I can see through the narrow opening. With Yevgeny's eyeglasses pushed atop my head, I watch the man pull out the bottom drawer on the left side of a desk. He withdraws a sheet of paper and closes the drawer. I lower the eyeglasses back onto my nose.

Wiping nervous perspiration from my palms onto my coat, I sidestep toward some shelves and pretend to inspect the varieties of loose tea displayed in glass jars. Behind me, I hear him lock the door.

The Chinaman shoves the paper across the counter. I examine the document, noting the word *Passport* in its heading, blank lines where identifying information would be written, and an embossed emblem at the bottom.

As I fold the paper and slip it inside the teapot, I dimple my smile. "I won't even bother you for a box for my purchase." I pick up the teapot and my muff and head out of the shop.

With the open door still in my hand, I stop midstride.

"What happened?" I shout down the lane. I pause as if to listen for the answer. "Oh, no! It's Misha!" I call to the Chinaman, my arm signaling for his help. "He's fallen and might be hurt. Please, please help me get him up. Do us a kindly favor. Please!"

The Chinaman reluctantly pulls a quilted jacket and fur hat from behind the counter, and with deliberate slowness, steps into his galoshes. He follows me as I rush to where the narrow lane intersects the main boulevard.

In a snowbank between the wheelchair and an enclosed carriage lies Peter, flailing like a turtle trying to right itself. The coach driver, a rheumatic old man who's all but buried beneath a heavy winter cape, makes ineffectual attempts to pick up the paralyzed man.

"If you'll please just help me, sir." The driver touches the brim of his peakless cap. "My back isn't what it used to be." Yevgeny lisps as though half his teeth are missing. "Between the two of us, we can get him in the carriage."

"Get him in quickly!" I entreat. "If he catches a chill, his lung condition will flare up."

Moving at the pace of cold molasses, Yevgeny lowers himself onto an arthritic knee beside Peter and signals the Chinaman to squat on Peter's other side.

My hand flies to my cheek. "Oh, no! I left my purse in the shop!" I place the samovar in the carriage and run back into the store.

Dropping Yevgeny's spectacles into my coat pocket, I race to the locked door of the back room. Thanks to years of experience with the door to Sophia Mikhailovna's apartment, I easily unlock this one using a hatpin. Then I discover the bottom left desk drawer is also locked!

Damn! Fear pounds in my ears.

I insert the hatpin into the lock, but it's too flimsy to do the job. I bring forth a larger one. It scratches around, but the lock won't budge. The skeleton key in my reticule is far too large.

Sweat runs down the back of my neck. *Think. Think. Think.* My hands tighten into fists. My nails dig into my palms. *There must be an extra key somewhere.*

I dash to the front room and crouch behind the counter where the Chinaman routinely stands. Three drawers. My clammy hands claw through the first drawer's jumble of papers, empty ink bottles, and rubber thimbles. In the second drawer, I find an assortment of paraphernalia, including a key ring with six keys.

Please be the one, I plead as I scramble back to the office.

On the verge of vomiting from fright, I try three keys. The fourth finally turns the lock.

Papers are filed in wooden slats, angled so the top few lines can be easily viewed. I grab some copies, perhaps a dozen, of the paper titled *Passport.* I also snatch a couple of the *Permit* pages as well as several *Decree* sheets. I roll the papers into a cylinder and jam it into my muff.

Voices filter in from the lane. Men's voices. The sound paralyzes me. This is a madcap scheme. I was crazy to agree to it!

When the voices retreat down the street, I thank a benevolent God.

My galloping heart can't endure any more. Lightheaded, I kick the desk drawer shut and lock it. Stepping out of the office, I lock the door behind me. Yevgeny's voice is approaching.

I still have the shopkeeper's keys.

One hand drops the key ring into my pocket while the other replaces the eyeglasses on my face. I sprint to the customers' side of the counter. "How is Misha?" I ask anxiously as the shop door opens. "He isn't hurt, is he?"

"He's fine, mademoiselle," Yevgeny lisps. "A little flustered, but just fine." Behind him, the Chinaman nods emphatically.

I lift my reticule off the counter. With my index finger, I hold its string next to my ear. "And my purse is safe and sound also." I glance about the shop, as if making certain I'm not leaving anything else behind. As I lean across the counter to check on the far side, I gasp, "Wait! What's that?"

I scoot to the far side of the counter and drop to my knees. I can hear the Chinaman's galoshes clomping across the wood floor.

Open the drawer, I instruct myself. *Silently place the key ring. Ease the drawer closed.*

I'm rising to my feet as the Chinaman rounds the counter. Dimples notch my cheeks, and my eyes roll at my own empty-headedness. "To think I almost lost this again! It must have fallen while I was searching through my purse."

A glove dangles from my raised hand.

As Yevgeny holds the shop's door open for me, he nods to the Chinaman and deferentially touches his cap. "Can't thank you enough, sir, for your help. Can't thank you enough."

CHAPTER 49

April
1873

I TURN THE passports over to Yevgeny, except for the one I tuck into a drawer of my vanity and the one I give to Athena. "You must use it to return to Greece," I tell the raven-haired beauty. "Promise me that you will. But do not ask how I came into possession of this. And do not under any circumstances tell anyone where you obtained it. Not anyone. Not a soul. Not even the women in this house. Make up a story—a customer gave it to you."

A week after the terrifying episode, I'm alone in the kitchen boiling some eggs. I warm my hands over the steaming water. Kurygina keeps the house cool during the day. Outside, the cold wind howls like baying hounds.

I hear the door open to Kurygina's apartment and exhale relief when her footsteps head down the hall toward the rear door. The woman has been on a rampage since the police raided the house last Saturday night and imposed a hefty fine for selling liquor. It was the first raid to take place in the five years I've been here.

A few moments later, the sound of fierce knocking comes from the Gentlemen's Entrance. When I unlock the door, I'm stunned to find Yevgeny.

"Just stopped by to share a bit of scuttlebutt in the newspaper."

I escort him to the kitchen, where he kisses my cheek, then tosses the *Russian News* onto the table.

"Care to read it out loud? Or would you prefer me to do so?" He wipes the fog off his glasses and takes the chair opposite mine.

"Read what?"

He points to an article, but his nerves are too overwrought to allow me to stumble through the written words. He snatches the paper and clears his throat. "'Yet another body was retrieved from the Moskva River, this one belonging to Moscow resident and respected law officer Viktor Viktorovich Shestov.'"

"Dead!" I gasp.

Yevgeny continues reading. "'The body was discovered early Wednesday morning by warehouse workers. The coroner determined that Shestov suffered a nonfatal blow to his head and was then pushed into the river, where he drowned.

The Chief Investigating Magistrate is putting the full force of his department into the inquisition. His fellow officers described Constable Shestov as brave, tenacious, and steadfast in his duties.'"

"So true," I drone. "Steadfast in his pursuit of innocent girls."

"'V. V. Shestov was a native of St. Petersburg, the son of the late Viktor Nikitich and Avdotya Osipovna Shestov. He obtained his law enforcement training at the capital, where he served as a prison guard. He transferred to Moscow in 1855. Although he has been offered many promotions, he always rejected them, insisting that a desk job would hinder his ability to provide service to Moscovites.'"

I drop my forehead to the crook of my arm on the table.

"'Officer Shestov remained a bachelor his entire life. V. A. Fedchenko, a well-respected retired police captain, was overheard saying that Shestov shunned marriage in order to devote himself to his many and various duties.'"

Yevgeny looks over at me and scoffs, "It's enough to bring tears to your eyes, isn't it? The article goes on to say that his black soul will burn forever in Hell."

"Don't we all hope." My forefinger pushes the newspaper in random circles on the table. "So, what do you know about this incident?"

He glances about the kitchen and lowers his voice. "As you and I know, Fedchenko is a miscreant in his own right—the key linchpin in a network of corruption that stretches across the city. A few years ago, Shestov—Fedchenko's low-level toady—entered into a dalliance with Fedchenko's teenage daughter. Something about stealing her virginity."

Yevgeny's fingers flutter airily beside his face.

"Fedchenko, renowned for his foul temper, ousted Shestov from his ring of vice. He also threatened that if Shestov ever touched his daughter again, he'd personally cut off his cock and shove it up his rectum. I suspect you'd be pleased to assist in the procedure."

My chuckle is sardonic. "I'd make sure the knife is dull and the slicing is slow."

Yevgeny nods his approval. "With time, Shestov wormed his way back into Fedchenko's good graces and the organization. However, Fedchenko *somehow* recently got wind that Shestov was double-dealing him—selling the ring's counterfeit documents on the side, thereby cutting Fedchenko out of the deal."

My eyes narrow.

"In fact, Fedchenko *somehow* came into possession of a couple bogus documents that Shestov had pirated. So . . ." Yevgeny pauses as a grin begins to emerge. "*Perhaps* Fedchenko was still harboring ill will over the deflowering of his daughter. And *perhaps* Fedchenko felt that he had put up with enough shenanigans. And *perhaps*, being a man unfettered by scruples, he decided to rid himself of the problem once and for all."

"So you framed Shestov?" I whisper.

Behind his glasses, Yevgeny's eyes are wide with feigned innocence.

"And Fedchenko had him killed? Isn't that rather extreme?"

Yevgeny shrugs a casual shoulder. "When big fish swallow little fish, they swallow them whole."

I start to ask another question, but he hushes me.

"The matter is closed. I don't want so much as a hiccup out of you about this, to me or anyone else."

My forehead knits. How could kindly Yevgeny so coolly orchestrate the destruction of another human being, even if it was Shestov?

Yevgeny rises. "I'm off to the bookstore, to see how the renovation of your future apartment is progressing. Then I'm on to Peter's for a stimulating game of chess and a rousing discussion about the smoldering miseries of Russia." His index finger taps the newspaper. "I'll leave this with you. To add to your keepsakes."

CHAPTER 50

April
1873

THE LOCOMOTIVE'S IMPATIENT whistle ricochets off the new station. The platform quivers with the train's eagerness. Sizzling bellows of steam harass the porters, passengers, and well-wishers.

Athena throws her arms around my neck and whispers, "Never I understand how you get passport."

I pat the arm that threatens to strangle me with affection. "Do not speak of it again. To anyone. What's important is to take that passport all the way to Greece and live a wonderful life."

Gratitude and hope shimmer in Athena's ebony eyes. "May the Almighty Creator bless you, Anna, all you do for me."

"It's small repayment for all you did for me when I first arrived at the house." I bestow the traditional Russian three kisses. "Farewell. And Godspeed."

Each of the other women hugs and kisses Athena and confers her best wishes.

"May your troubles be light," says Dunyasha.

"And your purse be heavy!" adds Dunka.

"Keep out of mischief!" advises Irina, the voice of experience.

We place Athena in the care of an attendant, who steadies her while she climbs the steps of the railcar.

"Step back from the tracks," orders a dapper guard with silver braid on his uniform.

The engine spews a fire-breathing hiss, and the drive rods begin to pump back and forth. Athena's arm waves wildly out the window as the clacking wheels take her on the first leg of her journey back to her native village.

I'm gladdened beyond all measure for my friend, yet it's a bittersweet moment. Women are leaving 903 Sviatoslavsky Prospekt like frogs leaping from the shore. First Maria. Then Matryna. Sophia Mikhailovna. Athena. And now, courtesy of Kurygina, Felitsa, Dunyasha, and Dunka are making plans to follow.

Irina, Dunyasha, Dunka, and I turn from the deafening roar of the seething beast and walk toward the cabbies hustling customers at the top of their lungs.

Suddenly, the world pauses even though my feet keep moving. The clamor is silenced. My face blanches cold.

I stare transfixed as a young girl leaps from a newly arrived train into the open arms of a middle-aged man in a gray cape—a cape that hung on the back of my door just three days ago. He swings the child in a joyful half circle before setting her down. Next, he welcomes a sprouting boy with a manly clasp of the shoulders.

The well-attired man pivots toward a smiling, dark-haired woman emerging from the train carriage, draped in a fox fur cape. She's carrying a striped hatbox and a small carriage parasol. My stomach muscles contract as the man offers his hand to assist the graceful woman as she descends the steps.

Once she's on the platform, he lightly kisses her cheek. A driver wearing a caftan and a red sheepskin cap takes the woman's hatbox. The woman locks arms with the caped man. They head away from me, their strides reflecting years of walking side by side.

Abram's family has returned from their visit to Kiev.

Blinded with jealousy, hurt, shame, and a host of feelings I can't begin to identify, I climb into our hired cab.

I see nothing as the carriage makes its way toward the south side of the city. Nor do I hear the chatter of my housemates. The scene at the station keeps circling around me, forbidding me to escape. The image of the doting husband and father overpowers my every thought, every emotion.

I strain for a clear remembrance of Leah. She seemed about my height, though perhaps slightly plumper. How plump? A little, but not enough to suit me. I wish the woman weighed enough to make the wood floors creak in their fancy house.

Stop it! I scold myself. It's childish to be antagonistic toward someone who has never wronged me in any way. It's simply a matter of fate that Leah chanced upon Abram before I did.

Nevertheless, my cheeks blaze with the flames of envy. I long to be the woman in the fur cape. The woman who knows what his favorite foods are, if he's grumpy when he rises from bed in the morning, how he spends his time in the evenings. The woman in the fur cape not only knows all those mundane tidbits, but undoubtedly takes them for granted.

A headache licks at my temples.

For the past two years, I've known my joy was one that could not be trusted.

But I had chosen to be blind and deaf to the truth. Observing Abram's perfect family in all their secure and happy glory was like a sharp slap across the face—a blatant and painful admonition that my daydreams are nothing more than foolish delusions. Someday he'll tell me goodbye, and I'll be left with nothing.

CHAPTER 51

April
1873

DESPERATE TO TAKE my mind off yesterday's encounter at the train station, I decide to organize the chaotic larder. I'm just finishing the task when Felitsa enters the kitchen, tosses *The Grainfield* onto the table, and spreads gooseberry preserves on a thick slice of bread.

I glance at the magazine. It's an issue I haven't seen before, dated October of last year.

"Where did this come from?" I ask.

"Athena found it while she was cleaning out her room."

I'm miffed. The women treat my magazines as their own, making off with them before I even have a chance to look at them. I reach for the magazine, but clumsily knock it off the table. As I retrieve it, a sealed envelope slips from between the pages.

It's from Petrovo.

The letter arrived in October, yet only now has it made its way into my hands.

I hurry to the privacy of my room. My trembling fingers press the envelope to my lips before I break the seal. My first communication with my family in seven years! When I unfold the beige paper, I find the writing that angles downward from left to right and lacks the curlicues that are popular in Moscow.

> Greetings from your home village,
>
> Your family received your letter. I congratulate you for learning to read and write.
>
> I am writing this letter as a friend of your mother's. I am sorry to tell you she died 2 years ago. She had a bad heart.
>
> Your Grandfather and Grandmother Vorontsov died some years ago. Your brother Ilya's wife had three miscarriages. The last one killed her.
>
> Elena Stepanovna Maximova is a nun at the ~~monestry monstery~~

orphanage. She is glad to hear you are well. Your cousin Platon studies hard in Sukanovo. He hopes to go to the university in Moscow after next year's harvest.

We had good crops last summer.

Feodor Nikiforovich Zhemchuzhnikov

I clutch the letter to my chest as tears of both joy and sorrow mist my eyes. Platon might come to Moscow next year! But my mother is forever gone.

I reread the letter, hoping to find a hint that Mamasha missed me. But there are no such words. Did Mama stay bitter over my one indiscretion until the day she died? Did she never forgive me?

Hurt and anger consume me in equal measure.

Do you realize, Mother, that you uprooted me from my home with the same concern you'd show a radish when pulling it from the earth? If you and the village wanted me to pay retribution, I've done so in the harshest way possible. I fulfilled the village's prediction that I'd grow up to be a depraved woman. But how much of that is truly my own doing? Didn't your actions and those of the village ensure the prophecy was carried out?

I read the letter a third time. The cold fact is, no one seems to miss me. My fingertips swipe away the tears. All those years of longing to return to Petrovo. All those wasted hopes.

A silent voice tells me that the embers of my youth are finally and conclusively extinguished.

CHAPTER 52

April
1873

STILL TRYING TO divert my attention from last week's scene at the train station, I plan to share the news from Petrovo with Abram. Won't he be surprised this afternoon to hear that Elena is one of the nuns who made those delectable candies! And that Platon might be coming to Moscow to attend the university!

But Abram is in no mood to listen to any of it.

Following a cursory greeting that offers no smile, he motions for me to sit beside him on the steamer trunk under the attic stairway. Fatigue pulls at his face, and his shoulders are slumped.

Ill-defined dread slithers through me.

Abram encases my hand in both of his, moves them onto his lap, and stares at the bundled fingers. The corners of his jaw tense and release, tense and release. With each passing moment, my velvet choker necklace feels tighter and tighter around my throat.

"I've mulled it over a thousand times, but I still don't know a gentle way to say this." He continues to focus on our joined hands. "I'm leaving Moscow. I'm moving my family back home."

My world drops out from under me, and I'm left dangling in the center of a boundless void. *Please God, no! I'm not ready for this!*

"Why?" My voice is small and weak, as if it had traveled halfway across Russia.

"Several reasons, so please hear me out." He swallows. "This is hurting me as much as it is you, and I ask that you listen to me."

"Go ahead, I'm listening," I say, even as I long to close my ears to his message.

His haggard eyes remain fixed on my small hand between his larger ones.

"Leah and the children returned from Kiev last week. After I met them at the train station, we stopped by the bank so I could sign some papers. While we were there, my uncle asked Leah about her trip. She couldn't stop talking about Kiev's booming prosperity. Fastest-growing city in Russia. New buildings everywhere. My uncle hung on her every word."

His head drops back against the wall, and he stares at the ceiling.

"You see, he's mentioned to me several times that he eventually wants to reopen his bank in Kiev. But on Thursday, he slapped me on the back and said, 'That settles it! You're going!'"

Everything inside me crumbles. "So you're moving to Kiev to open a bank?"

His eyes finally meet mine. "This is a once-in-a-lifetime opportunity. A large promotion. Very large. And both Leah's and my families live there. Isaak and Sarah will be able to know their grandparents, aunts, uncles, cousins. Leah is beside herself at the prospect."

My limbs take on a tingling numbness. I withdraw my hand from his, wrap it around the fingers of my other hand. I squeeze until both hands throb.

"Anna, please don't pull away from me. This decision is killing me."

My response is brusque. "It sounds to me like the decision has been finalized, and everyone is over the moon about it."

"I don't really have a choice. My uncle has been insinuating for some time that I should move to the Caucasus to keep an eye on the oil situation. He predicts a great future in Baku's oil. I kept putting him off and putting him off. It's either Kiev or the Caucasus. Staying in Moscow is not a long-term option."

"Well, then, *mazel tov* on your promotion." My sarcasm is low and mean. Although I knew in my heart of hearts that someday I'd grieve over our final farewell, I'm unprepared for the ending to be so soon, so abrupt. Rather than tears overflowing from my eyes, I feel resentment surging within me.

Abram's hand rises and spans the full of his face, his thumb and middle finger pressing his temples. "More things than you realize weigh into this decision. There's Isaak's and Sarah's well-being. Here in Moscow, other children call them names—names that wound them deeply. In Kiev, they'll have their cousins, plus other Jewish friends to play with. They'll be part of the community."

I relive the outrage I felt toward the Petrushka puppet and his prejudiced audience. Irrationally, I lash that anger toward Abram. "Jews will always be outcasts, no matter where you live. You and I discussed that very thing the first day we met. And several times since!"

As he lowers his hand from his temples to his lap, his melancholic eyes reach out for me like fingers. "My children are at the age when they should be surrounded by people of their own heritage, so they can learn what it truly means to be Jewish. Can you understand that?"

I hurt, and my instinct is to hurt him back. "Isaak and Sarah may be treated unfairly in Moscow, but so are the rest of us! The very day we met, you told me we mustn't let others' petty pride make us think less of ourselves. But you won't take the trouble to teach your own children that lesson!"

In contrast to my loss of control, Abram keeps his voice constrained. "Children learn the most from their parents. I want my son and daughter to obey the commandments of the Torah. I want a home filled with love and honesty and Jewish devotion. How can I raise honorable children when their father practices a life of continuous deceit? When he aches for a woman other than their mother?" His eyes, webbed with lines of exhaustion, implore me to absolve him.

When I offer him no such thing, he continues, keeping his voice staid.

"I can't pretend I don't love you. But I tried so hard not to raise false hopes in either of us. If I continue seeing you, sooner or later it will destroy my home and my career." His hand moves to my skirt, but I jerk my leg aside.

"My state of mind is very shaky right now." His pitch is high and unsteady. "Please listen to me. Please try to understand."

"I understand that you are running away. That's what I understand!" He's hurting me, and I want my words to hurt him back. But even in my addled state, I realize that malicious words will ultimately result in rancor and hostility—the antithesis of the eternal devotion and love I have always craved for us.

My hand darts to my mouth. I bite a knuckle while fighting back the scalding tears. I feel myself unraveling, like a loose yarn pulled from one of Fyedka's wool mufflers. I shift my gaze to the opposite wall.

Abram places a bent knee atop the trunk and pivots to face me. "Pretend with me for a moment that my uncle doesn't exist. That Leah and my children don't exist. Anna, I'm still Jewish, which means there's no future for you and me together."

Still receiving no response from me, he rises from the trunk and strides with heavy, measured steps to the window. He pushes aside the drapes and stares out, seemingly, at nothing.

In a burst of frustration, he slams his palm against the window's trim. "I'm the poorest example of a husband and father! Marriage is the primary institution of Jewish life, and I can hardly . . . can hardly be a husband to Leah anymore." He hangs his head like a man who has been whipped.

Now that he's put distance between us, even if it's only a half-dozen paces, a sense of urgency arises in me. "We can be happy together, I know we can! Please, Abram, give us a chance. Please!"

When he turns back toward me, I see a face that's tortured almost beyond recognition. His eyes slide closed.

I hear the loudest silence of my life.

I push myself off the trunk and scuffle toward the vanity. After lifting a handkerchief from the drawer, I stand like a statue, staring at the wall. He has obviously thought this decision through. Further hysterics would be futile.

I feel trampled by Abram and trampled by the world. I press the kerchief to my forehead and gulp in air, desperate to clear the whirling, painful bedlam inside me. "When will you leave?"

"A month from now." He hesitates. "I'll be back in Moscow on business a couple of times a year. Perhaps we could—"

"No!" I swing about to face him, bitterness boiling up from deep inside. "I'm not interested in becoming Sophia Mikhailovna, spending an entire lifetime waiting for a man who says he loves her but won't marry her. Oh, by the way, I neglected to tell you. She mentioned that if you happen to be in Kiev, feel free to visit her. You will pay her a visit, won't you? You should have plenty of time. A whole lifetime, in fact."

I toss my head in childish defiance. Handkerchief crushed in my fist, I punch the front of my thigh. Damn Kiev! Why must it take so many people who are dear to me!

With long strides, he comes to me. His arms encircle me, and he draws me close. I desperately want to push him away, but I can't. My anger has turned to shuddering bouts of anguish.

He whispers, "I'll treasure our time together for the remainder of all my days."

The certainty of his departure pounds through my heart, my head, my every fiber. Soon the cherished comfort of his arms will be nothing more than a fading memory. The feel of his suit's fabric. The coarseness of his beard. His serene countenance. Forever gone from me.

In my heart of hearts, I've always sensed this love story wouldn't have a happy ending. From the very first, I recognized the price of falling in love with Abram would be more than I could bear.

I take a step back and allow my blurry eyes to travel along his face. A brow that is a little too broad. A nose that is slightly too large. Heavy lidded eyes that are just a tad too close together.

"Prolonging the pain won't help either of us," I whisper. "Abram Abramovich, I give to you one final shavua tov. A good week. And a good life." My finger gently traces a weary crease from the corner of his eye, knowing I'll never again see those eyes crinkle with laughter.

"This is the hardest . . . " His eyes are dark pools of sorrow. "I'll think of you the rest of my life."

"As I will you."

With agonizing slowness, he brushes the back of his hand across my tear-soaked cheek, then gathers his overcoat and attaché case. I listen as his heavy footfalls fade away.

The gaping doorway stares at me. Once a warm, flesh-and-blood man had stood there. Now all that remains is my memory of him, a phantom of the love that once was. With painstaking slowness, I close the door and place my forehead against it. The past two years have led to this solitary moment.

Limp with weariness, I slowly pivot toward the room. Tears cloud my vision like frosted glass. But in my mind, images of the past burn as numerous and bright as a thousand votive candles.

A flute concert.

Pancakes dripping with honey.

Reading lessons.

A funeral.

Unexpectedly, but as real as if I'm standing in the tobacco shop, an earthy aroma cascades over me, so heavy it's almost suffocating. Silent tears burst into strangled sobs. My chest can't stop convulsing long enough to draw a true breath.

I stagger to the window and fling it open. Ever so slowly, the fresh air quells the rampage.

At the train station, I felt it in my bones—that this illicit affair couldn't continue. My instinct turned out to be not only correct but timely.

I recall the endless month when he was at the Fair in Nizhny Novgorod. How will I ever survive the rest of my life without those compassionate eyes that warmed my soul? How long before I can get through a whole day without aching for him? How many years will lapse before despair loosens its grip?

> Oh, your eyes are darker than the sea's darkest depths!
> Within them I see my dear soul's demise.
> In them I can see the flame of defeat . . .

CHAPTER 53

May

1873

I HAD CLUNG for so long to the dual hopes of being with Abram and of return-ing to Petrovo. They had become as much a part of me as my breath, my skin, my toenails. Not only were the two dreams mutually exclusive, but now both have blown away, like the seeds of a dandelion.

First came Zhemchuzhnikov's letter, its content clear that Petrovo holds no future for me. But that rebuff, hurtful though it is, doesn't drag at my soul as heavily as it might have. Somewhere along the way, I lost my simple-hearted naïveté. Life in Petrovo no longer seems like a halo of happiness. It more closely resembles a dry husk, empty of options and opportunities. Thank heavens Platon is breaking free of it!

Then, a week ago, came Abram's farewell. My love for him had swallowed me whole, allowing me to believe that my galloping fantasies were reality. But the coveting of a dream isn't enough to make it come true. I'm left with emotions that shall be forever scarred, and yet I must keep moving forward. The journey will be agonizing, but somehow, as I've done with countless other hopes, I'll put the prospect of a life with Abram Abramovich Segalovich behind me.

Last night as I yet again cried into my pillow, I faced the sobering realization that portions of a person's life are continuously passing through and out of it, never to return.

When you leave here, you'll be alone, Sophia Mikhailovna had prophesied.

Yes, Sophia, once again you were correct. But I have the wherewithal to keep pushing myself forth. I'm literate now. I can figure numbers. I have the necessary legal document. Plus I have the fresh start I need—at Yevgeny's bookstore.

Abram and I have bid our final shavua tov. And today's task will tie up the loose ends.

IN THE LATE MORNING, I join the teeming crowds on the bridge and cross to the north side of the river. A springtime cold snap has brought a blustery wind that stings my cheeks and forehead. But my brow is furrowed for a different reason.

I'm rehearsing the lie I'm about to tell.

And once that lie is spoken, I swear that I—not my family, not poverty, not fear, not the malignant ache for a man I can't have—I and I alone will shape my future.

But as I approach the bank building on Ilinka Street, my self-confidence ebbs. I've never stepped foot in a bank before. What if I look like a fool? What if he isn't there? What if Leah happens to be visiting? What if I don't have the mettle to go through with it? What if he knows I'm lying?

Bringing all my courage to bear, I place a hand on the polished brass knob and push open the enormous door. A rush of blood pounds my head.

The ceiling is so high. The floor is so shiny. The marble pillars are so massive. There are so many important people doing important things.

This is a horrible mistake.

No, it isn't.

Stop now, before it's too late.

Keep walking across the lobby.

As I pull off my gloves, a cordial young man appears at my shoulder. "May I assist you?"

"If you would be so kind as to tell me where I would find Abram Abramovich Segalovich."

"Is he expecting you?"

"No."

"May I tell him your name?" The young fellow is the embodiment of politeness.

"A. E. Vorontsova."

He tips his head toward me, then disappears behind a mahogany door.

Chairs are scattered about. Although I'm uncertain it's acceptable for me to sit in one, I decide I'd better do so before I faint dead away.

As I run the string of my reticule through my fingers, I wonder for the hundredth time if I should tell Abram that I'll be working at Yevgeny's bookstore. And for the hundredth time, I decide against the truth. It would be best if Abram believes me to be gone, completely out of reach, so that when he comes to Moscow on business, he doesn't have any crazy notions about trying to locate me. I need to banish this love affair like a stone tossed into Petrovo's river. After a bubble or two, nothing remains.

The building is warm. I open my coat.

Time stretches on. I feel something jabbing into my palms—my own fingernails. I open the tight little fists, stretch my fingers wide, and place one hand sedately atop the other. The next time I look down, they're balled up again.

The cordial young man offers me some tea. I decline.

I stare at a wall clock, its hands languidly moving forward. My head bows to one side, which makes the clock look as out of kilter as I feel, as if being askew might cause its pendulum to stop, much the same as my heart might do.

My skin grows hot and moist, but whether from the building's heat or the fervor of my own emotions, I can't tell. I remove my coat and fold it across my lap.

I roll my head back and around to loosen the tension.

There's a small stain on my skirt. I scratch at it with my fingernail.

The mahogany door opens. The man who will always possess my heart stands before me.

Concern is etched on his face, a face that is unexpectedly pale. *Ah yes,* I realize. Missing is his late-afternoon stubble.

"Anna?"

I rise and throw back my shoulders. "May we talk in private?"

"Of course." He leads me through the door and down a hall to a small but well-appointed office. As he takes my coat and hangs it on a coat tree, it occurs to me that I'll never again be this physically close to him.

My feet somehow move across the thick carpet, and I lower myself onto one of the two straight-backed chairs situated in front of a heavy desk of dark wood. Spanning its top is a leather insert with a gold-embossed perimeter. Atop the leather is an oil lamp with a green shade, an inkwell, and scattered papers.

My eyes flick over the glass-doored bookshelves, then freeze on the large fern in the corner next to the window. My breath catches in my chest, refusing to move in or out. It had slipped my mind that he had taken one of my ferns.

Abram closes the door and lowers himself onto the cushioned, high-backed chair behind the desk. "I'm sorry you had to wait so long. I was with a customer. In fact, it was the tobacconist a couple of blocks from you." He says the last words cheerfully, as if the reference to the tobacco shop wouldn't run a ramrod through my emotions.

I tilt my chin up slightly. "You're undoubtedly surprised by my presence. I assure you, I'm not here to embarrass you with hysterics."

"Yes, I'm surprised, but I also know you wouldn't be here if you didn't have good cause." He pulls the loose papers together and tidies them into a neat stack by tapping their edges on his leather blotter.

Is it my imagination, or are his fingers trembling?

"I have a couple of things to tell you. And one thing to ask of you." I push my shoulders back as far as they will go. "First, it seems you're not the only one leaving Moscow."

His eyebrows gather together inquisitively above his nose.

"Remember the letter I wrote to my mother last August? Her response was delayed, but I received it last week. The whole family is delighted to hear that I'm well, and they're begging me to return home. They suggest I seek office employment in the district capital." I strive for a sunny, bright-eyed guise. "It's the answer to my prayers."

He shifts in his seat as if scratching his back. "How wonderful that you'll finally return home. Isn't it odd that the letter should arrive at such an auspicious time?"

Is he doubting my story? I dimple my cheeks. "Fruit drops from the tree when it's ready."

"You'll be leaving soon?"

"As soon as my passport arrives." I give the slightest giggle. "I have to hurry home if I'm going to spend any time with Platon. The irony is, he's leaving Petrovo in the fall to attend the university here." I lean forward and deepen my dimples. "Moscow! Of all places!" I think this bit of trivia adds credibility to my tale.

He laughs, and his eyes crinkle at the irony. Lines from the poem come to me, unbidden.

> Oh, your dark eyes, eyes so passionate,
> Eyes that burn through me, eyes so beautiful.

Those dark eyes will haunt me the rest of my days.

I focus all my strength on steadying my breathing.

Abram's smile dwindles as he hunches forward over his desk. "You know I wish you only the best."

"I do know that. I truly do. That leads me to the second thing I want to tell you. I . . . I appreciate that you've always been straight-from-the-shoulder with me. You never promised more than you could deliver."

His lips part but release no words. He closes his mouth and tries again. Inside the oval, I can see his tongue flopping about. It would be comical under other circumstances, and it supplies me with the fortitude to go on. "The favor I have to ask of you is this."

He places his elbows on his desk and tents his fingers in front of his chin. It's a pose I've never seen him take before, possibly one reserved for business decisions.

"Hire Sonia and take her with you to Kiev. Give her a chance at a better life. She knows the alphabet and how to write a few words. She's sharp as a tack and honest to the bone. She'll be a good worker for you. I'll write a letter to Sophia Mikhailovna and convince her to offer Sonia a room in the Count's mansion until the girl gets on her feet."

His tented fingers fall and interlock. "That's a splendid idea. Tell her to come see me."

Thank you, I mouth, dismayed that my voice has deserted me. "I'd best leave."

When I rise, he gets to his feet and starts to come around the desk.

My hand flies up, palm out. "No!" I blurt, before subduing my tone. "I don't believe I could bear having you close to me."

He presses a clenched fist against his lips. The sunlight from the window glints off his wedding band.

I gaze at him, and he at me. There's nothing left to say. But the conversation isn't over. It continues, silent and painful, for an infinite moment.

I retrieve my coat and, without looking back, pull the door closed behind me.

The hallway stretches endlessly as jagged breaths wheeze through my open mouth. I can't cry—not here in the bank. I can't let that cordial young man see a woman emerge from Abram Abramovich Segalovich's office with tears decimating her carefully applied makeup. I yank on my coat and pull up its collar to hide my contorted face.

I bolt though the enormous door with its shiny knob. Bracing against the cutting wind, I run past the next building. Then another. And another. At the end of the block, I round the corner and am sheltered from the numbing blasts. I slump against a brick building, my chest throbbing. Bending forward, I brace my hands against my knees while I relive each word and each gesture.

After an eternity, my breathing slows. My tense muscles loosen. My rattled mind becomes lucid. It's as though the cold has chilled my heated turmoil and replaced it with transparent clarity.

I had started out in Moscow with my heart beating wild and scared, like that of a bird in the grip of a cat. I had no confidence in myself. But others did.

Fenechka.

Sophia Mikhailovna.

Madame Martynova.

Yevgeny.

Peter.

Abram.

And while I owe each of them a world of gratitude, I'm the one who turned my own life around.

The change is more than just literacy and arithmetic and confidence. It's something more elusive, yet more profound.

I arrived in the city as a vulnerable child and ripened into a mature woman. Soon I will make my own home and start building a career at Yevgeny's bookstore. The bone-deep truth is I am within reach of something that can't be taken away from me—independence and self-respect. Throughout my entire life, I never knew that either existed.

For the second time this morning, "Dark Eyes" circles of its own accord through my mind.

> I draw comfort from my own destiny:
> Everything fine in life that God gave to us.

Although my starry-eyed recollections of my time with Abram Abramovich Segalovich will pass, I'll never let go of the love we felt. And someday—yes, someday—I'll be able to view those two years with nostalgia rather than stabbing pain. I'll look back upon my time with him as a brief but remarkable interlude in my life.

Interlude? Imagine little Anna Vorontsova knowing such a word!

I pull away from the wall and stride headlong into the wind.

THE END

Reading Group
GUIDE

1. Compelling fiction is driven by conflict. *The Yellow Ticket* does not have a traditional human antagonist (bad guy) running through the storyline. What substitutes for the antagonist? What forces and situations thwart Anna's happiness?

2. For seven years, Anna chased the dream of going home to her village of Petrovo. Why does our childhood home resonate so strongly for many of us?

3. While hospitalized for syphilis, Anna longed to return to her old room at 903 Sviatoslavsky Prospekt. And during the second half of the book, she pined for a married man. Have you ever been unable to put aside a desire (be it a person, an emotion, an idea, an obsession, or a dependency) even though you knew in your heart that it was detrimental to your well-being? How did you move past it?

4. Initially, Anna thinks Yevgeny is an odd bird. However she learns to appreciate him, and eventually he supplies the mechanism that allows her to pursue a better life. Have you ever met someone you initially disregarded, only to later highly value his/her abilities or friendship?

5. France's model for regulating prostitution in the 1800s was adopted by many European countries, including Russia. Do you think such regulation achieved its primary objective, that is, to decrease the incidence of syphilis and other STDs?

6. The theory that disease is caused by germs didn't gain much traction in Europe and the United States until the late 1800s.

A. According to Anna, "The physician thrusts a cold, metal instrument into one sex hole after another, taking a quick glimpse in each." What effect did this supposed preventive measure have on the spread of sexually transmitted diseases?

B. If the organism couldn't be identified, how did hospitals know that a patient was cured of syphilis?

7. When were modern condoms invented? When did they come into common use in developed countries?

8. Anna was inoculated (vaccinated) for smallpox. When did routine vaccination against smallpox cease? Why?

9. Whose job is more dangerous—the prostitute's or the bouncer's?

www.ingramcontent.com/pod-product-compliance
Lightning Source LLC
Chambersburg PA
CBHW031647100726
47898CB00006B/2011